This book should be returned to any Lancashire
County Council Library on or before the date shown

0 1 APR 2021

By Peter Laws

THE MATT HUNTER SERIES
Purged
Unleashed
Severed
Possessed

POSSESSED

PETER LAWS

Allison & Busby Limited
11 Wardour Mews
London W1F 8AN
allisonandbusby.com

First published in Great Britain by Allison & Busby in 2020.

A CIP catalogue record for this book is available from
the British Library.

First Edition

ISBN 978-0-7490-2467-3

Typeset in 11.25/16.25 pt Sabon LT Pro by
Allison & Busby Ltd.

The paper used for this Allison & Busby publication
has been produced from trees that have been legally sourced
from well-managed and credibly certified forests.

Printed and bound by
CPI Group (UK) Ltd, Croydon, CR0 4YY

taps mic
Ladies and gentlemen, good evening. This next track's called
Possessed and I want to dedicate it to someone who I've admired
since – well – since birth. Yep, that's right, this is for my brilliant
brother, Norman, who's going to play bass on this one.
And it goes a little something like this . . .

'Be sober, be watchful, for your adversary the devil prowls around like a roaring lion, seeking someone to devour'

1 Peter 5:8

PART ONE

PROWL

CHAPTER ONE

The milk van moved quietly through the streets, or rather it trundled. Yeah, that was a better word, Phil Pepper thought to himself. My little milk van *trundles* along, morning after morning, dark hour after dark hour. Weaving a silent, gentle circuit through the cold and sleeping suburbs of Totternhoe, West Hertfordshire.

It was a March morning, at 5 a.m. That wonderful, sacred time, when all is quiet. The Sandman Milk Company had committed itself to keeping it that way. They were famous for their award-winning, low-noise guarantee, with a promise painted on the side of every van.

The first you'll hear of our milk is when it sloshes into your cornflakes!

It's why he wore special shoes with soft rubber soles, and why they had a whisper-only worker policy, and why all the metal baskets in the back were lined with specially made cotton buffers so the bottles didn't clink. And, of course, why the vans had electric, golf cart engines. Pretty crappy if you were trying to outrun a snapping pit bull, but quiet enough to do what the family company had prided itself on for nearly ninety years. It let the people sleep. Phil admired that goal, right from the start. When he did the rounds with his dad, who did it with *his* dad, before that. Because just as breakfast really mattered (ask your doctor), sleep mattered more. Without rest, people didn't function right, and more importantly, they couldn't dream.

So Phil made a hushed turn into Lowry Terrace. Then a graceful right onto Gibson Avenue, and a sharp, silent three-point turn into Felling Road. Which is where his smile vanished. He knew it would, because this was the road that he always drove straight through. Not a single customer on the longest street in town. And every year, who was he kidding, every *month*, streets like this were becoming the norm.

Back in the '80s, he and his dad would've stopped at pretty much every house. There was a whole fleet of quiet little trundlers back then. An army of white coats, tiptoeing a silent pavement ballet, tipping hats at one another from across the street. These days, however, Phil was in his mid-fifties, and he'd often deliver one single milk order to an entire hundred-home street. Some streets he'd drive past completely – like Felling. People preferred to stock up with hefty, plastic six-pinters, beamed straight from the mouse clicker to the supermarket to the doorstep . . . along with every other food-based wonder known to humanity. No wonder the Sandman Milk Company had dropped from twenty vans to two over three decades. And for the last six months, they'd reached one – which was Phil: the Last of the Milkhicans, he'd joke. Though he was yet to laugh when he said it. Pretty soon it'd be no van at all and then, he supposed, perfect silence would finally be achieved.

He whispered to his melancholy. Told it to 'Shhhh', because he was finally coming up to Pendle Street. Hallelujah, Praise Jesus on a moped, *this* was more like it. He had seven customers along here, and two of them were brand new. They'd signed up last month after his solo door-knocking campaign. He'd hated doing it, because it reeked of charity, but his wife's nag had been worth it. Two new customers! Maybe folks were getting sick of big business. Sick of using plastic and killing the little fishies. If vinyl bloody records could make a baffling comeback, why not nice-cold, ice-cold milk?

So he drove down his street of hope and parked by the postbox. He slid out through the doorless gap and let his soft-tread soles kiss the pavement good morning. He tugged his white coat into place and tapped his white peaked cap too. Just for the hell of it. So what if he looked like a relic. So what if an early morning jogger once gasped loudly at him, honestly believing that Phil was a wandering ghost from the 1950s. Legend says he roams the streets, searching for new customers! He allowed himself a silent laugh.

He did number 78 first. The Hakeems. Two semi-skimmed and an orange juice. He set the bottles down on the doorstep and gave a gentle, friendly tip of the cap to the window above. Mr and Mrs Hakeem would be warm under their duvet right now. Faces and lips pressed against marshmallow pillows.

Dream on, my friends, he smiled, *dream on*.

Back at the van, he grabbed the next crate. His heart sank a little.

The Bensons lived at Number 81, just across the road. Mr Benson was a grumpy old goat, who was *not* impressed when his wife signed up for a delivery last week. He remembered how Mr Benson shouted at her, when the door closed. Not a nice man, by all accounts. Maybe he just needed more sleep.

So Phil moved towards the front door and very gently set four pints of milk and two choco-milks down. He leant over and turned the bottle facing out, just like his dad always did.

Then, somebody laughed.

Phil paused with a finger on the last bottle, his other hand dangled like a mannequin.

Oh? The Bensons are up earlier than—

Again, somebody laughed. Muffled and quiet. It wasn't coming from the house.

He stood up straight and turned, soft soles revolving. A dirty greenhouse came into view, just near the pavement. As soon as he stopped turning, the laughter came again. But this time the giggle felt different. It was a giggle *against* something. A laugh into the hand. He pictured Mr Benson in there, ready to come striding out to hit him with a plant pot. He'd had crazy customers before.

Time to leave. He took a hasty step towards the path. There were other, kinder people to serve after all, and Weetabix tastes like chunks of cardboard without a fresh bottle of—

'*Help . . . help me . . .*'

He froze.

That voice . . . no way was that Mr Benson. Was that a *kid* in there?

'*Pleaaaasssssse . . .*'

Heart rate rising, Phil took a step towards the greenhouse door. Then another. He whispered, 'Hello?'

Another giggle, followed by words that weren't the type you'd normally giggle about. '*Help . . . help . . .*'

What if that wasn't laughter? What if the poor little tyke was crying in there? One of the Benson kids maybe. Maybe daddy was easy with his fists, and this was where his kids liked to hide. Especially when he was so furious at all this overpriced choco-milk.

Phil gently set his empty basket down and curled a finger around the cold handle. It was way too dark to see through the grimy glass, so he pulled at the metal-framed door. Just one tug brought the whole thing gliding open in a helpfully silent, recently oiled arc. Phil leant his head into the gloom inside, jaw tight, every filling touching. He couldn't see anybody, just shadows.

'Where are you?' He stepped inside and winced at the smell. He had no clue what alien vegetable was rotting in there, but holy smokes, something absolutely *stank*. He saw a tall, long, metal shelving unit on his left, rammed with pots and tools and a hanging piece of tarpaulin. There was a low wooden table on his right, too. It was filled with herbs sprouting from plastic pots and . . . carrots. Jeez-Louise. There were *stacks* of carrots, caked with soil.

'*Come here . . .*'

The voice, closer now, sent ice sliding down his spine, and he span back to see the greenhouse door. The spring hinges had already closed it. So silently that he hadn't noticed.

'*Come here . . .*' the voice said. '*Down . . . here . . .*'

He squinted towards a low metal shelf where a dark roll of plastic sheeting was hanging from the third shelf, draped down across the second like a curtain. And he knew immediately that this was where the hidden giggler lay.

'Hey . . .' he whispered. 'Are you okay?'

'*Help me out . . . Pleeaaaassse . . .*'

Crikey, that was a kid.

He dropped to his knees and slowly reached for the sheet, fingers trembling like they had on his wedding day. Getting closer. Take a breath, Phil. Do the right thing. Almost there.

He snapped his hand back.

Yuk.

There were slugs crawling around the hem of the canvas. Four of them, all bunched up and wriggling together. Then he stroked his throat with a grimace as he watched a very strange thing occur. The slugs started to move in time with one another, and they were working together, tugging at the canvas so it might silently slide down. It did, and quickly too.

Ffffffffffffft.

It fell into a heap on the floor, and behind it Phil could see something now visible that both relieved and devastated him, all at once.

The crying voice was real. Not a ghost, not a clever carrot, but what looked like a naked teenage girl, bunched up and lying on her side on the second to bottom shelf. Her long black hair hung from the edge and her dirty slug fingers were now wriggling across her kneecaps, hugging them towards herself, head folded in. He couldn't see her other hand.

'Bloody Nora . . .' he said, oblivious to his breaking the no-whisper policy.

She was a knee-hugging ball. He thought of kids shouting 'Geronimo!' when they leapt into a swimming pool, but then thought she was more like a giant embryo instead. Because the closer he got, the more he saw her glisten with some sort of gloop. Sweat?

Under all that wet, bedraggled black hair, he saw her other hand. She had it splayed, wide across her face. The way he used to play peek-a-boo with his daughter in the park. He was so taken aback by this, the splayed hand, that it took him a few seconds to realise that this shivering, wet, Geronimo ball was already growing bigger. It was unfurling.

He couldn't move, and he couldn't speak or even whisper, either. He just took off his hat like a hearse was passing by, and he stared at this bizarre ball of limbs flowering. He whispered, in his kindest, most gentle voice, 'I'm gonna put you on my milk float. I'm gonna get you some help . . .'

His absolute best guess was that he'd stumbled onto Mr Benson's prisoner child. Like those reports he'd seen of young girls kidnapped and stuffed into cellars for decades. And Phil even had time to picture himself on the BBC News tonight. The silent, cautious milkman who sneaked a kid to safety, and kick-started a nationwide turn back to doorstep milk deliveries – the hero's option!

Until one skinny leg splayed out, then another, and he saw something that didn't compute. Those legs were bizarrely long for a young teen. Like this was one of those Russian contortionists who could dislocate their bodies just to fit inside a tiny box. The head was still down, with that hair-strewn hand still clawed across it, but the other arm started peeling away from her knees. The arm folded jaggedly outwards. His brain pretended he could hear pencils snapping, but he knew. His ears were filling with the audible cracking and grinding of bones.

All this hypnotism stopped when the bare foot hit. It made a steady slap on the concrete floor. That's when Phil blinked, because the foot had hair on it. And that shoe size was almost as big as his own. With the body still on the shelf, the other foot slapped next to the first, and Phil's gaze rolled up that long, freakishly long leg, to see the blossoming of a crotch, covered in sticky pubic gloop. Then something else that made him dizzy again. This wasn't a little teen after all, and it certainly wasn't a girl. This was a skinny man, half-covered in blood, who had a terrifying ability to fit into tight places.

One long arm lolled out and started grasping.

Phil went to run, but he couldn't. Because when he looked down, his wrist was locked inside those slippery, blood-soaked slug-fingers, whose touch had flung his entire body to the coldest peaks of Everest. All he could do was yelp and yank himself free, while this thing, gripping something at last, finally started to fully uncoil. The other hand, the one under all that hair, finally pulled away, and Phil now saw a face – though he dearly wished he couldn't. It was still at an angle, pushing through the black strands. A brow, and a pair of eyes slid through the doorway of the wet fringe, and he saw the grimacing thing being born. A cheek slid and stretched along the shelf towards the edge, and he thought he even saw one tooth, grinding a line in the metal. His first thought had been correct. He hadn't heard whimpering or crying at all. The skinny man was giggling *like* a child. He could hear the cold air of laughter, fizzing through the dry lips.

It was the first time Phil made any real, unrestricted noise.

He wailed loudly, and then he slammed himself back against the wooden table, yanking his clamped wrist as hard as he could. All that did was drag the naked man fully out, so that his horribly long body slid free and dropped. It slapped onto its side on the floor, with a nauseating, stomach-turning crunch. A man-sized beetle, with its limbs flailing out quickly, grabbing the world for balance. Phil's jawbone lost all strength when the strange skinny man pulled himself into an upright position. Now fully open, Phil saw everything, but it was the man's stomach, just beneath his belly button, that held the real horror. The most furious cuts and gashes he'd ever seen. Like a tyre mark, like a pattern, like a . . .

A word.

He saw a word, *carved* into this man's pulsing stomach. A wound-word that even now was pumping out fresh fuel for what was becoming a growing, sticky lake on the greenhouse floor. Phil looked up at the ceiling in panic. The morning sunlight was finally seeping through the grime. When he looked back he saw the man *staring* at him. Eyes filled with desperate fear, even as he enthusiastically tugged at the ragged word in his belly and laughed.

'*Let me out . . .*' the man mumbled. '*Let me . . . out . . .*'

'Who are you?'

'*I . . . I roam the earth . . . One. Three. Three.*'

'You want me to call someone?'

'*Three. One.*'

'Do you like orange juice? It's fresh?'

'*Six. Six. Six. Six.*'

'I'll—'

'*One. Three. Three . . . hushhhhh little baby, don't say a word . . .*' The man's teeth suddenly snapped at the air, and the lips peeled back in an awful, bony smile. '*Open your mouth, friend . . .*'

'Why?'

'*Cos, I'm gonna climb in.*'

Phil yanked as hard as he could. It was on the third, grunting pull that he finally dragged his own wrist free. He heard the wet slide of it. The splashing of drops and the whip of skin pulling. He grabbed a shelf and pulled himself up, clambering to his feet in a hailstorm of pots and carrots. When he slammed the greenhouse door open, two of the panes immediately smashed, though Phil wondered if that might have been from the man's roar. Dear God, Phil thought. Was there anything ever so loud?

'*Let me ouuuuuuuuuutttttt . . .*'

Phil staggered out into a rectangle of light, which wasn't from the sun. It was Mr Benson's bedroom. He looked up and saw him up there, fat, shirtless and shouting silently at the glass, clawing at the window locks to open up. Phil just spun around and ran. He accidentally kicked his milk basket across the floor and sent it flying. He left it behind. His feet crunched down the gravel path, as loud as meteors crashing against the house, and he flung the gate open with a clanging metallic rattle.

He ran straight past the milk van and raced down the street, just as the sun was turning the black sky purple, and then the purple sky pink. Gasping, wheezing, but refusing to stop, he saw the other street lights flicking off, as the day began. He saw many people at their windows, holding the curtains back and wondering what Mr Benson was shouting about, and why on earth the milkman was running down the street screaming.

And why . . . somewhere, amongst it all . . . a strange and not-right voice could also be heard wailing and crying and laughing all at the same time.

CHAPTER TWO

Professor Matt Hunter walked towards the filing cabinet with his arms folded, running his eye across all the framed diplomas that were fixed to the wall. He clocked the institutions, logged the dates, then he ran his eyes over the cube of an office, with its dull, bare blue walls, two tub chairs and a ceiling fan, slowly whirring.

'No offence, Jeff . . .' Matt said, 'but this room . . . It's a bit sterile, don't you think?'

Silence.

'A bit clinical? A bit cold?'

Silence.

'Probably a great place to negotiate a mortgage, I guess, or I don't know . . . do an autopsy.' Matt chortled into his fist, then coughed. 'Sorry. I just mean it's . . . well . . . it's a bit . . . you know . . .'

Silence.

Matt sighed and looked back at the filing cabinet. A Newton's Cradle sat on top. He leant towards the suspended chrome balls and saw his reflected face stretch. He opened and shut his mouth a few times, just to see the gaping black space. He reached a finger towards the first ball. 'I made one of these at school, but I got the weight distribution all wrong. When the teacher tested it out, all the balls fell off. Totally screwed it up. I can still remember the sound of them rolling.' He attempted the noise with his mouth. 'Got a big fat "F", Jeff . . . but you know something? I wasn't that bothered, because it made me and everybody else laugh, and at the time that felt more important. Guess you should probably write that down on your little pad. It might be significant.' Matt moved his fingertip a little closer. 'May I?'

Silence.

'I'm going to take that as a massive, enthusiastic yes.' He lifted the ball with his finger and thumb. 'You're really sure?'

Silence.

'Well, if you insist . . .'

He released his grip and the time-bomb metal clacking began. 'Wow, Jeff. That's a perfect weight ratio. You'd have gotten an A for that, no doubt about it.' Matt watched the balls ticking for a moment, then he blew out a breath and folded his arms again.

He took a slow walk past the blinds. Tesco car park was out there, somewhere. He could see bright, sunny lines of it through the gaps. He shrugged and sat down instead, sinking into one of the unpleasantly cold chairs.

'I just always imagined a therapist's office to be cosy and sophisticated. You know . . . a couple of Ansel Adams landscapes on the walls. Soothing shots of pretty woods, mysterious lakes . . . cleansing waterfall metaphors. And pot plants too. I always expected those. And now you mention it, where's the tilted couch for the crazy . . . sorry, I mean . . . where's the couch for me to lie

21

back in? That was the only part I was looking forward to. This tub chair's like leather-wrapped cement.' He bumped a fist off the arm and shook it out in mock pain, laughing. 'I mean, come on . . . ow!'

Silence.

Matt crossed his legs one way, then the other, then he nodded at the diplomas. 'So you qualified in 1976, the year *Star Wars* came out. I was minus eight that year. Please tell me your office was cosier than this in the '70s? Therapists had carpets on the wall, back then, didn't they? You seen much Woody Allen, Jeff?'

Silence.

Old Jeff sat stiffly, looking like a broken theme park animatronic. He was always in the same position: one leg crossed over the other so that it lifted his cream flannel trousers. Matt saw a sock (also cream) reaching up a thin line of hairy, bony, shiny shin. He had a yellow pencil and a black Moleskine pad resting on his kneecap.

Suddenly, Jeff blinked.

Was that the first time he'd done that in this session? In his entire life, even?

'Look . . . I don't want to be rude but . . .' Matt sat forward, elbows on his knees. 'I'm just filling the gaps cos this is my first session with you and you don't seem to speak . . . So how about you say something, just to get us going, eh? *I'll* take over after, I promise. How about we start really easy like . . . um . . . I don't know . . . what's your favourite processed meat, Jeff? Hot dogs or burgers . . . go!'

Silence.

'Ahoy there, anybody on deck?' Matt let his cupped hand drop away from his mouth. 'I'm hot dogs by the way. Better write that—'

'The preliminary report you gave me . . .'

Matt made a mock lean back into his chair. 'Glory be. He lives!'

Silent seconds passed. Matt counted thirty of them. Then Jeff said, 'The report said you're being troubled with nightmares.'

Matt's smirk drooped a little. 'Actually, the report said I was *having* nightmares. Not that I was troubled by them, per se.'

'Tell me about your nightmares.'

'What do you want to know, exactly?'

Silence.

'I *knew* you were going to say that. Well . . . okay . . . the nightmares . . . well, let me see. They're usually just me living my life as normal. I'm eating dinner with my family, I'm watching TV with my wife, when all of a sudden, they just . . . walk into the room.' Matt looked across at the blinds. He heard the rumble of engines beyond them, the clink of trolleys, the slamming of car doors. '*Who* walks into the room, I hear you ask? Well, Jeff, let me tell you.' He leant forward again. 'I've seen a few dead people in my life, Jeff. Back when I was a vicar, they were kinda par for the course. I wouldn't exactly call them a perk of the job, but they're certainly part of the package . . . and I guess I thought I'd left all that behind when I jacked church in and became an academic. Though there's a couple of students in my lectures that look like rigor mortis has set in . . . know what I mean, eh Jeff?' He laughed again but then his eyes dropped when Jeff's pencil suddenly started scraping.

Upside down, Matt read: *Humour . . . defence mech*.

Jeff quickly covered the rest with his hand, and just looked back up with his unblinking, amphibian eyes.

'So, yeah, I thought the death stuff was behind me. But since I started helping the police my corpse quotient is *Through. The. Roof.* And that's who comes to my house – in the dreams, I mean. The corpses. The victims. From Hobbs Hill, from Menham . . . and I had a fresh crop turn up from that crazy night in Chervil. I guess you read about Chervil . . .'

Silence.

'Only they're not your classic corpses, you understand. These guys are up and standing and doing stuff. Or they're sitting in the back row of my lecture hall or they're standing behind my car when I set off for work . . . Or they're crawling. When I'm in the bath they're just crawling along the floor, and the ceiling too. They're very agile, these corpses. And they're looking at me, of course.'

'Is it always just corpses?'

'Just?' Matt laughed.

Silence.

More silence.

No more smiles now. 'That's an insightful question, because no, it's not always corpses. In fact, it's often just shadows. Things in the corner that vanish when I turn around. Animal things, human things. A mix, I guess. Heck, sometimes I need a wee in the middle of the night. You know how it is, Jeff. I'm mid-thirties, the end's coming. I cross the landing in the dark night and then I hear one of them scrambling up the stairs after me. A big, tall rabbit, only it's also a man and . . .' Matt nodded at the scrawling pencil. 'Haaaang on. You're clear I'm talking about the dreams, here. Like I don't mean I see these shadows in *real* life . . . obviously. Like when I'm asleep. Or half-asleep.'

Jeff blinked again. It was a slow and laboured fall of lids. Like his decades-long therapy radar had just picked up Matt's first lie. What he'd just said *was* a lie, after all. Matt's gang of corpses and shadows were a loyal and sociable bunch, and true they mostly stayed in dreams. Mostly. But now and again, when the mood was right, they'd slide into the waking world too. Usually quite subtle. Like the stench of burning hair that might suddenly fill his nostrils in a restaurant. Or the dull and distant singing of dead folks holding hands in his garden, standing up on the picnic bench. Or that splashing wave of teenage blood that would totally soak the windscreen of his car, until he blinked again and it was all gone. And like now, as he looked in Jeff's glasses and saw something tall and spindly, and not quite human. The tall black rabbit reflected and standing behind Matt's left shoulder.

Jeff set the pencil back and tapped his chin for a long moment, but of course, he said nothing.

'I'm not surprised by any of this, by the way. I don't think I'm defective for being . . . affected by the things I've seen. My wife too. She was in Chervil and frankly it'd be pretty weird if we weren't impacted by some of this. It's not even that I'm *particularly* troubled by it. It's all just chemistry and biology, really, and most of, it's just classic tricks of the light.' Matt tapped his temple. 'Pretty fascinating stuff. But look, Jill Bowland thought it'd be a good idea for Wren and me to chat to somebody about it, because . . .' He trailed off, and looked across at the blinds. 'Cos call me old-fashioned, Jeff, but it'd be nice to sit at a Sunday dinner for once and not see my mum's chopped-up face glaring at me . . .'

Matt caught his breath and noticed that his chest was heaving. He put a palm against it and glanced at the clock. Still twenty minutes left. 'I've never been one of these macho robots, who keep on trucking. So, here I am – ta-dah' – he did jazz hands – 'I'm sitting here in counselling, as instructed. Coping with the lack of inspiring art on the walls and I'm ready to be counselled. So if you fancy hitting me with some nifty breathing technique. Heck, even a low-grade pill you'd recommend, I'm up for trying something, cos I need the sleep. Just no juju chants or prayers to a deity, if you don't mind. I have an allergic intolerance to bullshit, after all . . .'

Silence.

'A few tips, Jeff. Come on. You can do it.'

Silence.

'Oh, for fuck's sake, forget it.' Matt was shocked at how loud his voice came out in a boom. He pushed himself up and scooped his jacket from the floor. He went towards the door and paused. 'Which means I'm going. Unless you have some actual advice. Do you?'

'Tell me about your mother's face.'

Matt cringed. 'Oo, yeah, I'd *love* to tell you about that. All while you appropriately stare back at me like a week-old corpse. But you know something? I've had enough of those already.'

Silence. 'Same time next week, then?'

Matt laughed. 'You, my friend, are an absolute riot.'

'Next week, then.'

'Why? What's the point?'

'Burgers.'

'Huh?'

'Burgers are my favourite processed meat.'

Matt paused, one hand on the door handle. 'If I ever do come back, I'm bringing you a pot plant, and I'm going to tickle you for the first ten minutes, just to see if you can smile. Deal?'

Silence.

'Thought so. Feel free to power down now. Bye.'

Matt closed the door behind him and didn't move for a moment. He just leant against the frame and got his breath back. Funny that he hadn't noticed his heart was galloping. He could hear blood pulsing through his ears. He started walking down the corridor, passing three other doors that led to three more counselling rooms. From one, he could hear muffled shouting. From another, the vague pulse of crying, and from the final one, the most important one, he heard silence. He couldn't tell if that was bad or good.

He considered waiting for Wren right here. He could just sit near the exit, ready for her coming out. If the door slammed open and she stomped out unhappy with her session, he'd be ready with a hug. But these doors sounded way thinner than they ought to be, and he didn't want to eavesdrop, even by accident. And besides, they'd arranged to meet in the supermarket cafe after, not in the corridor.

The thought of seeing her again was already dropping his heart rate. She was reality, she was normal life, and that was soothing to him. This . . . in here . . . was an excursion into the brain, which was a bit of a wild west.

So he tugged his jacket into place and hurried to the exit, stopping only once. The fluorescent tube was flickering above him. When he looked up at the frosted glass case, he saw a fly crawling around in there. Aimlessly moving in a circle of eight. Probably looking for another bug to chat to, but finding nobody.

'Good luck with that, amigo,' Matt said, and pushed his way outside.

CHAPTER THREE

The mid-morning crowd in the Tesco cafe was thin and scattered. Sure, there were one or two lone parents tapping phones with one hand and rocking buggies with the other, but he had his pick of the seats. He sat a few tables down from a wizard on a lunch break – an old woman with fairy-tale long white hair. He couldn't help but notice her eat. Who knew that somebody could chew one single mouthful of sausage for a fortnight?

When she looked up and saw him, he smiled at her and he gave one of those gentlemanly nods he'd assumed people did in the 1940s. Her attempt at a smile back turned into a loud, hacking, wet-sounding cough.

He tried not to wince and looked away. Which is when he saw Wren.

It was the flash of red hair outside, gliding past the glass of the cafe.

Her bright, some would say shockingly bright, hair was always his fast-track way to find her in a busy place. Like a kid with a balloon, or a tour guide with a raised umbrella. You could spot a Wren Hunter right in the throng of a huge concert crowd, and you'd be all the better for it.

He watched her slow to a pause at the window, then cup her hands against the glass. She squinted inside, searching. Their eyes met, and smiles bloomed. He pointed a finger down to the two hefty slices of carrot cake on the table. She threw up an eager thumb. She mouthed the words *get me a cappuccino* and started jogging round. Her red hair vanished behind a concrete pillar and earth plunged back into its dull, submarine grey.

He was already at the till when she found him inside, just as the coffee machine spluttered froth into two cups. He waited to pay while she stepped up to him and kissed his cheek. Her lips felt chilly on his skin. Back at the table, Matt slid the humongous slice of carrot cake towards her. 'The treasure you seek.'

She jabbed her fork in and shovelled a hunk of buttercream through those cold lips. 'God,' she spoke through sponge, with instant hamster cheeks. 'I needed this.'

He took a bite of his. 'So, was your session all you dreamt of and more?'

She covered her mouth, mid-chomp. 'I'm busy. You first.'

He took a slow sip of coffee. 'My guy was sooooo quiet. I mean, he barely said a word.'

'Really? Mine was quite chatty.'

'Well, mine just looked at me like this, the whole time.' He flashed his eyes into a hypnotic, panto-villain glare and started leaning across the table, gradually zooming his face towards hers. 'No words, just this, for like forty minutes straight.'

She wafted him back. 'I'd have hated that. You'd think they'd have the same approach.'

29

'Depends on how they're trained. In the therapist lottery I think I got myself a full-on psychoanalytical. They're supposed to act as a blank screen, so they barely say a word. It's up to the patient to bring up anything important. I've read about that method being delivered by machines.'

She stopped chewing. 'So are you saying it was a waste of time?'

He swallowed. Set his fork down. 'Did you talk about Chervil?'

'Yep. And I wasn't expecting to cry straight off the bat, but she was passing me tissues like five minutes in.' She set her fork down, too. 'I'm glad I went. I'm booked in for four sessions at first. Maybe you could ask to change your therapist?'

'Maybe. We'll see.' He caught her eye. 'But don't worry. I'm still up for trying. It'd be good to process all this police stuff I'm doing. Especially because . . .'

'Because?' She slid a hand across the table and held his. Then she caught his eye. Saw the look in it. 'Hang on. They've called you, haven't they?'

'This morning. They've asked me to drive up to Watford this afternoon.'

She let his hand go, but he could see her taking a breath. Fighting the urge to resist this stuff and instead to accept it. Matt may well be a university professor, but the police consultancy part of his job was just a part of life now. 'Don't tell me.' She grabbed her fork. 'A Baptist's dressing as Jesus and he's crucifying all the Methodists.'

He laughed. 'Not quite. They've found a delirious man in a greenhouse this morning. They say he's silent and won't talk to anybody.'

'So why call you?'

'Because he's written one thing down so far . . . the name of an ancient biblical demon.'

He saw her blink. The sign of a brain making a conscious

decision. 'Oh, the old ancient biblical demon routine. Bet that happens all the time.' She smiled at him. Or tried to. 'Will you be back for dinner, dear?'

He laughed. 'Depends. Hopefully.'

She nodded to his carrot cake. 'Better load up on sugar, then, just in case. You'll still be at Amelia's school play tonight. Right?'

'The Great Fire of London? Absolutely. I'll just meet you at the school.'

They ate for a while in silence, and every now and then she'd check her phone when another email came through. She was an architect, and her latest client was the blow-into-a-bag nervous type, constantly seeking clarity. Back in the car, she said she could drop Matt at home, then head off to yet another reassurance meeting. He said fine. He'd gather some books for the police visit, grab his own car and go. She said fine. It was only when they were pulling out of the car park that she brought the therapist back up again. She was looking at those four windows where the counselling rooms were.

'You know, if the police counselling isn't working for you, we can just pay for someone else.'

'Maybe. Or I could just read some books about it. You know. Get a few tips on healthy living. Sleeping well. That sort of thing.'

'Hmmm.' Her voice was quiet. She turned away from the window, and was now tapping the dash, filling the car with music. He saw four windows against the wall of the police building. All but one of them had their blinds wide open.

CHAPTER FOUR

It took him forty minutes to get there, chugging along the motorway at a steady clip. The automatic wipers slid every few minutes, trying to catch what only ever amounted to a tease of indecisive rain. After an idle flick through the radio channels, he stopped on Radio 4. A technology doc was asking if we should be more polite to our digital assistants, lest we wind up as a nation of hopelessly boorish and rude slave drivers.

'Hey, Siri. Play me some funk . . . ya scumbag.' He went to add the word 'please' but he was too late. Isaac Hayes boomed through the stereo at full blast. 'Thank you ever so kindly.'

He pulled off the motorway, drumming his fingers to the wacka-wacka guitar sounds of Shaft, and followed the signs through Watford city centre. The traffic lights made the journey a constant flow of stop and start, but when he finally pulled up into the hospital car park, he was ten minutes early.

He clicked the horn section off and hopped out, dragging his heavy backpack from the back seat. When he slung it over his shoulder, the weight made him stagger to the side. A passer-by laughed at that, so Matt laughed right back, and loudly too, with Shakespearean levels of sarcasm. He heaved the bag through the car park, squinting up at a fat sun that now hung over the hospital building. He slowed down, pulled out his phone and read his text.

Meet DS Martin Fenn at Mendip Wing, Block B. TO THE LEFT OF A&E. Officer Marriot waiting to collect you.

He weaved through a few more cars and saw an older-looking uniformed officer. She was standing stock-straight in front of a small, rectangular building, which stood separate from the rest of the hospital. She had her arms folded and was utterly still apart from a permed blonde mane that shivered to the left in the breeze. As he approached her, she clocked his face. She pulled out her phone and looked down at it. Then up again. She did this twice in a swift snap. 'Name, please?'

'Professor Matt Hunter.'

'And you're here to meet?'

'DS Fenn. And you're PC Marriot.'

'Bingo, he's expecting you inside.' She smiled and held out a hand. Matt saw the hint of a bird tattoo on her wrist. 'Now, can I just have a quick looksie in your bag? Make sure it's not loaded with illegals, eh?'

'It's just books.' He dumped it on the bench next to her, and she started to rummage. He winced as she dragged out tome after tome, watching on nervous tiptoes. 'If you could be careful with the covers. Couple of those editions are pretty hard to find.'

'Oh, I see. Sorry.' With an instant delicateness she turned an old book in her hand. 'These look a bit creepy . . . is this one Latin?'

'It is indeed.'

She whistled, pleased with herself. Then she zipped the bag up again and hoisted it towards him. 'Get a Kindle. It'll save your spine.'

He steadied it on his shoulder while she swished a black key fob across a panel in the door. 'This way.'

There was a second set of secure doors inside. She typed a code into this panel, then they stepped into what looked like any other hospital corridor, lined with a few chairs, a drinking fountain and a coffee machine at the far end. What felt different were the CCTV cameras. They were in every corner, buzzing and turning, red lights blinking in a constant flash.

'What is this place, anyway?'

'It's the secure unit. Some hospitals have them. It's where they look after patients who might be a danger to themselves and others. Naturally, it's used for a lot of violent, mental health cases. And offenders come here too, of course. If we arrest a murderer with a stab wound, he still needs stitching up – if only to stand trial.' She laughed and paused at another door. 'Right . . . here we are . . .'

She knocked. Three hard raps with a single knuckle. While they waited Matt heard a mechanical drone of a CCTV camera twist on its hinge. He looked up and watched it stop on him. He stared into the twitching lens, then the door clicked open.

'Heeeeyyy!' A large, happy fella in a grey suit filled the gap. Everything about him was round. His body, his face, the frame of his glasses. His yellow spotted tie was as loose as a lounge-singer, so he yanked it into place before thrusting out his hand. His smile was filled with little teeth and his hair looked like a rat had died while crossing a beach ball. But gosh, was he jolly-looking. 'You're the demon guy, I take it?'

Matt laughed. 'That's one way of putting it.'

His grip was hard, and Matt felt his own wedding ring being pressed painfully into the next knuckle. Then before he could move, he felt himself tugged quickly into a forward step.

'Come on in. I'm DS Martin Fenn.'

CHAPTER FIVE

'Park your bum.' Fenn nodded to the empty chair at the desk, then waddled to the other side where open blinds let the sun flood in. An open laptop sat on the desk, speckled with shiny dust, but Matt couldn't see the screen. Fenn had his eyes on it though, as he went to sit. His hefty rear made an audible creak of plastic and chrome.

PC Marriot appeared with two machine coffees in plastic cups. She rummaged in her pocket and carefully set a sealed custard cream in front of each of them.

Fenn's mouth dropped, 'Awww . . . out of Bourbons, Pamela?'

''Fraid so, sir. NHS, sir.'

They shared a sad, nodding glance, and she left.

Fenn tore his biscuit packet open. 'Hey, thanks for coming out.'

'No problem. How can I help?'

'Well, like I said on the phone, we have a man in custody. No ID, nobody recognises him. No fingerprints on file, either.' He dipped his biscuit so deep into his coffee that his fingers got wet. He shoved the sodden lump into his mouth and wiped his hands on his trousers. He spoke through food. 'Chap's a mystery.'

'Where was he found?'

'In a domestic greenhouse this morning. In Totternhoe.' He must have caught Matt's blank face. 'That's a small-ish village, just out of Dunstable. We have no idea how he got there and neither do the homeowners.'

'Who found him?'

'A milkman called Phil Pepper. It's why we're calling our mystery man Ernie for now.'

'I don't follow.'

'You know . . . the fastest milkman in the west?' Fenn dropped his jaw, horrified. 'Benny Hill?'

Matt grabbed his biscuit. 'That's a bit before my time. Sorry.'

'Well, that just about makes me want to kill myself. Anyway, Pepper was out on his rounds when he heard . . .' Fenn held up finger quotes, '*creepy laughing* from a greenhouse on Pendle Street. He goes inside and finds Ernie totally naked and wailing for help. But he's aggressive too. He's reaching out, trying to grab. Like this . . .' Fenn started stretching his arms out across the desk, demonstrating.

Matt pulled back. 'All right, all right. I get the picture.' He lifted the biscuit to his mouth.

'Oh, and he was drenched in blood.'

He set the biscuit back down. 'You definitely didn't mention that on the phone. Whose blood was it?'

'We think it's his, but we're looking into it. Still, though, we're pretty eager to find out what our Ernie was up to last night. We doubt he's from Totternhoe and it doesn't look like he got there by car either . . .' Fenn leant forward, his gut spilling over the desk. 'Why are you frowning?'

'I'm just curious how a butt-naked bloke gets himself to Totternhoe without being spotted by someone. Or by CCTV, at least. Unless he just dumped his clothes on the way, I guess.'

'Pendle Street backs onto fourteen square miles of fields and woodland. Plus, Ernie's feet were absolutely shredded by twigs. Like, in ribbons, I mean.'

'So he walked through the fields?'

'Crawled too from the looks of his hands. Probably did it all night. Which means the cows and sheep may well have seen Ernie's wang a-wavin' but he could have easily skipped past human folk for *miles*.' Fenn sighed, and that small-toothed smile faded with it. 'He could literally have come from at least three to maybe five different villages or towns. So as you can imagine, tracking him down is getting on my wick . . . which means it's annoying me, by the way.'

'I know that phrase. So . . . I take it he's on that screen?' Matt nodded to the laptop. 'You keep looking at it.'

'Correct. This is the feed from next door. Here . . .' Fenn spun the laptop round to show a grey CCTV image. The camera was looking down on a man in hospital pyjamas. He had long, straggled black-looking hair, which hung ragged around his jawline. It covered his face. He was handcuffed to a metal bar in the centre of the desk, bandaged hands clasped together.

Matt tugged his chair a little closer and frowned. 'Why just a still image?'

'You're the second person to say that, but no. This isn't a still. It's video, right now. He just hasn't moved a single muscle for hours.'

Matt stared at the motionless man on the screen. 'What's the psychology report say?'

'Total mental collapse. He's shut down like an off switch. So, as you can see, we have very little to go on apart from this weird word that he wrote. The one I mentioned on the phone.'

'Ah yes . . .' Matt said. 'And did he scrawl this name on the greenhouse itself? On paper? If I could see it and check the spelling . . .'

'No, mate, he wrote it on his body.'

'Oh, I see. Where on his body?'

'On the stomach area.'

'Wrote it, how?'

'With a razor blade.'

Matt winced.

'Brace yourself. Picture coming . . .' Fenn pulled a photograph from his desk drawer, but he paused midway. 'You're okay with cuts and stuff, right? It's a bit grim, but they tell me you're a tough little bugger.'

'They do?' Matt laughed. 'Slide it over.'

'Good lad . . . just haven't got the time for a fainter right now. It's a bit messy, but you'll get the idea.'

Matt saw a midriff drenched in blood, and a navel filled with it. Like he'd done a belly flop into an entire pool of the stuff. Amongst it, he saw the source of the flow. A furious set of jet-black lines, slashed at angles, and along the bottom of the shot, a tufted line of dark pubic hair, sticky with clotted gunk. 'What's wrong with Post-it notes, eh?' Matt said. It was all he could think of.

These were letters, gouged deep, and at an angle too, so that they could be read the right way around to an onlooker. No curves at all, just sharp lines slashed against sharp lines. If Ernie did this himself, he had a shockingly steady grip. He pictured the utterly still man on the screen, reaching for a razor blade, patiently slicing his own skin as calmly as cutting through sandwich ham.

In the picture, the coagulating blood had stuck and gathered, making the letters harder to read – but it wasn't impossible.

39

Especially when a cloud outside decided to open a pathway in the sky. The entire room suddenly lit up with sun.

The word was there, carved amongst the blood.

And the word was *Baal-Berith*.

CHAPTER SIX

Fenn took a slow sip of his coffee. 'So, I typed this Baal-whatnot into Google but I just got reams of academia back and I can't make head nor tail of it. All I know is that it's supposed to be some sort of God, which isn't my strong suit, to be honest. So I called for this famous Matt Hunter I keep reading about.'

'Famous. That's hilarious.'

'Well, Mr Professor . . .' With his fingers woven behind his head, Fenn leant back. 'Please fill my life with enlightenment. Who the holy hell is Baal-bloody-Berith?'

Matt grabbed his backpack from the floor and hoisted it onto the desk. It landed with a deep thud. 'Come round my side.'

Fenn didn't stand. He just wheeled his squeaky chair in jerks, all the way around. Matt made some room.

'Okay, so I'm not surprised Google confused you because the

history of Baal is really complex. Especially because Judaism and Christianity really muddied the waters for him. There's a lot of theories, as you'll see . . .' Matt started pulling each book out, setting them on the desk, side by side. *The Malleus Maleficarum*; *The Praestigiis Daemonum*; *The Key of Solomon* and more.

'Erm . . .' Fenn looked at the growing book pile. 'I'd appreciate just the bullet points.'

'Bullet points. Sure. Then we start here . . . the Bible.' Matt picked a hefty King James Version up and flicked through its pages. 'Forget Baal-Berith for a second, and just focus on Baal. The Bible says he's an ancient Caananite God who was worshipped back in Old Testament times. He had cults, temples, priests, prophets, the whole shebang. Quite the established religious system, by all accounts.'

'Goodie or baddie?'

'Depends on who you ask,' Matt set his finger on a thin journal. 'I could show you ancient Ugaritic texts calling Baal a mighty hero, a good guy. But the Hebrew Bible – what Christians call the Old Testament, and the New Testament – they present Baal as a false God, an arch-rival to God himself. You could say the Bible demonised Baal.'

Fenn turned it over in his mouth. 'And the Berith part?'

'Well, Baal simply means "lord", and there's a bunch of Baals in the Ancient world. We get Baal-Hamon, Lord of the Multitude, Baal-Shalisha, The Lord of Three, Baal-Gad, The Lord of Fortune. Some say they're separate Gods, others say it's just different aspects of the *same* God. Whatever the case, the Bible paints the Baals as an evil distraction. Heck, the Hebrew texts say that Baal is even into child sacrifice. I guess the most famous example would be Baal-Zebub.'

Fenn silently mouthed the word, then his eyebrows sprang up. 'Oh . . . Beelzebub . . .'

'Yup. Where Baal means lord and Zebub means flies.'

'Lord of the flies . . .' Fenn stared at the photograph of slashed skin. 'I'm not liking where this is going, but carry on.'

'Okay, so Baal-Berith means the Lord of the Promise. Which sounds quite sweet really, but by the Middle Ages the Christian PR machine got well and truly established. So we see the rise of Christian demonology. That's a bunch of self-proclaimed experts mapping out the elaborate networks and hierarchies of demons. It's all pretty whacky. And in demonology, this ancient Canaanite deity called Baal-Berith goes from an obscure, possibly benign "Lord of the Covenant", to being thoroughly demonic. Look at this . . .' Matt opened one of his Christian demonology dictionaries and flicked through to find his marker. A Starbucks receipt. 'And I quote . . . *Baal-Berith is the keeper of the archives of Hell and also the curator of its infernal library. He is a powerful second order demon with enough majesty to officiate at many of Hell's key ceremonies.* And according to this he's even *a co-signatory to Satan, who formally certifies pacts with the Devil.*'

Fenn was folding his arms and chewing on his lip. Looking nervous.

Matt grabbed another book. 'Then he starts cropping up in demonic possession cases. Like this one from seventeenth-century France, where a—'

'Possession?' Fenn groaned. 'Oh, great.'

'Afraid so. Look, the short answer is this. Baal was seen by many as a benign God. But the church, inspired by the Hebrew Bible, ended up categorising Baal-Berith as this arch demon who tempts humans in two specific ways . . .'

'And what are they?'

'Blasphemy, and murder.'

Fenn whispered '*Shit*', under his breath.

'So I might be jumping to conclusions here, but you should definitely get those blood results back. Because if he's writing that specific name on himself, then maybe that's not all his blood on there.'

Fenn blew out a long, weary breath. 'Well, Professor. It's wild, but I do think this'll help press my boss to get a few more officers deployed. Work out where he's from.'

'You know, I could always pop in there and speak with him.'

Fenn thought about it, then his face scrunched. 'Nah. He's dangerous, and besides, he'll just stare at you in silence. He's done that to every other officer I've—'

When the door crashed open they both jumped. It was Pam, stumbling through, breathless.

Fenn stared at her. 'What on earth?'

'It's Ernie, sir. He's speaking. He—' Her eyes bulged when she saw the screen. 'Sir!'

Matt looked back at the desk.

The silent laptop screen showed the same feed as before, but now it was different. Ernie, the fastest demon in the west, may still have been cuffed to the table. But without either he or Fenn noticing, he'd now managed to crawl up on top of it. He was crouching and . . . Matt leant towards the screen . . . *swaying*. Frantic bare toes wriggled through the bandages on his feet, but his hanging hair still kept him mostly faceless. Even from this angle Matt could see Ernie's jaw was moving. Saying the same, silent thing over and over again.

'What's he saying?' Matt asked.

'He's whispering. He keeps saying . . .' Pam cleared her throat. '*Send him in, send him in.*'

Fenn grabbed something from his desk. 'Pam? Me and you better go and have a chat.'

'And me?' Matt said.

'Sir, look!'

Ernie's head shifted on the screen. It moved in a slow upwards creak towards the camera. Like a lizard on a rock hearing a fly scuttle across a leaf. And now they were all staring straight into Ernie's face.

'Oh, my . . .' Pam said. 'His eyes.'

They looked like two fuzzy black scribbles, scrawled by a troubled child. Two deep, ragged black holes.

'Jesus,' Fenn said.

'Relax,' Matt said. 'It's just the light. The shadow from his brow.'

Ernie instantly shifted again, his head cocked so his ear was towards the lens.

Pam looked at Matt. There was a definite shiver to her voice. 'It's like he heard your voice, Professor.'

Fenn's shirt had pulled out a bit. He started tucking it back in as he headed for the door. 'I've changed my mind, Matt. You can come in with us. And bring your books.'

CHAPTER SEVEN

Matt and Fenn stood in the corridor, while Pam tapped the code into the keypad. There was a small window in Ernie's door, but her blonde mane blocked it from view. Just before she reached the last digit of the code, her finger hovered over the final number.

'Press it,' Fenn said.

'Erm . . .' She didn't move.

'Press it, Pam.'

'Sir?'

'Yes?'

'He's still on the table.'

'And?'

'He's still talking.'

'*And?*'

'He's looking right at me.'

'Oh . . .' Fenn stepped forward and patted her on the shoulder. There was a tenderness to it. A signal that she ought not be embarrassed. Then he tapped the final number in himself. A locking mechanism clicked and the red light turned green. Pam stepped back and shook her uniform into place.

Matt hitched the bag on his shoulder. 'I'm ready.'

Fenn whispered, 'I'll start the conversation, Matt. You just sit in the corner and observe. But *if* he talks to you, then talk back. And watch me for signals. Got it?'

'Got it.'

Fenn tugged at his tie. 'You don't believe in this sort of thing, do you?'

'In demons? Nope. You?'

Fenn's voice said, 'No.' But his face said something quite different. He turned and peered through the little window in the door. 'Must be murder on his knees, crouching up there like that.' Then he took a deep breath, turned the handle and went in.

A few seconds later they were all inside, breathing Ernie air. And Ernie air, it turns out, smells like, Matt sniffed . . . like soil. It smelt like soil.

Three soft chairs were waiting to receive backsides in the windowless room, but no backsides seemed keen to touch them. Everybody stayed upright instead, staring at the crouching man on the desk.

Ernie stopped that weird whispering the second they'd walked into the room.

Come on, Matt. He thought to himself. *It was the second YOU walked into the room. That's when he stopped.*

In the flesh, Ernie's dark and hooded eyes weren't the shadowed, messy holes they'd been before on low-grade CCTV. That was no shock. But what did make them all stiffen was that the eyes were open. *Wide* open. It's not often you enter a room where someone is staring

47

quite so intently at you. But Ernie's gonzo eyes lolled out through the curtains of black hair. The look would have been slap-your-thigh hilarious if wasn't so damn unsettling. So Matt just nodded a polite and silent hello in response, then he looked away. He hitched his bag around for a bit on his shoulder, like it needed altering. It didn't.

He grabbed a chair and dragged it into the corner. He sat, just as he'd been told. When Pam closed the door she gave Matt a complicated, sweet look. Like she was both deeply relieved, yet genuinely upset that Ernie had chosen to glare so fixedly at Matt, and not her. And he really was staring, because once Matt sank into his chair he looked up and saw those same bulging eyes had slid a fraction in the dry-looking sockets, just to follow him.

Matt lowered his gaze to Ernie's midriff. He thought of the gashes under his hospital pyjamas. The name, *Baal-Berith*, sliced under there. The very moment he thought that, a smirk turned Ernie's mouth up at the edge. Then his eyes flickered and finally shrank into a more normal-sized stare.

Fenn, still standing, broke the silence. 'Hello friend,' he said with a smile.

Nice work, Fenn. Go for the cheery approach. Maybe do some balloon modelling for him.

'Is there anything you need? Would you like a drink, perhaps? Some food? There's a vending machine right outside this room. Lots of chocolate. My treat.'

Silence.

'And how about the temperature in here? Just say the word and we'll get it just how you like it.'

Silence.

All this time, Ernie just squatted up there, not like a man but more like a bizarre oversized puppet, hunched on the table. He seemed to be waiting for someone in the ceiling to grab his strings and to scoop up a pole so they could yap his jaw open and shut.

Fenn cleared his throat, 'You said *send him in, send him in* earlier. Is there someone you'd like to see?'

Silence.

'Somebody you'd like us to call? I can bring a phone—'

'Are *yooooouuu*?'

It was a shock to hear it.

A shock to see those chapped, smirking lips peel and tear slowly apart, then form a bottomless hole on the elongated 'oooo' sound. And from that hole came a groan from a throat so dry and brittle, it must be packed with dirt and sand and gravel and . . . cemetery soil. That's what it smelt like in here. Not just soil, but cemetery soil. Etched into Matt's nostrils from presiding over many graveside funerals.

'Are *yooouuuuu* thirsty?' he groaned the words out, directly at Matt. 'Wanna drink?'

Matt threw on a smile. 'I'm good, thanks. I had a milkshake in the car. But I appreciate you asking.'

Ernie's lips seemed to have paused on the 'k' sound of the word 'drink'. Like he was stuck on the last syllable he'd said.

'How about you? You sound absolutely parched,' Matt said. 'You should have some water. Okay?'

Ernie didn't answer but the 'k' shape in his mouth finally changed. It collapsed slowly into a slit, which may have been a smile, it was hard to tell. He started nodding slowly. Slowly and repeatedly, without stopping.

Fenn called back to Marriot, 'Get this man some water.'

She shot through the door, eager for clean air, and Fenn caught Matt's eye. It appeared that Matt now had the floor. Fenn gave him a nervous-looking nod to proceed.

CHAPTER EIGHT

'So . . . anyway, I'm Matthew. And I'm pleased to meet you.'

Still staring. *Still* slowly nodding. Stuck again on his last answer.

'So what's *your* name?'

Silence.

'Do you have a name?' Matt went on. 'I'd like to—'

'Pleased . . .' the word wheezed out of him. 'Very pleased to meet you, indeed.'

'Likewise.' Matt heard the sound of metal clinking. It was Ernie, gently tugging his cuffed hands away from the bar on the table.

'We should shake hands . . .' Ernie's voice was odd. It sounded, at times, like a buzz. 'Gentlemen shake.'

'I don't think that's allowed.'

'Oh? But that's what gentlemen do. They shake hands.'

'Yes but—'

'I like to be the gentleman.'

'That's nice.'

'I like to wriggle fingers into fingers.'

Matt looked back at Fenn briefly. 'Yes, but we don't actually know if you *are* a gentleman yet. None of us do. I mean you were found this morning covered in blood and we're a bit flummoxed about that, to be honest. We don't know how it happened, and we don't know your name. What is your name?'

A long silence followed, with the occasional clink of metal on metal.

'It'd be really gentlemanly if you could clear that up. Or just tell us what happened. Can you remember what happened?'

The metallic clinking stopped. 'Why did you ask for my name, just now?'

'I was being polite.'

'But you already know my name.'

'I'm afraid not. We haven't met.'

'We *have* met, Matthew.'

Fenn frowned, and so did Matt. 'We have?'

'Oh, yes.'

'Where?'

'Your house.'

'When?'

'Last night.'

Matt shook his head. 'I think—'

'In your bathroom,' Ernie started to tongue a line along his bottom lip. 'I'm in your bathroom.'

Matt laughed. 'You know, I'm pretty sure I'd remember meeting a fella like you in my bathroom.'

'I'm often there. You know that. I like it there. In the dark.'

'Anyway . . .' Matt said.

'In. The. Dark,' Ernie started nodding again. 'Oh, yes . . .'

Matt didn't speak for a moment, but Fenn kept urging him on.

'Well, I'll take your word for it,' Matt said, 'but back to my big question. What happened to you last night? And did you write that word into yourself?'

Ernie's toes suddenly broke into a flurry of movement, scrunching and wriggling against the desk. 'In fact, Matthew . . . why don't you switch all the house lights off one of these nights? Switch the lights off and go in the bathroom. Look into the mirrors and call my name. And I *bet* you'll see me . . . just like I see you. Then we can talk proper, about everything, and we can really wriggle our fingers together.'

Matt twitched as the door clicked open. It was Pam, creeping in with a white plastic cup. She handed the water to Fenn – there was no way she was going to hold it to Ernie's mouth. Fenn did, though. He reached over and set the plastic rim against his cracked and quivering bottom lip.

'Go ahead.' Matt smiled. 'Wet the whistle.'

Ernie immediately slid his tongue into the water. It pushed through his dry lips like a slug. Like a long tentacle of meat, which is all that tongues are, Matt supposed. Just Ernie's long meat tentacle that up till now had lain coiled in the deep caverns of his body, but was now unfurling. Pulling taut up his throat and slipping itself out into the light. Fenn tilted the cup on an angle, and Ernie started sucking and slurping the water, loudly. It dribbled down his chin. Nobody wiped his mouth.

'So what *is* your name?' Matt said, as Fenn stepped back and sat. 'Remind me.'

'I wrote it down.'

'On your stomach?'

The slow, smiling nod started again.

'So you're Baal-Berith, then?'

'Mmm-hmmm,' he closed his eyes and kept nodding. 'But I'd be grateful if you say it again, please.'

Matt frowned. 'Baal-Berith.'

'And again.'

'Baal . . .' Matt trailed off. 'Anyway, where were you last night?'

'I like it when you say it. Say my name again and I'll tell you where I was last night.'

Matt looked to Fenn. His face said, *Do it!*

'Okay,' Matt said. 'So where were you last night . . . Baal-Berith?'

His eyes flicked back open. 'Bathroom mirror.'

Matt sighed. 'Not that again.'

'No, I mean *after* I was in your mirror . . .' He curled a finger, so he was pointing at his own chest. 'I was in this one's. *His* mirror made of wood. His house. The man I'm in now.'

'I see. So you're speaking through his body?'

'That's true.'

Matt leant forward and pointed at Ernie's chest. 'So what's *his* name?'

'His name is Tom . . .'

'Tom who?'

'Tom, Tom, the piper's son . . . sucked the prick of an Englishman.' He snuffled a laugh into his shoulder.

'Well, that's a real shame you're being like that,' Matt put his hands on the arms of the chair. 'I hoped you wouldn't waste our time, but I think we'll just go—'

'Tom Leopold. This one's name is Tom Leopold.'

Matt spotted Fenn's face. The flush of excitement. He mouthed a frantic word . . . *where!* Ask him, *where?*

'Thank you for that. And Baal, where exactly was Tom—'

'Full name, please.'

'Sorry. Baal-Berith. Can you tell me where Tom's house is?'

'I can . . .' Another chuckle.

'Prove it, then . . .'

Silence passed, and eventually Matt put both hands on the armchair again.

'Easy,' Ernie said. 'It's Cheddington. Tom lives in . . . Chedd. Ing. Ton. And I live in Tom.'

'And the address?'

'Have you ever hurt anybody, Matthew?'

'Pardon me?'

'Have you ever *really* hurt anybody?'

Matt didn't answer right away, he just listened to Fenn's pencil scraping out the words Tom Leopold and Cheddington in a pad. He tore the sheet out and thrust it at Pam, whispering in her ear. She nodded and span away. He could hear her footsteps clicking on the corridor as she ran to call it in.

Tom, if indeed this guy really was called Tom, was oblivious to all this. All that existed was Matt, and the handcuffs, and the question. Which he said again, in almost a reverent whisper. 'Have you ever really hurt anybody? Let all that anger and bitter loneliness fill up your fists and turn them into claws? Have you done that, Matthew?'

Matt looked down and saw his own splayed hand pressing a man's cheek into the carpet of his dead mother's house. And then that hand curling into a fist and pounding that killer's cheekbone, which sounded less like the crunch of loud movie punches but more like the rhythmic slaps of skin. Over and over, stopping only to wipe the tears from his own cheek, then to start again.

'Yes, I've hurt others.' Matt swallowed. 'What about you, Mr Berith? Have *you* ever hurt anybody?'

'Oh, yes.'

'Did you hurt someone last night?'

'Oh, yes.'

'Someone at your house? In Cheddington?'

'Oh, yes. Mmm-hmmmm.'

'Who did you hurt?'

The slit smile was back.

'Who did you hurt?'

'I hurt . . . Jusssstttiiiiinnneeeeee.'

Matt and Fenn caught each other's gaze.

'Who's Justine?' Matt asked.

'Tom's sexy wife.'

'I see. And how bad did you hurt her?'

A sniff rattled things in his nose. 'Have you ever had a tongue in your mouth, Matthew?'

'All my life,' Matt said.

'I mean someone else's.'

'I couldn't possibly comment.'

'I had a tongue in my mouth last night.'

'Good for you.'

'I had Justine's tongue in my mouth.'

'Does Tom know?'

'But she was in the cellar at the time. And I was in the kitchen. Can you figure out how that was possible?' He started giggling. 'Because all things are possible.'

Matt looked away for a moment. 'So you're saying you killed her?'

'Tongues are much, much bigger and much, much heavier than you think. Much thicker than *lips* . . .' The meat tentacle pushed through again and tasted air. The CCTV camera seemed to buzz at that. Some deep circuit in the system was saying this was the right time to zoom in.

'We need an address,' Matt said. 'Now.'

'Then say it again.'

'Your name?'

He closed his eyes and nodded.

'Baal-Berith. *There* . . .' Matt said. 'So where—'

'And again.'

55

'For crying out loud, Baal-Berith . . . Baal-Berith. Now what's the address?'

'Say it again . . .' For the first time in this entire interview, Tom had torn his gaze from Matt. Now they were on Fenn. '*Both of you* . . . say my name . . . and then I'll tell.'

Matt and Fenn looked at each other. They said the name at the same time. It came out awkwardly. Like when girl bands announce their band's names in interviews. 'Baal-Berith.'

Tom's slit grew into a huge, toothy smile, and Matt could see that tongue of his was frantically pushing behind his teeth, trying to squeeze through the gaps. Matt looked away. The sight of that pink flesh, pushing with a mind of its own, wasn't good for the psyche. Perhaps the tongue was the only thing left of Tom Leopold, and it was fighting to get out. Tom's head slowly started returning to the place it was at the very start. The heavy eyelids closing half over, the forehead sinking, the cuffed wrists stopping their constant yanking. Then he said one more thing.

'Look for the cross,' Tom whispered. 'It's quite the pretty one. I'm tired now . . . okay?'

Tom was silent from then on, and no amount of Matt asking for a street name would help. Even Fenn said the words Baal-Berith another few times, hollering it out like he was trying to rouse his Amazon Alexa. But the ancient name fell through the air, a dud firework. So Fenn checked his watch and hurried out the door, not looking back.

'Hey,' Matt dragged his bag. 'Wait for me.'

'Oh, sorry.'

In the corridor, Fenn closed the door and tapped in the code. The lock clicked shut and the light turned red. Through the window, Matt saw that Tom or Ernie or Baal-Berith – or whoever the hell it was – was somehow back where he'd started. Off the desk and sitting in his seat, head down, unmoving. Matt pictured that long strip of tongue, sliding and coiling back into its dark cave.

'I'm coming with you,' Matt said as they hurried down the corridor.

'I'd appreciate that.' Fenn pushed into what looked like a reception area to find Pam just hanging up the phone.

'I've got officers looking through the files for Tom Leopold,' she said. 'And I've sent a car to Cheddington.'

'Good. Then tell the car we'll join them. Oh, and tell them to look for a cross.'

'What sort of cross?'

'A pretty one,' Matt added.

She frowned. 'Okay.' She thrust a sheet of paper at Fenn. 'That's a postcode for Cheddington High Street. Probably half an hour's drive from here. It's a small village. I should probably come with you.'

'No. I want you standing at Tom's door.'

Her eyes flashed. 'By myself?'

'Who else is there?'

'But . . .'

'Just stay at the door, and watch him, all right? And you call me if there's any change. It's all locked.'

She swallowed and nodded. 'And if he starts talking? Should I go in?'

'No. Just call me. And if he says anything, you write it down. And Pam? Best not look in his eyes.'

CHAPTER NINE

It may have been early March, but right now, the world felt a long, long way from spring. The afternoon was dull, cold and as grey as a gun as Fenn's car rolled slowly along Cheddington High Street. Matt leant out of the window like a motorway dog, and a gust of grim wind flapped his eyes into a flicker. He pulled back and resumed his methodical scan from house to house, to garage to house.

'Still no crosses,' Matt said. 'Plenty of gnomes, though. I've never really understood what people see in—'

The car jerked forward as Fenn hit the brakes.

Matt's cheekbone bumped against the window frame. 'Er, hello? Nearly chopped my head off.'

Fenn was rummaging a clumsy, fat finger into his ear. He dug his hands-free earpiece out and it bounced against his thick neck, tapping a flashing blue light against his shirt collar. He shook his head and slapped a hand on the steering wheel.

'What's wrong?' Matt said.

'He's taking the piss out of us.'

'Why? What's happened?'

'I've just been informed that there *are* no Leopolds living in Cheddington, at all.'

'How about a Leon?'

'Nope.'

'Leo?'

'Nope. Not in the records, anyway.'

Matt groaned. 'Let's just keep on looking, though. Least until we find the cross.'

'The cross? I'm telling you, he's taking the piss . . .' The engine moaned its own frustration as the terraced streets of Cheddington rolled by again. They passed a school on the right which seemed weirdly quiet for a Tuesday in term time.

After a while, Fenn started making small talk. 'So, come on, then. Did you really used to be a vicar? Like a proper one?'

'Yes, my child, I did. But it wasn't for me in the end.'

'When did you know, that it wasn't right?' The car rolled on, as they looked from house to house.

'Well, I knew I wasn't fitting in well at Bible college when I made a joke in the dining hall and it fell flat.'

He looked across at him. 'What was the joke?'

'Somebody asked me if I believed in a theological concept called Penal Substitution, so I put a banana between my legs and said, you mean this? I thought that was pretty damn funny, but nobody laughed. I think I was doomed from that moment.'

Fenn started chuckling.

'Seriously, that was a clever, multi-levelled joke, that.'

'I'm more of an agnostic myse—'

'*Stop.*' Matt slammed a palm against the dash.

Fenn hammered the brakes. The car jerked hard.

'Over the top of those trees. There.'

Fenn was shorter than Matt. A lot of people were. So he had to push himself up and press his slip of hair into the ceiling of the car. At first he saw nothing, but then his grimace of physical discomfort turned into a cautious, edgy grin. The engine surged again and he quickly pulled away.

The car reached the shaggy row of trees and he swung a hard right into a large concrete drive, scattered with three other cars. Fenn almost clipped the back of an old Skoda in his haste to get in. Their tyres ground to a stop, and for a few seconds, all Matt heard was the skittery hiss of the wind, whistling through a gap in his window.

'Out you get,' Fenn said. 'Chop-chop.'

When they stepped out into the cold, Matt noticed that Fenn had blocked all three cars in. Deliberately, he could tell. Fenn looked across the roof of his car and narrowed his eyes at the building, biting the inside of his cheek. 'Would you call that cross pretty?'

'Prettier than most, I suppose.'

They headed towards the little church, an old prefab, all wood and peeling roof felt. The walls were painted a sickly shade of flaking blue, and yet the front door was a horrendously insipid salmon pink. That door *must* have been a deep red once, only now it had become heavily sun-faded. If not, then the church had chosen their door to be the shade of an uncooked economy sausage. Surely that was reason enough to cancel all religious movements with immediate effect.

He watched Fenn walk forward to the door, but Matt slowed so he could look up to the apex of the roof. The cross was made of two thick strips of aluminium bolted together, and draped around each strip were fairy lights. The kind you'd buy in a garden centre to magic-up a tree on a darkening barbecue night. The bulbs twinkled on and off against the dull, cloud-packed sky above. The lights were cable tied and fixed, but not so tight that they didn't shiver a little in the wind. They made a clinking noise, and the thought occurred to Matt that this sound was a bit like (actually, it was identical) to Tom's handcuffs, tapping against the bar.

CHAPTER TEN

They stepped inside the cold church porch, each foot pressing into a spiky-looking welcome mat, which read: *Holy Spirit You Are Welcome Here*. He also clocked a noticeboard, bolted to the wall. It was filled with neat papers, including an A4 sheet. It proudly announced a cutting-edge outreach event this coming weekend – *Community Potato Carving and* BIBLE PUPPET SHOW*!* And a demand in oversized capitals: BRING THE KIDS*!*

The sudden sound of muffled voices made Fenn slap a finger to his lips, but they kept going, heading up the corridor towards a wooden door with frosted glass panels. When they went through, the voices grew louder, but not much. They found a simple church sanctuary with long wooden pews with Bibles neatly placed, and – what was wrong with these people? – salmon-pink carpets. The entire place was empty. Behind the pulpit onstage was another door, and this was where the voices were coming from. It must have been the vestry.

Nodding to each other Matt and Fenn both headed down the aisle. If this had been America, Fenn might be pulling out a handgun right now. Shoulders locked into a cool-looking, Kiefer Sutherland grip. But this was Cheddington, England, and so the only weapon they had was Fenn's podgy, clammy hand, reaching towards the handle of the vestry door.

He didn't open it. Fenn cupped his ear towards the wood instead, and Matt did the same. Matt knew those tones and rhythms instantly. People were praying in there. It sounded like the classic patting the divine back stuff – *Lord, we just want to say we love you. We just want to worship you, Father. We just, just, just . . .*

Fenn pushed the door and it swung open so silently that the man and two women inside didn't notice at all. In fact, for a long moment Matt and Fenn were able to just stand there and watch. The man and the two women were on their knees in the far corner, focused on a candle and scatter of papers on the floor. Harp music drifted from a Bluetooth speaker up on a filing cabinet.

Matt took a step further inside . . . and froze when he saw all the eyes.

A rack of puppets hung on hooks on the side wall. Biblical characters . . . Moses, Jesus, Mary, Peter, Centurion. And the token Random Blind Guy who was ready to be healed and made a 'full person', as if disabled people weren't totally human before.

Their felt mouths gaped open and their arms and little hands lolled with thin black rods hanging from them. Empty bodies just waiting for a hand to slide up inside and bring them to life. He tried not to think of Tom Leopold, and his own puppeteer, Baal-Berith – but it wasn't easy. Instead Matt considered how many churches had bought puppets in a bid to appear more normal and cool and less creepy. Oh, the irony. He stared at the goggled, bugged-out eyes of the apostle Paul, staring up at the ceiling, with a twisted neck.

Matt tore his eyes from the Muppet Bible Movie, because the prayers were moving into more interesting territory.

'. . . and just drag it out of him, Lord,' the man whispered. 'With the same power that made the world and raised the dead and flung all stars into space. With the kingdom authority of the Lord Jesus Christ, drag every ounce of darkness from his heart and set our brother free. For your glory, and for your fame, and in the blessed name of . . .'

Fenn coughed into his fist. The prayers stopped instantly.

Three heads whipped towards them. The women saw Matt and Fenn first. Each looked in their sixties, seventies perhaps. Their cardigans screamed the latter. A frown on each face tripled their wrinkles. Then the man's head turned, twisting around to see them. Matt saw a boyish face appear, with a crop of curly ginger hair and a neat ginger beard. Quite handsome with it, freckles and all. He wore a thick woollen jumper, in light green. Something that a farmer might like – only the cut was stylish.

'I'm terribly sorry but . . .' he cleared his throat. His accent was like a 1940s newsreader. Clipped and proper. 'I'm afraid this prayer meeting is rather private. But if you'd like—'

'Do any of you know a man with the surname Leopold?' Fenn said.

The two women clearly didn't. They looked at each other and shrugged.

But the man's reaction . . . now, that really was quite different. He didn't say a single word in response. He didn't have to. It's just that the colour vanished from his cheeks, like a switch flicked in his bloodstream turning all the red cells white. 'Who are you?' he said.

It took an awkward ten seconds for Fenn to dig his ID from his trouser pocket. He flashed it. 'I'm Detective Sergeant Martin Fenn and this is Professor Matt Hunter. And, Father, we need to know why you just gulped at the name Leopold.'

The man pushed himself up. 'He's a member of our church.'

The women frowned. One of them, who wore golden teddy bears for earring studs, shook her head. 'Since when?'

The other agreed. 'There's no Leopold here, Pastor.'

'Actually, Mary, there is.' He was up on his feet, wiping his hands down on his blue jeans. He blinked a lot, almost a squint, but not quite. His green eyes matched the wool of his jumper. 'Detective, I'm Simon Perry. I'm the pastor here and I saw him last night.'

'Where?'

'At his house. But I haven't seen him since. Is he hurt?'

'We just need his address. Right away.'

'Of course. He lives here in Cheddington. 22 Kerry Avenue.'

One of the women looked like she'd just swallowed a wasp. 'Pastor. I'm sorry, but that's not right. There's no Leopold at 22. That's where . . .'

'Where Tom lives . . .' he said.

'Yes, Tom . . .' The ladies shared a look of bafflement.

Matt had already walked towards the candle on the floor. He dangled an arm down to the A4 sheets. 'May I?'

'Go ahead.' Perry smiled.

Matt lifted a wedding photograph from the floor and saw a beaming couple sat against the white leather seats of a Bentley. Both were holding one another's hands, fingers laced together. Their rings were clearly in shot and the bride had long, thick, beautifully curled hair draped over her shoulder. The man, all rugged and smiling, had that happy glint of pure, unfiltered delight in his eye.

Matt stared at the man's face, and shivered. 'That's him. That's Leopold.'

'No . . . that's Tom *Riley*,' one of the women said. 'Everybody knows that. That's a picture of Tom and Justine on their wedding day.'

Justiiiiiiiinnnne.

Perry was leaning against a desk, arms folded. 'Mary, you're right . . . his name really is Tom Riley, but his father used to call him Leopold as a child. It was a nickname, and a cruel one at that. If you'll excuse for a moment, ladies.' Perry waved Matt and Fenn into the corner, and started to whisper to them, out of the women's earshot. 'Look, Tom's always had long blonde hair, throughout his life, even as a child, but his father mocked him for it. He called him Leo the Lion, then that wound up as Leopold. He's dyed his hair black since, and his dad's long dead but . . . where did you even get that name, anyway?'

'It's the name he gave us.'

He blinked. 'So Tom's with you? I don't understand. I thought you were looking for him?'

'I think it's best you grab a jacket, Reverend,' Fenn said. 'Wind's getting up.'

'I don't follow.'

'You're taking us to Tom's house.'

'Right now?'

'Right now.'

Fenn apologised to the ladies, while Perry reached over and tugged a dark blue duffel coat from a coat peg. The sleeve hit one of the hanging puppets and it slid off its hanger.

When Perry didn't notice, Matt said, 'Your Moses just fell off.'

One of the women was already scooping it up. She dusted off its white curly beard and held it for a moment, smiled, then placed it carefully on the hook. 'I love these little chaps,' she said.

CHAPTER ELEVEN

Fenn swung the wheel. 'It's left, yeah?'

'Right.' Perry nodded. 'Sorry. I mean that's correct. It's left. Turn left . . . he lives on the outskirts of the village, overlooking the fields.'

Matt was sitting in the back, still fumbling for his seat belt when Fenn surged into a sharp, three-point turn. He slid around the smooth leather back seat, then finally clicked himself in. All docked, Matt watched the houses slide past and asked, 'So, Reverend . . . why were you at his house last night?'

He turned. 'Tom just had a problem he wanted to discuss.'

'Which was?'

'I'm not really at liberty to say.'

Just as Matt opened his mouth, Fenn switched gears and said, 'Let's just check the house first and see what we're dealing with. We'll dig more after that. Okay, Matt?'

'Okay,' Matt said. A little voice from the back seat.

'Take this right,' Perry said. 'Then drive all the way to the end, then turn left. Where that rabbit is. Do you see?'

Matt looked from the window and saw a little black rabbit sitting on the edge of a kerb. It was sniffing the air, paws dangling.

'Bold little tyke,' Fenn said, 'coming into the streets.'

'Not really . . . we're right on the fields here. You see rabbits round here all the time.'

Matt watched the rabbit and the rabbit watched him, then the car drifted by and Matt sank back into his seat. The houses were getting more and more spaced out, and he started to see stretches of dirt paths winding off into vast rolling fields. He saw a washing machine on its side in a ditch. A dog's tail hung out of it, wagging.

They reached the end of the road. 'What's Tom do for a living?' Fenn asked.

'He's a chef at the Cross Keys pub in town. Best shepherd's pie this side of heaven.'

'And his wife?' Matt shared a cautious glance with Fenn. 'What does she do?'

'Justine? She's a mobile hairdresser, though my wife says she mostly cuts from home these days. She's set up a little salon for herself in the cellar. I bet she'll be in today . . .' Perry was looking at Fenn. 'Please tell me where Tom is. You two are worrying me.'

'He's safe, don't worry,' Fenn said.

Perry looked thoroughly unconvinced and turned his head to gaze across the fields. 'Just follow this dirt track and it's the last house on the right.'

The car started rocking gently from side to side as the ground turned from tarmac to dirt. Then Fenn pulled up to another police car that Fenn had called in. It was already there waiting. Two uniformed officers stepped out.

As soon as Matt stepped out, he looked across the vast open

space and felt a wave of wind push at his back and sweep across the fields. It was easy to follow its journey. It flattened out the tall grass, pressing the field like a wave, like a huge invisible hand, stroking the land. It rolled up into the distance to the top of the hill, where a crop of tall trees stood alone. Fenn had said that Totternhoe was somewhere over that hill, and the greenhouse on Pendle Street that Tom was found in. Matt clocked the distance and realised that a naked fella could easily cross that entire stretch and be missed.

Hair dancing, Matt turned to the house. Its white PVC door was spattered with dirt and soil from the field. In fact, the entire front looked hammered with the elements. The pink council bricks looked crumbly and jagged in places. Weather-beaten.

'Reverend?' Fenn asked.

'Yes?' His arms were in a tight fold as he stared at the house. His duffel coat had a hood, but he hadn't flipped it up yet.

'I'd like you to wait here for now. We're just going to have a quick little gander.'

'Sergeant?' Perry's voice dropped to a whisper.

'Yes.'

'Would you like me to pray, before you go in?'

'Do you think we need it?' Fenn said.

'I do . . .'

Matt came round. 'And why do you say that?'

'Can't you feel it?' Perry pulled his arms in tighter, staring at the house. 'Something not right. Look at the sky.'

Matt saw a swirl of dark cloud looming.

'Then pray it doesn't rain.' Fenn pushed on the gate and headed up the broken, breeze block path to the front doorstep. Matt noticed how slow he was walking. A measured stroll, so he could look left and look right, and stare down at the path for signs or evidence. Matt did the same, and couldn't spy anything quirky. No abandoned knives, no bloody, Tom-sized footprints soaked into the concrete.

Fenn reached the front door and knocked. Three hard, serious-sounding booms.

They waited, but all they could hear was the distant hiss of blades of grass sliding around and making room for the sky. Fenn took a pencil from his inside pocket and used the rubber end of it to lift the metal lip of the letter box. He called through the gap. 'Mrs Riley? Mrs Justine Riley?' His voice sounded strained in that position. When he heard no reply he cranked up the volume. 'Are you there, Mrs Riley?'

Matt turned back and spotted Reverend Perry. He'd finally stopped hugging himself, and the biting wind had forced him to put his hood up. Now his hands were locked into a ball, tapping off his chin as he paced the dirt out there. He was whispering to God like an earnest monk, unable to look at the house.

'No cause for alarm,' Fenn shouted through the door, 'but this is the police, and we'd like to talk to you . . . or anybody else who might be in there.' Fenn's voice dissolved into a strained groan. He could crouch no longer. He shot a hand out and Matt helped him up. 'Got a dodgy knee,' he whispered. 'Sports injury.'

Matt gave him a sympathetic nod.

They tried another option and walked towards the tall wooden side gate. Fenn pressed the handle down and was about to speak when the handle suddenly whipped from his fingers. The gate flung inwards with a loud and snapping crash, and they all braced themselves for whoever had dragged it open. But there was nobody there except the wind that seemed to enjoy taking humans by surprise. An overstuffed wheelie bin spat out bits of torn cardboard, swirling into the air.

The house had a side door, and it was wide open. Matt could see the blood from here.

CHAPTER TWELVE

Fenn held up a finger of caution and started walking towards the door. The other officers followed, and so did Matt. They started to see the kitchen lino, which had two thick smears of crusting red, sticky with dried leaves from outside. Fenn pointed to the ghost of bloodied fingers that had grasped the door handle as Tom, no doubt, had sprung out of it and vanished into the garden, and off into the fields.

The other officers headed through first.

The blood on the kitchen floor looked like pure spillage, but as they crept further inside they saw the messy outline of bare feet.

'Matt,' Fenn said. 'Don't stand in it.'

I wasn't planning to, Matt thought. He nodded and took a deep breath.

They followed the prints into the hallway and found a thin yellow carpet punctuated with dark, ragged footmarks. The walls, painted with classic magnolia, had intermittent prints of a single bloodied hand. Always with a sharp smear off the fingers. It gave the impression that the hand must have had claws. Though in reality, it must have just slid each time, dragging trails of blood from the fingertips.

One handprint had smeared across a glass picture frame, toppling it to the floor. It lay shattered on the carpet, and as they passed through in a deep, solemn silence, Matt saw Justine Riley's distorted face, beaming up through shards of glass. She was smiling with pride, getting some sort of hairdressing award on a stage.

They'd been silent up until now, so when Fenn called out her name again, it filled the hallway with a grenade of deafening sound. 'Mrs Riley?' he hollered, and Matt blinked. 'Mrs Riley? Can you hear us?'

The bloody footprints stopped at a door under the stairs, and Fenn nodded to the officer to tug it open. Matt braced himself for a hoover, ironing board, or a sliced-up corpse to come tumbling out. But it opened to some stairs, descending, and a long strand of fairy lights, wrapped around the bannister. They were switched on, beaming a pulsing, cosy glow. Only some of the bulbs were red. They were soaked in red.

He could smell hairspray. Lots of it. But it mingled with the now heavy stench of blood to nauseating effect. And he could hear music too, as they all headed softly down. The soft slink of panpipes and synth pad, and in the background, the occasional cry of whale song. The steps creaked as they slowly reached the bottom, and Matt saw two hairdresser chairs, and two mirrors, framed with bright, glowing, showbiz bulbs.

Matt's heart ached a little, just then. He pictured Justine fixing up these lights, and hanging all these black and white, Toni and Guy headshots on the walls. He glanced at the sweepable lino floor and the hand-painted sign she'd hung across the mirrors that simply said 'Headmasters by Justine'. Which was both corny and sweet and profoundly heart-breaking all at the same time. Because he could smell her in the air. Even though he'd never met Justine Riley, and never really would, he knew the smell of her now. The reek of her. All it took was to follow the trail. The whales sang on, like sirens guiding men to a cold, rocky, dangerous shore.

There was a moment. A very brief, blink of an eye moment, that Matt had a dumb, cruel sense of hope. Because there was a curtain covering a recess, and he assumed she might be hiding in there. But when the officer slowly pulled it back, they saw nothing but brooms and a hoover and a stack of Tresemmé conditioner still sealed with cellophane. There was a long mirror in there too, and a light switch, which Fenn clicked—

Oh . . .

He saw her. Trapped and screaming forever in the mirror.

They all stared at the reflection, the new light now showing a previously blacked-out corner behind them. It was now bathed in trendy, harsh spotlights. He heard himself mutter a loud trembling gasp against his wrist. The other two said nothing of reprimand. No mockery that a civilian should react with a great, gulping yelp. Because they had sucked all their own breath in too, in their own way, when they saw her in the mirror.

They all turned at the same time. The world's worst boyband, spinning for their final, funky close-up. They twisted on the sticky lino so they might find their audience of one. The flipped reality of what the reflection had promised.

Sinks.

There were two white sinks, near to the wall. Where Justine could stand and stroke the hair of local ladies, and listen to their plans and irritations with their husbands, and their thoughts on this year's *X-Factor* line-up, and how they missed their long-dead mums so very much.

Justine wasn't washing hair today. She wasn't massaging this time. It was her turn to sit in the chair.

Matt's hand was on his mouth. It was all he could do to stop what might at any moment rush up from his stomach and hammer past his lips.

Justine, with clothes torn open and underwear showing, lay splayed on the chair, her left arm idly dangling. This left half could have just been her relaxing in her backroom, dreaming of the future of her growing business. But the right arm had been snapped back and completely broken with horrendous, savage force. And the legs too, had the same, vile pattern. Her left leg, naturally bent and sitting, as innocently as any other leg that had ever sat in this chair. While the other, her right, was rammed wide and open as far as it would possibly go, so that the bones of her inner thigh must have cracked very loudly down here. Like he was pushing her legs apart so they might meet full circle round the back.

It was the face, though, that's what made Matt look away. The ragged cheek and, Jesus Christ . . . the hair. She had a luscious, beautiful head of hair in those photographs, that no doubt wowed the crowds on her wedding day. And must have filled her customers with so much confidence, because their hairdresser had the follicle prowess of a Hollywood star. Now, he saw great matted clumps of it lying on the floor, scattered around her bare feet, still attached to skin.

Tom must have torn her hair out with his bare hands.

The tongue too. Not that he dared look.

The others were doing that. He could hear them creeping forward, shaking their heads in utter disgust and peering down into her mouth, which was open very wide. Her jaw pulled down so hard it had dislodged completely. It would never close again.

Let them look, Matt thought, as he moved towards the stairs in something not quite a walk, not quite a stagger. *That's* their *job,* he thought. *They're the ones who get paid for this. Not me. Let them be the ones who check if the tongue is indeed gone, and they can tell me later, when I'm far away from this place, and when I can't smell it.*

He started walking back up the stairs on rubber legs and he put both of his trembling hands up to cover his ears. He just wanted to block out that damn new-age music that kept on playing. There was no point in him staying any longer to watch. And there was certainly no need for him to watch what they were doing, gazing down that deep cavernous hole. But still the music played on and he could hear the rising song of that ancient demon Baal-Berith. Who, it turns out, moans with the voice of a lonely, desperate, beautiful whale, trapped in the deepest, coldest ditch of the ocean.

CHAPTER THIRTEEN

'And what time did you arrive?' Fenn splayed both hands flat on the desk. '*Well?*'

Reverend Perry's face was now so paper-white that even his freckles seemed to have faded, but his ginger hair and beard looked redder than ever. He took a long breath in, and his green eyes fixed on the top corner of the interview room. The same spot he'd been staring at from the moment Matt and Fenn scraped their chairs up and started firing questions.

'Hey,' Fenn leant forward. 'I said what time—'

'Sorry.' Perry's eyes flickered. 'I just . . . you haven't . . . you haven't told me how she . . .' His eyes bore into the corner. '. . . how she died.'

Matt went to speak, lips ready to say *in total fucking agony*, but instead he said, 'Reverend Perry. I appreciate this is traumatic but—'

'Moody organ players, yes. Difficult church meetings, fine. Arguments, premarital affairs, even . . .'

Fenn's face crunched. 'Huh?'

Perry dragged his eyes from the corner and looked at them both. With a nod of understanding, Matt pushed the glass of water towards him. 'I guess that's the level of issues you expected as a pastor, right?'

'Yeah . . . funerals, weddings, grumpy old people who hate drum kits, of course . . . but not this. Not *murder*.'

'It's a lot to take in. Have a drink.'

'But you still need to answer our questions,' Fenn clicked his pen as Perry glugged. 'So just give us a picture of your movements yesterday. I want the timing.'

He tilted his glass and gazed into the dregs. 'I took part in a funeral for one of my old Bible college tutors. That was in London. I was there for most of the day. I didn't get back to the village until 6 p.m. Then I went straight to the pub to meet my wife.'

Fenn looked down at his sheet. 'That's Claire Perry?'

'Yes. We meet in the pub every Monday because—'

'Which pub?'

'. . . because couples need to invest the time. Are you married, Detective Fenn?'

'Which pub?'

He sniffed. 'The Merricot. We had a few drinks. Soft ones. We didn't stay long.'

'And did anybody see you?' Matt asked.

'What sort of question is that?'

'A routine one,' Fenn said. 'Were you seen?'

'Of course we were seen. We didn't drink in the cellar . . .' He bit his lip. 'I'm sorry. That came out sarcastically. It wasn't meant to. May I have more water?'

Matt reached for the jug.

'We left the pub at about 6.45 p.m.'

'You're quick drinkers,' Matt said.

'I promised Tom I'd visit him. He was struggling and I'd been supporting him, pastorally. I dropped Claire at home, then I got to his place at just after, hmm . . . 7 p.m. Yes. Seven.'

'Was Justine home?'

'No. She volunteers at the Brownies. She'd have been there until eight-thirty, I think. Later, perhaps. I hear she's very community-minded. I left Tom's house at about 7.40 p.m., before Justine came back, certainly. I went straight home and spent the evening watching television with my wife. I can tell you precisely what programme we were watching.' He blinked then sat bolt up, the thought occurring. 'Gosh, Claire. She'll be worried about me. Can I—'

'Soon,' Fenn said. 'And you were with your wife the entire evening?'

'Yes. After TV we went to bed and that was that. Call her and she'll confirm everything I'm telling you.'

'We already have. Your times all match.'

'Really? Oh . . . well, there you go,' Perry said.

'Okay, we've got the timing . . .' Matt said. 'So how about you tell us what happened at Tom's.'

'That's rather private.'

'I think we're past the point of privacy.'

'But Tom spoke to me in strict confidence.'

'Somebody is dead,' Matt said.

'I appreciate that, but it's a delicate pastoral—'

'Reverend Perry.' Fenn put his pencil down. 'Justine's hair was torn out in clumps. It was ripped from her scalp and left scattered on the floor. And now it's sitting in sealed cellophane bags a few rooms away. I think you need to tell us everything. Do you understand?'

Perry's eyes had already closed on the word 'clumps'. Now he finally opened them and reached a shaky hand for the water. 'I feel sick.'

There was a litter bin near Fenn's foot. He reached down and upended the few tissues from it. Then he slid it with his foot towards Perry's chair. It made a scrape. 'As you were saying.'

'Er . . . okay . . .'

Matt said, 'Take a breath.'

He did, a deep one. It seemed to reset him. 'So, Tom and Justine were having issues. He said they were growing distant . . . they didn't spend much time together.'

Fenn turned his finger in the air. 'There's more.'

Perry pursed his lips. 'Fine. He was convinced Justine was having an affair. He'd worried about it for months. And yet there was no evidence to base this on. I told him if he was so sure of it, he should confront her, but he refused.'

'Why?'

'He was never one for an argument. Tom avoided conflict to an unhealthy degree. You know, I never saw him raise his voice. Not once. I think he didn't want to be like his dad, who was very . . . shouty . . .' Perry shook his head. 'But inside . . . I could tell Tom had this rage, which he never let out. I told him that bottling it up wasn't good for him. I was worried for his mental health. I told him to go to his GP.'

'And did he?' Matt asked.

'He did. In fact, I went with him, for support. He was diagnosed with intense anxiety and was put on pills. I think they helped at first, but there was something deeper going on.'

Fenn and Matt shared a glance and Fenn's voice came out low. 'Carry on, Reverend.'

'I saw it most when I prayed with him. That rage of his. We'd read scripture together and I'd see his face start to twist and contort, like he was in a great deal of pain. He'd even swear sometimes.'

'Lots of people swear,' Matt said.

'Not Tom. He was the sweetest, quietest man you could ever

meet. I'd never heard a crude word from him in my life, until the last few months. And he only swore when we prayed. Little words at first, but then it just started pouring out of him. A torrent, and terribly vulgar too. Unrepeatable things. It was like the Devil was reaching up inside of him and working his eyes and flapping his mouth. Well, I don't like to admit it, but . . .'

'Please do.'

'He frightened me. The way he'd sit in my office in his usual gentle, demure way. And he'd be chatting about a new recipe he was working on for the pub's winter menu and then I'd see this flash of something in his eye. And he'd focus on me with a terrible intensity. He'd start asking me questions. Scary questions like if I was happy with my life, and if I ever wished for more.'

Matt laced his fingers together. 'Why are those scary questions?'

'Because it was like if I ever said I did want more in my life, he'd have some way of giving it me. There was just something *wrong* about it. I'd see him singing the hymns in the pews on a Sunday, just like anybody else, but then I'd catch his gaze and he'd start smiling at me, only it wasn't even a smile. It's hard to explain, but it chilled me. I saw him . . .' He swallowed. 'I saw him lick the Bible once, during the Eucharist. He did it in a . . . how can I put it . . . a sensual way. I guess that's when I realised his problems were beyond the medical.'

Matt poured himself some water. 'Intense anxiety and depression can manifest in unusual ways.'

Perry just frowned at them both like this was obvious. 'Look, gentleman. I know depression. I've seen it up close. My own mother was bi-polar and my brother, God bless him, suffered from anxiety for years. But this thing Tom had . . . it was something else entirely. It came from a different place. So I knew that the real solution to his problems wouldn't be found in a bottle of pills . . .' That made Perry trail off for a moment, and he clasped his hands together like he

80

was praying. 'I'm saying he needed spiritual deliverance. He needed something very particular.'

'And what's that, exactly?'

'Why exorcism, of course. He needed exorcism.'

CHAPTER FOURTEEN

Exorcism.

There it was. The word Matt could tell was coming at some point in this conversation, just as sure as a cloud will cover the sun. The hissing repetition of the 's' sound fizzed in the air. *Exorcism, Possession* . . . both words sound like they're being interrupted by white noise. Or was it more appropriate to say, entwined with a serpent's *hissssssss*.

'So you believe Tom was demonically possessed?' Matt said.

'Absolutely. I started reading up on it, so I knew what to look for. And my goodness, the evidence was undeniable. The aversion to Christian symbols, the foul language, the swings in mood.'

Matt shrugged. 'If that's the criteria, then I'm as possessed as they come.'

Fenn put a silencing hand on Matt's arm. 'So you told Tom this?'

'I suggested it was a distinct possibility, yes.'

'And did you perform an exorcism on Tom?'

He was staring down into his empty cup.

'You did it last night, didn't you? At his house.'

He looked up at the corner of the room again and nodded. 'When I arrived, I could tell something was wrong. It was dark and very cold outside. *Exceptionally* so. The winds were coming over the fields, harsher than I have ever seen in my life. I parked and noticed that his front door was open, and I mean wide open. The light was shining down the path. So I went inside and I called his name. I heard Tom calling up for me. He was in the cellar . . .' Perry cleared his throat. 'In the salon, I should say.'

'So you went down?' Matt said.

'Of course. It was dark down there. Pitch-black, in fact. I nearly lost my footing on the stairs, but he must have realised because he flicked a very small lamp on. I found him standing near the sinks. I noticed that even the little lamp was making him squint. He covered his eyes with his hand. Like he'd been down in the dark for quite some time. He was turning one of the taps on and do you know what he said?'

Matt and Fenn both shrugged.

'He asked me if I'd like my hair washed. He said *your hair looks a little greasy, let me wash it for you.* I remember that very vividly, because I thought it was the strangest thing for a man to ask another man.' He gripped his arms to himself and shuddered. 'Naturally, I said no and so he just turned off the tap and started chatting about buying some wood from Poplars Yard. He wanted to build Justine a love seat. He'd seen them in garden centres and thought it'd be a nice gesture. That it'd bring them back together. He suggested they'd finally try the marriage course at church, and I'd have been relieved to have heard that, but something wasn't right. He was saying all these things – good, constructive things – but he had a smirk on his face when he did it. Do you understand? He was chatting about measurements and designs for the love seat and he was asking if carving a heart in the back panel would be too much . . . but simultaneously, that icy coldness was there in his eyes. I had a Bible in my pocket. A small New Testament, and I touched it. That's all I did, I just touched it, because . . . well, because I was afraid of those eyes. I'm not ashamed to say it, gentleman, but I'm a religious man, and I needed to feel it in my hand. And here's the thing . . . he wouldn't have even known it was in my pocket, but as soon as my finger was on it, the very *second* I touched it, I saw his mouth start to twitch . . .' Perry whispered the rest. '*God . . . I can't get his face out of my head. His eyes . . . they were sparkling down there. He was excited . . .*'

Fenn sloshed water into his own glass and swigged.

'I pulled out my Bible, and I held it in front of me. I told him the truth, that he'd become a victim of a demonic force.'

Matt resisted a groan. It wasn't easy.

'I started commanding whatever was in him to leave. I cast the demons out.'

'Have you ever performed an exorcism before?' Matt said.

'No, but there was nobody I could call to do it,' Perry shook his head. 'You see the Catholics, the Anglicans . . . they're better organised with such things. But I'm a Baptist. We're hopelessly untrained for this stuff. They didn't even cover it at my Bible college, but they ought to. By God. I'll be telling the Baptist Union in no uncertain terms that they *must*.'

'So you just . . .' Matt opened his hands, '. . . gave it a go, then?'

For the first time, Perry's sad eyes turned defensive. 'Yes I did. Because if there's one thing us Baptists do believe, it's in the priesthood of all believers. Which means there was no reason at all why I couldn't just do it myself. Or indeed, any Christian could do it. And besides, since I started to suspect this of Tom, I'd watched quite a few videos on it. There's a lot on YouTube, which will really open your mind to—'

'YouTube?' Matt crossed his arms and leant back. 'You learnt it from YouTube?' His mind filled with visions of cutesy video tutorials, while smiley millennials cast out demons to a jolly, ukelele soundtrack.

'Yes. So what?' He sat up, more confident. 'And who cares where I learnt it from, because it worked. I started calling evil spirits out from him, and there was an immediate reaction. He was swaying and scratching himself, and clawing his stomach, and I really mean *clawing*. Like this' – Perry started dragging his bent fingers across his own belly – 'so I did what the videos said. I called out the demons by name. First I cast out the demon of suspicion, and straight away he gasped out a breath. It was like something was coming *out*. Then I called out the demon of fear, and he gasped that out too. He'd stagger after each time, like I'd given him a physical blow. It was astonishing. And the demon of vulgarity and foul language and lack of faith, they all just left him. And sometimes it was a gasp, and sometimes it sounded like he was being sick, but they were leaving, praise God. And the more I did it, the more I could see flashes of Tom, still trapped in there.' He caught a sudden breath. Tears were brimming in Perry's eyes. 'And bless him, he was so close to the surface. I could *see* him in there fighting to get out. So I called out the final spirit I could think of, which was blasphemy. But he didn't gasp that time. He just fell to the floor and lay on his side in a heap. I sat there for ten minutes, praying. He kept looking at me the whole time, like a lost little boy, like little Leopold all those years ago. Then he shuddered, and he just sat up, and was talking again, saying that he felt better than ever.' Perry sniffed, and now the tear that was brimming finally ran over his cheek, lost in the red bristles of his well-clipped beard. 'And he really did look better. His face, his voice, his eyes . . . he looked lighter. He hugged me, and he felt warm, but he was exhausted, and gosh, so was I. I said I'd come back and pray for him the night after, and he said that'd be a wonderful idea. He put two thumbs up at me, and I left that place brimming with hope and faith. It was amazing . . .'

'Um . . .' Matt drew a lazy circle on the table. 'Then he brutally killed his wife.'

The room ticked with silence for a while.

'Which rather suggests,' Matt went on, 'that this exorcism of yours didn't—'

They all jumped when Perry smacked his palm on the desk. 'Don't you dare blame me. I was trying my very best, and I thought he was free.'

'Oh really?' Matt said. 'You put a mentally ill guy through an ancient ritual you'd learnt on YouTube. And then you just moved on, right?'

'I didn't move on. I spent the next afternoon praying for him. You saw me at church, doing just that, today. I'd planned to visit him again tonight . . . but it's obvious now that I simply missed something.'

'And what was that?' Matt said. 'Calling the doctors?'

'I told you. He tried those, and they failed.'

Fenn said, 'What did you miss?'

'I missed two demons. I called out the spirit of blasphemy, but he didn't gasp, see? I thought it had left, but clearly it hadn't.'

'And the second demon?' Fenn asked.

'Well, that's rather obvious now, don't you think? It was the spirit of murder. I never even thought to cast it out because I never imagined Tom could do such a thing . . .' He shook his head. 'In fact, I *still* don't believe he could. Not unless something else made him . . . so there you are. There are dark forces at work here, I don't know how else to put it. I tried to help. My biggest sin, perhaps, was tiredness. And before you dismiss this, Mr Hunter, as I can tell you will . . . perhaps you should consider these words . . . *the irony of the enlightenment is that it has brought no light at all – on the contrary, it has paved the way for the most malevolent forces of darkness.*'

'That some sort of quote?' Fenn asked.

'Yes it is.' Matt nodded. 'It's Bernie Kissell, isn't it?'

Perry's eyebrows shot up. 'You know him?'

'I know *of* him.' Matt turned to a confused-looking Fenn. 'Kissell's a big deliverance minister in the US. He's a freelance exorcist, basically. He gets paid big money to cast out demons. He does it on Skype sometimes.'

'And in person too,' Perry added. 'Pastor Kissell travels the world setting people free. What could possibly be wrong with that?'

Matt leant forward. 'What's wrong, is making vulnerable people even more unstable and confused. Which is probably exactly what you did with—'

'How dare you,' Perry glared at Matt. 'I told you I took Tom to the doc—'

'Whoa there.' Fenn raised both hands, calming two horses. 'Wind the volume down. Both of you. Reverend Perry, thanks for being so candid. We'll talk more, but for now,' Fenn checked his watch, 'I think you need a break.'

'You mean I can go home? To my wife?'

'Yes,' Fenn said.

Matt looked up, confused. 'Shouldn't we keep going?'

'That'll do for now. Thanks for your help, Reverend.' Fenn pushed his chair back and stood.

Perry shook Fenn's hand then turned to Matt. 'Mr Hunter? I was only trying to help.'

Before Matt could speak, Fenn patted Perry on the shoulder. 'Come on, Reverend. I'll walk you out.'

CHAPTER FIFTEEN

Fenn was missing for five whole minutes, so Matt just sat at the desk, thinking the conversation over. Walking back through every word and sentence. When the door eventually did swing back, Fenn flopped in with his phone pressed to his head.

'Thanks for the confirmation.' He set his phone on the desk. 'Right, I've just had some preliminary comments from the autopsy. They're still working on her, but they've confirmed that it's Tom Riley's DNA, skin fragments, prints. They're all over her. Not exactly a shock, but it's good to get confirmation.'

'Anything else?'

'Well, this isn't pleasant, but they reckon Justine was alive for quite a while. When he pulled out her hair, I mean. Something in the follicles means they can tell these things.'

In the silence that followed, Matt squeezed the bridge of his nose. Then eventually, he said, 'What was the cause of death?'

'Heart attack. Poor girl. Forty, fit, healthy and she has a bloody heart attack at the sheer terror of it all. At least they reckon he pulled the tongue out, after.'

'That's very considerate of him.' Matt grabbed the water jug for a drink, but it was all gone. 'Why did you let Perry go?'

'Because he didn't kill anybody. He had an alibi. His times match up with his wife. Justine was seen by multiple people at Brownies when he was at Tom's. Then he went back to his wife all night, just like he said. Time of death's been confirmed at a little after midnight, so Perry wasn't present at all.'

'Yeah but his *influence* . . . that was present. Isn't that the point here? That all this demon talk flipped an already mentally disturbed man over the edge?'

'Well, we'll explore that. Course we will. But believing in the Devil isn't a crime and the bottom line is, the real criminal is in custody, and he's clearly psychotic. Though, it's interesting, isn't it?'

'What is?'

'The two demons Perry said he didn't cast out of Tom. Blasphemy and Murder. Didn't you tell me this morning that's exactly what this Baal-Berith is famous for? Isn't blasphemy and murder his *thing*?'

Matt shrugged. 'According to the whackos, yeah.'

'I found that interesting . . . well, listen.' Fenn slapped his hands together and rubbed them. 'I'll be in touch, but thanks for all your help today. There's no way we would've found out who Ernie actually was so quickly if it wasn't for you. He really opened up when you walked in.'

'Demons get super chatty with me. It's a gift.'

Fenn smiled and put out a hand. 'I'm not sure it's a gift I'd want. But thanks all the same. You up to much tonight?'

'It's my daughter's school play.'

He smiled at that. 'Aw, I miss those.'

It was cold outside in the now windswept police station car park. Every tree, and every strand of Matt's hair swayed as he snaked through the cars to find his own. When he did, he crawled inside and shut out the groaning air. He fired up the heater, and the stereo too. He needed some banal chat or wallpaper music for distraction.

It was only as he was pulling out of the car park that he saw Reverend Simon Perry again. That duffel coat of his was an easy spot. He was sitting on a bench by a lamp post, legs crossed, with his head clasped between both hands. Distraught with the events? Finally feeling some guilt or remorse? Hopefully. When he rolled his car past him, he saw that Perry wasn't in despair at all. He just had a mobile phone clamped tightly to his right ear, while the other hand blocked out the wind to his left. He was so absorbed in his phone conversation that he was oblivious to Matt as he came past.

Matt considered calling out, but by then he couldn't help but notice the fat sun was sinking behind a crop of spindly, leafless trees. It looked like a huge, glowing ball hovering over Perry, pulsing bright behind a wooded ribcage. Matt didn't care for the look of it, and how it made him feel, and how the wind moaned through his own car, dragging him back to the whale-song of Justine's cavernous throat.

She'd been alive for so much of it . . .

Horrible. Horrible.

'Home time,' Matt said out loud. He pumped the accelerator and rumbled out of the car park. He kept clicking up the heater but it was already full blast. He tapped it, wondering why it was taking so long to kick in.

He took one last glance at Perry on the bench. He was in the same position as before, head in his hands. Only now the leaves were spinning up around him in a tall funnel, and the light was starting to die.

So Matt shrugged, tapped the oddly faulty heater again and drove away.

CHAPTER SIXTEEN

'Oh my word. Wow,' Matt said, as he pulled into the school car park. He couldn't believe his luck. He found a parking space in the first, most favoured row of them all. Finding an empty slot in this car park, especially on a school play night like this, really was the miracle of all miracles. As he slid out of the car, he saw parents on the other side of the school gates. Unlike Matt, they hadn't risked the school bays and they'd parked in the nearby streets instead. It meant they had to walk the long way around. When they saw him through the bars many paused mid-trudge, staring with either sneering jealousy or watery-eyed nods of astonished congratulation.

He winked at them, then hurried along the covered walkway to the school entrance. In a few minutes time, the crowds would fill up every inch of this floorspace.

He spotted them standing near the main doors. Lucy was on her phone, thumb moving so fast it was a creamy-pink blur. Wren, on the other hand, was leaning over a bush and running her hand across the cement walls of the school. She often did that around buildings. When they were shopping. On the way to the pub. She had this compulsion to touch stone, and prod concrete and slide her fingers across wooden beams. Homes, offices, supermarkets and car parks were giant kittens she just had to stroke.

Architects. They're a little odd, sometimes.

'Behold,' he jabbed a thumb over his shoulder. 'Best parking space ever.'

Wren pushed both hands off the wall and span away from the bushes. Her mouth dropped when she saw the car. 'You lucky swine.' She leant in to kiss him. 'This means we get the front row before . . . *them*.'

He followed where she was pointing to see hundreds of parents now flooding through the school gates, far off. A zombie horde, shuffling and stumbling over each other, ravenous for a seat with good photo lines of their kid.

Wren shoved Lucy's shoulder. 'Switch your phone off. Let's go and see your sister.'

Lucy said, 'Bet you weren't this eager at my school play.'

'I most certainly was. Now move.' Wren nodded to Matt and they sprang off to the doors.

'Please,' Lucy winced at them both. 'Don't *jog*.' She walked up after them, shaking her head. There was a smile in there somewhere, too.

They stepped into the bright entrance hall where the walls were filled with the pupils' art attempts. They were evidently learning about a husky dog called Togo, and some of their work was surprisingly decent. But skill levels meant that most of the dogs were hideously deformed, with uneven eyes, and woefully out-of-perspective hind legs. These were the mutant canines, fresh from Outpost 31, but it was a good effort all the same.

Their shoes squeaked a path to the main hall, and when they flung the doors open Wren tutted loudly. They weren't, in the end, the earliest, but then . . . they never were. There were always a few adults who took parental eagerness to creepy, knee-rubbing levels. The centre front row was already stocked with parents who must have turned up an hour early. The type who'd have gladly brought a sleeping bag and a camping stove here last night, if hanging around a school wasn't classed as a crime.

Amelia would be backstage now. She'd advised them to sit on the far left of the stage. That'd be the best view of her character, she'd said. This was good, because there were still some seats on that far side, even at the front.

They squeezed adult backsides into skinny, plastic chairs, and instantly his leg touched a stranger. There were little programmes on each chair. Just a single A5 sheet, in appropriately garish orange, announcing that tonight's play about 'The Great Fire of London', was going to be 'hot stuff'. Ha. Good old PTA.

The sound levels changed just then, because the hallway outside grew thick with the loud, muffled shuffles of the horde. Then the doors slapped open, bodies spewed in and filled the room. Like the blood from that lift in *The Shining*.

They sat for twenty minutes like that, about two hundred people hip to hip, and eventually the headteacher came out and did her usual welcome. When she shared the fire procedure, some guffawing, cockney bloke shouted 'Fire procedure? Ya should'a said all this at Puddin' Lane? Eh, love?' His joke was followed by a gaunt, awkward silence because a room full of modern parents weren't sure if it was okay to laugh at a man calling a woman 'love' these days. The quiet of the hall, and the pause from the headmistress, was so excruciating that Matt had to press a full palm across his mouth to keep his laugh in. Especially when the man shouted, 'Eh, love? Eh?', two further times, to no reply.

Then they were off.

The squeaky curtains screeched open and a bunch of kids came marching out dressed like typical Londoners of 1666. Which meant, ironically, a plethora of Victorian cloth caps. But who was he to complain at the historical accuracy of the headgear? Or the buildings. Or indeed when the fateful fire was depicted by a bunch of kids flashing torches on and off, while the rest sung 'Great Balls of Fire' to a slack-mouthed crowd.

Then it was the big moment. The *Amelia* moment, when Matt, who'd filmed everything so far, made a bespoke zoom to the left-hand side of the curtain. She said she'd emerge from there, so he waited for his cue: the end of 'We Didn't Start the Fire' by Billy Joel. And on she walked, taking long strides, dressed as a bearded man and holding the lapels of a fur coat. It was so big it looked like she was wearing a werewolf's pelt.

Matt caught Wren's eye. They beamed simultaneously.

She was playing the Lord Mayor of London. Sir Thomas Bloodworth, a part she'd requested because Amelia thought his line was funny. It was true too: he'd actually said these very words – or something close to it. When he was woken to be told of the great fire, Bloodworth didn't take it seriously. She strode up to the left-hand side of the stage, where some boys were rushing up to her, saying, 'Lord Mayor Bloodworth! Look at the fire, sir! Whatever shall we do?' To which Amelia responded by putting her hands on her hips, throwing her head back and laughing out a line from somewhere in her elasticated beard: 'That fire? *That* fire? Pish. I bet a woman could wee on that and put it out. I'm going back to bed!'

Laughter swept the crowd.

Line delivered, she stomped off, as kids and teachers broke into 'Firestarter' by The Prodigy. As she vanished behind the curtain, he resisted standing and cheering and clapping with gusto. That'd be odd, and unfair to the other kids, but man was there a huge hug coming for her. She was, after all, the greatest actress who ever spoke a line.

The rest of the play passed slowly. So slowly, in fact, that there were moments when Matt could feel his clothes going out of fashion, but eventually they were done and, when it all finished, the kids came running out to their seats, still in costume. Amelia smothered all three of them in furry, hairy kisses.

'Peasants!' she said, still in character. 'Was I awesome?'

'You were amazing.' Wren squeezed her.

'She's right,' Matt said. '*Brilliant* projection.'

'And Lucy, what say you?' She swooped dramatically close to her sister, eyebrows pushing up and down like Groucho Marx on speed. When that didn't work, she pulled her beard up and down too and kept going. 'Well? *Wellll?* What say you, peasant?'

'You were . . .' she fought a smile, '. . . you were fine. Now can you stop talking like a loser?'

'Aha! Fine, she said!' She stuck a finger high in the air. 'Then my fee, peasants, is a hearty doughnut! Proceed.' She pointed to the doors where the crowd was clambering towards the dining hall. Signs said, PUDDINGS FROM PUDDING LANE – THIS WAY!

It was just as they left the hall when he felt something in the air shift. There was a murmur in the crowd. Words that went beyond simple questions of whether folks had remembered to bring change or if the mikes hadn't been loud enough. Something was happening outside and it was causing a lot of frowns.

'What's going on?' Lucy pushed up on her tiptoes.

Amelia started jumping up and down to see, beard flapping. 'Bet a grandma's collapsed. They do that, sometimes. Back to my doughnut, though.'

Matt was about to say something, when a rippling wave of

teachers' heads started turning in his direction, each catching his eye. One raised a hand to beckon him to the main doors. Then another.

Wren scratched her cheek. 'Why do they want *you*?'

'Oh dear,' Lucy's mouth dropped, half smiling. 'I bet you parked in the headteacher's space.'

Amelia gasped. 'You'll hang for this, peasant.'

'I didn't, honest!' he said. 'Listen I better go over and—'

'Announcement.' The PA system screeched out feedback and everybody looked up. 'Can Matthew Hunter please come to the headteacher's office immediately. Thank you.'

'Gonna get *spanked*,' Amelia said.

He looked at Wren and noticed her smile had dropped.

'You better go,' she said.

He nodded and started pushing against the flow, heading towards the staff corridor, near the entrance. Eyes were on him, he could feel that, and he heard the tail end of whispers as he made his way across. Then a teacher in a tracksuit gripped his elbow and guided him to the head's office. She was there, Mrs Wraithe, standing at her office door and beckoning him to come with a frantic hand.

He trotted towards her. 'What's going on?'

'Mr Hunter. Have you seen what's happening outside?'

CHAPTER SEVENTEEN

'Come on,' she shoved her backside against her door and it swung open. Then she walked away from him to a closed set of blinds at her window. 'Could you switch that light off, please?'

Matt frowned. 'I'm totally confused here. I've been watching the play.'

'The light, please?'

He clicked it and the office plunged into darkness. He had to navigate around scattered chairs to reach her. She was using one of her long nails to open a gap to see through. She pressed an eye against the opening slit. 'They're asking for you, and they won't go away.'

'Who are they?'

'You need to get them to clear the car park as soon as possible, some parents want to leave and they're completely blocking the path.'

'Who are you talking about?' He leant forward, squinting through the gap, then his face sank. 'Oh, crap . . . I'm sorry about this.'

'Just get them off school grounds? They're up on kerbs and blocking cars. It's a health and safety time bomb.'

'Will do . . . and again, I'm sorry . . .' He headed for the door.

She called after him. 'Funny old life you lead, isn't it, Mr Hunter?'

'Oh, it's a laugh a minute.'

He rushed back down the corridor, trying to ignore the crowd of other parents whose eyes literally bulged with curiosity. He pushed through the revolving doors and stepped into sudden lights, shockingly bright, clicking on and flinging his huge shadow against the school wall. He squinted into the beams and saw silhouettes of figures lurking behind. The figures rushed towards him, and he held up a hand to block out the light.

'Professor Hunter? Any comment?'

He was so tempted to say, *Certainly, the school play was a triumph!* But instead he just said, 'Comment on what?'

'On Tom Riley . . . and the demon murders.' A camera lens rushed in, flooding his face with light. 'You were with him today, does he really believe he's possessed by Satan?'

'I'm not talking about this here. Let's get off the school grounds first, then maybe I'll—' he stopped. 'What do you mean *murders?*'

'You haven't seen the news?'

'No . . .'

'Tom Riley. He's killed somebody else tonight.'

'That's impossible, he's in custody.'

'That's where it happened. In a hospital secure unit. He's killed a female police officer. They say he cut her throat.'

The ground. It moved.

Matt felt it shift beneath him.

He swayed for a moment at the thought of it. Knowing. Just

knowing who that female police officer was. It was PC Pamela Marriot, from earlier this morning. She of the blonde curls and the custard creams and the twitchy fear, whenever Tom Riley looked her way.

'Professor?' the reporter said, and then offered another question that seemed to make the earth spin just that little bit faster. 'Who is Baal-Berith? Professor? Professor? Are you all right?'

CHAPTER EIGHTEEN

Matt had always assumed it was the magical repel-mantra for journalists the world over. Yet no matter how much he flapped his lips to say 'no comment' they just weren't going to budge. As long as he was standing there, physically in their space, this little troupe of reporters were going to stand there too, jaws hanging, microphones poised, waiting for Matt to throw them a tiny fish of information, or better yet, a frustrated, emotional outburst.

He also knew that if he went back into the school, they'd probably just follow him in. Or just as bad, they'd hover out here until he came back out. And in the mad crowd rush one of their big vans would back into a little kid from Year 7 and break both of their legs. The most popular, most sporty kid in school, no doubt. Meaning the Ofsted *and* the Olympic hopes of the school would be recklessly dashed because of Matt Hunter's kooky, spooky life.

He swivelled his head to look back at the building, where his car was blocked by a house-sized Land Rover. And beyond it, he saw parents in the school, cupping their hands to see out. Confused faces, irritated faces, and the most prominent one of all was fogging up her office glass with many huffs and many puffs. Mrs Wraith kept making a shooing motion with her hands. *Go*, she mouthed. *Go. Go.*

There really was only one option left. Run away.

Matt twisted his shoes on the pavement, 'I told you . . . no comment. So . . . um . . . I'm going now.' He started a fast power walk towards the gate. He heard them trotting behind, so he broke into a jog. Their footsteps only sped up too, and they called out their loud questions after him. Stuff like 'Why are exorcisms on the rise today?', 'Did Tom Riley speak with the devil's voice?' and 'Was there vomit?'

His escape pod was waiting just outside of the school gate, perfectly timed.

The local bus jerked to a stop and the doors unfolded with a loud hiss. He hopped straight on board and slapped his debit card against the reader. 'Could you close the doors, please?'

'Come again?'

'The doors. Those guys aren't with me.'

The bus driver gave a slow blink, then he craned his neck and spotted the coming commotion on the pavement outside. He shrugged and hit a button. The doors folded shut, just as palms pressed against it. 'So, mister . . . are you famous in a good way, or famous in a bad way?'

'Neither,' Matt said, and the bus engine rumbled into life.

Matt grabbed one of the bars for balance and watched the dwindling reporters on the kerb. They were shaking their heads and giving up, but he saw the headlights of their vans lighting up behind them. They'd be out on the street soon.

He sank into a seat and thought, wow. I'm like James Bond escaping a Russian tactical squad. Only my getaway car isn't an Aston Martin. It's the number 105 to Amersham. 'Can you just let me off round the corner, please?'

'Shame. That was the shortest getaway in history,' the driver mumbled, as he started to swing the bus round.

The doors opened and Matt leapt out. He slipped through a gap in a metal fence he'd seen earlier this evening, on the way in. A faulty street light had turned it into a murky, but handy, black hole. He ran through, churning up the smell of damp wood chips under his feet, and found himself in a playground. Around him were swings, a long metal rocking horse and a climbing frame with a little wooden house on top of it. All in blackness. And then a sports field that led to the back of the school.

He saw the twin lights of the media van, twinkling at speed through the tree trunks to his left. They'd be round the corner soon.

He scurried up on the metal frame, said 'bugger' when he clanged his kneecap against a pole and then he quickly crawled inside the tiny wooden box. It stank of urine in there, even though the floor was dry. He hoped – and this was a very pure and earnest dream – that the stink was only canine.

Keeping inhalation to a minimum, he pulled out his phone and saw a string of missed calls, all from the last hour. He didn't recognise some of the numbers, but the other was DS Fenn from today. He dialled him back and pressed the phone close to his ear, crouching into a ball at any hint of headlights outside. The glow from his screen threw a dull light across the graffiti in here. Well, fancy that, Matt thought, as he waited for the phone to pick up. Apparently, THE POPES NO DOPE COS THE POPE SMOKES DOPE.

Fenn's voice fizzed into his ear. He sounded troubled, breathless. 'Matt? Where are you?'

'A bunch of reporters just chased me out of my kid's school play. So I'm sitting in a pool of dog piss, hiding in a playground. You?'

A swift sigh on the line. 'Dammit. I'm sorry about this.'

'It's okay. But listen . . .' He felt his eyes close, tone dropping at the question he dreaded asking. 'They're saying Tom attacked someone at the unit. That a policewoman's dead. It isn't Pam, is it? From this morning?'

Nothing.

'Fenn?'

'She's not dead, they're wrong on that.' His voice was low, quiet, lost in a sudden crackle on the line. 'We thought she might be, but it wasn't quite as bad as we thought.'

'How, though? He was handcuffed.'

'I went back to see Tom, after we interviewed Perry. I wanted to formally arrest him for suspected murder. Pam was guarding his room, just like I asked her to. She said he'd been totally silent since we left him. He'd just sat completely still the whole time, but though he couldn't see me arrive, the second I walked into that corridor, and Matt I mean the *second*, he started wailing and screaming in his room like a madman, and he was calling out . . .' Fenn paused. 'Sorry, mate, but he kept calling for you.'

Creeeeek.

Matt blinked when he heard it. The sound of metal scraping and starting to grind.

Matt's mental filing system was pretty good with sound. So this metallic creak was instantly understood and duly categorised. Someone was settling into one the swings out there, though he couldn't see from inside this little hut.

'He was furious that you weren't with me,' Fenn went on. 'He's like, where's Matthew? Where's Matthew? He just kept screaming it. And I mean Matt . . . he was frickin' livid.'

Creeeeek.

'So I said you weren't coming and he just had some sort of seizure, like a fit . . .' Fenn said. 'But not like any fit I've ever seen before.'

Matt's head reached the little doorway, and slowly, really slowly, he pushed his face into the breeze.

'We were looking through the window at him, and I saw his whole body twisting and bending. I swear I heard a bone crack. His arms, his head . . . the angles of it . . . shit. It'd give you nightmares.'

Creeeeeeek.

Matt saw the empty swing slowly rocking itself to a stop, like somebody had just slipped off it. Matt quickly scanned the shadows around him, and out across the gloomy void of the field. He saw nothing. Nothing except a bitter night wind curving the tips of the trees at a considerable angle. The same wind that probably pushed the swing in the first place. Yep. Just some wind, pushing one of the swings and somehow not the other. He watched it rock to its final, gentle stop.

Matt slid off the climbing frame and crunched into the woodchips, eyes in a constant, nervy scan. He found a roundabout and sat against it. It slowly started to revolve under his weight. 'So . . . what happened?' His voice was a whisper, he noticed.

'He just smacked his head off the bar. Like hard as hell. Split his forehead wide open. Blood everywhere, and he went to do it again. So me and Pam just got in there and grabbed him. I'd already called for some nurses. I heard them rushing up the corridor prepping a sedative, but me and Pam thought we had him under control, then he bit her.'

Matt blinked. 'He *bit* her?'

'Right in the throat. Just locked his damn teeth in. Me and the two nurses, male nurses mind you, we couldn't get his jaw open. Then he pulled away from her really hard, teeth still together, and Pam just dropped, blood everywhere. He just kept laughing and spitting and demanding to see you, and that we should all do as he said, because he was the great Baal-Berith and Baal-Berith gets what he wants. So I told him to fuck off and almost throttled him. The nurses dragged me off.'

'And Pam?'

'Intensive care . . .' His voice started to crack. 'I should have waited for the nurses. Dammit, I should have hung back. And I'm sorry about the reporters, Matt.'

'That's nothing, but I just thought we were keeping this demon stuff under wraps? How did it get out so quick?'

'How do you think? It was Perry. The second he left us he called the papers.'

Matt pictured Perry in the car park, wrapped in leaves and stuck on his phone. 'That little turd.'

'Yep. And he's shouting about this case from the rooftops now. He's everywhere. I've heard him on local radio, he's on TV tonight and he's told them *all* about you. That you saw her body. That you were with Tom. He's calling it the Demon Murder, and folks are lapping it up. He wants to raise awareness.'

'Of *what*?'

'He calls it "The Great Devouring".'

Matt sighed, and jabbed a shoe to the ground. The roundabout jerked to a stop. 'That's Kissell.'

'What?'

'Bernie Kissell. The famous exorcist he mentioned. That's one of his phrases. The Great Devouring.'

'Yeah, well, he's warning everybody about it. Telling them to turn back to the church, cos Tom Riley is just the start of a whole wave of possessions that are sweeping the country. It's making headlines, put it that way. Especially when he's insisting that Tom's completely innocent. That something else took him over.'

'What a mess.' A breeze rolled across him. 'So I take it with the media, I just say no comment?'

'No, no, no. You do *not* say no comment . . .'

'What?'

'I *want* you to comment. I want you to comment *a lot*. You're respected, Matt, you're known. And what's more you've spoken to Tom and you've seen what he did in that cellar. So if any reporter asks you, you tell them. You say Tom Riley has serious mental damage, and that's all there is to it. You balance out all this nutty satanic stuff with common sense.'

'You know most people aren't going to fall for Perry's mass possession idea.'

'I'm not worried about most people. I'm worried about the minority who *do* believe it. So just help me redress the balance, yeah? Cos I don't want this kicking off a bunch of wannabe exorcists, hunting for demons. That's not going to end well.'

'Agreed. What about Tom? Should I come in? See what he wants?'

'Screw Tom Riley,' Fenn shouted down the phone. 'He's being transferred to prison for now, so he can sit in there, wait for his trial and rot. And when he's convicted of Justine's murder, and what he did to Pam, he can go back in there and rot a bit more.'

'Fenn, I'm so sorry,' Matt said.

'Then just help me nip this demon stuff in the bud, okay? It's making me nervous . . . oh, and Matt,' he paused for a while, like he was considering whether to speak or not. 'You know he whispered something to Pam, just before he got her.'

'Could you hear it?'

'Yes . . . he said, *your baby's in hell*, and I didn't know what that meant because Pam doesn't have kids . . . but she still got upset and distracted. And that's how he got her. I tell you, it makes me nervous.'

Neither of them spoke for a while. Matt just watched the black shadows of the rocking horse becoming the slouched body of Tom. Looking away at the black field didn't help. He saw tree trunks turning into the usual watchful corpses, and quivering bushes becoming crouching black rabbits. Stupid brain of his.

Fenn said goodbye, and even though the phone hiss vanished from Matt's ears, he still didn't feel like he was alone. He frowned and turned from the park to look back across the field. He saw throngs of parents in the distance, going home, but there was no sign of the reporters anywhere. So at least his little escape plan must have—

Creeeeeeeek.

He spun back, losing an entire breath on the turn.

His eyes sprang through the black, assuming he'd catch the wind in the act, causing that swing to move again. But the swing was moving because somebody was in it.

He saw a dark figure, perched on the seat, with hands curled high around each metal chain. A human-shaped hole, cut into the world.

The figure, knowing it was now seen, started pulling itself up to stand.

The shadow came towards him. It spoke with a woman's voice.

'Good evening, Professor. I hope I didn't scare you.'

CHAPTER NINETEEN

'Do I know you?'

'No, we haven't met . . . but I've been hoping we would, tonight. May I?' She came closer and a light suddenly bloomed from her hand. The torch from her phone. 'Is that better?'

She was an Indian woman, maybe late forties, hovering in a cloud of extremely potent perfume. She had immaculate make-up and a long, thick rope of black hair. It hung in a swoop to one side, as did a long grey scarf dangling from her neck. It kept drifting in the breeze. The glow of the phone flashed its reflection in the military-style buttons on her long, meticulously tailored jacket. She nodded towards the hut, and her hooped earrings swung. 'I didn't want to interrupt your call. So I waited.' She put out her hand. Black leather gloves. 'My name is Anupa Parekh. Call me Nupa.'

He shook it and her wrist immediately jangled with bracelets hidden up her sleeve. 'Nupa, it's nice to meet you but I'm not in the habit of just running into random people in the park at night. No matter how nice they smell.'

She laughed. 'I'm a TV producer—' She clocked his expression and held up a leather palm. 'But before you scamper away, let me say that I totally understand why you're avoiding the media tonight. Makes sense.'

He glanced towards the bus stop. 'You saw my big exodus, eh?'

'I did.' She nodded. 'And bravo. You lost them all.'

'Clearly not *all*. Let's sit.' They walked to the swings and sat down, hands automatically grabbing the chain on each side, like they were ten. 'So, Nupa . . . what do you need?'

'Right, well, I'm a documentary producer. I work for the BBC, Netflix, PBS but I'm also involved in an ITV show called *The Exchange*. It's an hour-long debate programme. It's on 11p.m. every Tuesday. It's presented by Freya Ellis.'

'Freya Ellis. National treasure.' He started to rock back a little on the swing. *Creeeeek*. 'I've actually watched that show quite a bit,' he said. 'It's . . . um . . . feisty.'

She chuckled. 'That's a fair choice of word. The live audience certainly adds spice. Then, as you'll know, we cover the day's news events and exchange views on them. Which means that later tonight we're devoting a full half-hour, that's half of the entire show, to the Demon Murder of Cheddington Village today. We have a few guests lined up already—'

'Such as?'

'Someone who claims to be demonically possessed for a start and then there's Reverend Simon Perry. He's involved with the Cheddington case. I understand you know him already.'

'I do.'

'Well, I can see from your escape that you're clearly not keen on the media right now but we really think the show would

111

benefit from your balanced perspective as a guest. And while's there no fee, we can certainly transport you there and we'll be glad to—'

'I'll do it.'

'—drive you back . . .' Her eyelids fluttered a little. She tilted her head. 'You'll do it?'

'Sure.' He glanced down at his watch. 'Though I guess we better scoot into town pretty soon?'

Her surprise clicked into a relieved smile. 'Well . . . that would be fabulous, thank you.'

'I just need to let my family know.'

'Of course. You can call them from the car.'

'And can we get a coffee on the way? I'm parched.'

She smiled and nodded. 'Absolutely.'

They headed out of the park, Nupa's phone lighting the way. He hadn't spotted her heels in the wood bark of the playground, but they sounded surprisingly loud on the pavement outside. Nupa tossed her scarf over her shoulder and waved a hand at a BMW parked across the street. The headlights clicked on and it slinked across the street slowly. It rumbled up to their kerb. The door opened automatically.

'All aboard,' she said, shaking off her jacket.

He climbed inside and slid along the smooth cream leather. She followed him in and tapped the headrest in front – a signal to pull away. She started peeling off her gloves, tugging at each fingertip in turn.

He called Wren, but it went to voicemail. He told her he'd be back late and to tell Amelia he was sorry he had to leave, and that he hoped he hadn't caused hassle with those crowds. He hung up the phone, just as they started rolling through the street at pace, which was when a thought occurred to him. He never actually asked this woman for any sort of ID. What if this was the most polite, and finest smelling, kidnap in history? But then she started handing him multiple release sheets to sign. Then she flipped open her laptop and started running through potential questions on the topic of possession. She seemed genuinely fascinated by his answers.

The driver was called Dom – Matt made a point to ask, and Dom grabbed three coffees from a service station for them. Through the window Matt could see a large TV hanging above the till, on the news channel. It didn't display what you might expect. No weather maps and no sombre-looking folks in business wear, gazing into an autocue. Instead, there was something he would never have expected to see on a news channel. It was a grim fifteenth-century painting that he knew well. The Devil himself was dancing and raking clawed feet into the backs of the damned, pushing them into the fiery mouth of some giant amphibious beast, and he was holding a banner aloft. He had the head of a bat, leering and glaring, while in his bare stomach was the staring and trapped face of a man.

Nupa saw him staring at it, and she shook her head in a kind of baffled wonder. 'You'd think demons would be a figment of our past by now. That we'd be over them.'

'You'd think.'

'Do you know the painting?'

He turned to her. 'It's by Hans Memling from the end of the Middle Ages.'

'And that banner the Devil is holding? Is that Latin?'

Matt nodded. '*In Inferno nulla, est redemptio* . . . In Hell there is no redemption . . . I believe the painting's called *Hell*.'

She sighed. 'Well, that's a very fitting title for *that* picture, wouldn't you say?'

He thought she was referring to the Memling, but when he turned back to the window he saw a brick house on the TV screen instead. It was looming against a concrete sky, sitting at the edge of a vast, windswept field. It was Tom Riley's house, standing defiant in the wind. And as he watched it, he wondered if those eager country breezes were now carrying the lingering stench of Justine's blood across town. Like the fallout from a nuclear catastrophe. And rolling across the bottom of the screen, the banner headline, white text on red, simply read – DEMON MURDER: LATEST.

CHAPTER TWENTY

'Scrunch again.'

Matt wrinkled his nose as Jackson, the freakishly tall make-up guy, leant over like a palm tree. He was dabbing Matt's face with a little hand-held brush. Matt, fighting a sneeze said, 'Are you *sure* I really need—'

'Shhhh.' Jackson pushed his lips forward in concentration, his accent Australian. 'Just because someone has good skin doesn't mean you have good *TV* skin. Kapeesh? Now . . . *eyes*.'

Matt closed them and for ages felt the brush bounce and swish around his temples and cheeks. When he finally opened them, he dreaded seeing a white-faced mime artist staring back. If anything, he looked slightly more orange. Yay. He'd just gone two or three levels up the Donald Trump skin scale.

'So, Jackson,' Matt reached for the tea they'd made him, 'what else is on the show tonight?'

He spoke through a comb in his teeth, pluming and picking at Matt's fringe. 'Second half's about working mothers and depression. Which, don't get me wrong, is important. But it's not as rock and roll as your bit is it? Satan, demons . . . *murder*.' He whistled as he freed the comb.

He leant forward as Jackson manhandled his head, and Matt wondered if he'd watch tonight's show on catch-up. Or rather, he wondered if he'd admit that he would. He flicked his eyes to the huge countdown clock on the wall.

Twelve minutes to go.

The door swung open just then, and in walked something he didn't expect: a little boy, about seven years old, with jet-black hair and a Super Mario backpack. He was holding someone's hand, who he tugged through. The hand became an arm, the arm became an elbow, then a shoulder. It was attached to a young Asian woman with incredibly long straight black hair. It hung over her white gypsy blouse, ruffled at the collar, all the way down to the waist of her jeans. She moved inside with a tentative step, then she caught Matt's eye and gave him a nervous smile. She couldn't have been much more than twenty-five.

A chunky researcher pointed her to the empty styling chair next to Matt, and then she had to let go of the boy's hand. She watched as he was taken into a corner, where a depressed-looking crew member in dungarees was setting up the game Connect 4, ready to play.

Now alone, the young woman made a cautious move towards the chair. 'I'm sorry I'm late. I couldn't get a babysitter.'

'No worries, I'm just about done . . . grab a seat.' Jackson slid his fingers out of Matt's hair, then he tilted his head, nodded and said, '*Fin*.'

Now Matt was complete, he swung his chair round to the woman, who was now sat bolt upright before Jackson, armrests gripped in a dentist's clench. 'Hiya . . .' Jackson said, but when he looked at her head on his voice trailed off and his mouth dropped. 'Jesus, you're bloody beautiful . . .'

She scrunched her nose and laughed. 'Bet you say that to everybody who comes in here.'

'He didn't say it to me,' Matt said.

Jackson tilted his head. 'So you're what . . . Japanese?'

Her eyes bulged in mock horror. 'I'm Vietnamese.'

'Whoops. I'll shut up.'

She laughed as Jackson got to work. Since she had to keep her face forward, she asked her question to Matt's reflection. 'So . . . are you the presenter?'

'Ha, no. I'm a guest.'

Her shoulders dropped. 'Phew, me too. I thought I was the only one . . .' She lifted her head as Jackson brushed around the perfect line of her jaw. 'I've done a few photo shoots, but I've never, ever done anything like this before. You?'

'Bits and bobs.'

'Advice, please.'

'Relax. Enjoy it, and even if you don't, remember that it'll be over in a flash.' Just as he said that he became conscious of his own raised heart rate. These media things were always a mixture of nerves, adrenalin and that constant dread of cracking a joke that'd get him crucified on Twitter.

'Eyes,' Jackson said suddenly.

'Sorry?' She frowned and looked at Matt's reflection again. He blinked back at her, over and over. She mouthed *oh*, then closed them. She smiled. 'I'm Abby Linh, by the way.'

'Matt Hunter. And who's the mini-me?'

'My son, Tuan. And yeah, I know I'm keeping him up late, but I had insane sitter issues. I'm a terrible parent.'

'That's nothing. I had to leave my daughter's school play for this.'

'Oooo, that's cold. Makes me feel better, though.' Just then

Tuan cheered as a winning plastic game piece fell into place.

'Well, he looks pretty hap—'

The door cracked against the skirting as it swung open. They all looked up to see a black man with a clipboard, headset and bleached blonde hair.

Jackson quiffed Abby's fringe and stood back. 'Stunning. *Fin.*'

Abby blushed.

The crew guy tapped a sharp set of knuckles against his clipboard for attention. 'Okay, folks, my name is Foster, and I need everyone appearing in the demon segment to follow me . . . oh . . . hold up . . . two seconds.' He pressed a finger into his ear and started talking quietly into his mic.

Matt went to stand and turned to Abby. 'Well, nice to meet you, and good luck for later . . .' He frowned when she stood too.

'I'm coming too.'

'Oh . . . I presumed you were here for the working mother's bit.'

'Well, I qualify, but nope. Afraid not.' She trotted to Tuan, dropped to her haunches and kissed him on his head, lips buried in his hair. 'I'll be half an hour, okay? Then it's . . .' she winked at him '. . . *ice cream.*'

'Kay . . .' Tuan's eyes were fixed on the game, but then something made him blink, and he pulled his eyes away. He looked up at her. 'You can do it, Mama.' She gave him an *aren't-you-adorable* smile, but then he added something else that made her mouth drop at the edge. Just a little. He said, 'Just be yourself, Mummy? Be *you.*'

Foster's hands clapped together. 'All right, they're ready. Let's *go,* people.'

They headed out into the bustling corridor and entered a busy and swift slalom, weaving through backstage workers and randomly placed trolleys filled with wires and kit. Over the speakers was the constant soundtrack of the TV news report, now playing live. As

118

they slid through arms and shoulders Matt leant into Abby and said, 'Forgive me for assuming before. I'm embarrassed.'

'No problem at all . . .' She caught his eye. 'So, does this mean you're possessed too?'

The comment slowed him for a moment, because she'd put a hand on his arm when she said it. She looked like someone lost in the woods, desperate for fellow travellers.

'Actually, I'm just here as a stuffy academic. I'm a professor of sociology of religion.'

She looked disappointed at first, but then she smiled and looked him up and down. 'Professors ought to have thick glasses and crazy white hair.'

'One day, hopefully.'

She laughed as they started walking again.

'So, Abby . . . are you? Possessed, I mean?'

'Seems that way . . .'

'Have you tried a doctor?'

She nodded. 'Course. She gave me some meds and they help a little but . . . only a little. I reckon I just—'

'Hey!' Foster was way up the corridor and had only just noticed them lagging behind. He was waving frantically to hurry them. They picked up the pace and he ushered them backstage, a netherworld place filled with tall black curtains all the way from the floor to the very high ceiling. Matt thought of the long temple curtains of ancient Judaism. The tearing open to reveal the holiest of holies.

'Wait,' Abby grabbed Foster's arm. 'I saw a TV in the make-up room.'

Foster tutted. 'So?'

'Well, can you make sure they're switched off? I don't want Tuan . . . you know . . . hearing the details.'

Foster nodded. 'Not a problem.'

'I'm serious. Switch them off.'

119

'I'll do that as soon as you're sitting, I promise. This way.'

He led them through a slit in a black curtain, and then through another. Each step increased the dull murmur from the studio audience who waited unseen in the gloom. Then, after speaking into his headset, Foster pulled back the final curtain.

He saw Abby squint under the hefty spotlights, and he did the same as they were led on set. He saw the studio audience now too, sitting to his left. About one hundred of them, perched on an ascending slope. They muttered to one another as they came past, sharing their disappointment that this man and woman were not famous. Foster led them to the three high-backed swivel chairs, and told each of them precisely which one to sit in. But before they sat a couple of crew members lifted Matt and Abby's arms, like a search for drugs at the airport. They were rigging up a lapel mic.

It was as he was standing there, arms out Good-Friday-style, that Matt did a double take. The presenter was right there.

Crikey, he thought, *it's Freya Ellis. Off the telly!*

The veteran celebrity was standing near a cameraman, arms out in the same position, while some greybeard roadie-type was fiddling with the national treasure's bra. He was tugging a lapel mic through her neat blue suit. Her trademark hook nose looked even more pronounced in real life. They say the reason so many politicians cracked under her pressure was that nose of hers. Some sort of witch's power.

Matt was so busy staring that he didn't even notice the curtains opened behind her. But then a figure walked right up to her and grabbed her hand, shaking it with both of his. It was Reverend Simon Perry and Matt thought his lips formed what looked like *Amazing to meet you*. Ellis smiled and pointed at the chairs. Perry turned, and Matt noticed that he'd ditched the folksy jumper and jeans. He was now in a full clerical collar. Grey shirt, black trousers, black shoes recently polished. His well-trimmed beard sparkled with some sort of oil, and when he looked up into the lights, he did it in a kind of slack-jawed wonder.

Abby whispered, 'Who's that?'

'That's Simon Perry, he's the vicar from Ched—' He turned to her. 'What's wrong?'

She was staring at Perry. Eyes locked on him as he was shown to his chair. That sweet smile of hers had totally drained now. She kept watching him as his mic was rigged up. Perry's eyes were on the crowd, and Freya Ellis mostly. Yet when he sat, he finally turned to his fellow guests. Abby was in the next chair and Matt was at the end. He waved at Matt and nodded a polite and chivalrous hello to Abby. She looked away.

'Are you going to be okay?' he asked her.

'Fine . . . I'm just nervous.'

'Right. Just don't worry about him. He's harmless.'

She attempted a smile. The type a kid does, when you leave them at a birthday party where they don't know anybody. That trying-to-be-brave face that you see framed in the soft-play window, just as you drive off.

A floor manager suddenly hollered out, 'Quiet on set. Rolling in one minute.'

Freya Ellis – her name sounded like a Hogwarts magic spell – was standing alone now, directly in front of a camera. She kept tugging her jacket into place.

'Here we go,' Abby whispered out the corner of her mouth. 'Good luck, Matt.'

He whispered back, his own heart shifting up a gear. 'And you.'

CHAPTER TWENTY-ONE

'We are live in five . . . four . . .' The sweaty-looking producer only said the first two numbers. He silently mouthed the rest, theatrically counting the seconds with his fingers.

Four . . . three . . .

The lights went out.

Two . . . one . . .

Boom.

Hefty speakers burst into life, filling the studio with an instantly recognisable theme tune. The industrial drums (that global signifier of serious current debate) thumped and pounded as the spotlights faded up.

And suddenly, here he was, a fly trapped in live amber, securely set into the fake-believe world of hot lights and cross markers on the floor. A huge screen behind them suddenly flashed up an . . . *oh great*, he groaned inside . . . that iconic image from *The Exorcist* movie. The silhouette of Max von Sydow standing in a shaft of eerie light, spewing from a possessed girl's bedroom window.

A POSSESSION EPIDEMIC? read the bold, capitalised, in-your-face, *dammit-be-worried-people!* lettering.

A camera, fixed to a long mechanical arm, did the show's trademark swoop across the heads of the audience. It gathered up their eager applause and delivered it to the single spot in the centre of the flow, where the presenter stood bathed in a perfect circle of light. Freya Ellis had been a newsreader since the '80s. She'd won awards for her fieldwork in Afghanistan, but for the last decade she'd really found her post-retirement niche in studio-based warfare.

The music dropped to its usual low beat for her opener.

She looked straight into the camera, arms folded, nose pushing straight through the screens of Britain. God help anybody watching this in 3D. Her voice was so husky you'd think she'd just caught a terrible strain of sexy bronchitis. It had been her 'sound' for decades, and it still made her the delight of grandads everywhere. 'A think tank warns that working parents face unprecedented levels of pressure and are more at risk of depression or suicide than ever. Are those who juggle kids and career really the forgotten casualties in mental health? But first, a chilling murder case in Cheddington, Buckinghamshire today, which raises a topic one might expect to find only in the Middle Ages. Yet why are requests for exorcism *growing* today? Could we really be on the cusp of a . . . possession epidemic? That's tonight, with me, Freya Ellis . . . *this* is *The Exchange*.'

Boom-ba-boom.

The lights instantly dimmed, and the screen had a new image on it. An epic, heavily filtered drone shot of rolling countryside hills, and then a house on the corner, Tom Riley's place. Next shot, a reporter, standing at the front gate, her white shirt collar flapping like fishtails in the wind. She told the story of a local chef who had been 'demonically driven' to murder. Every sentence went up at the end into an implied question mark. It was their way of appearing balanced, Matt assumed. The screen now lingered on that wedding photo of Tom and Justine.

The scene switched to Reverend Perry sitting in a church pew, looking grave and serious. Only this wasn't filmed in his own modest little clapboard church. There were no goggle-eyed puppets on these walls. It was the main Anglican church. Perhaps Perry wanted to make himself look higher up in the Christian food chain, or maybe, and Matt suspected this, the producers had seen that pink salmon carpet in Perry's church and insisted on a more divine-looking backdrop. Whatever the case, he now sat, one arm resting casually on a pew, and he was beautifully lit by a stained-glass glow. Perry was in his early thirties, but on screen he looked five years younger.

His posh, old-Etonian accent boomed from the speakers. 'The spiritual state of our country suggests that what happened to my friend Tom Riley will not be an isolated incident. The chances of another demonic murder, or indeed *many*? I would say they're high. Great Britain . . . be on your guard.'

Boom-ba-boom.

Matt saw a camerawoman swing across the studio floor, like a dancer in the dark. Then Matt, Abby and Reverend Perry were slowly born under the rising of spotlights. He saw a tiny red light on the camera, pointing right at him, which made Matt's mind explode with sudden questions.

Had he left his zip down?

Was there a hideous and unforgivable flake, quivering in his nostril?

He had a fierce urge to cross his legs and sniff hard, but now that other-worldly human – who he'd seen on screens since he was a kid – strode her long, and very real, trousered legs towards Perry, headmistress arms folded.

'Reverend, you say that even if the police prove that Justine Riley died at the hands of her husband, you still claim he is innocent of any crime.'

Perry nodded, without nerves or hesitation. 'Tom Riley was as much of a victim as she was. And the solution is not incarceration. It is a full and comprehensive exorcism.'

That word threw a nervous murmur into the audience.

'And what makes you so convinced that Tom Riley was . . . as you say . . . possessed?'

Perry started reeling off the exact same reasons he'd given to Matt and Fenn today. Almost word for word. Tom's aversion to religious symbols, the blasphemous licking of the Bible. As he listed these devilish symptoms, Matt looked across at Abby.

She sat there, listening politely, smoothing her jeans down, tilting her head in a patient, attentive way. He decided that sometimes you can just tell when people are nice, and decent. He could see it in her. Like a glow. But at times, when Perry said certain words, her eyelids fluttered. A barely perceptible twitch in the right corner of her lip. A microsecond of downturn, when the glow would fade. He kept a mental note of when these little spasms happened, and within about sixty seconds he'd built up a clearly discernible pattern. It was any time Perry mentioned the name Jesus or Christ or Lord or . . .

'Abby Linh.' Ellis took a step towards her. 'You're a healthy, twenty-five-year-old single mother. You work for a successful office cleaning company, but you've done a bit of fashion modelling. You hope to do more. Correct?'

'*Yes.*' It came out as a barely audible croak. She cleared her throat. 'Sorry. Yes.'

'And yet, you've recently requested an exorcism from your local church. Do you really believe that you are possessed?'

The audience shifted in their chair. Forwards.

'Abby?'

'When you say it out loud, it sounds crazy. And maybe I'm not possessed. Maybe it's just in my head. But I might be. All I can say is that something's changed this year.'

'Tell us . . .'

'Well . . .' She glanced at the camera lens and slipped some of her long hair behind her ears. 'I can't step into a church any more. I have to cross the street to avoid priests. The thought of prayer or the sound of hymns makes me feel physically ill. I've felt a presence in my bedroom. And yes, I sometimes have horrible thoughts.' She sat suddenly upright. 'Though obviously nothing like this Tom Riley guy. Like, I need to make that clear. I'm not a danger to anybody—'

'What about to yourself?'

She bit her lip, then slowly shook her head. 'That's not how it is with me. I don't want to hurt anybody. I just sometimes feel there's something with me, or . . . *in* me. And if I touch a crucifix my fingers ache. I mean they *throb*. It's very weird and I don't like it.'

'So, you requested an exorcism, from a church?'

'Yes, but they refused.'

'Why?'

'They said my issues were pastoral. That exorcism was a dangerous relic of the past. They said I should just join them at a Sunday service, but I can't get near the place. I mean, I see the entrance and want to throw up.'

'Interesting . . . so we have a demand for exorcism and yet not all churches seem prepared to help.' Ellis turned towards the camera again. 'Well, we have two experts with us tonight, both from opposing sides of the argument.'

Here we go, Matt thought, and he turned his chair towards Perry, ready for a theological, one-on-one rumble. Only it turned out that the other expert wasn't Reverend Perry at all. It was somebody else.

'So, ladies and gentleman, may I introduce you to the world's leading exorcist . . . Pastor Bernie Kissell.'

CHAPTER TWENTY-TWO

Matt blinked with genuine surprise, but when he glanced across at Perry he seemed very chilled about it. He must have known Kissell was going to be on. Matt looked towards the curtains, waiting to see the infamous exorcist come striding out, but he saw Freya Ellis walk towards the screen instead. The camera followed her.

'Over the last five years,' she said, 'Pastor Bernie Kissell has become one of the world's leading deliverance ministers. Unaffiliated to any major denomination, he claims to have performed independent exorcisms on thousands of people, both face-to-face, but also, and perhaps controversially, over YouTube Live and Skype. Speaking through screens is therefore not new to him, which is just as well, because tonight he joins us live from Pittsburgh, Pennsylvania. Pastor Kissell, are you there?'

The *Exorcist* image faded from the screen, and in its place came a backdrop video of a sunny city park. Superimposed in front of it was a skinny, smiley figure in a white, open-necked shirt. He had a comb-over which, considering he must be pushing sixty, was a deep, dark brown and almost certainly dyed. His wispy sideburns, however, were flecked with grey. He wore glasses too. Big aviator things with clear glass and thin silver frames. Maybe he'd just stepped off the gun range.

When she said his name, he smiled. Forget that . . . he *beamed*. Eyes wide, eyebrows up, mouth open in delight. Like a sweet old grandpa spotting his kids at the airport, or a jolly geography teacher seeing his birthday cake. What he certainly didn't look like was the type of guy who'd drag a spitting demon from the souls of the damned. Forget Max von Sydow. This was the happy-go-lucky ship's doctor from *The Love Boat*.

'Mr Kissell,' Ellis said, 'welcome to *The Exchange*.'

'Hey, call me Bernie, everybody does. And good evening, guys . . .' He gave a goofy, kids' TV show wave. 'Though it's actually pretty early here in the Keystone State. Behind me by the way, you're seeing the beautiful Point State Park. And the joggers are jogging. It's making me feel suitably out of shape, Freya.' He slapped a hand off a stomach that lacked any excess fat at all.

'Well, thank you for joining us on a cold, British night. So Bernie, in your recent book you claim that the demand for exorcism is exploding today. Which isn't what we'd expect in a modern, secularised society.'

'Well, the numbers don't lie.' He reached off camera, then raised a copy of his book for the screen. 'My book, *The Great Devouring*, takes a Christian standpoint, sure, but only in the second half. In the first I've simply collated government statistics, health surveys and secular demographics, which do indeed show that the demand for exorcism not only persists today, it's *growing*. Rapidly. And I don't just mean here in the US. I'm talking about the entire globe. Including over there in England. Beautiful country, by the way. I *adore* your queen.'

Matt slid a quick gaze to the audience.

One or two looked bored or sceptical. They had that chewing-the-inner-cheek thing going on. Maybe they were just holding out for the promised fun of the depressed parents segment. But most were listening to Kissell intently. Some on the edge of their seat, and many . . . many looked scared.

Kissell went on, 'Exorcism stats are up all across Europe, actually. For example, last month I was in a French region called Île-de-France, just out of Paris. Now, about a decade ago the church in that region was performing fifteen exorcisms a year. That's still a lot, sure . . . but in the last few years that figure has shot up to fifty each year. That's five-*zero*. It's a huge leap. Or look at Italy. The Vatican have had to set up a telephone helpline to cope with the exorcism demand. You know, Father Vincenzo Taraborelli recently told the press that five hundred thousand people in Italy requested an exorcism in 2015. That is a mind-boggling number. Oh, and your own think tank, Theos, in the UK. Their recent report called the growth in exorcism demand "astonishing". That's their word, not mine. So, like it or not, and however you want to explain it, the *fact* is that it's happening. Growing numbers are claiming to have been oppressed, or even *possessed*, by a demonic entity.'

Ellis glanced at the audience. 'What you're suggesting is rather disturbing, don't you think?'

'Absolutely, but these folks are not monsters. We're talking about afflicted people in pain. That's what truly matters here. Human beings who need freedom . . . freedom in Christ.'

As soon as he said that, Abby pulled back in her chair.

Not by much. Just a slight and swift push back, and Matt saw that her left hand was trembling. She put her right hand over it. Like one hand was in charge, and the other wasn't. He considered leaning over and asking if she was okay, but then, without warning, she spoke.

'Mr Kissell?' Abby said to the screen.

'Hey kid.' He smiled at the screen. If he was next to her he might have ruffled her hair. 'You just call me Bernie, okay?'

'Okay . . . I just wanted to know. Aren't you scared? When you go head to head with these things?'

'Often, yes. Heck, I've seen stuff that'll turn your hair white. I'm not ashamed to admit that I sleep with the lights on some nights. But I know I'm safe with the Lord. And my mom always used to say a calling is a calling, and a need is a need. And that need is growing. I refuse to just dismiss or laugh off the pain of others. Like your pain, Abby. You know it just about breaks my heart to hear your struggle, and to think that your church wouldn't even help you . . . dang. That's cruel. That's cold. You are a precious child of God and you're doing the right thing by at least *trying* exorcism. I mean, come on, what harm can it do?'

The presenter did a swift turn towards Matt. 'Professor Hunter, let's bring you in here. You've heard the statistics. What's your take?'

'Well, good evening, and thanks for having me.' Matt cleared his throat. 'You know, I'd say that Pastor Kissell is quite right. The demand for exorcism is rising. I've been keeping an eye on the stats for a while now. Which is troubling, to say the least.'

'Would you go so far as to call demonic possession a modern trend?'

'Well, it's not exactly this year's fidget spinner' – titters from the audience – 'but yes, the rise is significant. It's the reasons for that rise where I differ. I see the cause lying with psychology, not spirituality. In the brain, not the soul, if you will.'

131

Abby turned her seat towards him. 'So you mean we're all just mad?' There was no malice in it. No defensive snap. Just a worried young woman, biting her lip.

'That's not a helpful word. I just mean the real answer is in counselling or medication. There's no shame in that.'

Kissell smiled. 'So why is demand growing? Oh, and hi, Professor.'

'Hi,' Matt said. 'Well, what's particularly interesting is the theory that demand is rising because being possessed can be a more attractive prospect than being labelled mentally unwell.'

Reverend Perry leant forward, aghast. '*Attractive?* Are you kidding?' He threw a horrified look at the audience and shook his head. 'Folks, I saw what possession did to Tom Riley, and it was anything but attractive.'

Heads nodded in agreement, but up on the screen Kissell tapped a knuckle off his chin and said, 'I'm intrigued, Professor. Carry on.'

'Well, as I'm sure you'll discuss in the second half of tonight's programme, we have stigmatised mental illness in our culture. So much in fact that many of us are deeply fearful of ever being labelled with words like depression, anxiety or personality disorder. Now it's completely normal for some of us to struggle with our mental health, just like our physical health. There's nobody to blame and yet we live in a blame culture. So when we're given these labels some of us blame ourselves. We say it's *our* brain or *our* personality at fault. Now . . . by contrast, imagine that someone tells us that we're not suffering from any mental illness at all. Instead, we're told we're demonically possessed. That our negative and unpredictable behaviour is not because of the inherent architecture, or the native chemistry of our brains. The problem isn't inside of us. It's an external foreign invader. Now that's freaky and scary, don't get me wrong. Yet for some it can be a liberating thought. They can blame someone else and not themselves.'

132

Abby's shoulders dropped. 'Are you saying I *should* blame myself?'

'Absolutely *not*. I'm saying we needn't blame *anybody*. Not ourselves, not a fictional demon. And yet we're trapped in this blame culture. We are constantly looking for scapegoats.' He looked across at Perry. 'And I say this respectfully, but religious world views are notorious for blaming others for problems. Be that other humans who don't believe, or when they blame mythical devils. Christianity itself throws all its pain on Jesus on the cross. The cosmic scapegoat, but, I digress . . .'

'So what about the appeal of exorcism itself?' Ellis asked.

'Well, think about it. A mental health diagnosis can feel like a permanent, lifelong label. Yet exorcism claims to cast the problem out for ever. And afterwards, you're welcomed back into the community, because the evil has gone away. By contrast, somebody labelled as schizophrenic may not feel that same sense of welcome. And hey, if the demon comes back, just do another exorcism. I know this sounds odd, but I'm just saying the growth in demand is real . . . except it's a lot more complex than lazy theories like we've taken prayer out of schools or legalised gay marriage, so the Devil is therefore more rampant.'

Ellis started pacing, with one arm across her. 'So could exorcism work as a psychological placebo then?'

'Theoretically yes, but should we therefore encourage exorcism? Absolutely not.'

Kissell tapped his glasses up his nose. They seemed to slip down whenever he got animated. He frequently got animated. 'Forgive me, but if you're saying exorcism can work, then what does it matter what's behind it? Surely, we just help people, no matter what?'

'Well, for a start, exorcisms *don't* always work, hence the repeated requests for more and more of them. This can cause great distress and confusion in the patient. But also, and this is crucial, the mere *idea* of exorcism can keep people from the treatment they really need.' Matt clocked Perry's glare. He tried to speak gently. 'I interviewed a woman once. When she was a child her parents refused medical help because they were convinced her frequent seizures were demonic possession. She had temporal lobe epilepsy. Whenever she felt a fit coming on she'd hide herself in the family bathroom. Just in case her parents saw it and started casting out demons. She could have died in there, having a fit, alone. Eventually she got out of that family and got the help she needed. But can't you see how damaging and dangerous that was? All that needless delay of treatment. And *that*, Reverend Perry, is the real crux . . . read the news . . . people die during exorcisms. And sometimes it's children. Plus, this ritual can exacerbate unstable, violent people who desperately need medical help . . .' He looked across at Perry. 'I believe that's what happened to Tom Riley.'

'Excuse me?' Perry sat bolt upright.

'I believe you should have persisted with the medical support, and not confused his mind with—'

'Dammit, I was helping him, and I'll tell you exactly how . . .'

Perry started ranting, but Matt quickly phased out from the words because something was happening over the reverend's shoulder. Bernie Kissell had been quiet for a while. Matt, perhaps foolishly, had assumed this was because he was listening to Matt's points. But the reason Kissell was silent was because he was praying. Head down, comb-over hanging. In fact, as Perry droned on, Matt saw Kissell lift both hands towards the camera lens. And as he did, a slow, hissing whisper began slithering from the studio speakers. Prayers that were spoken in Pittsburgh were being beamed through space, and were now firing through the amplification system of a cold, English TV studio.

And he said, '*I call you out. In the saving name of Christ, I call your name and command you to leave this wonderful person. Out. I call you out. OUT!*'

Reverend Perry had already trailed off. He started pointing instead. Not at Abby, like Matt had expected, but towards the audience instead.

'Look!' Perry gasped in horror. 'There's one of them now.'

A woman in the audience started to scream.

CHAPTER TWENTY-THREE

Matt's head, every head in fact, snapped to the middle row, where a huge, muscled chunk of a man was sitting in a baseball cap. Matt had noticed him before, when he first walked in, looking bored and distant and impeccably toned. But now he was reaching one of his huge, trembling hands up his chest. Thick fingers were spider-crawling towards his own throat.

People were already pulling and leaning away from him, including the screaming woman, who had been trying to yank her long cream cardigan free. The end of which was clamped in the man's other massive fist. She must have seen how much his biceps and chest were bulging through his muscle top, so she'd already given up. Now she frantically climbing out of the wool altogether, yelping as she did it.

Matt heard the rapid footfall of security just as the guy in the cap pushed his chest forward with a sudden spasm. A huge globule

136

of spit sputtered across his lips and covered his chin. More people screamed, but at least the woman was now free. She clambered and crawled directly across the plastic seats, just to get away.

'Sir!' one of the security guys shouted, one hand outstretched.

It was too far away for Matt to fully see the muscle man's face, but that didn't matter, because his close-up was already on the big screen. The man couldn't seem to turn his head. It was trapped in an invisible, shivering vice. But his eyes moved. They slid in their sockets towards the oncoming security guards, and his gaze lacked any sense of aggression or threat. Just the watery-eyed, desperate fear of a man drowning. Something was creaking, the man's plastic chair perhaps?

An older woman in the crowd clearly knew him. People were holding her back, as she sobbed and dropped to her knees. She reached out, shouting, 'Richie . . . Richie love . . . *stop* it.' His mother.

Kissell's prayers filled the studio speakers. And now, Reverend Perry was doing the same.

'Sir, *sir*.' The guards started treading up the stairs slowly. 'You need to calm down, right now.'

'*Calm down?*' Matt whispered to himself, then he sprang to his feet and hollered across the studio in frustration. 'He's having a seizure. Call an ambulance.'

The guards ignored him. They stood gawping as the man's hand kept crawling up the side of his own face. The grasping fingers slowly tugged the baseball cap away. It dropped, bounced off his shoulder and fell to the floor, revealing curly black, mid-length hair over a receding brow. It was matted with visible droplets of sweat.

'Call an ambulance,' Matt shouted again.

A gruff voice shouted back from the dark. 'Shhhh, we have.'

The man's lips opened a little. The screen zoomed to show his top and front lower teeth grinding against each other. God. That was the creaking sound he could hear. Like dry rope on an old ship. His teeth might burst into dust at any second.

137

Freya Ellis stood stock-still through all of this, simply taking in the chaos. Her eyes were methodically drifting between the man in spasm and the frantic floor managers as they guided the panicked crowd towards the exit. She didn't say a word, and Matt quickly realised why when he saw her head tilt. She was listening to her producer in her earpiece. Would they cut to something else, or would they keep with this?

The latter. This was ITV.

The voice in her ear must have given the word, because she blinked and then erupted into action. The remaining cameras that were trained on Matt and the other guests suddenly span around, every lens in the room swooping towards the muscle man, Richie, whose neck now bulged with many visible pulsing veins. He could have been lifting five hundred pounds right now, but he was just sitting there, one arm lolling by his side, gripping the loose cardigan, and the other crawling across his own body like a hungry fly.

His lips started moving just as that roving hand gripped his own T-shirt. He tore it, and the front collar fell open in a triangular tear. The ripping sound was surprisingly loud, until Matt discovered why. A nervous member of the crew had already rushed up the stairs and was dangling a boom mic over the guy's head.

Ellis barked out a massive, 'Quiet, everyone. He's talking.'

The whole room dropped into an intense, throbbing silence.

A hiss grew on the speakers, and a little whistle of feedback too. Somebody in the gallery was cranking up the mic, and slowly, very slowly, a strained and whispered South African accent started coming through.

'. . . *walking . . . walking . . . I am . . . walking . . .*' There were gaps in his speech. Pauses in which the man's face crunched in pain. '*I am . . . roaming . . . walking . . . to and fro . . .*'

Freya Ellis frowned at this. Perplexed.

Matt noticed Perry out of the corner of his eye. He was on his feet digging into his inside pocket, like he had a gun in there. But it wasn't a gun. What he had was just as destructive, though, a tiny New Testament. Matt wondered if this was the same one he'd touched last night, when Tom Riley finally lost control.

He held it forward, aimed at the trapped man across the room. A crucifix to a vampire. 'Messiah!' he shouted, wiping his beard of sweat from the spotlights. 'Christ! Set this man free!'

Instantly, the man jerked his back with a hideous, painful yelp, like he'd just been kicked directly in the spine. It was a shocking, heart-stopping moment, and Matt could well imagine folks at home, spitting out their late-night takeaway. The man's tongue now pressed out between those lockjaw teeth. Any more of this and he'd bite it clean in two.

Matt had had enough. He ran across the studio floor towards him. 'Dammit, help him. Support his head—' A security guard grabbed Matt and shoved him back hard. Matt staggered and ran to Perry instead. 'Hey.'

'Satan!' Perry shouted. 'Release this man.'

'Stop. That's enough.'

'Satan! Can you hear me?'

'Enough.' Matt grabbed Perry's arm, and the New Testament fell from his fingers. Perry stared at it in cold terror as it dropped through the air in slow motion. As it fell, Richie's whispers suddenly roared into the speakers, at an ear-splitting level.

'*I am walking to and fro, through the earth, through the soil . . . I am in the soil, I live in the fucking soil . . .*' on the screen, in wild, terrible close-up, the man's eyes and nostrils flared like a horse, and then he screamed, '*I am in my box, but I am roaming through the earth!*'

The picture suddenly flicked to Kissel, who was now much, much closer to the lens. His serene face had filled most of the screen, cheeks now a shadow from the closeness of the camera. When he spoke, it sounded like it was through tears. 'Leave this wonderful man. Demon, be gone.'

The muscle man roared at this, the type of sound that could split things in his throat, then he burst into a massive, shuddering spasm.

Matt pointed at Kissell on the screen and yelled, 'Switch him off!'

They didn't switch Kissell off, because this was clearly too good. A TV first, perhaps. A spontaneous, live exorcism on national TV.

Clearly ignored, Matt threw up his hands, and turned back to Abby still in her chair. He rushed back to her, and said, 'You okay?'

It was subtle, he supposed.

She was just sitting there, staring at all this chaos in a gaunt, white-faced kind of shock. And to everybody watching, they'd have probably said she was reacting no differently than anybody else. But when Matt dropped next to her, he could see her lips. She kept licking them, and now it wasn't just her left hand trembling, it was both. Fingers slowly, slowly, curling inwards, like claws.

'Abby?' He said her name in a sharp whisper. When she didn't reply he put a hand on her forearm and shook it, like waking her from a dream. 'Abby?'

Her head, her trembling head, turned towards him, just as a tear trickled a line down her cheek. 'Make him stop, Matt.' Her frightened eyes stared up at Kissell on the screen. 'Make him stop.'

Matt shouted one more time, only this time he yelled directly at Freya Ellis. 'That's enough. Dammit, you've got *enough*.'

Ellis turned to him and, to his surprise, she nodded. She lifted an open-fingered palm high into the air, which must have been the signal to wrap this up. The sound of Kissell's whispers vanished mid-sentence, as did the whispering from Richie, the muscle man. Perry was the only one still shouting, but a crew member put a firm hand on his shoulder and spoke into his ear. His voice trailed away, and now the only sound left was something horrible. Richie was weeping. Hands went to mouths, as people looked at the sobbing man, alone on the chairs. He'd covered his face with one hand and his shoulders were rocking. Somewhere, in the silence, his voice, no longer low and grating, came through the tears. 'Why'd you stop?' he said. 'It was coming out . . .'

Matt jumped when Perry grabbed his shoulder.

'Professor, you had no right . . .' he whispered to Matt. 'You can't just force your world view on other people. He needed help. He needed *this* . . .' Perry pointed across the room. 'And look how you've left him.'

Richie's face was now totally covered by both of his hefty hands, and the studio pulsed with the most pitiless and bitter sobbing Matt had ever heard. He felt a confused beat of anger and then a guilty stab of shame. Which became anger again, when Ellis walked into the centre of the studio. She turned to the camera and stood upright.

Holy shit, they were *still* filming.

She walked towards the lens, slowly, and he saw that her chest was rising and falling with the breath she'd just lost. She raked a rogue strand of fringe back in place, with a trembling hand. He had no idea if any of that was real or fake; he just heard her voice.

'Ladies and gentleman. As I'm sure you understand, we need to take a short break. I'm told that the ambulance has arrived, and we can assure you that the audience member will be given all the help he needs. We apologise for the bad language, and we will update you just as soon as we can . . . I'm Freya Ellis, and this . . . is *The Exchange*.'

The red light vanished.

There was no *boom-ba-boom* from the speakers.

Freya Ellis's long and well-postured body immediately clicked into a sudden stoop, and with a hand in her hair, she drifted on shaky legs towards a growing clan of producers gathered on the floor. Maybe she was scared, after all.

Perry was already at Richie's side, handing his cap back to him, and holding his hand as the paramedics rushed up with oxygen.

Matt and Abby were left on the stage, and when he turned his chair, her chin was trembling, eyes brimming.

'I'm scared,' she whispered. 'I'm really scared.'

'You're going to be okay. Let's just find your son.'

Her face crunched and she nodded. 'Okay.'

He took her cold and shaking hand in his, and they both walked quickly towards the black curtains. Perry's voice called out, 'Bless her, Jesus!' And for a moment, he felt her slow down.

He squeezed her fingers and tugged her away. Wafting his hand through curtain after curtain, like an eternal maze, impossible to escape from.

When they finally reached the dressing room, Matt pushed through the door and what he saw seemed to perfectly solidify all the stress, frustration and anger he was feeling right now. Foster, that crew member, had *not* done as Abby had asked. The TVs were still on and there, by the now abandoned Connect 4, sat Tuan, her little boy. He was staring at the screen, jaw lolling open. He slowly turned and looked at his mum, which made her step back. For a moment Matt thought he might screech out in fear and run away from her.

But instead, he immediately slid off his chair and raced towards her. He flung his arms around her legs, then he looked up and laughed. 'Mummy! Did you see that man just now? What a total, *total* nutter!'

PART TWO

SEEK

CHAPTER TWENTY-FOUR

Matt plunged under, raking the water back so he could skim his chest along the bottom of the pool. He liked doing that. Had done since he first cracked swimming as a kid. Going so low that he felt his belly bounce off the lowest possible tile, then up, up and away, micro bubbles doing a giddy slide across his goggles until he crashed up through the surface, like the mighty, sleek sword of Excalibur (in his mind) or a gasping, flapping, semi-fit fella in Star Fleet swimming shorts (reality). But for the last few years, he always picked something special up on the way.

Amelia was on the surface, lounging back in the water, staring up at the high lights of the vaulted ceiling, until Matt burst up around her, scooping her in an explosion of water and giggles. That's what always did it. The unexpected timing of it. The thought that the Great White was coming, only *when*? Every time they came swimming she'd requested 'the Shark game'. Funny how Matt's passing idea during a toddler swim session should now be a firmly bolted family tradition.

She wriggled out of his arms. Like she always did. He put up a token fight. Like he always did. Then he raced her to the shallow end, like they always did, him swimming with head down and palms up together to make a shark's fin.

When he finally snapped a shrieking and laughing Amelia, Wren was coming to the end of her lengths too.

'Nice form there, Wren.' Matt applauded as she splashed up next to him. Amelia went off to do handstands. He lifted his goggles. 'Spied a few forbidden angles under the water, too.'

She flicked drops at him but didn't speak yet. Her chest was heaving. 'Did you see . . . that old lady beat me?'

'You mean the *super* old one? In the flowery cap?'

She nodded. 'She's like two hundred years old, and she's faster than me. I hate my life.'

'I bet she's got webbed toes. And gills too. She's a mutant, Wren. Don't envy that.'

She slid a wet arm around his side. 'You two, done? I *need* a latte to celebrate.'

'Celebrate what?'

She shrugged. 'Giraffes?'

Eventually they climbed out, battling through the predictable stroppiness from Amelia, who would have stayed swimming in there for the rest of the decade if she had her way. Coldness hit him as they trotted a wet trail to their lockers. Shivering, he rummaged for his towel and washbag and found an unoccupied shower. It was while he was in there, while hot water pounded his hair into a bubbled, marshmallow Afro, that someone knocked hard on the door.

'Just a second,' Matt called through.

Another knock.

'Almost done.'

Another knock, only this time followed by a voice. 'Professor Hunter?'

Matt's fingers stopped in his hair.

'Professor Hunter?'

'I'm in the shower.'

It wasn't easy to hear them over the gushing water. 'Can we chat?'

'While I'm butt-naked?' he hollered. 'Give me a sec—'

'Professor Hunter?'

Tutting, Matt turned the valve and the water finally stopped. He threw his towel over his shoulder and opened the door up a tiny gap, blinking away the running drips. Through the haze Matt saw a spindly guy emerge in skinny-white jeans and a blue T-shirt. Mid-twenties probably, but he'd fast-tracked his hair to the future. The whole cut, quiff and all, had been dyed a funky shade of cool, silvery grey. He was wearing blue deck shoes too. No socks, and he had the biggest Adam's apple Matt had ever seen in his life. It bulged as he talked, pushing through the rim of his collar. He looked vaguely, *vaguely* familiar.

'Sorry to bother you.'

'While I shower in a public swimming pool?' Matt smiled. 'Not at all.'

'Then we'd like to talk to you.'

Matt leant out and looked left and right. He whispered, 'Who's *we*?'

'Oh. I'm Ethan.'

'Okaaay.'

'I'm from Stiff Media. We make TV shows.'

'About men showering?'

He looked confused and shook his head. 'My boss, she's in the cafe. She told me I *had* to grab you before you left. There's a time frame element. Can you meet her?'

'Can I be unreasonable and dry my crotch first?'

He bit his lip and actually checked his watch.

'I'm gonna dry myself, okay? Then I'll meet you in the cafe. How about that?'

'And you won't leave?'

'Promise.' Matt saluted as he closed the door. He looked down as he started scrubbing his towel through his hair, and for a split second he saw a clump of someone else's hair on the tiles below. Yuk. He stepped back and saw it was a thick clump of blonde hair, with streamy rivulets of pinky red blood, sprouting like veins fading into the plug hole. He closed his eyes, just so that he didn't have to see Justine Riley's hand reaching from the next cubicle to get her hair back. Trying to lift it with her snapped wrist. When he opened his eyes, the hair was gone. He caught a glimpse of his face in the curve of the tap.

'Dimwit,' he said to himself.

CHAPTER TWENTY-FIVE

Matt slung his bag over his shoulder and paused when his phone buzzed. Wren had received his text message.

He'd written: *Sorry. Random work meeting in the cafe. Grab your drinks and I'll join you soon.*

And her reply was. *Absent father!*

He noticed she was typing again.

JOKE! That was a joke!

He laughed and pushed through the turnstiles. He headed towards the white leather sofas and scattered tables. A tattooed dad was trying to stab a disobedient straw into his kid's Capri-Sun, and he saw five red-faced women tightly wrapped in garishly patterned Lycra. They were hi-fiving for another hardcore gym workout. Celebrating, naturally, with only a *mid*-sized latte and only a *mid*-sized cupcake.

Sitting on a circular table, in the far corner, was Ethan talking to someone. And when he turned, Matt saw it was Nupa. The TV producer from the park last night. She'd ditched the long black jacket, and now wore red leather trousers and a chic white shirt, patterned with thin, but still bold black lines. She wafted her black mane back like a shampoo advert and stood.

'Hey, Nupa.' He put out his hand. 'Come for a swim?'

'Never. My hair despises English pools.' She tugged at his hand. It felt more like a pull down to sit than a handshake. 'Now, can I get you anything?'

He dumped his bag to the side. 'Do you know what? I'd love a vanilla milkshake.'

'Done.' She turned and randomly made the peace sign to Ethan. Matt frowned until he realised it wasn't the peace sign at all. It was a drinks order. He sprang off on his deck shoes towards the counter, each hand plunging the minuscule pockets of his skinny jeans, rummaging for money.

'So, Nupa . . .' Matt said. 'About last night.'

'That was a pretty astonishing bit of TV. It's causing quite the buzz.'

'It was dangerous. I saw a mentally unstable man having some sort of seizure. Is he okay?'

'Mostly, though he's disappointed. As you know, he wishes you hadn't intervened.'

Matt said nothing.

'Don't you wish you'd let Kissell finish?'

Those nearby women suddenly erupted in a mad cackle. Matt looked across at them and said, 'Even if I had, I'm pretty sure his medical issues would have only returned.'

'If indeed it *was* only medical . . .'

He looked back. 'So if you're not here for a dip . . .'

'We're making another programme on this subject. A follow-up.'

'In the studio again?'

150

Her hooped earrings were heavy enough to drag her lobes down when she shook her head. 'No, this will be different. A documentary. A fly-on-the-wall look at the subject of exorcism.'

Matt groaned. 'Do you mean one of those corny supernatural shows? With the night vision cameras and the idiots?'

She laughed. 'No. It's not that at all. Far more serious. This one is for BBC Two and BBC America, and we'd like you on board.'

'For what, background research?'

'Partly, but actually you'd be on-screen too. A fair bit, I hope.'

'With *this* hair?' Matt pointed at the growing frizz.

She smiled. 'This will be fifty minutes, exploring *both* sides of the exorcism debate. And the central focus is going to be Bernie Kissell's visit to the UK.'

Matt felt himself sit up a little. 'He's coming here?'

She nodded.

'When?'

She checked her watch. 'Well, his flight was about three hours ago, so he'll be over the Atlantic by now. He's really looking forward to meeting you. He talked about you a lot.'

Ethan appeared with two very full milkshakes in hand. With an edgy sense of focus he set each glass down with no spills.

'Thank you.' Matt took a sip. 'So why's he coming?'

'To save England.' She gave him a wry smile and took a delicate sip of her drink. She wiped her lip with a napkin after. 'He says that what happened in Cheddington yesterday, and in the studio last night, proves that England's demon problem is out of hand. He thinks it's about time someone sorted it out. He's already got a waiting list for British Skype exorcisms.'

Matt shook his head.

'He's decided to do their exorcisms here in the flesh, all in one go. And we'd like to film that.'

'Well, what could possibly go wrong?'

'It's going to take place at The Reed Institute, in Cambridgeshire. Have you heard of it?'

Matt bit his lip in concentration. 'Isn't that where all the celebrities go for rehab? I thought it'd closed down?'

'It had, but it's been bought by Faith Fire now. They're a UK megachurch—'

'Oh, I know Faith Fire.' He thought of trendy hipsters, supping on craft beer and lifting their hands to 'Jayzuz' their 'save-your'.

'They're reopening The Reed as a big Christian retreat centre in a few months, but Kissell's booked it for this weekend.'

'You're kidding. *This* weekend?'

'It's short notice, true. But you can get a lot of footage in a few days.'

'Yeah, but what about his' – Matt searched for the word – 'his *clients*? What about psychiatric assessments? Have they seen doctors first?'

'We'll try and push for that, yes.'

'You'll *try*?' Matt set his shake down. 'Nupa, I don't want to tell you how to do your job, but if you guys are going to bankroll something like this you take on a duty of care. These are vulnerable people. They could wind up exploited or damaged . . .' He trailed off when she held up a palm.

'We're not paying for it. Any of it. A bunch of private donors, religious types, they saw the show last night and the news about Tom Riley. They were horrified. *The tide is turning*, is how Kissell put it. They want to nip this possession boom in the bud, so they're paying for him to come over and they've hired The Reed. And remember, all of these clients were prepped to pay Kissell a fee for a Skype exorcism, anyway. They'll pay a fair bit more when it's done face-to-face.'

Matt shook his head. 'I bet that'll be the crux of all of this in the end. The money.'

'You don't know that. Besides, the programme isn't out to prove or disprove possession. We're impartial. The point is that we're not organising this at all. It's going to happen with or without us being there, but he invited us. Surely you agree it'd be better to at least *be* there, than leave them on their own?' She leant forward, hands clasped. 'Come aboard, Matt. You can offer the alternative perspective, like you did last night. *Be the voice of rational science in the face of the mystical.*' She ran a hand across the air. A poster tag line. 'Or at least, just give his clients, as you call them, a bit of balance. They deserve it. And besides, Kissell's very keen for you to take part.'

'Why? If I'm opposed to what he's doing?'

She blinked slowly. 'Because he's convinced that by the end of it, you'll believe.'

Matt snorted into his milkshake. 'He doesn't know me very well . . .' He took a gulp, swallowed, then he scrunched up his face. 'Sorry, but I'm not sure about this. Maybe you should ask somebody else.'

'It's not just Kissell who wants you there.' Nupa tilted her head. 'Remember Abby from the show last night?'

'Crud. She's going too?'

'Yep. He offered her a free exorcism and she's accepted. I think he wants to make her a focal point of the whole event, but I can see she's in two minds about the entire topic. She said she might benefit from you being there.'

Matt let out a long breath and sat back.

'She needs you, Matt. The programme needs you.'

'You're making it sound like a poster for war.'

'Isn't it? The battle between rationality and superstition?'

He glanced at her, annoyed at how she was trying to play him. So he looked away for a moment and saw Wren and Amelia over his shoulder. They were now in the queue for drinks, red cheeks glowing, hair a mass of drying straw. Wren waved, though she didn't smile.

'Beautiful family you have there,' Nupa said.

'You don't expect them to be involved, do you, because I—'

'No, just you . . . but, your daughter over there, just gets me thinking. Abby has a young son. Tuan.'

'All right, all right. You can lay off the guilt trip. Just email me details, and I'll think about it.' Matt went to stand and put out his hand. 'Well, thanks for the drink, Nupa. I'll let you know.'

'When?'

'Tomorrow?'

She shook her head. 'We'd need an answer soon. Kissell's plane lands at four this afternoon and we're filming his arrival. We'd want you there to meet him. Then you can have input into the event planning for The Reed. He's calling it *Free Indeed*, by the way.'

'It's not that free for all those folks who are paying for it.' He blinked. 'Hey, do *I* get paid for this?'

'Yes. Quite well. We'll be hiring you as a consultant.'

'Well, Nupa, why didn't you say that at the start?'

'So, you'll do it?'

'Just send me the details and give me a couple of hours to think about it. How about I call by three this afternoon?'

She nodded. 'Okay. But you'd be mad to say no. I think it'll make for a fascinating hour of television.'

'It's better than another damn talent show I guess . . .' He tipped his head. 'Thanks for the milkshake.'

His glass was still half-full so he took it over to Wren and Amelia where they talked through the rest of the day's plans. He was supposed to be sorting out the garage at home, while the girls were heading into town to meet with Lucy. They were taking Amelia for a haircut, and they kept talking about fringes a lot, scrolling through Google Images. He did a pretty good job at keeping his attention through all of this, nodding at the different styles and putting his thumbs up at the right times. But it was hard not to sip his milkshake and think of Abby Linh. He pictured her sitting at a kitchen table, fingers bent into claws while her frightened son called her name over his cereal. Pleading for her to be . . . *her*.

A call you have, a Call you Have. A CALL YOU HAVE!

The phone crashed into his mind and he quickly killed the Yoda ringtone. He pressed it to his ear and turned from the girls.

'Matt, it's me, Detective Fenn, I mean, from yesterday.'

'I remember who you are, Fenn.' He walked towards the huge glass viewing window overlooking the pool. The glass was so thick he couldn't hear anything from the water. He just saw people splashing in a weird silence.

'Right. So are you busy today?'

'I *might* have something at four. Why?'

'Four this afternoon gives us plenty of time. Look, I'm heading back to Cheddington today. Reverend Perry's wife has a video of Tom Riley. Says it proves he was possessed.'

Matt turned to the girls, who were already finished and reaching for their coats. Wren tapped her watch and hooked a thumb at the door. *We're heading off, okay?*

Okay, he mouthed back to her, then turned his ear back to Fenn.

'Do you fancy it?' Fenn said.

'You know what? Yes, I do,' Matt said, just as a child dive-bombed into the pool, mouth open in a silent wail that could have been a scream or a roar of joy. Without the sound, it was impossible to tell. The child's face stuck in Matt's mind as he headed out to the car. He wasn't sure why, though he could guess. The jumping kid's face stayed with him all the way up the motorway. Lodged in a mid-air plunge, lips peeled back from his teeth, mouth setting a black hole between two pink cheeks, and eyes all wide and wild and staring, with either happiness or panic. Maybe even both.

CHAPTER TWENTY-SIX

She had both of her bay windows wide open, so that the cold air from the Cheddington fields sucked her mustard curtains out across the sill. Hems flapped against the pebble-dashed walls while Matt and Fenn watched her from the doorstep outside. Oblivious to them, Reverend Perry's wife just slid the noisy hoover back and forth, back and forth, her face expressionless. Her short brown hair was cropped into a pixie cut.

Fenn sighed and pushed the doorbell again. Nothing.

'Maybe it's not working.' Fenn stepped off the path, and almost clipped the *Keep off the Grass* sign with his foot. His shoes pressed into the damp, perfect lawn as he reached the bay window. Matt could smell the faint smell of manure in the air from the fields. A hard knock on the glass did nothing, so Fenn leant his head through the open gap instead. 'Mrs Perry?'

She hoovered on. Her mouth a perfect, unbroken line.

'Mrs Perry!'

She spun and spasmed when she saw Fenn leering through the window. He tried to set her at ease with a wave and a toothy smile. It only made him look like a happy killer, rather than a glum one. 'Mrs Perry,' he hollered. 'We spoke on the phone? The video?'

Her shoulders, as arched as a cat on the M1, dropped a touch, and she quickly yanked the plug. The wincing drone of the hoover dropped to silence and she threw a cold stare at Fenn. 'Please, *please* get off our lawn. It's only just been laid.' She stepped over the hoover and moved towards the door.

He tiptoed back to the path and Matt shook his head at the Bigfoot tracks he'd left in the muddy grass. Fenn shushed him and frantically scraped dirt off his shoe, as the lock of the door rattled and slid. When she opened up, she was pulling a grey cardigan over her yellow T-shirt.

Fenn flashed his ID. 'Hiya. I'm Detective Sergeant Fenn.'

She leant forward and squinted. There weren't many lines around her eyes. Simon Perry was early thirties, but she looked five years younger. And that hair of hers was pretty funky. He wondered if she'd had it cut by Justine.

'Come in.' She stepped back and opened the creaking door wide. She led them to the lounge where she pointed at a terribly worn, brown leather couch, full of cracks in the fabric. It looked like spider webs.

'Would you mind closing the windows, Mrs Perry?' Fenn sank with a shiver. 'It's a bit nippy.'

She blinked, then looked across at the windows, as if she'd only just realised they were open. She shut each in turn, talking to the glass. 'Call me Claire, please.'

'Will do. Thanks for seeing us, Claire.'

She sank into a high-backed armchair covered with throws and the definite curve of cat hairs. 'I have to ask. Why is *he* with you?'

'This is Profess—'

'I know. He's the man who called my husband a murderer on TV last night.'

Matt tilted his head. 'I didn't *quite* call him a murderer, I just—'

'Blamed him for Justine's death?' She crossed her legs and brushed some dust from her knee. 'Which is why I think it's fair to ask . . . why are you in my house right now?'

This wasn't easy for her, and what he said next seemed to make her soften. 'I apologise if I came across too harsh last night. And I don't believe your husband is a murderer. However, I do have a legitimate concern that—'

A slap to Matt's knee cut him off. Fenn smiled. 'Matt is purely offering a few . . . theological insights to the investigation. Cos, to be honest Claire, all this demonic possession malarkey didn't really feature on my police exam. Matt's just my walking Wikipedia. Okay?'

'Maybe you should use my husband for your information instead. At least he's wise enough to know that it's not malarkey, for a start.'

Fenn nodded. 'Sorry. My bad.'

'Where is he?' Matt asked. 'Your husband, I mean.'

Wow. Strike up the band. Call the press. A flicker of a smile rose at the edge of her mouth. 'In a posh hotel in London right now, being wined and dined.'

Fenn whistled. 'And what's the occasion?'

'He's taking part in a big TV show about Bernie Kissell. He's flying over to England today, and they want *Simon* to be his right-hand man. How about that?'

Matt had already told Fenn about his own involvement with the show, but Fenn wisely kept that back. 'Then your husband's an important man.'

She nodded. 'Simon always said God was going to widen his ministry.'

'Well, I'm pleased for him,' Fenn said. 'But about this video?'

Her smile stopped.

She reached under the coffee table and pulled out a chunky-looking laptop. Matt noticed streaks of something black around her wrists. Was that dirt? Ink? Maybe paint? When she caught him looking, she instantly pulled her arms back. 'This old thing takes eons to start. I'll make tea.'

She vanished into the kitchen, while Matt and Fenn looked across at the framed photographs hanging from the walls, mostly of Keswick, in the Lake District. A large wedding photo sat on the mantlepiece showing the brand-new Claire and Simon Perry, snapped on church steps in a cloud of laughter and confetti. Her hair looked down to her waist back then. Perry's looked as red as a balloon.

She timed it perfectly, because when she set the brewed tea in front of them the Windows screen had finally loaded. Her wrists, he noticed, were now clean. She waited an age for each mouse click to register but eventually a row of video thumbnails appeared. She hovered a finger over the space bar. 'Okay, so these are from our camera above the door.'

'Wait,' Matt said. 'Why do you have a camera?'

'The couriers dump our packages on the doorstep sometimes, and they're easily stolen. It happens a lot round here. Simon and I got one of these doorbell cameras, and he loves his gadgets. It's handy, but we didn't expect it to pick up this . . .' She tapped the space bar and sat back. It took a full thirty seconds for the black screen to finally flicker into something else.

The screen filled with a fish-eye view of the doorstep Matt had only just been standing on. Only it was dark and the night vision camera had turned everything into a strange, bluey-grey. It was a clear view of the path all the way to the wooden garden gate, set between two high hedges. The time code read Tuesday, 18th February, 3.10 a.m.

They waited and sipped. Waited and sipped. Until Fenn saw it first. 'Ooo . . .' He leant forward, squinting.

'What?' Matt frowned.

'Something's wriggling under the gate.'

Matt shuffled forward on the couch and Claire pushed the laptop towards him with a scrape. 'Oh . . . I see it.'

They looked like worms. Like tiny black tentacles reaching under the gate. A baby octopus slithering through town, knocking on doors and seeing who was home.

'What *is* that?' Fenn said.

Claire said, 'Watch.'

As soon as she said it, the gate opened incredibly slowly and beyond it was, confusingly, just the black road. Until the road writhed and moved and started spilling through the gate. Slowly, very slowly, a figure was crawling up the pavement.

'Is that Tom Riley?' Matt asked.

'Yes. Or at least, it's his body, being moved.'

Matt stared at the reaching, grasping, crawling shadow, making its way towards the house. It kept so incredibly low that it looked more insect than human. And for a little while, Matt felt very cold indeed. The thoughts of his own garden and his own house and his own bathroom, coming to mind.

'Yep, that's him . . .' Fenn said, 'look at the trousers.'

Matt squinted and saw it getting clearer as it came nearer the light. The black and white chequered squares of a chef's trousers.

'Remember this is three in the morning,' Claire said. 'That's *hours* after his shift ended. So if you think this is just mental illness, Mr Hunter. Keep watching . . .'

The crawling spider was so near the doorstep now that it vanished out of sight. Looking for cracks in the wood. When nothing happened for a while Matt was about to ask another question. Then, suddenly, the screen filled with the eyes of Tom Riley, for the briefest of seconds, before the gaping hole of his mouth covered the lens. From then on, all they saw was a dark, blue, pixelated hole that would occasionally flash with a row of glistening teeth, or the swish of a wet tongue lolling. In seconds, the mist of Tom's hot breath turned the image into a smeared, foggy haze.

Fenn spoke through his teeth. 'How long does this go on for?'

'It's forty-two minutes from start to finish.'

Matt and Fenn's eyebrows shot up.

'He just crawls away at the end, but you can barely see him leaving cos the camera's smeared with his spit. All that gloop broke the damn thing. The ringer doesn't work any more. We're getting a new one.' She leant forward, elbows on her knees. 'There's something *crude* about it, don't you think? The way he's doing it?'

'You mean crude as in sexual?' Fenn said.

'Yes . . .' She stared down at the flicking hole on the screen.

Matt nodded. 'I admit it's disturbing, but you don't need to be a demon to lick a doorbe—'

'Do you know the name Baal-Berith?' Her eyes narrowed.

'He's a demon,' Fenn said.

'Bravo. And did you know he's the lord of blasphemy and murder?'

'We're aware of his work,' Matt said. 'Why?'

'Because when we got up the next morning, that name was scrawled across our front door, and we both had to look it up. It was written in . . .' She looked to the window, shaking her head.

'In what?'

'In shit.'

Matt felt his face contract. 'Urgh.'

'Yeah . . . so you see, Tom really was beyond the scope of doctors and psychologists. Tom needed an exorcism, and Simon was the only one who cared enough to help.'

'What about his wife?'

'Justine wasn't exactly . . .' she trailed off.

161

Matt frowned. 'What?'

'I don't want to speak ill of the dead.' Claire saw them both staring at her, pressing her. 'Fine. Justine wasn't a Christian. She had no time for church. She was too wrapped up in that salon of hers and I thought that was a sad thing to focus on. I mean her job . . . a beautician.'

'There's nothing wrong with beauticians,' Matt said.

'I know, but they make masks for people, don't they? They encourage women to be obsessed with themselves. I'm not sure if that's healthy. It makes us insecure. I suppose what I mean is . . . Justine spent so much time looking in the mirror, she probably never looked up . . . to God. That sounds terribly judgemental.'

Matt nodded. 'Yeah, it does.'

'I'm sorry. But my point is that she wouldn't have prayed for Tom. She was never at church. So he must have been a desperately lonely man, until Simon came along.'

'Why didn't you call the police and show them this video at the time?' Fenn said.

She thought about it, her eyes lowering. 'Maybe we should have. Maybe not. But the Pastor Kissell videos say that bringing in non-Christians can just make things confusing and worse for the person possessed.' She bit her lip again. 'All I know is that no matter what you say, Professor, and no matter how guilty you try to make me feel, I've never seen someone with depression do *that*.' She pointed a stabbing finger at the laptop screen. For a moment, Tom's flicking mouth seemed so frantic, there could have been two tongues in there.

Fenn asked her to skip to the end of the video but by then Tom's crawl away was lost in a mass of smeared spit on the screen, so she closed the laptop, sat back into her chair. She stared at them both for a while.

'Claire?' Fenn said. Then again, 'Claire?'

162

She blinked. 'Yes.'

'The report says you and your husband met at the pub on the night of the murder.'

'Yes. He'd been in London all day. He came straight to the pub from the train.'

'And what about you?'

'What about me?'

'Where were *you* that day?'

'At home,' she frowned at Fenn, like it was a ridiculous question. 'I was *here*.'

'All day?'

'Of course. Then I went to the Merricot and met Simon at six. Simon went to see Tom after and that's . . . that's when the exorcism happened. We were together all night after that.' She turned something over in her mouth. 'And Mr Hunter, can I just say that I think you're being rather unkind to my husband. He really did try the medical approach. It just didn't work. He performed that exorcism on Tom from a pure, loving heart. Doesn't motivation count?'

'It does . . .' he said. 'But people can still do destructive, terrible things, even with the noblest of aims.'

'Is that true for you, too?' She watched him.

'It's true for everybody.'

Matt jumped when Fenn clapped his hands together. 'Well, listen, thanks for the tea and the video, but we best be off.'

'Wait.' She stood with them. 'How's Tom doing?'

'Why do you care?' Fenn said.

'Excuse me?'

'After what he did to Justine, and to an officer of mine. Why would you care how Tom Riley is?'

'Because we all lose our way, sometimes.' She looked at Matt. 'Don't you think?'

163

'Tom Riley is fine. Now goodbye, Mrs Perry.' Fenn shook her hand, very briefly, and they headed back into the hall.

It was just as she was undoing the latch that Matt spotted a side door, open a crack. But it was the handle that really caught his eye. He saw those familiar black smears again that he'd seen on her wrist.

'Uh-oh.' Matt pointed at the handle. 'You missed a bit.'

She stared at it and tugged her cardigan close.

Fenn was clearly intrigued by that look of hers because he was already pushing through the door.

She shot a hand forward. 'I'd rather you—'

The door swung open into a small, dark room, with a set of blinds firmly closed. In the centre were two small wooden stools. One sat in front of an easel, with a large canvas propped. It was scraped with three charcoal lines. Like claw marks. And on the walls, there were about seven more hanging. He saw the smeared shapes of what seemed like strange, shimmering faces.

'You're an artist?' Matt said.

'No . . .' she said. 'I . . . attempt.'

Matt caught all the shadowed eyes looking back.

'They look like skulls,' Fenn said, quietly.

'They're faces. People I know. People I love.'

'People you love?' Fenn's brow crinkled. 'Did that doorbell video inspire you?'

'Certainly not.'

'What are the wires?' Matt pointed to the little black cords hanging from the frames. They each had a switch.

Before she even opened her mouth, Fenn flicked one of them on. Suddenly some sort of hidden clockwork mechanism started moving, and the canvas started to ripple and protrude. For a moment, the face was alive.

'Wow,' Matt said. 'That's actually pretty clever.'

She shrugged. 'Simon helps with that part. He's the clever one.'

Fenn stared at the pulsating skull, face twisting in disgust. 'Do your parishioners know about these . . . things?'

'No. They're private. Now please . . .' She reached for the handle and tugged them back into the hallway. She pulled the door shut and all those gaunt black eye sockets vanished. He could still hear the one motor whirring. 'Now, can I please get back to cleaning my house?'

'We're sorry for intruding, but may I say . . .' Matt said, as she ushered them out onto the doorstep. 'It's refreshing to see Christian art that isn't all rainbows and doves. You're very good. So anyway, thanks for . . .' He turned to say goodbye, but he just saw the door rattle shut in his face.

Fenn was already halfway down the path.

Matt jogged up behind him and they reached the gate. Matt turned, standing in the same place that Tom the insect had crawled a few weeks ago. He wondered how long it took to get the smell of shit out of a door.

He shivered when he realised she was watching from the lounge window, staring out like a doll in a trance. It was just as he opened the gate that she seemed to blink herself to life, and then she raised a hand. Her wave looked strange and sallow. A ghost in the window. Then she turned away and walked back to her hoover.

'Bet she's great fun at parties,' Matt said.

Fenn shook his head. 'She gives me the creeps.'

CHAPTER TWENTY-SEVEN

They sent a car. A sleek, black BMW that made Wren whistle when it rolled up at the house. The driver didn't get out. He just beeped his horn twice and Matt's phone pinged with a simultaneous message.

Ready, it said.

Matt zipped up his hefty bag, stuffed with demonology books and a notepad, and he wondered if they'd have a camera on him, just to film him walking out. Nupa did say they wanted a lot of footage. He leant towards the hallway mirror to fiddle with his fringe. He tutted to himself.

'You look hot,' Wren said.

'Hot as in temperature or hot as in—'

'Hot as in *hawt*. You look great. You'll *be* great. And hey . . .' she kissed his shoulder, 'you did the right thing last night on TV.'

He caught her eye, and they held each other's gaze for a moment in the reflection. Then he turned and kissed her. 'I'd rather they didn't film our house. I don't want the nutters knowing where we live.'

'Especially the possessed ones.' She opened up the front door and he looked down their long path to the gate and the black car, purring there. 'If they *are* filming, do you dare me to slap your arse as you leave? Like, proper old school.'

'Wren don't.'

'Do you dare me, though?'

'Wren *don't*.' He grabbed his bag, then he kissed her one last time. 'I'll see you tonight.'

'Do you dare me, though?'

Laughing, he trotted quickly away from her. But he went a little too fast, a little too eager. His half-zipped-up bag slid off his shoulder and almost upended. He slapped it with his hand, pinning it midway down his leg. His papers didn't flutter out, but if they were filming, he'd already ticked the 'nerdy professor' box with great skill. He hitched his bag back up and turned. She was standing on the step mouthing the word, *Smooooth*. But she added her patented wink too, and so he winked back.

He loved that comedy wink of hers. The one that to passers-by looked like little more than a bit of ribbing, but to him, was always the codeword reminder to not take life too seriously. That she'd be there at the end of it with wine and smiles and *real* reality.

There were no cameras. Just the driver opening the door and reaching out a hand for his bag. 'I can take that, sir.'

'Careful it doesn't leap from your hand.' Matt handed it over. 'I think *that* bag's possessed, don't you?'

He looked at Matt, in complete confusion. 'I'm afraid I don't follow.'

He heard Wren snort with laughter on the doorstep.

'Er . . . let's just go.'

Not long after moving off Matt tried to make conversation, but

167

his driver, called Ray, was a one-word-answer type of fella, so Matt got bored of trying after a while. He just sat in the back and took in the sickly new leather smell.

Just enjoy it. And relax, he heard his own advice to Abby Linh last night. *And if you don't, it'll be over in a flash anyway.*

It took a good hour to reach Heathrow, which gave him time to read over a bunch of psychology reports he'd gathered on so-called possession cases. A consistent theme was that so many of the slam-dunk evidences of demonism – vulgar language, aversion to religious symbols, seizure-like writhings – could all be easily faked. Or if not faked, then acted from a purely subconscious belief that a demon was lurking inside.

And those evidences that were more difficult to explain – levitation, vomiting metal nails and pins, or having secret, almost psychic knowledge about others in the room – they were never convincingly caught on record anyway.

All these case notes just solidified his natural thinking on the topic. That possession was, to use the technical term, the very poppiest form of poppycock.

When the car pulled up to Arrivals, he saw the silver quiff of Ethan, the guy from the swimming pool this morning. He was waiting on the kerb, both hands plunged into the pocket of a denim jacket with a thick collar of sheep's wool. He was doing his usual, impatient two-step, nervously staring at his watch. And next to him was a young woman with blonde pigtails. She was holding a hefty-looking camera.

As soon as Matt's car pulled round the turn, she swung it up onto her shoulder. *Yikes*, he thought. *Here we go.*

He tugged his jacket into place, and some dangerous imp of mischief in his brain insisted he step out of the car like a Hollywood diva and strike a *Vogue* pose, just for the larks.

Do you dare me, though?

Don't, he told himself, *don't*.

'Least you're good-looking,' Ray suddenly said. 'Ready for your close-up?' It was the longest sentence Ray had probably said in his entire life.

CHAPTER TWENTY-EIGHT

Matt got used to the camera fairly quickly. Mainly because this was so different to his usual experience with news reporters. Nobody was thrusting a mic into his gob, asking him constant questions. Ethan just greeted him and they walked into airport arrivals together while the camera just kinda . . . hovered around. The pigtails woman would either film from behind, or she'd suddenly burst into a dash ahead of them, to get a shot from the front. She was a master at walking backwards without looking, though she still made him deeply nervous around pot plants.

Yet within minutes she, and the camera in her hand, faded into the scenery. It was scary how quick that happened. Then Ethan said they had half an hour before Kissell would appear, which was when the camera finally dropped. She put out her hand and became a person, rather than a living tripod. They shook as they walked, though she tended to spring along. 'Hey, Professor, I'm Suzy.'

'Hi . . . and please, call me Matt.'

'Cool. Cool. Then guess what, Matt?'

He mirrored her wide-eyed, cheery gawp. 'What?'

'I've read your book.'

He stopped walking. 'Yeah?'

'Well, audiobook, but I still think that counts. And I *really* liked it. Like, I am totally with you on all this supernatural stuff.' She shook her head. 'Demons. I mean, come on . . .'

He smiled. 'Then, Suzy, you can stay.'

The closer they got to arrivals the more dense the crowd became. This wasn't really surprising, since it was often packed. But Ethan's model face looked worried at just *how* rammed it was. They saw the usual little kids holding hand-painted signs for 'Grandpa' and grumpy drivers in ill-fitting suits holding up clipboards saying 'Metrogenics' and 'The T. T. Group'. But then the atmosphere changed. Because the signs changed, and as soon as they did, Suzy's camera swung back up.

Bible verses.

He saw Bible verses being pushed up into the air. Some just scrawled with pencil onto A4 sheets, others carefully printed at home on laminated, shiny A2. Various bits of scripture were being thrust up, but by far the most popular was *1 Peter. 5:8*

'*Be sober, be watchful. Your adversary the devil prowls around like a roaring lion, seeking someone to devour.*'

Yeah, that's just the type of thing you should say to someone with depression.

He spotted Nupa just then, standing in the crowd. She was wrapped in a long black coat, quietly observing it all. She was speaking into a phone clasped in her gloved hands. Soon after, Matt saw three different cameras shimmer out of the crowd. If anything was prowling, it was them. Then the final lens, which Nupa seemed the most interested in, was instructed to follow a commotion that was now coming through the crowd.

Maybe he should have guessed.

It was Reverend Perry, in full clerical collar again. He had a phone to his ear too.

'Here he comes, everybody,' Perry called out. His voice sounded whiny when it was loud. 'Here he comes.'

The applause was telling. The sheer loudness of it. Up till that moment, Matt had assumed the Kissell welcome party was about ten to twelve strong, but that was only the ones with banners. The sudden roar of cheers and clapping made it shockingly clear. Thirty or maybe forty people in this crowd were not here to pick up their sister from a Disney trip. Their eager faces and tiptoe stances were all for Pastor Kissell, whose sudden appearance was marked with a collective happy gasp.

In reality, Kissell simply stepped out of the crowd like everybody else. But to most people it looked like he'd just kind of materialised under the arrivals sign. He wasn't there one moment and was clearly there the next, dressed in dark blue slacks and a light blue polo shirt. He looked like he'd just stepped off the tennis court, but instead of a racquet, he had a little leather doctor's bag hanging from one hand. The flock took his appearance as a bona fide, science-busting miracle. Then Kissell, skinny little fella that he was, opened both arms wide and hugged the air, hips swinging. With a mahoosive and goofy grin he shouted, 'Hello . . . hello beautiful England!'

Rev. Perry. *Sheesh*. He almost tumbled over his own eager feet pushing towards Kissell. He was helped when a few burly men, clearly part of the TV crew, opened up a channel for him and his personal camera guy to get through. Matt wasn't close enough to hear their greeting, but he could see it well enough. There was a sudden flash of nerves on Perry's face, as he stepped into the same breathing space as his idol. But Kissell rushed over and smothered Perry in a hearty, reassuring, back-slapping embrace.

It was during this hug that the crowd of voices moved from monotone cheers to the beginning of a melody. And before he knew it, singing started to rise. The airport arrivals hall quickly revealed its world-class acoustics. Voices from the thirty or forty harmonised together, and Matt saw other passengers, amused and baffled by this, lifting their cameras. This probably looked like a bizarre flash mob. Or perhaps folks were asking what sort of international rock star turns up at an airport to the strains of 'Onward Christian Soldiers'.

Kissell. He was a total pro. As the singing swelled, he vigorously shook hands with his supporters, always using two hands clasped over theirs. If there'd been babies to kiss, he'd have done it. At one point, he even put a holy palm on a few spiritually hungry foreheads. It made them shudder and spasm and giggle with happiness.

Matt looked across at Nupa who had climbed up onto a little wall, to watch. Arms folded she scanned the crowd, the singing, the prayers, the thoroughly awkward frown on Matt's face – which he only now remembered was being constantly captured in Suzy's lens. Through all this Nupa started to smirk. This was, to be fair, a pretty solid opening scene for a TV show.

'Matthew!'

He turned to see Kissell striding his bandy legs towards him. With every step, the singing died down into, finally, silence. Kissell walked up with his cameraman gliding, and Matt took a step forward, with Suzy's camera next to him. Matt put out a hand and said, respectful and polite, 'Pastor Kissell. It's nice to meet you in the flesh. And I have to hand it to you, you really make an entrance.'

'Now, Matthew . . .' He put one hand on his hip and waggled a finger at him. 'I insist you call me Bernie. All my friends do.' Up close you could see his age, particularly around the eyes behind those huge glasses of his. But that smile was so filled with boyish wonder that it was like a young Huck Finn was living inside of Kissell, beaming at the wonders of the big, beautiful airport.

'Okay, Bernie it is . . .' Matt said. 'So how was your fl—'

Matt couldn't finish, because the wind was knocked out of him with Kissell's huge and crushing hug. He smelt mostly of coconut. The two nearby camera lenses started to revolve around this embrace. Which could make a fella really overthink his own mid-hug facial expressions.

Then just as soon as the hug started, Kissell pulled away quickly. 'Aww, darn it. Forgive me, Matt.'

'Something wrong?' Matt said.

His nod looked sad. 'No rest for the wicked.'

The crowd fell suddenly silent.

Kissell's eyes narrowed, as he stared into the crowd. Scanning, scanning, scanning and then *snap*. He clicked his finger and raised his hand. He moved the palm slowly from one side and then to the other, suddenly locking into one position.

His fingers curled in, leaving one finger pointing.

'Valac!' he said.

Hands flew to mouths at the sound of this name and immediately it sounded like something heavy had slumped in the crowd.

'Over here,' someone shouted.

Another, 'Let the pastor through!'

'Friend?' Kissell put a hand on Matt's shoulder. 'You should see this.'

They walked through the opening channel in the crowd, cameras hovering as close as flies. And soon, in the centre of the floor, Matt saw a woman in her fifties in a pink T-shirt and flowery leggings. She was curled in the foetal position, grunting the words, 'Fuck a dog, fuck a dog.'

Oh, for crying out loud, Matt thought, halfway between despair and hilarity. *This is so dumb.*

Kissell started rummaging through his little doctor's bag and quickly pulled out a thick wooden cross. 'Valac!' he shouted. 'What are you doing in there?'

The woman started to moan and shudder, 'Fuck a dog, good and proper.'

An unseen child in the crowd burst into laughter.

'You have no right to be in this kind-hearted lady,' Bernie shouted. 'Valac! I *command* you to leave.'

Over the heads of the crowd, Matt saw two confused-looking airport security officers pushing through, lips pressed against their two-way radios. But before they could get much closer, it all hit its crescendo.

Bernie dropped to his knees and placed the simple wooden cross against her. Not on the woman's head, like Matt had expected, but against the base of her spine. Her strange moaning clipped into a jerking stop, like a hiccup. Then her face lit up with a Christmas-morning smile. Matt had to look up to make sure Nupa hadn't arranged some sort of spotlight beam to be aimed at her face. She hadn't. The now bright-faced woman looked up at Bernie Kissell like she was at the feet of Christ himself. She blinked the tears away. 'He's gone. Hallelujah, he's gone.'

The security guys finally got through, and after staring at this in bewilderment, they started dispersing the crowd, telling people they were causing an obstruction. After a few hugs from Kissell, Matt saw the weeping woman getting collared by one of the crew. They pulled out a release sheet for her to sign, so they had permission to use the footage. She happily scrawled her name. Now she was standing, he noticed what the slogan on her T-Shirt said. *Cat Addict: Help Meowt!*

Nupa appeared at Matt's shoulder. 'Let's get moving.' She nodded for Perry and Kissell to walk towards the entrance.

As they went, Kissell trotted up to Matt. 'Would you like me to explain who Valac is?'

Matt said, 'Isn't it the winged baby-demon who rides on a dragon?'

Kissell's eyebrows went up. 'Hot dog.' He pronounced it 'dawwwg'. He turned to Nupa. 'He's good.'

Perry stepped between them, a smile lifting his red beard. 'And isn't Valac from the *Malleus Maleficarum*?'

'Not quite,' Matt said. 'It's from the *Lesser Key of Solomon*, am I right?'

Perry's shoulders dropped a little.

'Bullseye.' Kissell was wide-eyed. 'You know, with your sort of knowledge, you'd make an excellent exorcist.'

'Ha. I just lack some of the more fundamental qualifications, don't you think?'

Kissell laughed and slapped a hand on Matt's shoulder. 'I'm glad you're involved, Matt. I'm pleased you said yes.'

'Well, I just want to make sure your clients aren't hurt in any way.'

'Does *she* look hurt?' Perry pointed towards a doughnut stand. Cat Addict was laughing her head off, standing like a celebrity, while people lined up to not only hug her, but to get selfies too.

They reached the kerb outside, where it felt warmer than usual. Pleasantly so. The sun had broken through the clouds and the entire airport car park seemed to blaze under a lazy, pretty light. Nupa gathered them all together, by the pleasant trickling of a fountain.

'Okay, so here's the plan. We drive to London and get a bite to eat in Bernie's hotel. But we all drive together so we can discuss the show. There's a lot to talk through, but I'm very confident we can put together a fascinating . . .' She trailed off when she saw Kissell raise his hand. 'You have a question?'

He nodded. 'I don't want to go to the hotel straight away.'

'Oh?' She frowned. 'What would you like to do?'

'I need to see Tom Riley.'

Matt and Nupa exchanged a glance.

'He's in custody,' Matt said.

'Then, I'll visit him in custody.'

'I'm not sure if that's possible,' Nupa said.

'Surely prisoners can have visitors in England? You haven't chained him in ye olde tower, have you?' He grinned at them.

Matt waited for Nupa to speak, but she was too busy looking at the pavement, pondering it. So he said, 'Problem is, Tom is dangerous. He seriously wounded an officer while he was restrained so I—'

'And that's *precisely* why he needs me. Now.'

Matt bit his lip and turned to Nupa. She was on the phone.

Kissell slid off his glasses and started cleaning them with a handkerchief. His eyes looked freakishly tiny without the lenses. 'And forgive me for correcting you, Matt, but technically speaking, it wasn't Tom who did anything. In my own, humble opinion, of course.' He lifted the glasses and looked through the lenses at arm's length. Then he nodded, slipped them back into place, and smiled, 'That's better.'

Two cars and what looked like a plush-looking minibus rolled up. They all climbed inside the bus while Nupa stayed out on the pavement, pacing with her phone. It looked like the A-Team van inside, with a bunch of comfy grey seats that could swivel and pivot so they could discuss things together. As they waited for Nupa, Matt kept advising Kissell that seeing Tom wouldn't achieve anything, though in the back of his mind he knew full well that it'd probably make a good scene in the show. Still, he couldn't imagine it being allowed, anyway. A thought that faded rather quickly when Nupa climbed into the back with them and stuck up her thumb.

'Buckle up.' She did her patented hand slap on the back of the driver's headrest. 'Get us to Whitemoor Prison, Cambridgeshire. We'll grab some food on the way.'

The journey was the polar opposite of the one he'd had with Ray. That was an hour of silence, but here it was constant talk as the motorways whizzed by. They talked through the logistics (and *potential* – that word kept cropping up) of the world's first mass exorcism on TV. Whenever they stopped for a rare breath, Matt would grab his chance and speak up. He'd point out the danger of all this. He'd list all the ways a mass exorcism might potentially go haywire. They listened politely, but he couldn't help but notice that whenever his mouth was moving, their fingers were drumming. Then, once Professor Chicken Licken had delivered his warning, they nodded sagely and with thanks they turned back into their huddle and the car would fill with sound again.

In the end, Matt watched the trees whizzing by instead, in a smudge of grey and green and in time he noticed a high-pitched moan coming from outside. Just a 70 mph motorway wind, pushing itself through an unseen gap in the glass. Despite multiple button prods to raise the window, that groan of air was an insistent companion. Like a very quiet scream.

When he turned from the window, he saw Kissell was looking at him, smiling. He put a thumb up and mouthed the words, *You okay?*

Matt shrugged, and nodded back.

CHAPTER TWENTY-NINE

The van barrelled along the motorway while Nupa, Perry and Kissell made furious lists and plans for the weekend. They'd been doing that for almost thirty minutes now until Matt made a coughing noise, and raised a hand, 'Excuse me.'

Faces turned to him. Voices sank to silence.

'I have another question.'

Nupa's pencil hung from her teeth like a cigar. She took a breath, then, 'Go ahead.'

'Well, I notice that you haven't locked down the numbers yet.' He looked at Kissell. 'You really need to decide how many of your clients are going to attend this . . . event.'

'I have a question.' Perry raised his hand too, his voice a little mocking. 'Why are you calling them clients? I'm not keen on that word at all.'

Matt shrugged. 'What's your preference? Exorcees?'

Nupa pulled the pencil from her mouth. 'Go on, Matt. How many . . . people . . . do you think is manageable? Give me a number.'

He looked at Kissell. 'Four. Maybe five at the most.'

The van erupted with moans as Perry and Kissell shook their heads. Nupa wasn't impressed either.

'*Four?*' Perry wiped his hand across his beard. 'You want to ration out healing? Since when was Jesus stingy?'

'If you take on too many people it might descend into total chaos. Remember, some of these people aren't exactly stable. No offence. Oh, and by the way, Jesus was a pretty heavy rationer of healing.'

'He was *not*,' Perry said.

'Read the gospels. He never zapped an entire crowd. He healed specific people, not everybody at once.'

Bernie Kissell shuffled forward in his chair. 'What about Matthew 15? Doesn't he heal the *multitudes?*'

'Ah, but the multitudes brought the sick people *with* them. So by definition there were less sick people than—'

'Ahem,' Nupa coughed. 'As fascinating as this is, we do need a number. Bernie . . . how many possessed people do you have on your waiting list?'

'In the UK? Thirty-one. The Reed has plenty of space for all of them.'

Matt's jaw dropped.

'And don't forget we'll have security on hand,' Nupa said.

'And psychiatric nurses too?' Matt tutted.

'We've got that covered.'

He looked at her. 'Nupa, that's *way* too many. It's dangerous.' He saw her stony gaze and took another road. 'Besides. Don't you think that's a few too many faces for the viewers to keep track of? You don't get thirty contestants on *Strictly Come Dancing*, do you?'

'What an odd comparison . . .' she said, but then she immediately started tapping her pencil off her chin. He noticed the van was coming off the motorway and heading down a slip road. 'We *could* cut those numbers a bit.'

'To four,' Matt said.

Perry groaned.

'Not four,' she said, 'but yeah . . . not thirty-one . . . how about twelve?'

'I think five's a reasonable—'

'Ten?'

Matt winced, and bit his lip. 'That's a *lot*.'

'Tell you what. Let's come back to the numbers later, eh?'

Kissell turned to her. 'Not to be rude, Nupa, but we can just do this event ourselves and have no number restriction at all.'

'True. Or you can do it with us and share your mission with the entire world. And hey, if it works well, we could do another episode for the rest.'

'Ooo . . .' Kissell's eyebrows leapt above his glasses. 'Could be a whole series.'

She nodded. 'But let's move on from numbers for now. We need to talk cameras. I want as much footage as possible of the entire weekend. We'll lose the hand-held cameras and go for discreet, fixed cameras instead, scattered throughout the complex.'

'You mean like a reality show?' Matt said. 'This sounds like Big Brother from hell.'

Perry spoke from the corner of his mouth. 'Big Brother was always from hell.'

Matt and Perry shared their first ever chuckle together. The man had a great, infectious laugh, once you found it.

'There's one other thing.' Matt looked across at Nupa. 'How about I test the clients beforehand?'

Kissell frowned. 'Test?'

'They could come to the university and I run some experiments. It

181

might help them consider more rational explanations for their condition.'

Perry wasn't laughing any more. 'How on earth do you prove something like *that* in a lab?'

'You test the supernatural claims. The aversion to religious symbols for example. I have some ideas.'

Kissell leant forward, elbows on his knees. 'I sincerely hope you don't want to make these people look stupid, do you?'

'Absolutely not.'

'Because they don't deserve that.'

'I know they don't. But they deserve evidence for an alternative explanation.'

Nupa was nodding. 'You know what? I like that. I think that could work . . .'

Kissell and Perry shared an uneasy glance.

'Anyway . . . almost there.' She slapped her notepad shut just as the van started heading down a leafy road. Matt saw some tall wind turbines over the tops of the trees. And just like that, his cruel mind dragged one of his dead faithfuls out of his subconscious. It often happened like that, in a split second, with no build-up. Somewhere in the crunch of gears, he could hear the sound of a teenage boy bursting open in the grille of a fast-moving train. He closed his eyes and willed his loyal ghosts away.

Focus.

It was just after six, and the light was slowly dying. Just physics with its cosmic syringe, carefully extracting the warm colours of day and dutifully reinjecting the world with the cold, grey promise of night. And set against that fading sky was a large block of orange and cream bricks.

Whitemoor Prison.

He watched its lines slice the sky. The architect must have had no desire to emulate the old Victorian prisons of old, built to scare and intimidate folks out of crime. Yet equally, this was no contemporary statement of progressive incarceration either. These bricks and angles weren't built to inspire. Whitemoor just hovered in the midway space where functionality was God, which was fine by Matt. It was a category 'A' facility, after all, housing five hundred of the most dangerous murderers, rapists and terrorists in Britain. If ever you wanted a building to be fully functional, it was this one. Their convoy of cars pulled into the car park and they all climbed out. They joined the gang of camera operators and sound technicians gathering on the tarmac. This felt like a school outing, and there was a conflicted part of Matt that found this undoubtedly quite fun. But then the chatter died down and the double entrance doors were pushed open. A thick-thighed lady came striding out, hips the size of watermelons. The strained hem of her light blue, ill-fitting trouser suit looked dangerously close to an epic rupture.

She said she was Patricia Bryant, and after a happy hello, she insisted that external shots would only be permitted for the next ten minutes. There could be absolutely *no* filming inside until they reached the DSPD unit. She said that was the *Dangerous Severe Personality Disorder Unit*, which sounded just about right for a chap like Tom Riley. Perry shook his head at the injustice of it. 'It's not a personality disorder,' he whispered to Kissell. 'He needs a church.'

In security (a laborious yet near-giggly moment), everyone had to pull off their belts and shoes and raise their arms for a pat down. Then they all spent twenty minutes sitting in the waiting room, while the tech guys prepped the DSPD. As they waited, Matt spotted a plaque on the wall that said this place was opened in 1991 by that dazzling celeb: Norma Major, the wife of ex-Prime Minister John.

Eventually, the governor popped her head in and guided them all through a series of sterile and not particularly well-lit corridors. By the time they reached the unit doors, this felt less like a school trip, and more like a descent into a grim, depressing abyss. Tom Riley had torn his wife's hair and tongue out. That was repellent enough.

But the idea that he had almost killed a woman with his teeth, *while still in custody*, was an ever-present force. He saw the arms of the others. Riley may have been locked away and unseen right now, but the thought of him was still tugging up goosebumps.

'Okay,' Bryant said. 'Are you all ready?'

'A minute.' Kissell placed a palm against the door. Then he turned and started shaking out his arms and then his legs. Stretching his neck muscle on a tilt. Nothing like cranking up the spiritual mojo before a face-down with Baal-Berith.

Several cameras were filming this, from various angles. The theme from *Rocky* could work here.

Bernie finally stopped curling his fingers in and out, and then he said, 'I'm ready. Lead the way.'

Bryant opened up. They filed inside.

Matt was close enough to hear Nupa throw a hasty whisper to the camera guys. '*Do not stop filming. Do you understand me? No matter what happens, you keep filming until I tell you to stop.*'

CHAPTER THIRTY

Matt could tell right away that the secure psychiatric unit did not normally look like this. For a start, there was a mass of seats and tables stacked against the back wall, hidden from the gaze of the cameras. Yet in the middle of the room was a single, sturdy chair, empty for now. Two long and open leather straps hung from its arms. Above that chair the ceiling was studded with fluorescent tubes, but none of them were on. Spotlights threw light instead, casting shadows all the way to the back, where Matt saw the mysterious door from which Tom was set to come.

It could have been an exorcism. It could have been an execution. Whatever it was the room looked . . . staged. What it didn't look like was a normal prison visit, and that ticked Matt off. He looked across at Governor Bryant and Nupa, who was whispering to Ethan crouching on the floor. He was flicking on a few extra moody spotlights. With his hands in his pockets, Matt strolled over and said, 'Hey, Nupa. When do you start piping in "Tubular Bells"?'

'Pardon?' she said.

'I thought this show was going to be natural. You said fly-on-the-wall.'

Governor Bryant sighed and looked Matt up and down. 'You're the sceptic, right?'

'And proud of it.'

'Oh, I've heard of you, Mr Hunter. And that book of yours.'

Nupa saw Matt's mouth open and broke in. 'Matt, listen . . . we cleared the room because we need the space for the cameras to move freely around Riley but to not get too close. We can't have our guys tripping over tables and knocking down chairs.'

'And all these moody spotlights?'

Bryant laughed at him. 'There's no use in filming stuff if you can't see it on screen.'

'Yeah?' Matt cocked an eyebrow. 'One of those bulbs is green.'

She blinked, slowly, 'And?'

Matt frowned. 'Why are you even letting this happen, anyway?'

'Because we have a wide and holistic rehabilitation programme at—'

'*Exorcism*, though?'

Nupa's hand went up. 'Please, we need to start.' She checked her watch, then stuck a thumb up at Bryant.

Systems Ready. Load vile killer into torpedo bay one.

The governor nodded back and threw a half-lidded glare at Matt. He waved at her.

A few tense minutes ticked by, and most eyes fell on the far door. Suzy, however, had her lens trained on Matt. Hmmm. This constant lens stuff really made you organise your armpit scratches and nostril tugs. Heaven help him if he ever got an itchy arse cheek.

The mysterious far door looked—

The handle started to move.

Somebody sucked a breath in.

The handle was down and the door was slowly opening. *Oh come on*, Matt thought, when he heard the coffin-creak of the hinges. Did they deliberately un-oil this thing? Was the plan for the demon killer of Cheddington to come a'creepin' out from total blackness, like he had up Claire Perry's path? Or would he be wheeled out Lecter-style on a trolley with a flurry of flapping bats? Spotlights slowly started to rise, and they picked up two bare, bandaged feet on the floor. The toes pulsed and quivered. And then the lights picked up the legs and midriff and then the torso of the figure attached, slowly materialising as the dimmer went up.

And there was the man of the moment. Tom Riley in da house, in a grey prison-issue jumpsuit. The air felt instantly thinner. Two burly-looking male nurses guided him in, his face hidden under that straggled mop of long black hair he had, though Matt could see some sort of dressing across his forehead. That must have been from when he'd nutted the desk, just before he bit down on Pamela's throat. Matt's mind started painting the pictures of what the moment must have looked like. He shook his head so the growing lines of such an image vanished, like a shake of his old Etch A Sketch.

Tom's bare feet scraped along the floor in a haphazard, uncertain stagger. On one stride, an overlong toenail scraped along the light grey tiles. Matt felt his stomach fully quiver at that. The exposed heels of Tom's feet must have been very dry too because they made a noticeable hiss as they slid along the floor. Both wrists were trapped in handcuffs, but the fingers were wriggling and twitching with a life of their own. They were very weird, those twitches. It was like he was wearing two flesh-coloured rubber gloves, generously filled with cockroaches.

The whole time, Tom's shaggy head hung down.

The two nurses set Tom into the chair, and one of the camera guys swung around the side to get a good profile angle, but not too close. Not in biting distance, anyway. It turned out that the straps weren't for his wrists, but for his legs and chest. The male nurses dragged them into position. One held Tom's head back tight, while the other buckled him in. Wise move. There was no mouth guard or muzzle, which seemed deeply unwise, all things considered – until he realised that a mute Tom wouldn't be much cop on camera. Half the shock of *The Exorcist* movie was all that crazy demon dialogue. He wondered if Nupa had specifically asked for his mouth to be free. You could hear multiple spinal cords relax when the nurses finally stepped back, then Nupa hooked a thumb at them both to get out of shot. The two men went to wait by the side wall, arms folded.

For a moment, there was just Tom, bathed in the lights, with his head bowed, and Matt noticed how his skinny, bony body cast a huge and bent monster shadow across the back wall. His hair hung down at the sides, like the dangling ears of a lanky rabbit in silhouette.

Focus.

This'd make a cracking poster, this. A spooky thumbnail to stop folks flicking through the warren of Netflix recommendations. But then a voice spoke out, in a strange, guttural whisper.

Tom said, 'Helloooo . . .'

Perry spoke first, 'Hello, Tom. It's good to see—'

'Hello, Matthew.'

Nupa's eyes flicked to him. Everybody's did.

'Matthew,' Tom said. 'Mr Hunter. I see you.'

Nupa mouthed, *Answer him!*

Matt took an awkward step forward. 'Well . . . that's not that impressive, Tom. I'm standing right here after all.'

'I'm glad you came, Matthew. But do you know why I brought you here?'

188

'You didn't bring me here. It was my choice.'

Tom let out a low, rolling chuckle. 'Okaaaaaay. I like your house, Matt. I like your bathroom very much.'

'Okaaayyy.' Matt looked across at Nupa. She was putting a finger up to a frustrated-looking Kissell, asking him to keep quiet. She turned back to Matt and urged him on.

'So, um . . .' Matt said. 'Can we talk?'

'What about?'

'How about Justine Riley?'

'Oooo.' He sounded like he'd just been offered cake. 'What do you want to know?'

'Well, for starters . . . did you kill her?'

He snorted with laughter.

'Is that a yes?'

'Course I killed her.'

'And the police officer. The woman . . .'

'Mmmmmm. Delicious.'

'Why did you do that to her?'

'*Why?*' He started chuckling. 'Because it makes my cock stiff, how about that?'

Perry, who had already been chewing his nails, stopped dead in shock.

Matt raised an eyebrow. 'That's a very cliché thing for a demon to say.'

'Is it now?'

'Yeah, it is. I've seen a hundred horror movies where demons say that sort of stuff. You know what I think?'

'Go on.'

'*You* think you need to say that sort of thing, so you say it, because you think that's what demons talk like. But you don't. And by the way, it doesn't shock me if that's your intention.'

'I'd like to shock you, very much.'

'Well, swearing and groaning isn't going to do it.'

'Then how about this, silly? I killed Justine because killin' gives me a nice feeling right in my little tummy . . .' Tom's voice dropped low. 'And I bit that lady because her baby told me to bite her. Her baby's in hell and her baby hates her.'

Matt waited. 'Tell me the real, actual reason you killed Justine Riley.'

'You want the real reason I tore her tentacle out of her mouth and stuffed it into mine? Ooo . . .' He paused at that, and under the hanging hair they could hear the frantic sound of Tom's unseen mouth licking and lapping. 'I did it for you. It was all for you.'

Matt waited for a moment. 'No you didn't. You don't even know me.'

'Gosh, Matthew . . . you need to wake up.' His shoulders, which had been rocking with quiet laughter, stopped suddenly. 'I did it just so this would happen. So that I could be near you, properly, in the flesh. To hold your hand, remember?' His fingers and toes started to spasm again. 'I've killed sooooo many people on my way to you. And now you can smell me, and I can smell you. Oh, I could sing.'

'I'd prefer if you didn't. So, who else have you killed?'

'Golly, where do I start? I've drowned little girls and I've stabbed young men and I've strung up bitches and melted their tits off, ha. I've stabbed old ladies right in the scalp and took their words away, but hey . . .' Tom must have seen the look in Matt's face. His eyes flashed. 'Oooo, Matt. You don't look well, all of a sudden? Where's that smirk of yours gone, now? Why don't you make a joke, you handsome devil?'

Matt wondered how Tom could see him, since that shaggy head of his was still down. Those eyes of his must have rolled up, somewhere beneath that hair, painfully straining and staring in the sockets.

'Cat got your tongue, Matt?' That chuckle of his. Like an engine, idling.

'I don't believe the things you say.'

'No? But I've signed a million, billion papers. I've cast a lot of souls into hell. That's how I met her little babba. But every now and then I come up from the ground and I climb out of my little box, and I help fellas like you find their way back down. And that really fills my little tummy up—'

'That's enough.' Kissell stepped forward, doctor's bag in hand.

Tom groaned. 'Go away, please. This is a private con—'

It was just as Kissell unzipped the bag. That's when it happened. And it was immediate.

The slightest crackle of the zip and then . . .

Tom's jaw clicked loudly open, and from the hole came an instant, ear-stabbing scream.

Everybody winced at the sheer volume, especially the sound guy, who dragged the headphones from his head like each can had shot a needle into his skull. Then Tom's head was suddenly up. His chin had been pointed to the ground this entire time, but now it flipped positions. It strained and pushed to the ceiling, his Adam's apple bulging and his nostrils flaring like a horse.

Matt could sense the cameras stepping into action.

'Jesus' blood hasn't failed you yet!' Kissell shouted over Tom's screams. 'Jesus' blood will not fail! We're coming for you, Tom.'

Tom yanked his head from left to right, left to right, wailing out the most hideous sounding squeals. He was an animal, he was a slaughterhouse pig. Everyone was taken aback by it. Even the governor, even Suzy. Even Matt, to be honest, who joined everybody else in pressing fingers into his ears. Matt felt someone shove into him. It was Ethan, staggering backwards. He'd already been on the verge of pissing his white jeans before they walked in. Now he backed against the mountain of chairs near the wall, with a forearm across his mouth.

Still, the rage went on.

Kissell, a few feet from Tom, pulled the rest of his weapons from his bag. A bright, red leather Bible. He started waving it in time with Tom's wild head movements. A snake charmer, swinging left and right, busting out Stevie Wonder shapes. Matt could see the Internet memes forming already, after this was broadcast. Someone adding a beat to this, and pitch-shifting the screams into a jolly, toe-tapping funk track.

Then Kissell shouted, 'Out! I tell you get *out*!'

A long thread of spittle burst from Tom's mouth in a tall arch. He saw Nupa check the cameraman: *You're getting all this, right?* He'd never seen her look more content.

'In the power and authority of Jesus, I command you. Tell me your name.'

'You know my name,' Tom screamed.

'Tell me your name!'

'You know my name.'

'Tell me your name!'

'Ask Matthew my name.'

Suzy's camera lens lunged up to Matt.

Kissell yelled, 'What is your name?'

Tom started laughing, horribly, weeping, horribly. 'Matthew . . . old friend . . . tell him my name.'

Matt shouted, 'Your name is Tom Riley! You are the chef of the Cross Keys pub in Cheddington, who makes an amazing shepherd's pie. And we are here to help you, Tom. Just not like this. Now cut this shit out!'

Kissell threw a tight-lipped glare at Matt and he stomped forward, closer to Tom than was permitted.

The governor stood bolt upright. 'Whoa there,' she shouted, 'step back, Father.' She nodded at the nurses on standby to rush in, but he ignored them.

'What is your name?' Kissell shoved the Bible directly against Tom's forehead.

'I am Baaaaal-Berith, and I roam through the earth . . .' His scream seemed to warp into a bizarrely uneven pitch. 'I am Baaaaaalll.'

Even Matt gasped.

It was the *sound* of his voice that was so astonishing. How it doubled up into a windpipe-ripping, inhuman roar. Like an actual screaming hog had somehow learnt the beginnings of speech. For the briefest of moments, the very briefest, the doubled-up voice made Matt feel a flash of confused, horrendous doubt . . . until something else happened that explained that sound. A fountain suddenly erupted from his mouth. A pint's worth of pink vomit, splashing between gritted, grinding teeth. It spewed up through the gaps and the sheer force of it ripped the dam apart. Mouth now wide, the sick flooded across his chin and down his chest, dropping into his lap and onto the floor. It slapped loudly into a bubbling pool. Kissell yanked his Bible back, somehow managing to avoid slipping in the puke. The instant acidic stench was appalling. Cupped hands hit mouths and noses at the same time.

The door behind him was smacked open as Ethan ran rushing out, retching. He also saw Perry in the corner, on his knees, but he wasn't praying now. He was crying, trembling like he was in shock. By now, the nurses had pushed Bernie back to a safe distance, and that nuclear Bible of his was back in its bag.

Tom had stopped screaming completely, though his wailing still echoed, like tinnitus. No more screams though, and no more moving of his head. He just set his drenched chin forward, with a visible face at last. His eyes were darting around the room, blinking sweat away with utter confusion.

'Tom?' Governor Bryant stepped forward. 'Tom, can you hear me?'

He looked at her, chest throbbing.

'Tom, do you know where you are?'

He shook his head, then he caught Perry's eyes. He was a child lost on the ocean, finally spotting land. His eyes bulged. 'Simon?'

His voice, now normal, shuddered out of him, 'Simon, where am I?'

Perry smeared his sleeve across his face and rushed forward, and though the governor raised her hand for caution, Perry dropped to his knees anyway, trousers splashing into the filth. He took Tom's cuffed hands into his, fingers trembling but not wriggling any more. They looked like the hands of a different man entirely. Perry's sob was not for show. 'Oh, Tom. You are loved, do you hear me? And I think . . .' He looked to a gasping Kissell, who nodded back. 'I think you're finally free.'

Tom's face crumbled and Perry started mopping his soaked chin with a handkerchief.

The governor, clearly a little shaken, said, 'Cameras off. Let's get him cleaned up.'

The two male nurses took Tom towards the door he'd come in and Bryant followed. Matt noticed Nupa nod to the cameras. *Keep rolling*, she mouthed. Which was just as well, otherwise they might have missed what Tom said, just before the door closed behind him.

He looked back into the room and found Simon Perry's eyes through the closing gap. 'Simon . . . where's Justine? Where's my wife?'

CHAPTER THIRTY-ONE

They filed into Governor Bryant's office. Matt, Kissell, Perry and Nupa, dropping into the chairs in a kind of gaunt, stunned silence. Suzy sat in the corner, camera running. The stale smell of vomit hung in the air, on their clothes, in their nostrils. Matt had some tic tacs, which he passed around. Nobody refused.

As they all sat there desperately sucking freshness into their bodies, Matt saw a shelf behind the governor's desk. Between some books and a small cactus, he saw a neat coil of rosary beads, bunched into a little heap. Maybe she'd confiscated these from a prisoner as a hanging risk. Or maybe, and this was the one he'd put money on, she was a believer. Which would explain why she would let them do this bizarre ritual tonight, and no doubt why she was so icy with him before.

I've heard of you . . . and that book of yours.

'So can we speak to him?' Matt said. 'After he's cleaned up?'

Nupa added, 'And can we film it?'

'If he's willing, yes.' She leant back into her chair, thinking for a moment. 'You know, Pastor Kissell, if you can calm killers down as quickly as you did just then, I have a whole line of prisoners here who might benefit.'

Kissell caught Nupa's eye. 'Perhaps I could come back in a week or so? I'd be glad to exorcise whoever needs it.'

'Thank you.'

'Even if it's not real?' Matt said.

Bryant didn't even bother to hide the glare. 'Listen to me. I am not naive. I am not deluded. We have been trying to connect with Tom Riley since the moment he got here, all with zero impact . . . but placebo or not, what just happened there *did* something.'

'Matt . . .' Kissell was smiling. 'Surely after that, you're a teeny-weeny bit closer to acceptance?'

'There was nothing I just witnessed that couldn't be explained psychologically.'

They all stared at him.

'You *were* in there with us, weren't you?' Perry said. 'You saw the screaming, the swearing, the way he reacted to the Bible?'

'Yes, and it was all so . . .'

'So what?'

'Cliché.'

'*What?*' Perry's mouth was open again. It often was. 'And the inhuman voice?'

'Next time you're about to hurl, try and articulate a sentence. You'll probably sound like the Devil himself.' Matt shifted in his chair. 'Look. Culture works like a closed loop of reference. It tells us how to act in certain scenarios. We clap our hands at a concert, for example. It's a custom we've learnt and repeated over and over, without thinking. It'd look totally bizarre to an alien, but to us it's what appreciation looks like. Hollywood and pop culture make possession look a certain way. Vomiting, crude language. We see it on screen and it confirms our image of what possession looks like. So if someone *thinks* they're possessed, how else are they going to act? They follow the cultural signifiers, and the loop starts again. We think it's authentic exorcism, but what we just saw in there was . . . was *learnt* behaviour from culture.'

Perry narrowed his eyes. 'So Tom's lying, is he?'

'No. It's more like subconscious, psychological theatre.'

'*Jargon!*' Perry snapped the word, like it was one of the deadly sins.

'I think Tom has completely lost his mind and killed his wife. So he's subconsciously formulating some sort of disassociation technique to help him cope.'

'That's ridiculous.'

'And your theory *isn't?*' Matt said. 'And what's worse, you're facilitating his illusion with an exorcism. I'm sorry, but I still think it's entirely possible that you pumped the demon idea into his head in the first place.'

'How dare you.'

Matt thumbed his ear. 'Look, it's clear that you care about him . . .'

Perry listened quietly, appreciative of that, at least.

'But what if Tom was troubled already and he simply absorbed the possession narrative you gave him? No matter how innocently it was given. Just like they're *all* absorbing it. The cat woman in the airport today, or that muscle guy . . . Richie . . . in the audience at the TV studio. Am I the only one who can see they're taking all their cues from . . . from bad horror movies?'

The shrill ring of her desk phone burst into the room, and the governor quickly grabbed it. 'Yeah? Okay . . . okay . . . cheers.' She hung up. 'Tom's clean.'

Nupa sat up. 'So can we talk to him?'

'Yes, but no filming. At least for now.'

The noise Nupa made was the exact sound Amelia made whenever he said she couldn't have a hammock in her room.

As they all stood, Perry said, 'Governor? When do we tell him about Justine?'

'Not yet. Let's not risk him losing it again. For now, we just talk.'

CHAPTER THIRTY-TWO

Tom, Version 2.0, was in a bright room, quietly sitting in a much more comfortable-looking armchair. He was still strapped across his chest and legs, but this time he had his head up. His hair was swiped back into a long, stylish wave. Seeing his face meant you could catch the whole, paper-white haunt of it. A baffled man, he kept staring at his handcuffs with a silent, confused beat of dread. When they all walked in, Tom saw Perry and a heartbreaking smile broke across his face, but Tom kept his eyes mostly on Bernie Kissell.

'Thank you,' Tom said to Kissell as they sat down. It was so odd to hear a normal voice in his mouth. 'Thank you for saving me.'

'Thank him,' Kissell pointed to the ceiling. This made Tom nod with a sniffle.

Perry called to one of the guards. 'I don't think the handcuffs are needed any more.'

'One step at a time.' Bryant sank her hefty frame onto an overly creaky chair. 'Now, Tom, we just have a few questions for you.'

He nodded.

'Do you understand what happened to you, just now?'

'Yes. I've been possessed for a while, but now it's gone.'

'So you feel better?'

'I do.'

Matt smiled at him. 'Hi, I'm Matt. Can I just ask . . . what made you come to the conclusion that you were possessed?'

'It was obvious.'

'May I ask if Reverend Perry brought the idea up first?'

Perry muttered something in annoyance, but Kissell shushed him.

'No. I brought it up first because I knew something was wrong. I was having horrible thoughts. I couldn't bear the Bible any more. And I kept hearing his name in my head.'

'Whose name?' the governor asked.

'Baal-Berith,' Tom said. 'He's the demon who helps run hell.'

'How do you know that?'

'I read a book on it. Then I felt him, telling me to do things.' Tom looked at Perry, eyes lowered in shame. 'I turned up at Simon's house once, in the middle of the night. And I just acted really crazy on his doorstep. It was bad.'

'I see,' Matt said. 'And when did this all start?'

Perry shook his head. 'That's a pointless question, it's impossible to tell. The demon could have been dormant in Tom for years, or—'

'I know exactly when it started,' Tom said. 'It was the 4th of January.'

Perry frowned. 'Tom?'

'That's when it started. The 4th.'

Perry looked at them all, confused. He turned back. 'What happened on the 4th of January?'

'That's the day Justine bought the box.'

A beat of silence. 'What box?'

'I'm sorry I didn't tell you this, Simon. I tried to but he wouldn't . . . I mean the *thing* in me wouldn't let me.'

Kissell clasped his hands together and gently tapped them on his chin. 'Baal-Berith is gone now. There's no need to fear him any more. So . . . you must tell us. What box?'

After a moment he said, 'My wife bought a wooden box. A kind of small crate from a car boot sale. It had little padlocks on it. The man on the stall said it was an antique with a spooky history. He said the box was haunted, and we best not open it. She liked that kind of thing, so she bought it.'

Perry said nothing. He just started to shake his head in silent shock, but it was Kissell who gasped out a response. 'Why on earth would you let her have something like that?'

'I don't know. I was pretty down around then. I guess *he* made me. She brought it home and put it in her salon. I think she thought it'd look shabby and chic. But she soon lost interest because . . . well, Justine has phases. I just kept thinking about this box, though. Kept looking at it too. The old locks especially.'

'What was inside?' Matt said.

'Oh, I didn't dare open it.'

'Why not?'

'Because there was something in it. Something evil.'

Perry let out a long sigh. 'You should have told me this, Tom.'

'I'm sorry . . . but Baal-Berith . . . he wouldn't let me.'

Kissell was nodding. 'This makes sense. I've had a lot of cases that start with some sort of cursed object. The box was clearly demonically infested.'

Matt rolled his eyes.

'Justine got bored with it in her salon, so I put it in the lounge,' Tom went on, 'but then she asked me to move it out. She felt like it was watching her. So I put it in my workshop in the garage. I like to fix things. And some nights, I'd be doing some odd job and it felt like that box was looking at me. Sounds crazy, I know. It wasn't long after that I heard the voice start in my head.'

'Oh, Tom . . .' Perry said. 'You poor thing.'

Kissell shook his head. 'This is a classic infestation.'

'It said my name. *Sang* my name, even. I knew if I destroyed that box, whatever was in there might come out.'

'How did you know that?'

'Baal-Berith told me.'

'So what did you do with it?' Nupa asked.

'Next best thing. I buried it in my front garden at home. I bet it's still there right now, under the earth. But ever since I buried it, things just got worse and worse. Till I forgot who I was any more. Which is why I'm scared to ask my question.' Tom's eyes locked onto the floor. 'Where is my wife?'

'You really can't remember?' Matt said.

He closed his eyes and shook his head.

The governor turned to Nupa. 'I'll stay with Tom a while. Can you folks wait outside?'

Nupa looked disappointed, but she nodded, and they all rose.

'Reverend Perry?' Bryant said.

'Yes?'

'Can you stay for a little while? So Tom has a friend?'

'I'd be honoured.' Perry sat back down. 'May I hold his hand?'

Bryant shook her head. 'Best not.'

Tom was trembling now, his face filling with a stress so overwhelming that it was very clear that somewhere in his brain he understood what those cuffs meant. He looked up and said, 'Can the exorcist stay too?'

'Of course.'

Kissell bowed in service and sat.

When Bryant saw Matt and Nupa still hovering she said, 'I think *you* folks have got enough for today. We'll meet you in the car park. My staff'll show you out.'

Matt stepped into the corridor first, and noticed Nupa do something odd on the way out. There was a mat on the floor. She slid it back with her foot, so that it lipped over the door frame, just a touch. When the door closed, it was still open just a crack. The movement she made was so fluid, he just knew that she'd done that many times before. She grabbed her phone, clicked it to video, and set it against the gap. It was too small a crack to see, but they could still hear the talking.

'*Don't,*' Matt said.

Nupa slammed a finger to her lips, just as the sound came out. A slow, but growing wail of despair. It didn't last long at those levels. It dissolved into deep and bitter crying. Matt kicked the mat back, and pulled the door shut.

It was a depressing end to a bizarre day, and when they finally gathered in the car park outside, Matt was glad of the fresh air. When Perry arrived, he looked shell-shocked. He'd clearly been crying. As annoying as this guy was, Matt did pity him. He just hoped that some of the tears might be a sense of guilt. Of personal responsibility.

Matt assumed it was time to head home and so the blossoming thoughts of cosy lamps, a comfy couch and mindless sitcoms on TV with his wife felt like the sun blooming over very dark mountains. Plus, he had two more full days before the weekend at The Reed. Enough time to devise those tests he'd suggested.

But after they shook Bryant's hand and climbed into the van, Nupa checked her watch and swung her chair around to Matt, Perry and Kissell. 'Just one more stop, before home. Okay boys?'

'Huh?' Matt said. 'Where now?'

'Cheddington.' Her eyes sparkled. 'We're going to dig up that box.'

CHAPTER THIRTY-THREE

Places look scarier at night. That's not exactly revelatory. Just kill the lights, let the shadows roam and your brain is going to dutifully fill in the blanks. Inky voids in the corner become the burglar choosing his moment. Rolling, brittle leaves? Legions of cockroaches, scuttling hungrily for your toes.

So it wasn't really a shock to find that standing outside of Tom Riley's house at ten at night felt rather different than it did yesterday afternoon. Bathed in moonlight and standing black against a cloudy sky, Tom's house was positively gothic without the sun, especially with that wind still sweeping the fields around them.

Not that there was a lot of time to ponder what everything looked like. Most heads were down, not up.

Tom's front lawn was a mass of activity with Matt, Perry and other crew members thrusting spades into soil and scraping back dirt. They'd found a few shovels in Tom's garage, and borrowed some more from neighbours. The ground was so rocky that Suzy tried to get them all singing some old chain-gang song, only she didn't know any actual chain-gang songs, so she tried to improvise. Folks weren't in the mood anyway, and besides . . . Nupa made it pretty clear that out of tune singers attempting the Bee Gees 'Staying Alive' did *not* suit this particular scene of the show. So she shut all that down, and told them to dig in moody silence. This was punctured only by heavy breath and metal hitting the beetle-ridden ground.

The cameras watched it all.

Despite the icy breeze, Matt swiped sweat from his forehead, but he kept on going. He was determined to find this little hunk of junk and crack it wide open. Show Perry and Kissell, and the cameras most of all, that there was nothing inside this car boot sale box except a pair of old shoes perhaps, or a set of melted *Star Wars* figures. Or who knows, a bag of rusty antique medals that might be worth millions, which Tom could have sold on eBay to fund a pleasant round-the-world trip with his wife. As opposed to a crate of supernatural evil telling him to tear his wife's tongue out instead. It was so, *so* depressing, when Matt thought about it, so unnecessary. To pollute the already murky waters of mental health with a bloody great influx of ancient, theological poison.

He looked up when a huge gust of wind laid the fields out again. It rattled the roof tiles of the other houses in the street. Many of which had their bedroom lights on, so folks could stare out at the TV crew, whispering their theories to each other. Surely, this was a dig for another of Tom Riley's victims? The dawning of a serial killer next door. But none of them came out to ask. They were way too scared for that.

Then he heard something else instead. A crew guy called Barry. Barry normally fiddled with the sound recorders, but he was a trooper, and was helping dig like the rest of them. Only he wasn't even using a spade. He was digging through the ground with an upturned plant pot that he'd nabbed from the back garden. Impressively, he'd dug a deep trench with it. He'd be a world class whizz with sandcastles, no doubt. He was a whizz at finding haunted homeware too, because the rim of his plant pot hit something wooden, and he let out a giddy *woohoo*. 'Hey! Hey!' he yelled.

The cameras swooped across the front lawn like helicopters, search lights scrolling the ground. Matt let his shovel fall and he ran, fresh dirt flying. Suzy and her lens always at his side. He found Barry with his knees deep in soil. His fingernails, now thoroughly black from scraping around an emerging edge of wood. This was no false alarm. Barry reached the corner of the box and started heaving it out. Matt dropped down to help.

Perry and Kissell had been sitting on the doorstep, and Perry's wife Claire was with them. She'd turned up in a black quilted parka, and a thick woollen scarf. She not only drove here to offer her husband moral support, she brought his duffel coat too. The three of them sat up on the doorstep praying 'a hedge of protection' over the diggers. To Matt, that sounded like a pretty nifty way of getting out of manual labour. Now they'd heard Barry's yell, all three were rushing down the path. Everyone headed straight for the hole.

'Careful!' Perry's voice and outstretched hand was pure melodrama. He dropped to his knees. 'You cannot break it.'

'He's absolutely right,' Kissell said. 'This is where the spirit of Baal-Berith probably emerged from, before entering Tom. But after tonight's exorcism, we made Baal homeless. He may well have slouched all the way back here.' Kissell nodded towards the soil-packed box. 'Stands to reason that he came home.'

'To *reason*?' Matt said.

Finally, the box was out and Barry sat back into the dirt, dragging it up onto his lap. The old padlocks, four of them, rattled.

He brushed tumbling dirt boulders from the top. They showered and bounced onto his knees.

Nupa tapped Barry on the shoulder. 'Get it up on the table. Gently.' She hollered back, 'And get us some better light!'

There was a picnic bench in the middle of the lawn. Matt had seen it today, grey and warped from years of braving the relentless elements here. He wondered if Justine and Tom had ever sat here, on some rare summer evening, sipping beer, smelling barbecues, holding down paper plates in the wind. Now the bench was flooded with harsh light, as Barry placed the box on top.

It was amusing, really, seeing all these ears suddenly hovering right next to the box, listening out for demonic snoring. Especially Perry, who had both palms opened towards it, like a hobo around an oil drum fire. Kissell, at least, seemed more chilled. He just folded his arms and did a kind of slow march around the picnic bench. Stopping after two circles, he hinged forward at his hips and looked at the box straight on.

'Can you feel . . .' he said, 'can you feel . . .'

The love tonight? 'Feel what?' Matt asked.

'The *energy*.' He whispered it, then visibly shook the cold from his body. 'This is it. This is the source of Tom's trouble. Can you *feel* it, folks?'

Okay. So the wind was up. And okay, the moon had picked this exact moment to hide behind a cloud. Two perfectly natural events. However, it did feel like since the box had come up, the world had dramatically dialled its dimmer down on both light and heat. Things are always scarier in the *cold* dark, after all.

God, it really was cold all of a sudden. Even Matt would wear a duffel coat in this.

Perry had his hands jammed under his armpits, in a kind of self-hug. 'I think we should burn it. I think we should soak it in petrol and set it alight. Before it takes somebody else over.'

Kissell put a hand on Perry's shoulder. 'Easy, tiger. That's what we *don't* do. Throw it in the fire and the flames are gonna crack it open. We can't let this thing loose in the world. We have to exorcise it.'

'You want to exorcise a wooden box?' Matt said.

'What's inside it, yeah.'

'Well, that I'd like to see.' Matt stepped aside and folded his arms. 'Go for it.'

Kissell was slowly biting his thumbnail, thinking. 'No. Not here. This artefact is way too powerful. An exorcism like this needs preparation.'

'Then when?' Nupa said.

Kissell started walking again. He made one more full, folded-arm circle, his knuckle tapping against his chin again. He was a drama queen sometimes. Most times, actually. Then he stopped dead and raised a finger. 'That's *it*. We'll take it to The Reed. We put it front and centre, right in the very heart of our exorcism. It will be our . . . unholiest of unholies, if you will. And we either cast the demon out of this box, once and for all. Or we banish everybody else's demons *inside* it – and it will be their prison. Can't you picture it, Nupa? We put this up on a stage. Somewhere prominent for focus, and we deal with it then. After all, it started with this box, so let's end things with it too . . .' He looked over at Nupa. 'I think at the very least, it'd make for a striking image for the camera.'

Perry wasn't convinced. 'Sorry, but I think that's too dangerous. I know the folks at the funeral home. I could *cremate* it, not just burn it. Make sure there's nobody near at the time, in case anything comes out. Or . . . I don't know . . . maybe we wrap it in heavy chains and dump it in the middle of the sea.'

'And leave it to wash up on somebody else's shore? Simon . . . Baal-Berith will find a way.'

'Well, he seems fast asleep right now,' Matt said.

Everybody suddenly looked at Matt, horrified. He was picking the box up and holding it to his ear.

'Hey,' Nupa shouted, 'don't mess with it.'

'Maybe we could make a little crack in—'

'Don't . . .' Nupa said. 'Put – the box – down.'

Matt gave it a little shake, and people gasped. Then he shrugged and placed it on the picnic table.

Nupa's shoulders relaxed. 'You know what, Bernie? I like it. I *like* that a lot. Let's take it to The Reed. Make it the centrepiece of the entire exorcism.'

'Good call,' Kissell said. 'There's just the small matter of who's going to keep it in the meantime . . .'

Perry raised a tentative hand. Bless him, he was keen to be the hero. 'I'll take it.' But Claire quickly tugged him down again. She was scared and shaking her head, mouthing the word *no way* to her husband.

'Why not you?' Nupa said to Kissell. 'You could keep it in the hotel.'

'I need to be as pure as I can for the weekend, and frankly, Simon, you do too. This box might contaminate our prayers. I've covered this in my YouTube videos many times. The demon inside feeds on the fear of the holder. It's extremely dangerous. In fact, I advise that *none* of us keep it. Do we have a key to Tom's house? Can we keep it inside the—' Kissell cut himself off when he saw Matt's hand going up. 'Yes?'

'How about me?' Matt said.

'Pardon?'

'How about I take it? I've got an office at home. I'll just put it on my desk.'

'Are you sure?' Nupa said. 'And remember you cannot mess with it.'

'I won't, and yeah, it doesn't bother me. As long as I don't have to take it for walks.' He spotted Nupa's frown. 'Look, I promise I'll take good care of it.'

'You really mustn't break it,' Kissell said. 'And don't fiddle with the locks or—'

'I *won't*.' That last sentence had a teenage tone. Suzy seemed to zoom in on him for some reason.

'And don't listen to it, either,' Kissell said. 'No matter what it says. Don't let it trick you.'

Matt smiled. 'I can guarantee it won't do that.'

A small grin started to form on Kissell's face, 'You know what? *Yes*. You know best, Professor. If you really think there's absolutely nothing to what we're saying, then of course, take the box. Put it in your office. Keep it by your bed, if you really want.'

'Bernie . . .' Perry said. 'It's risky.'

'No, the professor's quite right. If there is nothing to this whole phenomenon, then there's nothing to fear. And if you're comfortable bringing an artefact like this into your family home . . . you do have a family, don't you?'

'I do.'

'Then go ahead. Bring Baal-Berith to your children. I advise against it, of course, but who knows . . . perhaps you'll discover that there is much to fear, after all. That perhaps you should be afraid, Matt.'

'Of demons? No. Of making people believe in them . . . now that *does* scare me.'

'Bless you, son,' Kissell started to laugh, but there was no humour in it. 'I like you, but there is . . . if I may say so, a foolishness in you.'

'I'm not the one scared of an apple crate.'

Nupa put a hand on Kissell's arm. 'It's late. Let's call it a night. Get some shots of the box on its own, and then Barry? Take it to the van. And make it secure.'

''Kay.' Barry nodded and walked Matt to the van. He slipped the box into a large, padded carry-case with Velcro straps. Somewhere in the techie car, a spotlight or two was going home naked tonight.

Perry and his wife Claire strolled towards him, arms linked together. It seemed like Claire's car was parked next to the van.

'Professor?' Perry said. 'May we talk?'

CHAPTER THIRTY-FOUR

Matt turned to them both and watched Perry unhook from his wife. He stepped forward. 'I know we've clashed a little. And I hope you forgive my sharpness with you.'

'Well . . . I'm sorry if I've been sharp back.'

'Thank you. That's kind of you to say. It's just been a very emotionally draining time for my wife and I. It's a lot of pressure, and . . . it's a frightening business. Professor, this box scares me just as much. I think you're being unwise taking it,' He reached out his hand and placed it on Matt's forearm. 'Think of your children.'

'We'll be fine.'

Perry let out a long sigh. 'Well, I admire your tenacity. I just hope, at least for your sake, that you're right. Claire, let me say goodnight to Bernie.' He turned away and left them both alone for a moment on the pavement.

Matt watched her eyes follow her husband, then she flicked the pixie cut behind her ear. She'd make a good elf. 'He's a noble man, you know,' she said suddenly. 'He'll help anybody in a crisis.'

'That's very admirable.'

'Yes, it is.' She folded her arms, leant against her car and looked up into the sky. Claire Perry seemed comfortable with silence. He liked that. He watched the fur on her collar quiver in the breeze.

'So how's the art going?'

She kept looking up, eyes on a cloud.

'I did like it, you know. You've got a—'

'Don't.'

'Don't what?'

'Don't patronise me.'

'That's not my intention at all.' He looked up at the cloud she was following. A huge flowing cruise ship in the sky, crossing a black sea, limitless in its depth. 'I can't help it. I liked your pictures. You should consider exhibiting—'

'Can you please just stop?' She pulled the driver's door of her car, and he had to step aside, just as another gust of wind seemed to push her towards the car. He grabbed the door, to stop it slamming on her leg. The footwell of the driver's seat was messy, filled with old scrunched tissue paper. Some of it blew out as she climbed in. She went to grab it, but it rolled away from her, tumbling along the pavement.

He ran after it, back stooping, arms in a grab. 'I've got them.' After a frantic, *Crystal Maze* flurry, he stood up panting, with a fistful of tissues. It was the first time he considered that she might happen to have a rotten cold, and now it was in his hand. There was a litter bin near the lamp post. 'Do you want me to chuck it in there?'

'No,' she said. 'Give it back.'

He looked down at the pile of rubbish, shrugged and handed it back. 'Suit yourself. Goodnight, Mrs Perry.'

'Goodnight.' She closed the door, the tissues piled neatly in her lap. She put both hands on the steering wheel, and just waited, staring forwards.

Perry's voice suddenly came sliding over the roof of the car, like he'd been lurking there the whole time.

'Now, Professor. You're not chatting up my wife, are you?'

'Well.' Matt drummed his fingers on the roof. 'That would make for a pretty interesting twist for the show.'

His eyebrow went up.

'Which means, no. I'm totally not.'

'Just as well . . . you know, I think on some other day, we might be friends. After all this is done, we should connect.'

'Sounds good.'

He smiled and went to get inside the passenger side, but paused halfway in. 'And Matt. Don't be a fool with that box. Or with any of this. I'm worried about you, you know? And your children.'

'I appreciate the concern.' Matt tipped an imaginary cap. 'Goodnight, Perry.'

'Goodnight.' He dropped into his seat and she cranked the engine. Matt stepped back as the tyres rolled off the kerb. She kept looking forward the whole time, tissues in her lap like precious artefacts.

He was watching the car drive off when Nupa slapped a hard hand on his shoulder.

'Jesus.' He jumped. 'Give me a heart attack, why don't you?'

'Sorry. I just wanted to say thanks for all your help today. We've got some cracking stuff. The airport . . . the *prison*, wow . . . And thanks for your input. We need that balance. That sense of lightness. And that convo you did with Baal-Berith. Lovely.'

'Been quite a day.'

'And it's only the first.' She winked at him. 'Well, look, I hope you don't mind but you'll be riding home alone. Pastor Kissell refuses to be in the same car as the box, and I really need to chat through some more prep before we drop him at his hotel.'

'No problem.'

'And you'll put those tests together for Friday morning?'

'Yep.'

'And is tomorrow enough time for you to get those ready?'

He laughed and felt a simultaneous beat of panic. 'They'll be ready to roll on Friday.'

'Well, okay . . . then just take this.' She handed him a small black bag with a strap on it.

'What is it?'

'Just a little diary cam.'

He groaned. 'Oh, you don't want me sat in bed at night do you, moaning about Baal-Berith being a dickhead or something?'

'No . . . but if anything *does* happen with the box. If you hear anything or feel anything, you get filming, okay? Use your phone if you must, but for the love of God and all that is holy . . . film it in *landscape*, all right? Never, ever, ever film anything in portrait mode. Like ever, in your life.'

'All right, calm down.'

'Just remember, the more tape we get, the more choices we have. Editing is all about choices. Got it?'

'If I see green smoke coming out, I'll start rolling.' He paused. 'In landscape.'

'You better.' She smiled at him. 'Well, thanks again. I'll be in touch about the tests on Friday.'

Matt climbed into the van, and found a new driver waiting for him. A compact little bloke called Dave, whose face crumpled like a dog when he smiled. Matt saw flakes of ash on the sleeve of his jacket, and the smell of tobacco came soon after. Dave was about to rumble into reverse when Nupa slapped her hand on the window. Matt jumped again and buzzed the glass down. 'Are you trying to kill me?'

215

'You dropped something.' She thrust her hand in. 'Just in case you need it for expenses.'

He took it from her and unfolded it. She was walking off by the time he realised it wasn't his. But he didn't shout out, because when he read the parking ticket, he caught the date. Monday just gone . . . the 2nd March.

The day of the murder.

'Ready to rumble?' Dave said, then coughed.

'Rumble away.'

How odd, he thought, as they headed off. Did this car park ticket just tumble out of Claire's car with the rest of her junk? If it did, then . . .

He flicked through the files in his mind, pulling out conversations. Didn't she insist she stayed home on the day Justine died? Didn't she specifically tell him and Fenn that she was at home up until she went to the pub with her Perry that night?

Maybe Simon drove her car that day, but wasn't he in London? Or maybe it *was* her ticket and she was lying. Or heck, maybe Nupa found a random ticket on the floor from a neighbour and all this was totally pointless. Still, though . . . he stared at that little ticket for a third of the journey home, glad to see that it had a registration plate number on it, and other codes. He'd contact Fenn about this. The police must have special computers for such car park sorcery. He'd probably solve this with one phone call.

Matt was snapped out of all this pondering when the van filled with the very un-evil sounds of Abba's 'Dancing Queen'. Dave leant back and wheezed, 'Sorry, mate. Pressed the wrong button.'

'Ah, leave it on. Fact, turn it up.'

He shrugged. 'It's your ride.' The driver cranked it up, and they drove on. By the third chorus, they were both quietly singing along and Matt was glad of the distraction. Especially when every now and then he'd glance down at his fellow passenger, who didn't join in singing. Evidently Baal-Berith was no Abba fan.

216

Barry, the crew guy, had tucked the wooden box into one of the seats. He'd even strapped it in with a seat belt, just in case it slid off, smashed and unleashed the hounds of hell. Safety was important, Matt thought, even when you're an ancient Babylonian demon.

When they finally came to a stop in front of Matt's drive, it was well after 11 p.m. He saw a light on in his bedroom. Wren must be up reading, most likely. Amelia's room was, unsurprisingly, cloaked in darkness.

Matt got out and went round to the other door. He reached in, unhooked the box, slid it out and stood up straight. At that precise moment a low rumble of thunder rippled across the sky.

'Aye, aye?' Dave poked his head through his open window, eyes on the stars. 'Devil's a stirrin'.'

'Don't tell me you believe in demons too.'

'Course I do. I'm married, aren't I?' He laughed loud enough to wake the street. Then his voice dropped to a whisper. 'And don't worry about that box, Matt.' They'd been on first-name terms since the A41. 'That devil in a crate stuff is bullllllshit.'

'Amen to that, brother.' Matt tapped a goodbye on the van roof. He watched Dave head off, the muffled sound of his stereo clicking back on. Then he turned to his house and hitched the box up on his hip. He checked his pocket for the car park ticket. Still there.

'Come on, Baal,' Matt said, as the drops began to fall and the thunder rolled. 'Let's go watch some telly.'

CHAPTER THIRTY-FIVE

Matt lifted the spoon and shovelled some more granola into his mouth. He liked this stuff with its chunks of coconut and squirrel-feed ingredients. They made his current favourite self-delusion much easier to believe: that this sugar-soaked bowl in his hand was somehow healthier than his usual, beloved Coco Pops.

He clipped his elbow on his second scoop and a single wet crumb of sultana, raisin or whatever the heck that was (rat turd?) scattered onto his paper. He picked it up with pincer fingers and set it neatly to the side. Underneath was his open A4 pad, covered in his chaotic handwriting. Wren once likened Matt's handwriting to a bunch of spiders marching across a pad, before someone slammed it shut and crushed them all.

He stared at the page and thought, *Behold! Roll up! For here lies the astounding and soon-to-be-world-famous Matt Hunter Tests for Demonic Possession! – patent pending.*

He sighed – and shivered a little too. Running such tests sounded like a good idea at the time. Cool, even. And the notion had come from a genuine hope that when Kissell's clients failed these tests they'd at least consider that wild and unpopular outside opinion he kept suggesting. That maybe Abby Linh, Tom Riley, the airport cat lady and even that baseball cap hunk Richie were just normal human beings who needed actual support, not hysterical prayers. That motivation remained, and that's why he was still going ahead with these elaborate TV experiments. Yet, as he stared at his list of challenges, with a spoon handle hanging like a cold cigar from his mouth, he knew his big contribution to this TV show could turn into a kind of laughable, satanic game show.

There was that other thought, too. That niggle.

What if they beat his tests somehow, even by fluke? Like test number three, for example. He'd planned on putting out five identical glass bowls. Four filled with ordinary tap water and one with Holy Water. All at identical temperatures. When he asked them to dip their fingers in, one at a time, what if they somehow flinched and squealed when they touched the blessed one? He took another gulp of tooth decay and upped the numbers with a shaky pencil. Forget five water bowls, let's make it ten. And heck, let's do that water test a further ten times. Ten rounds with ten bowls, and he'd mix them up every round. So the chances of getting all ten rounds right would be . . . he started jabbing the rubber on his calculator, and scrawled out the stats. Yikes. They'd have a one in ten billion chance of being right all ten times. A psychic demon of the occult might ace that test. There was no way anyone from the real world was going to consistently beat that.

The plan was to head into uni this morning and get all these tests set up. He had all of today and this evening to get them shipshape and standardised. Then at 10 a.m. tomorrow, Kissell's troop of demon-ees (and Nupa's troop of cameras) would trot in. A day after that, on Saturday, would be the big showdown at The Reed.

The cameras . . . he was getting used to them. This was an unnerving thought. When you're used to something you let your guard down. If his tests turned out to be dumb, the cameras would know. And the cameras would tell.

He checked his phone for a distraction, and after a brief flick through his email a thought popped like a bubble in his head. The car park ticket. He'd forgotten about it with all this test stuff, but for now he fired off a quick message to Fenn. He took an awkward few pictures of the ticket itself, making sure that the various codes were clearly readable. He said it might be nothing, but it'd be interesting to see where Claire Perry's car had been on the day she insisted she'd stayed at home.

He sent it off, sighed, and pulled the pad back towards him. He'd just started pencilling in a few ideas when the kitchen door swung in and slapped the skirting.

'Daddy!' Amelia was midway through getting ready for school, a slice of toast flopped from her hand. She was half in, half out of her school jumper. She swallowed and shook her head.

'What the emergency?' he said.

'You're on TV!'

He set the pencil down. 'I am?'

'Like, right now. Get in the lounge.' She span and ran off, hollering as she went. 'Like right *now*!'

He paused and considered English modesty for a moment. Then he quickly scooped up the half-full cereal bowl and ran too. In the lounge he found Wren and Amelia glued to the screen. Even Lucy had set her phone down. Their sixty-inch beast of a TV was showing one of his old lectures . . . on *BBC News*. Crikey. They must have grabbed that from the uni website.

'Well, check out Professor Studley,' Matt said, as he perched on the arm of the sofa. 'What a dreamboat!'

'Shhhh.' Wren tugged him down. She slid him off the arm to sit beside her, his hand across his bowl for spillage.

Lucy tapped the volume up.

'. . . on Friday, when Professor Hunter will carry out a series of intricate tests to prove that demonic possession is purely in the mind.'

Intricate? Don't call them *intricate*.

Matt suddenly vanished from the screen and they cut to disturbing clips of YouTube videos. People were shaking and writhing on the carpeted floor of a megachurch, under the outstretched hand of Bernie Kissell.

'Yuk.' Wren looked away. 'That stuff makes my flesh creep.'

Amelia shrugged and pointed at two women, jerking around in spasm, arms cocked behind them like chickens. 'Has anybody considered that these guys are just like, the worst dancers ever?'

Matt chortled into his spoon. 'Case solved.'

'Totally. Like this?' Amelia leapt in front of the TV and started copying their chicken walk.

'Amelia,' Wren snapped. 'Go and brush your teeth.'

'Can't . . .' She started jogging on the spot, with hands waving. 'The Devil won't let me.'

'Hey.' Wren pointed her magic finger at her, which always seemed to work. Amelia tutted and trudged off. At the door, she turned back, eyes rolling around in her head. 'Daddy, watch!' She started squawking and strutting.

'Move it!' Wren shouted. 'And grab a clean jumper. You've got butter all down that one. There's one in the utility room.'

The door clicked shut and the newsreader went on.

'Meanwhile, controversial exorcist and author Pastor Bernie Kissell is preparing for what is being called a mass exorcism event, taking place at The Reed therapy centre in Cambridgeshire. All this in response to the death of forty-year-old hairstylist Justine

Riley, who was brutally murdered by her husband Tom Riley some time on Monday evening. Critics of Kissell, particularly Professor Hunter, have warned of the intense psychological damage the ritual of exorcism can inflict. Kissell and his supporters, however, point to the astonishing success from last night, when a visit to Tom Riley in prison seems to have unlocked the thirty-eight-year-old chef from a mostly catatonic state. Riley has made a full confession for the murder of his wife and cites Pastor Kissell as the key source of healing. The mass exorcism, known as *Free Indeed*, takes place overnight on Saturday evening and will be filmed by a television crew for broadcast later in the month. In other news . . .'

Wren clicked the remote. The TV blinked to black.

They were all silent for a moment. Especially Lucy.

'You okay?' Wren said.

Lucy stared at the blank screen. 'Just a bit scary. The way they move and stuff.'

'It is. But it's not real,' Matt said.

She looked at him. 'So it's in their heads?'

He nodded. Wren kept looking at her.

Lucy swallowed. 'Fair enough. I'll go and brush my teeth too.'

'I'll do mine with you,' Wren said, even though Matt knew she'd already brushed. He saw her walking with Lucy up the stairs, a hand on her shoulder.

When minty-fresh Wren eventually returned, she found him at the kitchen sink, washing out his bowl.

He paused for a moment with the brush dripping. 'Is Lucy okay?'

'Yes. It's just the sounds these people make. The faces. And the murder, of course.'

'We should have switched it off.'

'Probably.' She leant against the counter, leant closer, and in a whisper said, 'You know, she said she saw Eddie's face like that, a few times.'

Matt immediately set the brush down and turned to her. 'Oh . . .'

Eddie Pullen was Lucy's real dad and Wren's ex. The violent piece of crap was now in prison, after almost beating Wren to death. Eddie Pullen was the closest thing to a demon that Matt could imagine.

'Lucy said Eddie acted that way sometimes. Like the people on the TV.'

'Really?'

'Now and then, when he was drunk. So seeing that just creeped her out.'

He hugged Wren, and he heard her sigh and squeeze him tight.

'Do you think I should chat with her?'

'No . . . it's fine . . .' She pulled back. 'What she did ask was if there is going to be decent security at this weekend thing of yours.'

He paused for a second, touched that Lucy would have asked it. He nodded. 'TV people say they've got all that covered.'

'And you trust them?'

He reached for a tea towel and realised that he had no idea if he could trust this TV crew at all. 'They've won loads of awards. They're a well-respected company.'

She looked at him blankly. 'Just be super careful okay? Cos this stuff can—'

'What the heck is this?' Amelia's muffled voice boomed from the utility room. Then after some hurried footsteps, the kitchen door opened. She was standing there in a new jumper, back to front. 'What is it?'

'What's what?'

'Why is there a treasure chest on the tumble dryer?'

'Oops.' Matt's teeth clenched and they all followed her to the utility room. They found Tom Riley's wooden box sitting on the top of the washing machine. It sat next to a big box of powder and a litre bottle of fabric softener.

'What is *that*?' Wren said, leaning through the door.

'It's nothing.'

'If it's nothing, then how come I can see it?' Wren wrinkled her nose. 'And smell it too.'

'You think it has a smell?' Matt said.

'Yeah. Like smoke.'

Amelia leant in, eyes on sticks. 'What *is* it?'

'Something for this show I'm doing.'

Amelia's eyes flashed. 'The demon show?'

'Shhhh.' He looked back over his shoulder. Lucy was still upstairs. 'They asked me to look after it, until the weekend. No biggie.'

'What's in there?' Amelia tried to push through. 'A ghost? The Devil? Let's open it up.'

'Amelia.' Matt grabbed her reaching hand. 'Don't touch it.'

'Why. Does it bite?'

'Course not. I just have to look after it and I'm not allowed to mess with it. It's a silly prop,' he turned to Wren. 'I was going to put it in my office last night, but it started chucking down when I got in.' His office was in a cabin outside in the back garden. 'I couldn't be bothered getting soaked, so I dumped it in here late last night. Sorry.'

Wren pushed her lips forward. 'Then put it in your office now.'

'I'll just fin—'

'Now,' she said.

'Okay. Will do.'

'I kinda like it. The little locks look cute . . .' Amelia said. 'Hey, you could put this in my room, if you like.'

Wren caught Matt frowning at the box and tilting his head. 'What's wrong?' she said.

'Nothing, just . . . did you move this, Amelia?'

'Huh?'

'Did you move it round just now?'

'No. Why . . .' Her eyes flashed again, a glimmer of excitement on her face. Countless hours of spooky YouTube clips had given her a taste for creepy things. 'Whyyyyy?'

He shrugged. 'No reason. I'm tired.'

'Put it in the office, Matt,' Wren said. 'Or I'll put it in the rubbish. How about that?'

He did what she asked. He lugged that thing across the garden and into The Cabin. His funky office that housed a lot of the geeky stuff that Wren didn't want in the main house. Said it would ruin the tone. Like his *Star Wars* Lego kits, and vintage '70s and '80s arcade machines, and now the banished box of evil.

He stared at it for a moment. Wanting to leave it alone but finding it hard to look away. It was probably just a standard storage or toolbox that someone had decided to kit out with rusty old padlocks. Intrigued, he rummaged in a drawer for his little Maglite torch. Squinting, he started shining it through the wood, but the gaps were just too thin to see through. There were no distinguishing marks. No stamps of origin (Made in Hell – that sort of thing.) No chirp of a Mogwai deep inside. He put his hand on the side of it and for a dangerous second he considered pushing it off the desk, just so he might watch it crack open on the floor. But then his finger slid across a corner and the tip sliced open on some splintered wood.

'Dammit.' Matt grabbed a tissue and wrapped it around the tip, just as a single bead of blood started to bloom.

'Why did you bring that home?'

He spun around, to see Lucy standing next to Donkey Kong.

'It's just a work thing.'

'Right. Can you drive me to school?'

'Sure.'

'It's just I don't want to walk today.'

'Course. No problem.'

She said nothing, just kept staring at the box.

'Lucy? I said I'll drive you.'

She swallowed, nodded. 'Okay. Cool.'

She waited outside on the grass while he slapped a plaster on his finger and locked up his office. They headed inside and neither of them looked back. He wanted to ask her a very simple question, he really did, but for some reason he couldn't. He didn't want to make her feel awkward or stoke any old memories of her real dad. The thought of Eddie looking possessed during his rages . . . that broke his heart and it scared him too. The thought of what they'd been through. So he said nothing as they headed to the car, and decided it might be best to avoid his question. To ask if Lucy was the one who had turned the box around. After all, he was sure that when he'd dumped it in the utility room last night, the locks were facing the wall.

CHAPTER THIRTY-SIX

Matt paced the floor of the university toilets and caught himself in the mirror. He straightened his back. Gave his shirt collar a tug too, for symmetry's sake, and was suddenly baffled as to how to set it. A collar sticking out over the jacket looked way too disco. Tucked too neatly inside had a vague whiff of the pervert.

You're overthinking this. You're nervous. Just get in there.

He nodded and tried to shift his own mood. He put a thumb up to himself like a pilot might, then he cringed because he'd put a thumb up to himself. The cringe made him chuckle, and that was the relief he needed.

Go.

Before he changed his mind he grabbed his clipboard from the edge of the sink and stepped back into the corridor. Suzy was waiting, camera ready. She'd told him not to smile at the lens so much, and to act natural. So he made a massive effort just to walk like a human being. She walked backwards, giving him the OK sign of approval.

He headed back to the large Merrill Hall – the university gymnasium that they were using today. He took a subtle breath before he pushed through the double doors and was surprised to see almost everybody had already arrived. Many faces turned and stared at him, and he was instantly conscious of the silence in there. This space was usually filled with the squeak of trainers and the grunts and cheers of sport. Now the only sound in the entire universe was the *clop, clop, clop* of his new shoes echoing across the gym floor. Suzy's gliding pumps made no sound whatsoever. Guess that's what made her the pro.

There were over thirty people in the hall, including a bunch of his post-grad students. They were eager for practical credits for helping out. He'd pulled in a few nurses from the university infirmary too, and the rest were from campus security. The only other member of the academic staff was Lisa Hammond – the veteran head of the psychology department. She was dressed in her usual funeral, let's-suck-all-happiness-from-this institution shade of black. She'd agreed to sit in and observe and boy was she doing that now. She gave Matt that slow, unsmiling blink of hers. Lisa was a master at the slow blink.

And then of course there was the TV crew, dotted all over the room and already filming. Lenses were pulling in reality and turning it into something else. Nupa, he noticed, wasn't there. She was tied up this morning with some prep for The Reed. It was the only part of the filming she'd missed, so far. Ethan was here, though. He'd pulled up a small chair and was watching from the corner, with his eye on Abby especially. Ethan had happily admitted the other day that he thought Abby was 'stunning'.

Matt didn't like the speed of all this, obviously. Hated it, in fact. Putting together a set of mini-trials should normally take months of planning. But the Bernie Kissell Express had left the station, and it was hurtling with pace towards the weekend. Matt, to be fair, was getting increasingly worried about that.

At least Perry and Kissell had agreed not to come. Matt had specifically banned them. Having those two lurking around with their prayer-soaked lips and underarm Bible odour would only confuse the subjects. It was certainly noticeable how calm, relaxed and *normal* these four clients seemed to be as they sat here in a pastor-less room. They'd gathered in a circle around the red centre spot of the basketball court.

Matt had read all of their files last night. One woman and three men, including the baseball cap bloke from the TV studio the other night. Having that one around put Matt on edge somewhat, but right now he was acting completely normally. He turned out to be a thirty-year-old personal trainer called Richie Gregor, with a history of drug abuse, two suicide attempts and what looked like a pathological obsession with weightlifting. He looked like a balloon, dangerously close to popping. But when he wasn't acting all demonic, like now, he had a bizarrely kind and delicate way about him.

Pavel Basa was twenty-three. A bald Romanian man in a red Coca-Cola T-shirt and blue tracksuit bottoms. Pavel worked in an abattoir, shooting thousands of cows point-blank between the eyes with a bolt gun – enough to shake anybody's mental state. The file said he'd been put on throat-slitting duty one day and had got an erection. He admitted this to his priest, and said it was purely from thinking about a girl he loved for distraction. The priest told him that no, this was an incontrovertible sign of bestiality and therefore evil infestation. Pavel, for whatever reason, seemed to be accepting this diagnosis.

The oldest was Deron Johnson, a Nigerian session drummer. The fifty-four-year-old had the type of Afro you could hide pencils in, and thick horn-rimmed glasses too. He claimed his mother-in-law was the Devil, which was less funny than it sounded. Especially when she'd been dead a year. She'd been mocking him every day. Telling him to drive his car up on the kerbs and mow down pedestrians.

Finally, of course, there was Abby Linh from the TV show the other night. She beamed with relief when Matt walked in, like they were old friends. Matt saw a lostness in her striking face that was frankly heart-breaking. For some reason, the fact that she'd worn a pretty summer dress on such a cold day made her confusion even more poignant. Her brown hair hung in a neat ponytail rope down her back.

He looked at them all, sitting there patiently and politely. Clearly a little scared, but perhaps hopeful too. Eager for insight and help for their condition. These poor people, Matt thought, as he walked into their circle. These poor, troubled people, who had so far been given answers that only pushed them deeper into despair.

He shook each of their hands (Richie's vice-like shake almost cost Matt a finger bone) and he thanked them all sincerely for taking part. He called them all by name, looked each in the eye and used the warmest smile he could summon. For a troupe infested with the Devil's minions, Richie, Pavel, Deron and Abby were a wonderfully polite bunch.

Matt chose not to stand for his speech. He scraped up a chair and chatted instead, setting his clipboard on the floor.

'I appreciate that this is an unusual scenario to be in. So thank you for coming. And please understand that although this afternoon involves a few basic experiments, you are not under any sort of judgement. This is simply an exploration of theories. A second opinion, if you will. Pastor Kissell believes . . .'

At the mention of Kissell's name, Richie immediately fluttered an eyelid. Just the one. He groaned and swayed in his chair. The cameras caught it.

'Mr Gregor?' Matt asked.

'Sorry,' Richie said, and sat up straight. 'Carry on.'

Matt nodded for one his students to bring some water over and he could hear the first scrawling of Lisa's disapproving pen on her pad. 'At The Reed this weekend, you will hear one theory on your current troubles. Namely, that you are somehow influenced, terrorised or even controlled by an external spiritual entity. Today I offer you an alternative idea. Take it on board, or totally reject it. That's your call. But I hope to offer at least some evidence that will suggest that you are *not* at the mercy of a demon or spirit. But rather that, just like millions of other people in the world today, you can be helped with more traditional medical methods. Therefore, I've devised a series of rudimentary experiments that will explore, and perhaps even challenge, some of the classic evidence for demonic possession. I've arranged with the university to offer you all a year of in-depth counselling, completely free of charge. I believe this will help you, but you are of course at liberty to take that offer or not.'

Pavel's fingers, his cow-killing trigger fingers, were trembling on his lap. 'What are the tests?'

Abby smiled at him. 'Will they be hard, Matt?'

'They won't be hard. It's not that type of test. There are no right and wrong answers. I simply want to observe your natural responses. We have four tests running at the same time, and we'll rotate you . . . which means I anticipate this will last no longer than one hour. Perhaps even less. After which, you'd be welcome to stay for refreshments. If at any time you wish to stop, come back into this circle. Are there any questions?'

Abby crossed her legs. 'Well, I'm sure this will be a very interesting afternoon. I'm ready.'

'Good, and thank you all for your participation.' He went to stand, just as the security guards and the student assistants

231

came to collect their designated clients. Matt was proud at how his students spoke, putting the subjects at ease, guiding them to the doors, but with hover hands and no physical touching, as instructed. As ever, the constant cameras went with them.

He gave them ten minutes to get started and then he slowly wandered through each of the five rooms, quietly observing the tests taking place, each observed by two guards. He walked into Room One, where the Latin test was already getting results. The drummer, Deron, was sat in a chair, legs crossed, while one of the students read loudly from what looked like an ancient Latin prayer book. Deron was starting to writhe and groan. The many rings on his fingers kept tapping against each other. 'No. *Stop it*,' he whispered, in a low kind of animal growl. '*I won't. I won't leave him.*'

Deron had been told this test was to record his voice – to see if they entered into any inhuman, animal-like frequencies. But the point of this room wasn't that at all. It'd be interesting to hear how Deron reacted later, when he learnt that what he was actually listening to wasn't an ancient book of exorcism, but yesterday's weather forecast being read out. Matt had laboriously translated it into Latin late last night.

Next, he strolled into the second room, where the cross test was already underway. Richie Gregor's bulk was perched on a chair, eyes gone behind a thick, tight eye-mask. Flanked by security and nurses, a student was methodically, and gently, pressing only the edge of a series of hard objects against his forehead, just under the superman curl of Richie's black hair. A pen, a chopstick, a toy sonic screwdriver from *Doctor Who*, a spirit level and a metal cross were the selections. Richie's notes said he had a vociferous resistance to holy symbols. But he only started squirming when the corner of the spirit level touched his head. The cross passed by without incident, but the chopstick prompted a sudden and sharp 'Fuck Christ' to burst from his lips.

Matt would have laughed, if it wasn't so depressing.

Next was Abby Linh and a simple test of psychokinesis. Demons were said to be able to levitate objects, and Abby's report said that some of her friends had seen this very phenomenon happen during her 'episodes'. Like a soup bowl that rose, hovered and smashed against her fridge. Even the possessed people themselves were said to sometimes rise off their beds and float. That he'd pay to see. So Abby was asked to sit in front of a tray filled with small objects. A small white spork, the plastic top from some deodorant, a paperweight, and a full salt cellar. This was the most ropey test of them all, he felt, but the students pressed ahead anyway, asking whatever was inside of Abby to lift something up. She sat there, looking awkward. She smirked at Matt as he came in. 'I think my demon has stage fright.'

Matt found Pavel in the fourth room, methodically dipping his fingers into those bowls of water. He snapped his hand back on almost every bowl, hissing like it was battery acid. At one point, he fell clean off his chair. It looked like Pavel was a solid fail, so far.

Yes, of course these tests were crude and rushed, and easy to dismiss if this was a purely academic study. But the point wasn't to offer slam-dunk proof one way or another. They just deserved a second opinion.

Thankfully, the security guards never had to do anything. The subjects' reactions were dramatic at times, but it was low level and nothing even approaching Tom Riley. The closest to that was Richie, who now and then snapped his eyes open and glared and hissed at people. But then he'd shake his head, apologise and then he'd be fine again.

When it was all done, they gathered back in the hall, and Matt thanked each of them. They seemed very relaxed for the most part. There were even a few giggles here and there. Matt suggested they head off for refreshments while he and his team went over the test results. He'd join them for doughnuts after and share the findings with anybody who was willing to hear them. The guards went with them, just in case.

It was around then when things went wrong.

He was sitting with his team, cross-legged on the floor of the basketball court. They were flicking through results and finding that yes, as expected, the subjects were hopelessly out in terms of detecting sacred objects and words. He felt an odd stab of self-satisfaction at this, immediately followed by an academic worry – that these rushed tests were built on a straw man premise. But then two things distracted him from this inner unsettlement. One was the two students who'd been shadowing Abby the whole time. They were still totting up her results, because they'd requested a few more minutes to double-check, then triple check their figures.

They looked up from their sheets and said, 'Professor. I think you better look at these.'

Then the corridor outside exploded with sound.

A man was screaming and glass was shattering.

Everyone blinked. Just a second to let noise travel from ear to brain and finally, to limbs. A whole army of shoes filled the gym hall with the slapping of soles as they barrelled towards the doors. They slammed through the double doors and looked left trying to find the screaming man, but what Matt saw was not what he expected at all.

It was Claire, Reverend Perry's wife, standing in the corridor.

CHAPTER THIRTY-SEVEN

Matt shook one of his student's shoulders. 'Get security . . . *now*.' Then he ran forward towards Claire Perry. She was standing alone, wearing black jeans and a black T-shirt, tucked in. One of her arms was raised up, pointing a palm towards the door to the toilets. The muffled screams were coming from inside.

'What are you doing here? What's going on?'

She ignored him.

Another pitiful scream split the air.

He winced and put a hand out to keep the students back, then he pushed the toilet door open wide. The first thing he saw was a doughnut on the floor. One of those Krispy Kremes he'd had delivered earlier. It was upended and fusing with a wet-looking tile. And just above the sink Matt saw a shattered mirror. For a brief second, he saw his own shocked face staring back, trapped in the honeycombed gaze of a giant insect eye.

But as he stepped further in, he saw.

Richie Gregor was thrashing his thick arms around, spine arched against the floor, teeth bared, eyes locked shut under horribly swollen lids. Two bauble eyeballs rolled madly against thin flesh. His baseball cap was tossed to the side, sitting soaked under one of the urinals.

Another shock was seeing that Reverend Perry and Pastor Kissell were on each side of him. Knees pressing into the wet tiles. Perry had his hand on Richie's shoulders, but Kissell's were slapped against Richie's sweat-soaked forehead. In the mirrors, he saw Abby reflected in the doorway. She was staring in shock and throwing a pill into her mouth.

Matt's shout was even louder than he'd anticipated. 'Get off him.'

'*You* . . .' Perry snapped his head back. 'Don't you think you've done enough?'

Kissell's cameramen swooped in, sensing blood, and Richie screamed again, only this time it was in sharp, jerking snaps. Kissell kept pressing his hand firmly against his forehead throughout the spasm.

'Out,' Kissell yelled. 'Out of this man. In the name of Christ!'

'Dammit, he's having a seizure.'

Perry rounded on Matt. 'Because of you.'

Matt glared at him. 'The guards are coming. I'll have them drag you off and throw you into the street.'

'No need,' Kissell said suddenly. 'It's okay. Look Matt . . . it's done.'

The screaming stopped, and Richie's spine was retracting to normal, which is when Kissell pulled his hand back. And that was when Matt saw it. The glimpse that changed everything. Not the final bubbles of spit spurting from Richie's lips. That's what everybody else was looking at. No, Matt was fixed on Kissell, who had chosen that spit moment to slowly pull his hand back and slip it into the

236

cream blazer he was wearing. There was something very odd about his palm. Like the skin was marked with an old blister or burn. Something smooth and flat, flesh-coloured and shiny, but not flesh.

A gruff voice in his ear said, 'Step aside.'

It was a security guard and a nurse. Matt, like a zombie, did what he was told, because his brain was too busy whirring with what he'd just seen.

'Clear a space,' the nurse said.

Matt shuffled back in silence.

Holy shit.

He had a rush of memory. Him and his mum in a seaside joke shop, pleading with her to buy a fake pool of plastic sick and a box of fake cigarettes that puffed out talcum powder, and a little black disc you could stick against your palm. That was the one his mum was saying, no, no, no to. Because there was simply no way any son of hers was going to shake people's hands and give them electric shocks.

Holy shit.

Matt blinked himself back, heart thundering as the guards gathered around the beast on the floor. Only he wasn't a beast any more. Richie was totally compliant and polite again. Hitching up and letting the nurse slip a folded cardigan under his head.

'He'll be okay now.' Kissell smiled at them all. 'Praise God.'

'Bless you, Pastor.' Richie spoke to the ceiling just as Claire rushed over to hug both him and Kissell. 'I really think it's gone.'

Kissell was beaming and started walking towards the door, but Matt moved with him.

'I'll go and tell the others, Richie,' Kissell said. 'I'll tell 'em you're free and . . . sorry . . . Matt, I can't get by.'

Matt stood stock-still in the doorway.

'Matt, I can't get through.'

'That's because I'm blocking the door.' Matt nervously looked at the guards. 'Can you search Pastor Kissell, please?'

'I beg your pardon?' Perry stepped closer. 'What are you playing at now?'

'*Playing?*' Matt almost laughed. 'Do it.'

The guards looked up, frowning, 'Search him for what?'

'A small device, flesh-coloured. Look in his pockets, his palm. I think he just gave Mr Gregor here a mild electric shock.'

Perry's jaw dropped. 'You are kidding me.'

'Do it.'

'I can't believe this.' Perry started to laugh. 'Don't do it, Bernie. Don't give him the satis—'

Kissell was already raising his arms. His tucked pink shirt tugged itself up and over his belt. 'Please go ahead. I have nothing to hide.'

Hands and fingers started patting him down, and with every passing second Matt felt his stress levels rising. The frantic review of images he'd just seen. The desperate categorisation of light and shadow. Without thinking, he grabbed Kissell's hand, and flipped it over, staring at the palm.

'May I have my hand back, please? I am rather attached to it.'

Matt dropped it, unable to speak.

The guard stopped patting him down. 'There's nothing.'

Richie was sitting up now, rotating his arm like he'd just finished a gym session.

'He's stable,' the nurse said.

Kissell tapped his glasses into place. 'Now, if you'll let me through, Matt.'

'Wait,' Matt said. 'You . . . you . . .'

'Are you all right, Professor?' Perry didn't just frown. He looked like his possession radar was going off. 'Are you affected? Dear God, the box. Did you touch it?'

'Screw that damn box. He must have dropped the device in here.' Matt marched to the bin that was in reach of Kissell before. He yanked the metal lid off the bin and flung it to the floor with a clatter. He dragged the black bag out and immediately shook it out on the floor. It took a while. They all just watched him as he jiggled the bag, as bits of old tissue paper fell with crumpled up receipts. By the swishing end, Matt dropped to the floor, and started frantically sifting through.

'Oh, Matt . . .' Perry said. 'Is there nothing there?'

Kissell looked over at Matt, sympathetically.

'Then search Reverend Perry,' Matt said. 'They were standing together.'

'Excuse me?'

'And his wife. She hugged them both.'

'*What?*' Perry's smarmy smile vanished. 'You leave her out of this.'

Kissell caught Perry's eye. 'If the professor saw something he should have the right to check it. It's important he eliminates the red herrings. That way he might get to the truth. Wouldn't you say, Matt?'

Matt was too busy scanning the room, and so did the cameraman. 'Where is she?'

'Claire?' Perry shrugged. 'She's already gone.'

One of the students was standing near the doorway. He nodded. 'She was scared. She needed air.'

'And I don't blame her.' Perry folded his arms. 'This was the first exorcism she's seen, first-hand. It can be very unsettling indeed.'

Matt rushed into the corridor to call Claire back, but saw Professor Lisa Hammond instead. She was leaning against the wall in the otherwise empty corridor, chewing at the inside of her mouth. Her phone was pressed to her ear and he just knew it, from that smug line of those thin, leather lips of hers. She was calling the principle and reporting Matt's unruly experiment, and now, his wild accusations.

Wearily, Matt turned to Kissell. 'What are you even doing here? You agreed to give me space today.'

'I apologise for the change in plan but we felt unsettled, Matt. We got a strong sense we were needed here, and look . . . we were right.'

'But they were fine.' Matt threw his arms in the air. 'They were all fine, until—'

'I wasn't fine,' Richie said, as the nurses helped him to his feet. Then he walked up to Kissell and said, 'I am now, though. I feel amazing. I really think it's gone.'

Wait. Matt span towards the camera guy. 'You were filming? The entire time?'

'Course.'

'Then I want to see that film as soon as—'

'Professor Hunter.' It was Richie, walking forward with a hand out to shake. 'Thanks for not stopping it this time. Like in the TV studio, I mean. I can't wait to tell my parents I'm better.'

Matt, his mind racing, looked down at that thick hand of his. 'I'm . . . just . . . I'm . . . I really think you should stay a while. You haven't heard the test results yet.'

'There's no point now . . . and . . . well, it's pretty clear which theory was right.' He looked back at Kissell, who was washing his face and hands at the sink. 'And don't worry, Professor, there's no hard feelings. I believe we're all on a journey, and I have a feeling you'll get there. You'll see the truth one day. And the truth . . .'

'Will set you free,' Kissell said, as he slipped his clean and shiny glasses back into place.

CHAPTER THIRTY-EIGHT

Matt sat in his dark garden, alone.

He had his head tilted back so he could watch the slow clouds creep past the stars, blinking distant suns off, then on, then off again. These chunky grey rattan chairs felt like a fake throne, but God they were cosy with all these bright-yellow cushions tucked around him. He and Wren often sat out here at night, when it was warm enough. Sipping red wine and discussing everything from the deep threat of climate change, to their shared grief at the passing of Saturday morning Kids TV.

But tonight it was just him. And it wasn't wine he was drinking, it was vodka in a highball glass. It wasn't even warm enough to sit outside, either. In fact, it was *cold*. So he'd dragged a starfield blanket from his office and wrapped it around him, up and around his head. He looked like a little Romanian lady, making doilies in the street. Like ET stuffed into a BMX basket. Yeah, he was really rocking this Friday night.

The leaves shook and filled the air with distant tambourines, and he took another gulp, a big one. He winced as it went down.

Damn, today was a mess.

He'd genuinely thought they were going to benefit from another angle on their condition. But after what happened to Richie Gregor, all of them – except Abby – had refused to hear their test results. He wasn't sure if that was Perry's suggestion or Kissell's, or if they'd decided it themselves over doughnuts, before the screaming had started. But Pavel, Deron and Richie politely declined. They feared the distraction might affect their faith and make them more vulnerable at The Reed. 'The tests themselves must have set Richie off, today,' Pavel had said. Such bizarre logic wasn't easy to follow, but in the world of the possessed, every tiny detail seemed to take on meaning.

It was so frustrating, and deeply embarrassing too. Whenever he closed his eyes, he saw Lisa Hammond pointing her fake nail at him, shaking her head.

And then there were the results. Or rather, Abby Linh's results. He was *not* expecting that.

He took another sip and glanced at the table. He'd put a garden rock on his clipboard, to stop Abby's stats blowing off. Though part of him wished they would. Wished they'd spiral up into the sky, and vaporise into a star, like they didn't exist. The breeze happily rattled those papers around the stone. Mocking him with their fluttering.

True, the male clients had spectacularly failed, just as predicted. With folks screaming at a pencil on their heads or hissing like snakes when they touched spring water from the campus Starbucks.

Yet now they refused to hear, or even release their results, all these colossal fails weren't even going to make the show. Though

Richie was glad to let the footage from his bathroom exorcism be shown. Of *course* they'd show all that stuff. They'd just leave out the part when he freaked out at the Holy Ghost power of a chopstick. But then there was Abby, who failed all her tests too . . . except the holy water.

He groaned at her figures.

She identified the bowl of blessed water out of ten bowls. Not just once . . . but eight times. Just hearing that figure in his head made him feel a bit sick. How was it even possible? He'd calculated that as a one in 2.7 billion chance. Everyone on the research team was talking about it. He just shook his head. Took another wince-inducing swallow. Good job he had the bottle here too. He topped up the glass.

So . . . tomorrow was the big day. He'd be heading off to The Reed with the exact same troupe of exorcees from the tests. As well as Deron and Pavel, Nupa had said there may be one or two others, but that'd be it. It was good to know there'd be at least one less, now that Richie was 'cured'. Star pupil Abby would be there, of course . . .

He jumped when his phone went off. Yoda, crying out across the garden. The neighbours must hate him by now for this tone. He snapped into focus. The email he'd been waiting for. From Nupa.

He squinted into the screen's glow, setting the sloshing drink aside. Above him, he thought he felt a single drop of rain on the back of his hand. A frantic thumb found the email.

Bathroom Footage.

Yes! Finally.

He ignored Nupa's message and clicked the file. He forgot to knock his volume down, so when the footage started, Richie's wild and jerking pig screams screeched into the garden. He tapped the volume with a frantic thumb, and in his tipsiness, dropped the phone on the grass. He winced when he saw next door's light come on. He scooped it up, and killed the screams, then he watched the scene play out in silence instead.

It was strange to watch an exorcism in pure silence. It looked like a dance. Like performance art. Or in other words, it looked like what it was.

The moment came. He held the phone closer for the money shot.

With a frown he tapped the slider back and watched it again. This time with a pinch-zoom and a hawk's eye. Another frown, another wind back. He watched it again. Then again. Then . . . he felt his grip on the phone tightening, because his brain was suggesting an alternative response. Throw this phone into the bushes and scream.

There was nothing. No sign of a device, only a brief moment when there *could* have been, but the angle was wrong. The camera, which never lies, was backing Kissell up, not him. He wanted to shout 'fuck' really loudly – like a possessed person might, and he briefly understood their attraction to it. Then he let his lips flap with bitter breath and read Nupa's note that he'd missed before.

We don't see any device, sorry. Take a look and see what we're missing.

He stared at the phone, thinking. Then he tossed a peanut into his mouth and started googling again. Calling up all the sites he'd found earlier this evening, in his frantic search for answers.

A picture of Kissell stared up at him, with his homespun glint and his 'hey-guys!' smile. Matt flicked back through the articles and profiles that charted the birth of his ministry, only about five years ago. An ordinary medical supplies salesman, whose wife had died tragically in a horrendous hit and run. When Kissell shared a tearful prayer during her funeral, someone in the pew had started writhing.

The rest, the articles said, was history. For whenever Bernie Kissell prays, the demons flee, which seemed like qualification enough.

Might as well call this salesman a pastor and be done with it. So people did. Matt stared at an old picture of Kissell and his wife, Sandra, standing on a cruise ship and waving to the camera. He was skinny and long, she was huge and round. Together they looked like the number ten. He looked so happy in the picture, champagne glass raised at the 'Sail Away' party. But her . . . there was a haunt in her eye. He drilled a little deeper, but found no more about her, other than the words 'hit and run'.

Matt sighed and tapped his phone off. The garden was suddenly thrown into darkness again. So he set the phone down and leant back, taking a final few sips. He heard her footsteps before he saw her. Just a crunch of trainers on the path. It was Lucy standing in her pyjamas. He turned to face her. She stood there, moon-coloured.

'Hey.' He quickly yanked that dumb-looking blanket off his head. 'Can't you sleep?'

She shook her head.

'Well, you're welcome to pull up a chair and watch the stars with me. I'll grab another blanket if—'

'Thanks, but . . . no. I had a question.'

'Okay.'

'That box . . .' The breeze blew suddenly and made her pause and look off into the shadows. Her hair rose and danced, and she slapped it quickly down. 'Is it still here?'

'It's in my office. Why?'

'When's it going?'

'Tomorrow. I'm away for the weekend. I'll take it with me.'

'I just think you should take it away, soon.'

'Lucy?'

She didn't speak.

'Lucy, did you touch the box last night?'

She waited.

'It's just I'm sure it was turned around when I—'

'I needed a lightbulb and I saw it. I was curious. Is it bad that I touched it?'

'Nah, it's just a box.'

'Is it bad that I picked it up?'

He went to stand. 'It's just a box.'

'Is it bad that I heard it sing?'

His face, which had been in some sort of sympathetic wince for her, slowly dropped. 'Lucy, I've had a crappy day. I'm not in the mood for a joke.'

She narrowed her eyes at him. 'Er, hello? Look at my face.'

He did, and then he felt cold. 'I'm sorry. Go on.'

'It sang . . .'

'Hey,' she let him take her hand, 'you're trembling.'

'Can you remember that ancient song? The one you used to sing when I was litt—oh, I mean . . . shit . . .' A beat of panic flashed in her eyes. That sometimes happened whenever she got her dads mixed up. 'I'm sorry.'

He squeezed her hand. 'Not a problem. What song?'

'That really old one? Hush . . . um . . . Hush . . .'

'Little baby?'

She shivered and nodded. 'My dad used to sing that to me, when I was really small. I don't know why I still remember it but . . . I do. And I heard it last night.'

'Are you sure it came from the box?'

'I think so. I don't know. I just . . . I just want to know if it was bad that I touched it?'

'It's absolutely fine you touched it, and there is nothing about that box you should worry about. Seriously.'

'Okay . . .' She turned before he could speak, and he watched her move to the sliding door. She paused when she touched the handle. 'But can you take it away tonight?'

'How about I put it in my car boot? Then in the morning it'll be gone.'

'Okay. Good.'

After she went inside, he watched the clouds cover the moon for a long time. He only took his eyes off them when his phone threw its feeble glow up into the dark air. An email from Fenn.

Matt. Re: Car Park Ticket. You're right, I've got Claire Perry's car placed at Melody Public Park at 13.20 p.m. on the day of the murder. That's in Sneddon, the next village. So she either lied, or someone used her car. I'll have a dig around. Enjoy your fifteen minutes of fame btw! Martin. PS. Pam's recovering well. Way better than we expected, thank God.

He set the phone down and looked up at the moon again. It was hidden now. As black and smudged as one of Claire Perry's creepy-looking artworks. *Why did Claire lie?* He sat there, thinking about that, and about Lucy, and the box, and Abby's results . . . until the shivering got too much. He dipped into his office and grabbed the stupid box, putting it into the boot of his car without incident. Then he went into the lounge where Wren was reading. She hadn't noticed Lucy come down. Or back up again.

Matt waved his half-full glass towards her. 'You want the rest of this?'

She screwed up her face. 'No thanks, comrade.'

'Then I reckon I might just go to bed.'

'Wait,' she had her eyes on the clipboard. 'Is that the test results? From today?'

'Yup.'

'Then why the long face . . .' She set the book down. 'Don't tell me they beat your challenges.'

'The vast majority failed them miserably.'

One of her eyebrows went up. 'And the minority?'

He shrugged. 'A fluke, I guess.'

'Show me.' She leapt up and grabbed the clipboard, running her finger through the figures.

'So I leave in the morning. This thing at The Reed runs overnight tomorrow, so I can leave mid-morning on Sunday. I was wondering if you fancy going out for a meal or—'

'This Abby woman . . .' Wren looked up, jaw hanging. 'She's psychic. She's Uri flipping Geller.'

'She did *not* pass everything. She didn't levitate anything. She failed the Latin a couple of—'

'This holy water stuff, though . . . that's creepy . . .' she said. 'Don't you think it's *creepy*?'

He shrugged. 'Maybe she cheated.'

'At *your* tests? If she did, then wouldn't that look bad, on you?' She winced. 'Sorry.'

'Why do you think I've got vodka?' He took a final swig and sloshed the rest out into the sink. 'I'm heading up.'

She watched him. She knew him well enough to know that this was one of those times that he didn't need a hug or a kind word. He just needed normalcy. 'Okay,' she said, 'I'll stay down here for a bit and keep reading my book. The president's about to steal a helicopter.'

He smiled at her and headed up.

He didn't sleep much.

Not only because alcohol had a tendency to keep him awake these days, but next door had their TV on too loud again. Even though they were detached, he could still hear their music coming from the trees. So he lay there, listening to the lullaby melodies from the neighbours. He listened out for Lucy's door too. Worrying that even though she wanted rid of it, she still might get up again, grab his keys and head out to his car. Just so she could find it and hold it to her ear. But Wren was still up, and she'd tell her to go to bed, anyway.

Unless . . .

As he fell into sleep he had a mental picture of them both,

Wren and Lucy, and then Amelia too, walking silently to his car, hand in hand, bare feet in the grass and following the pretty music. And the slow, in-and-out of his breath reminded him of when he was a boy on the storm-soaked nights on the Suffolk coast, counting the space between the thunder and lightning out at sea. Working out how far away it was, or how close.

PART THREE

DEVOUR

CHAPTER THIRTY-NINE

Matt sat in the back of the Subaru, feeling like his seat belt was on way too tight. Next to him, Nupa was rapid-chatting on her phone. She'd gone for the cream look today. Cream trousers, cream shirt, pointy cream shoes. Since the leather of the car was also cream he figured that if he squinted his eyes, she'd turn into nothing more than a floating head.

He listened to her prep for the shot of them rolling up in the car. She had quite a grating voice, he decided. Husky and strained. The kind of 'this-is-what-cool-women-sound-like' tone you heard constantly on TV shows and ads. She had a MacBook Air sitting on her lap, which she kept tapping incessantly. She played that thing like a concert piano.

Today's driver was Ray, who still didn't do conversation. With nobody to talk to, Matt leant forward and looked through the front seats. Kissell and Perry were travelling ahead of them in the silver minivan. He could see their heads talking and laughing. It looked like there was room for Matt in there but—

'Great. You're the best, Anders.' Nupa said it like she was announcing the top forty. *Playin all the hits!* 'See you soon.'

Matt turned in his seat and smiled at her. 'Okay, so can we talk now?'

She glanced at her laptop, shrugged, then closed the lid. 'I'm all yours.'

'So . . . I take it you're keeping me away from the pastors?'

'Yes, but that's because Reverend Perry said you weren't speaking to them. Not after what happened at the university.'

'*Not speaking?*' he said. 'I'm not twelve.'

'Then maybe I misunderstood. I still think it's best we keep things as calm as possible before the event. I saw that bathroom footage, Matt . . . It did get a bit . . . frisky between you three.'

'Yeah, but Richie Gregor was fine until they turned up.'

'You know, Pastor Kissell was quite hurt by what you said.' She leant closer. 'The accusation, I mean.'

'I'm telling you, I saw something in his hand. A device.'

'Did you see wires?'

'Those things don't always need wires.'

'And what colour was it again?'

'Flesh. Easier to disguise.'

'Maybe it was flesh-coloured because . . . it was just flesh.' She started to click her fingernail. 'Matt, are you absolutely sure you saw something?'

'Yes.'

'One hundred per cent positive, court-of-law style, on-your-kids-lives kinda sure? It was *hectic* in there.'

'I'm ninety per cent.' He saw her eyes roll. 'Which is pretty darn high, Nupa. It's just a shame he was so quick. Like he's good at sleight of hand.'

'Like a magician?'

He watched the van up front and nodded. 'That little flick back of his wrist. That was a practised move, you could tell.'

'You could ninety per cent tell . . .'

'Still pretty high.' He turned to the window where the motorway fields were now churning by in a blurred, yellow fuzz.

'Well, listen, we're watching him,' Nupa said. 'And at The Reed we'll be *really* watching him. So if he slips up, we'll see it from all angles. Until then, I think you should give him the benefit of the doubt.'

'Isn't that what this show is lacking . . . *doubt*?' He started drumming a rhythm on his knees.

'Don't forget Abby's still unsure. She has doubts.'

'Good.'

'You brought her results, didn't you? She's the only one who wants to hear them.'

He stopped drumming.

'Why didn't you tell her them yesterday?'

'There was too much commotion with Richie. I left it.'

'Well . . . go on, then . . . how did she do?'

He sighed, then opened up his bag. He handed her the sheet and waited patiently for the word 'wow' to come.

It did, quicker and louder than he expected.

'*Wow.*'

'There it is.'

'She did *way* better than the others.'

'On one test. I've got a theory on how she might have done so well. Just looking into it.'

'Yeah, well . . .' She clearly wasn't interested in his theory. She flipped open her laptop and stuck her phone back to her ear. 'These results are fascinating,' and just like that she was gone again, deep in conversation with one of her team.

The car came off the slip road and stopped at a junction. As he settled back into his seat, he saw a cow in a field nearby. It was chewing and blinking so lazily, it was like God had specifically created it not to give a shit about anything. He felt insanely envious of that cow, right now.

They hit some long country roads, with fewer and fewer houses. Then the buildings disappeared completely and were replaced by what seemed like a billion trees. In time, as they turned up a single narrow lane, he saw the pulse of signs begin to appear. THE REED CENTRE, in thin and elegant fonts.

Ferns and branches were now squeaking against the car doors. The woods were close now, and so thick. His reception icon had zero bars.

'This place really puts the "retreat" in retreat centre,' Matt said. 'How on earth did you get the camera trucks up here?'

'With difficulty, but they got through. When The Reed was a rehab place, it was supposed to make patients feel like they were stepping away from the world.'

'Feels like we're stepping away from the planet. I assume they have Wi-Fi? If we need to get in touch with earth, I mean?'

She laughed. 'Course they do.'

He looked out at dense forest. 'Feels a bit too isolated. A bit . . . vulnerable.'

She put a hand on his knee; it was the first time she'd done anything like that. She patted it, like calming a nervous puppy. 'You worry too much.'

'You don't worry enough.'

'That's not what my ex tells me . . . listen . . . just try and relax. And remember we've planned this to the nth degree.'

'Nupa, the whole idea for this only came up four days ago.'

She started laughing. 'We're always prepared in TV.'

Suddenly they both had to grab at the ceiling handles as the bumpy road started rocking them up and down. She laughed like she was on a rollercoaster. Then the road opened up again, and gravel was crunching under their tyres. They both leant forward to see something new. A fountain. A random, modern-looking fountain made of concrete. It looked like a giant concrete teardrop trickling out water from the top. And on the stone were thick metal letters, in brushed gold.

THE REED CENTRE – *Where Peace Lives*.

Nupa tapped the back of the driver's seat. 'Why are we slowing down?'

Ray jabbed a gloved finger towards the windscreen. 'The van's stopping.'

Matt and Nupa almost bumped heads as they leant together to look. Sure enough, the van was slowing to a stop. Then it just sat there, idling its engine near the fountain.

'What are they doing?' Matt said.

'Crap.' She grabbed her phone. 'Maybe they're having second thoughts.'

'God, I hope so.'

The van door opened, and he saw Kissell and Perry step out, stretching their backs and swinging their arms. Kissell was back in his blue polo shirt today, only now he'd added cream golfing trousers. Perry had gone more formal. Grey trousers and a tailored white shirt, neatly tucked. His outfit had a flash of the Mormon about him. Perry took off his blazer jacket and flung it over his shoulder as the two men started walking towards the fountain. 'What *are* they doing?'

They both plunged their hands into the bubbling water. Then Matt heard Perry call out to the van, curling a beckoning arm. Perry's wife Claire slid out. She hurried towards him, head down.

He groaned inwardly. 'I bet they're going to pray before going in.'

'Wrong.' She started laughing. 'Ha. They're taking selfies.'

Perry and Kissell smiled as Claire took various shots of them. At one point, Perry insisted Kissell stand by himself with his hands on his hips, looking valiant. The cynical Matt wanted to tut and shake his head, but the human part thought . . . you know what, fair enough. No matter what they might believe, this is a big moment for them. The sympathy was short-lived. He saw Kissell rake his comb-over into place with the palm of his hand and Matt thought of that device. Ninety per cent was pretty damn high.

'You should have been filming this bit,' Matt said.

'We are.' She lifted a finger towards the trees. A couple of wooden boxes stood by the road.

'I thought those were litter bins.'

'They are . . . with cameras inside them. Gotta catch 'em all.'

Matt shook his head as the pastors climbed back into the van. 'Should I skip showers this weekend?'

'Yep. And toilets for sure.'

His eyebrows shot up. 'You're kidding.'

She burst into laughter, then slapped the headrest. 'Drive.'

The engine rumbled again, and as they set off they heard a dull thud from the boot. Tom Riley's wooden box must have slipped from its strap and was sliding about in there.

'Careful up front,' she said. 'Important cargo back here.'

Ray stuck up a thumb and turned the curve more gently, and before them they saw the forest opening up. Splitting to each side to prepare the wide and open way for them. Like Moses slamming his staff down and revealing the watery passage to the Promised Land.

'Welcome to The Reed Institute,' she said.

And in a whisper, Matt said, '*Holy shit.*'

CHAPTER FORTY

It looked like a giant, concrete mushroom.

That was the first thing he thought of when he first clapped eyes on it. He saw this huge concrete column thrusting up like a single tree trunk from the ground, which eventually started to lean out, with hefty concrete struts open like mighty hands. Held in those thick, grey fingers, three storeys up, was the main building itself. A pyramid of glass and boxes, teetering on top of the column. It was widest at the lowest floor. Smaller for the second, and again for the third. There was a small box at the central tip that looked small enough to be one room. Yep. A giant mushroom made of concrete and glass.

'I've seen something like this before,' he said. 'There's a library in California . . . the erm . . .' he started clicking his fingers, to jog his memory, 'Geisel. That looks like The Geisel.'

She shrugged. 'Whatever it is, it looks fabulous on camera.'

The closer the car got, the more The Reed seemed to be sprouting slowly from the ground. It looked like a multi-storey car park with a futuristic hotel on top, planted within landscape gardens that looked golf-course-lovely and golf-course-fake. Those gardens made the surrounding forest itself look fake. Like the ancient woods were just a modern accessory. An indulgent flourish.

Their eyes were forced upward, the closer they got.

He stepped out to the sound of trickling fountains and birdsong, though he saw no birds. The flurry of tweeting was so busy, clear and constant, that he wondered if there might be hidden speakers somewhere, creating an unreal, retreat centre feel. Maybe he'd hear the flutter of a cheeky pan pipe next, or the solemn cry of a new-age whale—

As soon as he thought that, Tom's stupid box knocked against something again, and Matt span to see that the driver had accidentally clipped it, pulling it from the boot.

'It's fine, it's fine,' the driver said, to all the gawping faces. He carefully passed the box to two waiting crew members and a cameraman. They shared nervous looks and deep breaths before walking it off with annoying looks of reverence. *I should have smashed it open when I had the chance*, Matt thought.

They all watched Baal-Berith glide towards the mushroom, just as the clouds seemed to slow. He heard a cough, so he turned. Nupa stood with a backpack over her shoulder and a case in her hand. She was absolutely beaming. 'Showtime!'

They walked together up the long, landscaped path. The trundle of her wheeled case rattled the ground. Up ahead he saw Kissell, Perry and Claire. They were already standing by the concrete stalk of the mushroom itself. Suddenly, some doors opened, and Matt realised that the stalk was actually a lift shaft. Kissell and the others stepped inside, laughing, then the doors shut over and swallowed them whole.

260

They reached the shaft and waited for the lift. Somewhere he heard a speaker playing 'Amazing Grace' on a saxophone. Classy. The doors opened and they stepped in. There were mirrors on every side. He looked left and waved his hand. Infinite Matt Hunters waved back, with infinite nervous smiles. He stopped waving when he spotted a small white camera tucked up in a high corner.

The lift rumbled up, then it finally opened up into the main building itself. The ground floor – and largest floor – looked like a huge 1980s hotel lobby, with masses of thick red carpet, and gold-chrome floor lamps arched over big-leafed pot plants. A few doors led off into other parts of the building, but most of the walls in here were glass. The place was absolutely swamped with sunlight, yet the low, humming air con made the place feel cool. Or rather, cold, actually. The Reed felt cold.

The demon-possessed hadn't arrived yet, but there were various crew, milling around. They were all dressed in black T-shirts, and most had clipboards and head mics. Every one of them, it seemed, held a little cardboard coffee cup in hand, steam wisping up like ghosts.

Then Ethan appeared in a red lumberjack shirt and big Caterpillar boots at the end of his skinny legs. Jeans turned up at the ankle.

'Hey, Matt, good to see you,' he said. 'Is Abby here yet?'

'I don't think so.'

He sighed, 'Oh well. Let me show you to your room.'

The signs said the lobby was on the ground floor, which felt a little odd seeing as all the views showed them in line with the treetops. His room was on the next floor up, the first. As they headed up in the lift, he assumed his room was going to be jaw-dropping. Some sort of glass-lined platform, worthy of a Bond villain. In fact, he already had his finger on the button of his phone camera, ready to make Wren and the kids jealous with a shot of his luxury lifestyle. But when Ethan opened the door, he didn't bother. The rooms looked like student digs. Simple and nondescript with a green sink in the corner and bricked walls painted yellow.

'Make yourself at home,' Ethan said, then he spun away for other duties.

Matt dumped his bag. Stuck his new toothbrush in the glass by the sink, but he didn't unwrap it. Then after the customary bum bounce on the bed, he had a wander through the claustrophobic corridors that ended with full glass walls overlooking the deep forest. The next floor up, the second, felt a bit smaller, which made sense considering the design. He found a corridor with a few rooms running off it. A storeroom, a toilet, and around the corner, a small chapel. He swung his head in and his nostrils immediately filled with the smell of anointing oil. Anointing folks with oil was an old biblical tradition that was making a comeback these days. He tried it himself once, early in his career, though the bride-to-be had a slight reaction to it. Turns out olive oil was the wrong stuff to use. After cringing at the wedding photographs, Matt had vowed it would be a mistake he would only make once.

The lights in the chapel were off. Just a circle of cushions on the floor, around an unlit candle. He closed the chapel door with a sturdy, two handed pull and found another half-set of stairs that didn't lead to another floor, but to an unseen room, halfway up. He didn't go up, though. The steps were too swamped with hundreds of black worms and grey snakes. Cables and wires, ready to be plugged somewhere. He found the final set of full stairs and trotted up to what must be the top floor, the third, though it could barely be called a floor.

This was the peak of the concrete pyramid, and so it was naturally the smallest. He found only one single door with a glowing keypad. The door said ROOF. It was locked.

Satisfied to have scoped the place, he hopped in the lift and headed back down to the main lobby again, which felt enormous in comparison. He grabbed a passing crew guy and asked where the exorcisms would take place. He was led through some glass doors into a corridor with wires trailing into a set of wooden doors. He stepped over them to find The Ash Suite. A mid-sized auditorium with a stage and a lectern. The huge glass windows had been covered with black screens. Guess they didn't want to let the squirrels, or other prying eyes, see the devilish action taking place in here in a few hours.

He spotted Kissell stepping up on the stage too, squinting up into the stage lights. This was while Perry was nervously watching two guys place Tom's wooden box on a special plinth in the very centre of the stage. As soon as it was in place, a spotlight from above clicked on. The wooden box lit up.

What next? Would Baal-Berith get his own little theme song?

His smile dropped a little, as Lucy came to mind. Maybe he had one already.

Hush little baby, don't say a word . . .

'Impressive venue, isn't it?' It was Nupa, striding up behind him. She was holding a silver flight case.

'It's bigger than I expected. Especially for just a few clients.' Which is when she went quiet and picked up her phone from her pocket, even though it wasn't ringing. 'Excuse me.' She put it to her head, lugging the case towards the stage.

He should have realised then, but for some reason he didn't. He only really understood the crooked smile, when the sun started falling behind the trees. He was sitting alone, back in the lobby area, having an iced tea. He was waiting for the other cars to arrive and had perched himself very near the lift doors. He wanted to be ready to meet Pavel Basa, and Deron Johnson and of course Abby Linh from yesterday. He'd smile and grab them all a drink. He'd ask how they were feeling and he'd make sure they weren't overwhelmed by all of this. But then the lift opened and a complete stranger stepped out. She was holding a little suitcase. Another crew member perhaps? Someone from the press? But then he saw another and another. He kept counting. It was twenty minutes by the time Matt saw someone from his test group yesterday. It was Deron and Pavel, yet they had two strangers with them.

Deron and Pavel waved at Matt, and he waved back awkwardly. But when more started pouring from the lift, Matt slammed his drink down and marched back to the Ash Suite. He found Nupa on all fours in the aisle, pressing a cross of white tape to the carpet.

Matt stared at her.

'What's wrong?'

'You lied to me.'

CHAPTER FORTY-ONE

She looked up, tape in her mouth. 'What is it now?'

He felt an eyebrow shoot up. 'You said the numbers would be low.'

She set the tape aside, then did something odd. She looked across at a crew guy and closed her fingers shut, like she was catching a fly in the air. Then without getting up she said, 'Okay, so we upped the numbers yesterday. I'm sorry you weren't informed, but it's been a busy twenty-four hours. But don't worry, we're well prepared.'

'We agreed that numbers would be low.'

'No.' She raised a finger, and her voice. 'We heard your advice. And we heard Pastor Kissell's advice too. We came to a compromise between those two approaches.'

Matt opened his hands. 'Which is?'

'Remember he had a long waiting list of clients.'

'How many?'

'Don't worry, we've tripled our security team and—'

'Tripled?' He made the sort of groan ill people make; he pressed a hand against the back of his neck. 'Nupa, how many exorcisms are going to happen here tonight?'

She sighed and glanced back at her work. 'Twenty, all right?'

His hand dropped to his side.

'Which we can manage. So can I please get back to it?'

'Twenty?' He waited. Took the figure in. 'Twenty is *way* too many.'

'Like I said, we've tripled—'

'*Why?*' He threw his hands in the air, and noticed some of the crew looking over, and whispering. 'Why do you even have me here, Nupa? If you're not going to take my advice?'

'I told you, the show needs balance.'

'Exactly. And call me old-fashioned, but my balanced opinion is that the last thing the *Titanic* needed was an extra sixteen fucking icebergs. I mean, *come on.*'

'I said the *show* needs balance.'

'Which is precisely why . . .' He trailed off because the realisation sank in. He felt his shoulders drop, with a slow and dawning clarity.

They wanted the *show* to be balanced, yes, but the event itself? The core event of this show? Nope. Yes, the *show* would have clips of the rational point of view, to counter the crazy claims of demonism. Nupa didn't want to be accused of being one-sided. But now she already had her Matt Hunter footage. All those side shots of him expressing his thoughts and cautions. And his crappy set of tests, let's not forget those. There was plenty to edit in, to keep this from being skewed, because unbalanced shows don't get awards.

But the event itself, the mass exorcism? That was where balance got boring. That's when she wanted TV.

He felt, and it was a very real and humiliating feeling, like the old Matt Hunter, all of a sudden. The naive teenager in a church concert hall. Who straight up believed that what the shiny adults told him

266

about heaven and hell and holiness was true. After all, they were such experts and he'd had no exposure to any other world view. He ached at the sheer gullibility. The thought of him being so naive again didn't just embarrass him. It depressed him. It scared him. It made his fingers tremble.

'I'm an idiot,' he said.

'Don't say that. You're vital to this.'

'Then call it all off. Before someone gets hurt.'

'Matt, you're overreacting, and I really need to get on.' She finally went to stand. 'And hey, if it fails, then at least the world will see all your footage of you warning us. You can be Chief Brody, and I'll be the Mayor of Amity.'

Something clicked. He glanced at the whispering crew, hovering by the AV desk, then he looked up at the fixed cameras around the room. For the first time since he'd arrived, they had no red lights on them. He turned back to Nupa. He couldn't be certain, but he was sure he saw it. A smirk, lurking on her lips. 'If you'll excuse me, Matt.'

He watched her turn back to the carpet, and so he did what felt like the most natural option. He slid his phone from his pocket, clicked it into video mode, and held it up high.

Her smile stopped. 'What are you doing?'

He manoeuvred, so he could get both him and Nupa in shot. It felt a little juvenile to do it, but he couldn't think of what else to do. He cleared his throat and spoke.

'This is the late afternoon of The Reed event, it's . . .' he flicked his watch to check, 'just turned 5.14 p.m., and I'm recording this little extra footage, this bonus feature, to make it absolutely clear,' he raised his voice so everybody could hear, 'that I think upping the numbers of this event from around four to twenty is dangerous and irresponsible, and it should have been kept low, which I said from the very beginning. I have only just heard about this number increase and I have strongly advised the show against it. Thank you.'

He clicked it off and turned to her.

'Try and calm down, Matt.' She strolled towards him, arms folded. 'It'd be a shame to lose you, at this stage.' She looked at him for a long moment. 'Especially when I can't spare anyone to take you back.'

He bit the inside of his mouth and couldn't think of what to say. So he just walked out. He thought he'd just head straight for his room to think. Perhaps he could gather up his things, and his stupid new toothbrush (why did it embarrass him so much, buying that especially for this?) and just get back home somehow. Maybe he could message Wren to pick him up. If they ever gave him the Wi-Fi code. If she could ever find this bloody place, this planet.

But he had to pass through the lounge on the way to the lift and that was where he found all these extra clients filling up the plush couches and chairs. They didn't look particularly possessed. They weren't hanging from the chandeliers singing Black Sabbath backwards. They weren't chewing chunks from the sofas with rapidly revolving heads. Some were laughing and sharing tea. Others were cricking their necks to look at the trees that were oh so close to the glass outside. And some were nervously sitting alone, hands folded on their laps like nerds at the dance, wondering what on earth they'd been talked into, just like Matt was wondering himself.

Two of them were hugging, patting each other on the back like this was a pre-op good-luck party. Twenty people, who for one reason or another were no longer sure their body was their own. And yet they had all stumbled across Pastor Kissell on some late-night Internet search. The click had brought them here. Where they could be scared, confused and perhaps even hopeful. Together.

He saw Abby just then. She caught his eye and pushed herself up on tiptoes to wave him over. Wearing jeans and a cool-looking woollen sweater, thick and baggy, she was, as ever, Instagram-ready. Yet her face looked as lost as ever. She was sitting at a table with

Deron and Pavel. All the gang. All the big names. She frowned at Matt, confused at why he was just standing there across the room in a trance. She pulled out a chair and jabbed a finger into the centre of the table. She smiled at him. He saw a plate of chocolate biscuits stacked high.

The lift doors were behind him, and that was where sanity was, he supposed. Abby, and everybody else, was in front of him. And that was where all the human beings were, right now. People who were, perhaps, no more naive than he was. What was he going to do? Walk out, and leave them? Was it wise to allow Kissell and Perry . . . and Nupa, to be the only voices to be heard in this place? Wasn't *that* the most naive idea of all?

Twenty . . . he said to himself and let out a long, jittery sigh. And shaking his head, he trudged towards Abby's table.

CHAPTER FORTY-TWO

'Oh, Matt.' She threw a hug around him, and he felt her bones. 'I was worried you might have skipped it.'

'Nope. Still here.' He smiled and took a seat, nodding a polite hello at the others. 'And how are you all feeling about . . . all this?'

Deron tapped his temple. 'A little nervous, but to be honest . . . I'm ready to evict this loser.' To anyone else, it'd look like he was being hard on himself. But he wasn't. He was being hard on the foreign invader, lurking somewhere underneath that Afro. Which looked wet and glistening today.

'And you, Pavel?'

'We all just want this to be over, Professor.' Pavel shrugged and scratched his arm under his T-shirt. 'But listen. I think we'd all like to say . . . thank you for trying yesterday. With the tests, I mean. It was worth a . . . how do you say it . . . worth a shot?' He raised his

Dr Pepper in a toast. The others did the same. 'You said to consider all angles. Tonight is part of that, no?'

Matt smiled at him, then turned back to Abby. 'And are *you* still sure about being here?'

She opened her mouth, but a voice spoke for her.

'She's even more sure, now.'

They turned to see Bernie Kissell, standing by a pot plant. He was sucking lemonade through a ridiculously long straw. Perry was with him, drink-less. 'May we join you?'

Abby nodded. Pavel twitched. Deron stayed silent.

The pastors sat.

'And why is Abby even more sure, now?' Matt asked.

'Because she knows about the test results, Matt,' Perry said. 'We all do.'

Yippeee. The tests! 'So . . . Nupa told you already?'

'She did,' Abby scooped up her long hair into a super-tight ponytail. 'So I guess you've proved it. It's not just in my head. I can detect hidden holy water at twenty paces.' She tried to laugh.

'Yeah, about that. I've figured out why your test went that way, Abby. I specifically told my students to standardise the temperature of the water. But I—'

'Matt, Matt, Matt . . .' Kissell shook his head with a smirk.

'But I think the holy water could have been just that little bit warmer than the—'

'You're reaching.'

'—warmer than the unblessed water and I take full responsibility. But I think you may have been able to tell the difference, even subconsciously—'

'*Matt.*' Kissell snapped it this time. 'This stunning young lady here is scared and confused . . . don't make it more muddy for her.'

'I'm sorry, that is not my intention. I'm embarrassed, but I still think those results can be ex—'

'Well, hey,' Kissell said. 'Let's not dwell on it now. We're here at this wonderful place. Abby, Pavel and Deron need my help. And so do all these other beautiful people.'

'All twenty of them . . .' Matt's voice was more like a grunt.

'Cheer up, man. It's still not exactly the *multitudes* is it, and look . . .' He opened his palms. 'Nothing up my sleeve.' He pulled his hands back.

Matt stared at him, shaking his head.

'No hard feelings, about yesterday,' Kissell said. 'I forgive you.'

'And I'm sorry too,' Perry said, suddenly. 'I've been tetchy with you, and I think unkind too. I'm not proud of that, Matt.'

Matt sat there wondering if this was a genuine connection here or if it was some sort of spiritual detox. A clearing out of any bitterness or resentment, so he'd be match-ready for an exorcism. He caught Perry's eye and something told him that he might actually mean this.

'Just, be careful tonight,' Matt said. 'Especially with all these extra bodies.'

'We *do* care. Very much.' Kissell said. 'In fact, that's the backbeat of all of this. *Love* . . . that's all that matters in the end. Psychology, culture, religion, history, that's all well and good . . . but it's love, isn't it? That's the pure goal of all things. That's what we're doing here. We're loving people.'

Perry frowned, 'Um . . . don't you mean God? Isn't God the pure goal of all things?'

Kissell rolled his eyes, for an awkward moment. Then he bit his lip. 'Simon . . . love is the goal of all.'

'Yeah but God is more important than love.'

'God *is* love. Remember? 1 John, 4:8.' With a laugh, Kissell put his hand on Perry's arm, 'Gentleman. It's a little late for a theological debate. So, if you'll excuse us. Simon and I need some prayer sleep before we begin. See you all in the Ash Suite at 3 a.m. sharp.'

'Why 3 a.m.?' Abby said.

'Because Jesus died at three in the afternoon,' Perry said, 'which makes three in the morning a prime time for Satan to surface.'

Matt tried not to snort. The logic of these people was off the charts.

'I suggest you all get some rest too.' Kissell rubbed his palms together and stood. 'Three sharp. And just you wait to see the smiles this time tomorrow, wait till you see the *love*. Night, y'all.'

Matt watched the two men cross the room, Kissell whispering into Perry's ear all the way to the lift.

Deron leant into Matt. 'I think you're too hard on the pastors.'

Matt turned back. 'I don't mean to be.'

'Don't you?' Pavel laughed. 'This machine in Kissel's hand...must have been your imagination, no?'

'I don't think so.'

Deron spoke again, 'How could Kissell *not* care, after what happened to Sandra?'

'Sandra . . .' Matt said. 'That's his wife, right?'

'It is . . . and do you know how she died, Matt?'

'An accident. Hit and run.'

Pavel folded his arms and shook his head. 'It was no accident.'

Deron's voice dropped so low, it pumped an ominous throb into everything he said. 'She walked out in the road on purpose.'

'He told you this?'

Pavel nodded. 'Right into the motorway and *blam*. The truck didn't even see her. It hit her dead on. His poor wife . . . murdered.'

'You mean suicide . . .'

'Aren't you listening to us, Professor? Can't you hear what we're saying?' Pavel said.

He shook his head. 'No, I can't.'

'Then listen . . . she was possessed, just like us, and her demon killed her. Why do you think I'm so desperate to get this monster out of me . . . what if I do something I regret one day? I know you care, Professor, in your own way. Kissell cares in his. How

273

could he not, when his wife became a victim of the devil?'

Abby murmured something. It was the first time he'd realised how quiet she'd been these last few minutes. They all looked at her and heard the dull cracking of bones. They looked down at her hands. She was methodically tugging hard at her own fingers.

Click. Click. Click. One by one by one.

'Abby?' Matt said.

Click.

'Abby.' Deron reached for her hand. 'You okay, girl?'

Click. She was staring into the bright bulb of a nearby lamp. 'Right out into the road. Headlights comin'. . .' A low chuckle rolled against her lips.

'Hey!' Deron squeezed her hand, and she finally looked back at them.

'Sorry, what?' she said.

Deron looked at Matt and Pavel and whistled. 'Roll on 3 a.m., right boys?'

Matt leant into Abby. 'Hey. You're still on your meds, aren't you?' He waited. 'Abby?'

She frowned.

'I said you're still taking your medication, aren't you?'

'What time is it?' she said.

Pavel checked his wrist. 'About 8.15 p.m.'

'Then I better go to bed. We all should.' She went to stand. The others too.

'*Are* you taking your pills?'

'Not any more.'

'What?' he stared at her. 'Why not?'

'I want to be clear-headed, for tonight.'

'Tonight is precisely when you *should* take them. Do you have them with you?'

She bit her lip and nodded, eyes drifting.

'Take them. Please.'

'I'll take them, if you do *me* a favour . . .' She put her hand over his and leant her face closer. 'Don't do the thing that you really want to do.'

'Which is?'

'To leave. To go back to your family . . . please stay?' She squeezed his hand softly. 'Goodnight.'

He watched her and the others walking out and noticed some of the crew and other clients stepping aside to let her through. Perhaps word of her test results had done the rounds. People certainly looked at her with a nervous kind of awe. And in her wake, others were getting up too, checking their watches and forcing a yawn. Abby stopped at the lift door and turned to face him, then she waved and mouthed, *Don't leave.*

She turned and collided straight into Ethan, who was swinging around the corner with a headset on. Matt watched them both crash into each other, and Ethan seemed to wobble on his thick white Nikes, but he was grinning from ear to ear. She burst into a teenager's laugh and helped him pick up his clipboard. They seemed to look at each other for a moment, smiling. Then she giggled again and vanished behind the sliding, mirrored door. And yet when she turned back, her smiling face was that same blank mask again.

Alone now, Matt hopped up to help Ethan with the rest of his stuff.

'She's *very* pretty, isn't she?' Ethan said, staring as the lift doors closed. 'For a demon, anyway.'

'I'm worried about her.'

He stood. 'Yeah, well, it'll be over soon. You should get some sleep.'

'Have you got the Wi-Fi password?'

He rummaged in his pocket and pulled out a tiny card. Matt snapped a shot of it on his phone.

'See you later, alligator.' Ethan headed off with a wave.

Matt suddenly found himself alone in the huge lobby, and the only real movement came from all the frantic trees waving at the windows. They looked like they were eager to join the party in here. At least he *thought* he was alone, until he walked towards the lift and passed an armchair. From the corner of his eye, he saw a figure sitting in it, as silent as a shadow.

He was about to blink it away as usual. Just another old dead friend come to say hi, but just as he walked on the shadow spoke.

'Do you like me, Professor?'

Matt spun, and his face crunched in confusion. 'What are *you* doing here?'

CHAPTER FORTY-THREE

It was Mr Muscle. Richie Gregor, sitting there in a black tracksuit, man-spreading with both of his hands plunged into a hoody. He was watching Matt from under the rim of his baseball cap. Lips wet. Matt wondered why.

'Richie, I don't understand.'

'What don't you understand?'

'Why are you here . . . I thought you were better?'

'Better how?'

'The exorcism in the university?'

He blinked slowly, pecs bulging.

'In the toilets, remember? You said you were cured?'

He started to nod. 'I was.'

Matt looked left and right; the lobby seemed much, much bigger when it was empty. 'So why are you here?'

Richie sat up a little straighter. His Viking chest filled with air. 'My demon came back. The pastors said I need a little more work. That's all.'

Matt sighed. 'And I'm afraid it'll keep coming back, until you get proper help.'

'This *is* proper help.' He slid those hulk hands of his out from his hoodie and placed them on his knees. He could probably crush boulders with those.

Matt figured it'd be best to not be alone with him. 'Well, if this doesn't work out, call me. I'll get you that counselling I mentioned. But I better get going, okay?'

'Do you like me?'

'Pardon?'

'I said, do you like me?'

'Um . . . I don't really know you.'

'Do you like me now?' He smiled very widely, and Matt wished he would stop. He looked around again, still empty, still just him and Richie. 'You didn't like me at the TV studio, Professor. You didn't like me at the test but—'

'I never said I didn't like—'

'But do you like me, now?' Lips started to peel further back. Showing more teeth than any sane smile should.

Matt swallowed. 'Yeah, you're great.'

Richie's thick face bloomed, like a strongman who'd found a pretty flower. For the first time, he looked normal again. And pleasant with it. But then he lifted his fingers to his nose and smelt the tips for a few seconds. 'I'm glad you like me.'

Matt smiled, or at least he tried to. 'Well, if you'll excuse me.'

'See you later, alligator . . .'

Matt turned and walked at pace through the empty lobby, and he had that horrible notion that Richie was coming up behind him the entire way. One, maybe two footfalls behind. Though

278

Matt dared not turn. He entered the lift, with that persistent *thump-thump* inside his head. He turned to brace himself, but Richie hadn't followed him at all. He was still sat there in that high-backed armchair all alone, still talking to the air and looking up from under his cap. As if Matt had never left.

With a genuine shiver, Matt jabbed the button and the mirrored doors slid shut. Breath returned as he headed up. His corridor was eerily empty, and he passed rooms that housed either crew members or demoniacs, settling down for a nap. Dammit, Nupa. Why didn't they have stickers on the doors of the possessed? The puking emoji, maybe. Or a biohazard sign.

When he got to his room, he closed the door behind him, and noticed something he hadn't spotted before. There were no locks on the door. *What?* His arms prickled. Such a simple security oversight from Nupa and her crew. He wondered what others they'd skipped over. The lack of a lock made him decide to sleep in his clothes, even though the room was clammy and hot, with no sign of air con. In fact, he'd not bother with sleep at all. He'd just lie on the bed and keep an eye on the door. He wasn't quite elderly yet after all, and he'd pulled all-nighters before.

The fluorescent light panel above him was harsh, and Matt didn't like seeing a familiar-looking silhouette of a fly walking in circles on the plastic. So he tapped the switch by the door, and darkness came. There was no bedside lamp. He climbed onto the bed, kicking the overly thick duvet into a mountain at his feet. He lay there as the minutes clicked by and tapped the Wi-Fi password into his phone. The mobile connection here was still non-existent, and the Wi-Fi signal looked abysmal. He tried watching some videos of people falling over or squirrels riding skateboards, but the signal was too weak for even the first frame. But still, it seemed, a signal was there. He set the phone to the side and waited.

The door. It hovered there, like a creamy-coloured box in the shadows. The lack of a lock was making him picture glassy-eyed strangers, dragging bare feet along the corridor and then stopping, so they might turn that handle slowly. He thought of Richie, sniffing his fingers and coming up in the lift.

'Nope,' Matt said, and promptly slipped off the bed. He dragged the small wooden chair that sat at the desk and shoved it under the door handle. Satisfied it was secure, he climbed back into bed. Sweltering in the heat, he unbuttoned his shirt, and almost fell asleep when the phone suddenly lit up the room.

An email, from DS Fenn.

I looked into Claire Perry's car. It was definitely in Sneddon on the afternoon of the murder, but brace yourself . . . we've found CCTV footage of her meeting with Tom Riley, in the park. Something's fishy but I'm not sure what. I've been told she's up at The Reed with you all. Keep an eye on her. When you get back I'll pay her another visit. Cheers. Martin. (PS. TOLD YOU SHE GAVE ME THE CREEPS!)

Matt leapt in a spasm when the fly's spiky legs landed on his chest and scuttled at speed across his body. But when he jerked up and slapped at himself he couldn't find a fly anywhere. Which wasn't helping at all.

CHAPTER FORTY-FOUR

Turns out Matt Hunter was elderly after all, because sleep did come, in the end. The last few days of craziness had finally caught up. And closing his eyes brought a very strange dream with it. Matt dreamt that he was lying right here in this odd, stuffy room, only now the bed sheet was completely off him. He lay exposed, in nothing but his boxer shorts, with one arm lolling off the side, and he was listening to someone sing to him. It was Lucy, his stepdaughter, humming a melody from somewhere in the shadows.

It was nice to hear her, and he really wanted to call her name, but his back was locked to the bed. Each time he murmured a sleepy groan she just said *shhhhhhh* and carried on with her strange song. This dream went on for some time, and the only moment it changed was when Lucy stepped out of the shadows into a very dull pocket of moonlight from the window.

Then it wasn't Lucy's voice at all, but the bizarrely low and raspy whisper of Tom Riley. And Richie Gregor and . . . and Ian Pendle too. Fancy that. The schizophrenic lip-eater who murdered Matt's mum. Those three male voices rolled together effortlessly. As if they had always been one single voice all along. Which turned the room exceedingly cold. The man's voice was talking about what it was like to kill a woman. How thrilling it was to chew through lips and tongue. His voice sounded like a fly's voice might, if it ever learnt speech.

So he decided to tell the strange dream figure to go away.

'Go away . . .'

But when he spoke the words in the dream, he heard them in real life. Because he was, it turns out, awake. And he'd been half-awake before.

When he strained his eyes fully open, he saw a figure, not far from the bed, and it moved.

Matt's limbs shot out in a scramble backwards. He felt his bare back slap against the yellow brick wall. Loud and cold enough to make him know, beyond doubt, that this was real.

There was a figure in his room and it was covered in a white sheet. *His* white bed sheet, that now left him bare. Wait . . . bare? . . . Why were his trousers off? Did he kick them off in the heat? The quilt itself and his trousers were gone, and the chair lay upturned on the floor. The one he'd wedged under the door handle a few hours before.

The figure, standing like a cheap, fancy dress ghost, was swaying. Matt dragged a pillow over himself. As if that might protect him. 'What do you want?' he said, and his voice sounded deeply pathetic.

It just swayed a little more in the moonlight and also . . . yes . . . yes . . . he could see it now. The material was trembling at the face, just under what must have been the subtle jut of the nose. Where the mouth must be. Something was making the material flutter. Whispers perhaps.

282

It's the flicking of an unseen tongue.

'Hey . . .' Matt went for a strict parent mode whisper. 'What are you doing in my room? Who are you?'

The sheet rattled more frantically and a very low moan came back. It sounded like a man. Surely this was too small and skinny for Richie? Was this . . . was this Ethan?

'Get out of my room, right now. Or I'll . . .' he trailed off. Or what, Matt? What will you do? The guy could have a knife under there. Are you going to pillow-fight him to death, or maybe grab the chair and—

Shit . . .

The figure was changing. The material was being sucked and gathered into fingers, as they tugged the material . . . downwards. He heard the very low hiss of the sheet sliding up the man's back, towards his head. Going slowly (so *damn* slowly) up and up and up his spine. Matt wanted to call out for help, but some deep wisdom said, don't do that. Shouting's going to set this guy off.

Matt frantically looked around for a weapon. Now, why didn't retreat centres come with Samurai swords? All he saw was a half-filled glass of water. That'd have to do. He grabbed it and tried to figure out a plan in as cold and dispassionate a way as possible. Where on the head should he smack this glass? How about right into the temple? That seemed good. That should disorientate the weirdo long enough to get past him and run.

He knew it wasn't Ethan when he saw the tuft of long black hair spring out from under the sheet, and then as the sheet fell, her face emerged, eyes staring, mouth moving.

His voice came out as a gasp. Then, setting the glass down, he glanced at the door and back again. '*Abby?* What are you doing?'

Her whispers kept rolling, rhythmic, a mantra, the ocean.

'Abby!' he snapped, then he slapped his hands together in a clap.

The sheet dropped completely to the floor. She was standing in her

283

flannel pyjamas of pink tartan doing something exceedingly strange. She was leaning forward, awkwardly. Now free of the material, she kept curling her wrists, sometimes forwards, sometimes backwards, so that her fingers and hands were turning and swirling.

He immediately recognised the movement. He'd seen it in some security footage that went viral a few years back. A troubled Cantonese woman in a hotel lift, Elisa Lam. She was last seen curling her wrists *exactly* like this, staring at someone unseen through the lift doors. Then she went missing. A couple of weeks later, hotel guests complained about their tap water looking black and tasting vile. They found Elisa's naked corpse in the water tank, up on the roof. She'd suffered from bipolar, but of course the Internet was convinced she was possessed.

Had Abby seen this video too? Had she presumed this was how possessed people act? An unhelpful, sleepy voice (that lacked the logic of morning light) whispered in his head, *Or is she just possessed by the same demon as Elisa Lan was . . .*

'Whoa . . .' He shook his head. 'Don't do that.'

She'd pulled her still twirling hands back and had started to tug at the top button of her pyjama top. She mumbled, 'Where's Pavel?'

'Huh?'

'Where's Pavel?' She started smirking. The top button popped open and her strange, undulating fingers immediately moved to the next one down. 'Where's Pavel?'

'That's enough.' Matt's bare feet hit the hot floor.

'Where's Pavel?' Another button pinged open. 'With the cows, perhaps?' Her chuckle chilled him.

'Stop it.' He pushed past her, and the narrow room meant his arm slid past hers. It dragged her pyjama top down a little. Her bare shoulder gleamed in the moonlight.

She raised her free hand up to her face and it was so strange. She let her hand revolve against her mouth. She laughed through her moving, spinning fingers. 'Where in the earth is Pavel?'

Not where *on* the earth . . . where *in* the earth.

Matt had to step over the strewn chair. He turned back to see her, and just like Richie before, exactly like him in fact, she was still just standing there, talking to the bed as if Matt was still in it. Laughing, and moving down to the next button. Her other sleek shoulder now uncovered. 'Do you like me, Professor?'

'Abby, please, you need to leave.' He yanked his door open. 'Now come—'

Ethan was standing in the corridor, yawning with one arm held up and ready to knock. He wore Pokémon pyjamas, so that fifty screaming Pikachus were all over his body. 'What's all the rack—' He saw Abby, standing by the bed, and snapped suddenly awake. Ethan's goggled eyes skipped from Abby to Matt, who stood there in the doorway looking mortified, in nothing more than his boxers.

Ethan's mouth flatlined. 'Plot twist.'

'You misunderstand.'

'Oh, do I?' He bit the inside of his mouth, in anger. 'Yeah, thanks Matt. Thanks a lot.'

'Hey, wait—'

'No, you wait. Wait till I tell Nupa.'

'Seriously, she just came in and . . .' He trailed off. 'Wait. Where's Pavel's room?'

'Who?'

'Pavel Basa. The Romanian guy in his twenties? From the tests yesterday?'

He shook his head. 'You're *married*.'

'Dammit. Pavel Basa. The erection in the abattoir guy? Bald?'

Ethan kept looking over Matt's shoulder. 'What about him?'

'We should check he's okay.'

Ethan wasn't listening, but his eyebrow was rising. 'What's she *doing* in there?'

'Sleepwalking, I think.' Matt turned and saw her still working down her buttons. He grabbed a shirt and trousers from the cabinet. By the time he was tugging them on, Ethan was already filming her on his phone. 'We need this.'

Matt glared at him. 'Don't do that. Jeez.'

'Relax. I'm not filming you.'

'*Still don't.*' Matt put a hand against the phone. 'I think she's asleep. Now let's check on Pavel. Okay?'

Matt stepped into his shoes and turned back to his room; Abby was still in her trance. Only now, it looked like her pyjama top was hanging fully open, though he couldn't see. She started climbing onto the bed, face first, beautiful hair hanging. The sound of her laughing did not sound like a young woman at all. It was as if there was a pervy old man sitting in the corner in there. Some filthy old cockney called Frank, who smoked a lot and drank ten pints each night and was rubbing his knees right now. If *that* guy was in this room, laughing right now, he'd believe it. Throwing his voice into hers.

'Abby,' Matt shouted at her. 'Wake up!'

She moaned and buried her face into Matt's cushion. When she pushed her hips into the mattress, he turned away.

'Ethan. Snap out of it. Come on. And radio your security guys. See if they've got any footage of Pavel.' They started heading down the corridor, where other doors were now opening. Other sleepy heads were slowly craning out, squinting like moles in the light.

'We're looking for Pavel Basa. Does anybody know which room he's in?'

He checked his watch as they went.

It was just after 1 a.m.

CHAPTER FORTY-FIVE

It turned out that there were a *lot* of Kissell's clients staying in Matt's corridor. In fact, it rather looked like he'd been slotted into the 'possessed' tier, thank you very much, while the rest of the unpossessed crew had joined Kissell in the floor above. As Matt started knocking on the doors, calling out for Pavel, more strangers came stumbling and yawning from their rooms, scratching their heads.

Deron Johnson came out wearing nothing but what looked like white speedos and a pair of golden-coloured flip-flops. Impressively, his chest had about three times more Afro than his head. 'You're looking for Pavel?'

'Yes. Do you know his room number?'

He scratched the curve of his hairy gut and shook his head. 'I'll message him . . .' He leant behind the door and came back with a tiny-looking phone. But he frowned and held it up in the air. 'Wi-Fi's gone.'

Matt checked his, and it was the same. He looked across the corridor and saw others doing replica forehead crunches at their own phones. 'Has *anybody* got reception?'

A smattering of shrugs and shaking heads followed.

Into all this, Kissell himself appeared. He came around the corner in his long and red silky dressing gown, or rather he swung around the corner, with a blatant sense of 'ta-dah!' He tapped his glasses into place and stood to attention, hands clasped behind his back. Bare feet in tan leather slippers. Some seemed to relax at his arrival. He was, after all, the spiritual leader with all the answers. But others broke out into their predictable demonic twitches. It was like possession was an allergy, and Bernie Kissell was a fistful of butt hair from a dog, stuffed right into their faces.

Kissell unclasped his hands and swung his skinny hairless legs in a march up to Matt, tying his dressing gown cord tight as he went. 'I am here to help, reporting for duty.'

'Okay,' Matt said. 'Then we're looking for—'

'Pavel, I heard. How about we—'

Everybody froze when Ethan's radio squelched. A voice fizzed in the speaker. 'Ethan? You there, bud?'

'Go ahead.'

'We've checked the cameras. We've got Mr Basa walking towards the woods in his pyjamas. That was about an hour ago. Hasn't come back since.'

'Shit, *shit*.' Ethan started pacing, hand lost in his silver quiff. 'We need to get him back. I'm coming down.'

'Good idea. I'll get Simon and pray.' Kissell swung around and the swirl of air lifted his thin gown, flashing both of his bony kneecaps. Not exactly Marilyn Monroe on a New York street vent. Matt followed Ethan to the lift and so did Deron, who didn't bother grabbing any clothes. Deron wedged himself next to Matt in the lift. Speedos and flip-flops. What an outfit.

'Shouldn't you get dressed?' Matt said.

Deron blinked at that, and just kept staring at his own reflection all the way down. He seemed to periodically frown at himself, like there was some other naked black guy staring back at him. Who looked like him, but wasn't him.

When the doors finally slid open, the night breeze rushed against them and he and Ethan stepped out into it. Deron, however, didn't move. He stayed standing in the lift, even as the doors closed over. Matt and Ethan shared a confused glance but said nothing. Odd behaviour wasn't statistically odd, around here.

A long pathway led to the boating lake. A perfect, unnatural circle of water, gouged by bulldozers from the ground. Around it, Matt saw the forest. The tips of the trees looked like black knives, dragging across the dark belly of the sky. The normally silent woods were now punctuated with the regular shouts of 'Pavel' from the security guys, already searching out there.

Matt and Ethan, still in his pyjamas, jogged down the pathway, and joined the others in the woods. But after a while searching, twigs cracking underfoot, they both found themselves back at the lake. They saw two little boats bobbing on the water, just black shadows against the rippled, reflected moon.

'Maybe this was all just too much for him,' Matt said. 'Maybe he just ran away.'

'Maybe . . .' Ethan pulled a torch from his pocket and flicked it on. The white beam danced across the still, silent water. Apart from the occasional bubble of air from an insomniac fish, there was nothing. 'Unless . . .'

'Unless what?'

'Unless he's under that water.' He clicked the beam off. 'Matt . . . ?'

'Yeah.'

'Are you and Abby a thing?'

'What? No. Absolutely not.'

'She really just turned up in your room?'

'Yes. Why? Do you really like her?'

'Course I do, she's stunning.'

'Do you know she has a son?'

'So? I don't mind . . . it's not just her looks, though . . .' He shrugged. 'I feel really sorry for her.'

'Me too.' Matt stared at the water. 'For all of them.'

A sudden shout made them both jump. A figure back at The Reed was leaning out of the lobby window, with hands cupped around their mouth. 'You two, back inside.' It was Nupa.

Matt looked back towards the woods, and saw the torchlight from the others flashing between the tree trunks. Scientists hunting down the misunderstood alien in *ET*.

'God, I hope they find him,' Ethan said, then he hurried back.

Before he turned, Matt noticed the moon, trapped in the surface of the water, while the forest kept calling that name, echoing up into the night.

Pavel, Pavel Basa? Pavel?

Matt turned and jogged back.

It was 2 a.m.

CHAPTER FORTY-SIX

Back in the lobby area, he saw a large crowd gathered. Most of them were Kissell's clients, and they were looking very twitchy indeed. Some of them, Matt noticed, kept skipping their eyes from one corner of the room to the other. One woman was chewing her fingernails with a rat-like enthusiasm. That was not a pleasant thing to witness, at all.

Deron Johnson was there too, and he was finally dressed. In fact, he'd dressed *up*, with a black T-shirt, black blazer and a velvety blue scarf hanging from his neck. He'd exchanged his flip-flops for trainers, and was pacing those Vans back and forth, mumbling to himself, or rather *at* himself. A few of them caught Matt's gaze and shrank away from him. Others narrowed their eyes.

The entire atmosphere was . . . he grabbed the best word he could think of . . . edgy. Like a boiling pan of tension, bubbling

291

under the lid. And where was Nupa? Best to look for her first. He turned to head back to the lift when he felt a heavy hand clamp onto his shoulder. Oh great. It was Richie Gregor in his baseball cap. 'She's crying. Did you know that?' he said.

'Who is?' Matt turned.

'She's crying, look.' Richie pointed to Abby in a nearby armchair. She'd changed clothes and was now fully dressed. She had that same ruffled white gypsy top she'd worn in the TV studio, and jeans. She was barefoot. Kissell and Perry were on either side of her, both in full dog collars, hands on her shoulders in prayer. The others sat around her, or were cross-legged at her feet, staring up at her face. In fact, everyone in here seemed to look at her.

'Abby?' Matt said. 'Where's Pavel?'

Perry flicked his head back and walked over, fast. 'Can't you see she's upset? And I wonder *why*, Matt?'

'What's that supposed to mean?'

'She's young, she's vulnerable, and you had her in your *room* tonight?'

The eyes of the crowd seemed to flash at that, in delight. One of them started moaning.

'Wait . . . what?' Matt shook his head. 'She just came in.'

'Oh really?' Perry said.

'Did you touch her?' A voice from the crowd. And then an eager moan that turned into groans. This was crazy. This was getting out of hand. Where the hell was Nupa? Matt took a step backwards towards the lift. He felt his back slam into Richie's chest.

Crap.

'Who knows, Professor?' Perry glanced down at Matt's crotch. 'Maybe you've got a demon of your own, coiled down there.'

'Shut up,' Matt said. 'Abby? Tell them.'

She looked up finally, wiping a tear from her cheek. 'I'm sorry. I don't remember. I just woke up in your bed.'

Perry smirked, 'Did you hear that everybody?'

Matt leant closer to Perry and whispered, 'Stop. Seriously. You're riling them up. They're not stable.'

Kissell wasn't saying much, but his eyes kept springing from person to person. He looked pretty nervous. But when he caught Matt's eye, he seemed to snap into life. He brought the moment into focus with a single clap of his hands. 'Enough!' His tone was loud, deep and final. 'We are getting distracted from the task here. Matt is right, things are losing stability. So let me tell you what we need to do.' Kissell quickly checked his watch. 'I'm bringing the exorcism forward.'

'What?' Matt tried to ignore the sudden hiss of busy, excited whispers from the others. 'We have to call it off. Pavel's missing—'

'No. We do it right now,' Kissell said. 'Pavel must have run away and now he won't be healed. So we need to help these people who are still here, before they run too.'

'What if they want to go? What if they're scared? And where's Nupa?'

'Here,' she called out from across the room.

He turned to see her standing by the glass doors. The doors that led to the Ash Suite corridor. Maybe it was his imagination, or maybe she was tired. But Matt could have sworn she looked more rattled than he'd ever seen her before. She'd kept her distance from the group, and she had her arms folded – her gaze shifting from one possessed person to the next. 'I think we better do as Bernie says. Let's just get this done.'

'You heard the lady,' Kissell shouted. 'Let's go!'

He started shepherding them towards the doors and Perry grabbed Abby's hand to pull her with him. Matt went to speak to her, but Richie's massive hand shoved his shoulder back. 'Let the lady through.'

'Please, all of you.' Matt set his shoulders back. 'This is making things worse.'

Abby's sobbing voice broke through everything. 'We just want it to stop. We're so tired . . .' She let herself be dragged away by Richie and Perry, just as Kissell rushed up to her and put a hand on her forehead.

'Don't worry. It'll end tonight,' Kissell said. 'Now feel the power of God!'

Abby's head and shoulders suddenly jerked.

The crowd gasped.

'Do you feel him, Abby?' Kissell had the nod of an eager dog. 'Do you feel the Holy Spirit?'

Tears rolled through her squinted eyes. She nodded and jerked again under his hand. 'I feel it. I *feel* it.'

'Then let your hope rise, everybody. Let freedom ring! Let's finish this! Love wins!'

Kissell swept through the noisy crowd, putting his hands on their shoulders and arms and heads and with each touch every single one of them jerked and spasmed. Matt saw their faces warping from smiling hope to agonised fear, and then back again. The whole time, Perry and Richie just kept herding them like livestock towards the double doors, heading to the hall. Kissell reached the doors and stood like a rock in a stream, touching them and letting them jerk under his fingers as they swept eagerly around him.

Which was when Matt buried both hands into his hair, because it was so shocking and yet so, so predictable.

'Take them in.' Kissell's voice was victorious. 'They'll be free soon.'

As the crowd started to vanish through the doors, Matt rushed to Kissell and yanked his arm to the side.

'Get off him, you heretic,' someone shouted.

Even Ethan's mouth dropped. 'Matt. Calm down. Let him be.'

Matt ignored him and shoved Kissell against the wall.

'What the fuck?' Ethan gasped.

Whispering into Kissell's ear with a desperate, rattled, frightened breath, Matt said, 'What are you doing?'

'I'm helping.'

'What are you *doing?*'

'I'm setting the captives—'

'Dammit. I *saw* it. Do you hear me? I just saw it in your hand. Now stop this—'

Hands, many hands, started dragging Matt off, though he couldn't see whose they were.

'I'm helping, Matt, you'll see,' Kissell said, but there was a flash of fear there.

Perry shouted to the few members of the crew. 'Keep the professor out of the hall.' Then he whispered to Matt, 'I really hoped you'd see this. I hoped you might believe.'

The moment was so mad, so insane, that Matt supposed his own repeated shouting simply blended with the madness. And no amount of him calling it was ever going to stop them now. Even the crew, even Nupa, seemed oblivious to Matt's ranting. Because after all, this was the moment. This was the TV first. The mass exorcism. This was the spectacle that this entire show had all been hurtling towards like a plane with no pilot. Still though, he felt a deep and profound coldness inside him when he saw them doing Kissell's bidding. The exorcist and the possessed and, bolted to the walls, the watchers of the possessed, safe at home. Everyone as eager as each other to get into that room, where Tom Riley's box was calling the world.

So all he could do was to keep shouting it, as vain as it was, as they disappeared into the hall. He just kept shouting it for Abby, for Deron, for all of them, for the cameras, for himself and his throat raged with pain with the loudness of it.

'Check his hand. Check it! This isn't real. Check Kissell's hand!'

CHAPTER FORTY-SEVEN

He was parched from all the shouting. Like, crawling-through-the-desert, lick-tears-off-the-floor level parched. So the first thing he did after they all vanished into the Ash Suite was to grab a mug in the now deserted lobby. He shoved it under the coffee machine and jabbed the choco-milk button. He listened to it gurgle and spit. Every few moments he'd snap his head over his shoulders, mostly whenever a crackle of the machine sounded like the nearby footfall of a pissed off demoniac.

As he glugged it down, all alone, his eyes flicked from corner to corner, from door handle to plant pot, and especially to all the big sofas that could easily hide . . . a croucher.

Then he heard it start. The muffled wailing. The moan of the possessed, in the next room, which was punctured every now and then with a chilling, drink-spilling scream. They sounded like they were all falling down into very deep and bottomless holes.

He paced the floor, glugging, wondering what the hell he should do. Wishing he'd driven here by himself because he could taste the buzz of violence in the air. The sheer throb of unpredictability. He considered just holding up in his own room, but with no locks on the door what was the point? Maybe if he found somebody to drive him home. Or heck, maybe grab some keys and steal a car . . . leave them all to it.

Crap.

He felt that inconvenient throb of guilt. Duty of care, and all that.

And besides . . . what if Kissell was right? What if this ridiculous placebo ritual might actually calm these folks down, until morning at least?

At one point, curiosity got the better of him, and he crept up to the doors to the Ash Suite corridor. Those glass doors must have been pretty thick too, because pushing them open just a tiny crack brought the wailing groans to eye-wincing levels. Two security guys were in the corridor inside, standing watch at the thick wooden doors that led into the hall. They looked like bouncers in the wildest nightclub on the planet. Both looked jumpy. Both looked white-faced. And both looked like they wished they'd never said yes to this job, guarding the gates of hell.

One of them caught his eye. 'Mate. You shouldn't be here.' A message to himself, perhaps.

'Relax. I'm going, I'm going.'

Matt let the glass door close, and found himself back in the lobby, still unsure what to do. He figured he might be the only person left who was still worrying about Pavel, so maybe he should head down in the lift again. Go looking for him. Or better yet, just head down in the lift and get the hell away from this place. He'd decide at the bottom. So he pressed the button, and the lift doors immediately slid open.

A rabbit hopped out.

A *black* rabbit.

It was like the world paused. Like he couldn't do anything else but become a slack-jawed mannequin smelling the dirt it had tramped in with it. It was, after all, Matt's nightmare animal of choice. Rabbits had been clawing across his psyche ever since that dreadful time in Menham, south London, though at least this time, it wasn't standing tall, like a man. But he still staggered back when he saw it. In fact, he felt his knees buckle and he hit a chair and landed hard into it. He heard the air of the leather cushion puff out in a sly, swift hiss. Though it could have been the rabbit, hissing words to him. His mind rabbits often did such things.

Slumped in the chair, he watched the black rabbit start to creep along the carpet towards him and then it stopped to twitch its nose and look around. The room span with a massive internal collision of logic. This was no big deal, technically speaking. There were probably lots of rabbits in the woods, and this one just sprang into an open lift, and that's that. Bet it happened all the time.

It sat up on its hind legs. Wow, it was big and—

It's a hare, Matt. It's a hare.

—it was twitching and tilting its large, stiffening ear towards the sounds of lament. How eager and content it looked. How well nourished it was, by the sounds of pain.

It flicked its head at Matt. And sniffed. In the other room, he heard a dozen people call out the name Baal-Berith in unison.

Click.

The rabbit broke into a mad gallop towards him.

Matt leapt off the chair and ran. Across the room, in the other direction, feet pounding the carpet. Conscious of his reflection in the glass, but not wanting to look at it. Not wanting to see the pursuer growing tall.

Until his shoes clipped a pot plant and Matt thought . . . what the hell are you doing?

He locked his knees and staggered to a panting stop.

It's a rabbit, ya big dope. It's Bugs Friggin' Bunny. He turned and saw the rabbit hadn't followed him after all. It was over by the reception desk, burrowing its nose into a strewn pack of crisps, near the glass doors to the dining hall.

See? Matt . . . *see?* You can let your heart rate drop back to—

A figure was watching him through the glass doors.

Matt swallowed. Hard.

The figure saw him looking, and now it spun around to step back and he knew who it was on the turn. Because the light seemed to catch her short little haircut, and he wondered if she'd been watching him the whole time. Or had she been watching the rabbit instead? Either way, he saw Claire Perry, eyes raw as if she'd been crying, turning away and vanishing into the dining room.

And then the rabbit was gone too. Hopped off behind a couch no doubt, or it had burrowed back into the deep folds of his subconscious. As if it was never really there in the first place. Still, as he went after Claire, he could smell it in the air. The soil.

CHAPTER FORTY-EIGHT

Matt followed the corridor around to the dining hall. The lights were off in there. He heard nothing but the low buzz of a vending machine which threw a dull glow across the dark room. The only other light was the tiny blip of red from the static cameras they'd placed in here. Funny, he thought, he'd totally forgotten about those being—

Crap, crap, CRAP!

A sudden crashing realisation made him cringe, and he saw a prophetic vision quite vividly. Of the show being finally broadcast, and people on their sofas slapping each other and laughing, as they watched him spasm in fright and run for his life from a harmless, oversized, and possibly even invisible rabbit.

His sigh sounded like an airbed deflating.

Focus.

Like most of the public spaces at The Reed, the dining hall was surrounded with glass walls. So with the lights off, the usual internal reflections on the glass were gone. He could see the dark forest outside clearly now. The branches were no longer swaying. Actually, the trees were as still as a painting. So strange. He would have dearly liked to have switched the lights on in here, but something said it might be better if he didn't. Better to lay low.

Something caught his eye.

He turned his head to the far corner of the hall, and immediately dropped into a crouch. A thin line of light was spilling from under a door. The kitchen, he remembered. He'd been in there earlier looking for a fork, because they gave him a slice of carrot cake with a spoon. A bloody *spoon*. He should have known these guys were totally unprepared for this when they thought that was kosher.

He moved across the dining hall, eyes becoming accustomed to the darkness, and he spotted something odd as he went. There was a long table that he hadn't seen before, filled with neat rows of bottles of . . . he squinted and confirmed it . . . of champagne. Alongside them sat an entire fleet of crystal glasses, ready to be filled and clinked. Next to them, white sheets were draped over unseen bumps and bulges. Body-shaped, he thought, and for an icy moment he wondered if that might be Abby again, doing her pound-shop ghost routine. No, he told himself, those were bowls of crisps and nibbles.

A breeze rippled the sheet.

He sped up the pace and put a hand against the kitchen door, deciding that even if she wasn't in here, it didn't matter. While he was here he'd grab a rolling pin. Or a meat hammer or a plain old knife, in case things' kicked off.

She was in there all right, alone. As the door swung in, she sucked in a swift breath and pushed herself up from a table like she was trying to get away. She saw him and froze halfway up. For a second she was a strange photographic tableau of a pasty-faced pixie surrounded by stainless steel. He saw a half-finished glass of milk and a jug. Her cheeks looked raw.

'Wait,' Matt said. 'Don't go.'

Claire Perry hovered for a while, one hand splayed against the metal table.

'You've been crying.' He took another step.

'Leave me alone.'

'You were watching me.'

She said nothing. Another tear fell. She sank back into the chair.

'Claire, what is it?'

'Maybe I should have listened to Simon and not come.'

He went to sit, keeping one eye on the door. 'Why *did* you come?'

She pressed her milk to her lip and spoke into the glass. 'To offer support . . . to be a good wife.' That made her chuckle for some reason, but the milk drowned the laugh.

'What's so funny?'

'Cos I'm not a good wife . . . I'm not a good person.'

He noticed her other hand was on her knee, unseen. He was eager to see what might be in that hand. But a subtle lean back found nothing. Nothing obvious, anyway.

'What if demons are way better at hiding than we think?' She looked at him. For a moment, they were a doll's eyes. 'What if demons are all bundled up and bedded down where you least expect them?'

He let his eyes scan the room and spotted knives stuck to a magnetic strip on the wall. None were missing. 'Claire. Were you in Sneddon on the day of the murder?'

The odd smile vanished; her breath caught.

'And did you meet with Tom Riley?'

She whispered it. 'How did you know?'

'You should clean your car out more.' He saw her frown. 'The car park ticket?'

302

She closed her eyes.

'Why did you see him . . . and why did you lie?'

'Cos I'm selfish. Cos, I'm cold. It's my fault she died . . .'

'You mean, Justine?'

A sob escaped her mouth.

'Talk to me, Claire.'

'Tom wasn't himself . . . so we can't really blame him . . . but me . . . I wasn't possessed, was I? I could have chosen the right thing. The good thing . . . but I didn't. I did what was right for me . . .'

He leant forward, though he wasn't keen to get too close. 'What are you telling me?'

A sudden flurry of noise made her look towards the door, and he looked too. A totally unexpected sound was filling the dining hall. Laughter. Hearty and jubilant, laughter. Not just one voice, but many.

'Finally.' She pushed herself up.

'Wait. We need to talk.'

'Sounds like it's over.'

'Claire,' he put a hand on her wrist. It felt cold and dry. 'Why is it your fault she died?'

A voice boomed from the dining hall, loudly praising God. Simon Perry.

'Shhhhhh.' She pressed a hard finger of panic against Matt's mouth, crushing his lips. Then she walked to the kitchen door. But she paused with her fingers on the handle and turned back. 'Did you really like my art?'

He nodded. 'Very much.'

She smiled, only this one didn't disturb him. It broke his heart. He saw another tear roll down her cheek, and then she smeared it with her palm and nodded at him. Then she was gone through the kitchen door, vanishing into a cloud of laughter.

He went to follow her, but he slowed his step for a moment.

He didn't like the idea of it, but he did it anyway. He leant towards the magnetic strip and grabbed a short stubby knife. Something he could wrap in a little kitchen roll. Something to dull the edge. That way, it wouldn't cut one of his balls off when he sat down. He slipped it into his pocket, just in case.

He jumped when a huge roaring cheer lit up the hall outside, and Matt frowned when he heard music start.

You're kidding me.

'We Are Family' by Sister Sledge.

'That proves it, Jeff, I'm going nuts.' Matt said it aloud to his therapist, who was just as silent when invisible as when he was actually in the room. Then he slipped the kitchen roll-covered knife into his front trouser pocket and headed through the kitchen door.

CHAPTER FORTY-NINE

Matt walked out into a crowd of pulsing disco lights and happy faces scooping up glasses and sloshing champagne. Some were hugging and slapping backs, while others were letting their hips sway to the music. He saw about fifteen people here, not counting the relieved-looking crew weaving in and out. So a few of the possessed were nowhere to be seen. But most were here.

Perry, who'd now removed his dog collar, caught Matt's eye and his face lit up. 'Professor! Join us.'

Matt made a cautious move towards them and was startled when he felt a hand tug at his elbow. It was Deron, face thick with sweat, but smiling. 'Hey, fella! Come and dance.' He'd already flung his jacket away, but he still wore the scarf. He started grooving backwards, wagging fingers and pointing them up like rhythmic pistols to the ceiling.

Matt was no stranger to dance floors at parties – Professor Hunter's break-dancing attempts were legendary – but he politely declined with a raised palm. Deron shrugged and turned his backwards slide into a body pop, then he started moonwalking across the makeshift dance floor in the middle of the dining hall, and people cheered. Perry must have seen Matt's bafflement. He sidled up next to him with a grin on his face and he slapped a warm hand on his shoulder.

'Hey, amigo,' Perry said. 'You look confused.'

Matt shrugged. 'I genuinely had no idea that the deeper stages of possession . . . was disco.'

Perry threw his head back and laughed. 'Nawwwww. This is the *celebration*. This is the thanksgiving. Look at them . . . they're finally free. Isn't it a beautiful thing?'

Matt watched them twirling and hugging, but most of all, they were laughing. So much *life*. 'I never knew exorcisms had an after-party.'

'Kissell's always do. And I think it's just perfect. Here' – he grabbed a flute of champagne for Matt – 'drink with us. Celebrate.'

'Thanks, but . . . no.'

'Oh, come on, amigo, just one—'

'Why do you keep calling me amigo?'

Perry stared at him with his mouth open, and then his red beard burst forth laughter again. 'Because I'm happy, Matt. And they're happy too. And guess what . . . newsflash . . . this just in' – he cupped his hand around his mouth – 'you're allowed to be happy too. Just because you lost doesn't—'

'Lost?'

'Sure. All those tests and things. But look at them now.'

'Perry, this wasn't a competition.'

'Well, it wasn't in my eyes . . . but are you really sure that's not how you saw it? Hmmm? But look, no hard feelings. Bottom line is that this whole exorcism thing has been a raging success . . . and there's only one way to sum that up.' He thrust his glass towards the ceiling and threw half of it down his throat. 'Praise Jesus!'

'Yeah, but . . .' Matt caught his eye. 'How long is this going to last, amigo?'

'It'll last. You'll see.'

'Richie had to come back for more, didn't he? Where is he, by the way?'

'Last I saw him, he popped out for a stroll. Said he wanted to see the Milky Way and thank God direct . . . he's cured, Matt.'

'And Abby? And what about Pavel for crying out loud, he's still miss—'

'Pffft, you atheists are no fun at all.' Perry shook his head and downed the rest of his drink. 'But us Christians, we know how to loosen up. We know how to partaaay.'

Don't . . . Matt thought. *Please for the love of all that is right and noble, don't, please . . .*

Perry started to jerk his shoulders up and down to the beat and he made a subtle (but not subtle enough) chicken bob with his head back and forth. Then he broke into a form of dad dancing that was, ironically, the closest proof that Matt had so far seen that demonic possession truly did exist after all. He spoke up, to prevent the horror. 'Perry? Where's Kissell. And the others?'

Perry froze his repellent flapping. 'They're still in the main hall. Guess some demons are more stubborn than others. In fact . . .' He checked his watch. 'Ooo, that's a shame. I better toddle back in and lend a hand.'

'Is Abby still in there?'

He broke into a huge smile just at the mention of her name, then he pointed towards the window. 'She's right there!' She was standing at the window with Claire Perry. Both of them hugging. 'You know she was one of the first to be set free. She just walked up to Tom Riley's box and went to touch it. But Bernie took her hand instead, and he prayed for her. She screamed, she cried, she smiled, she sang. Oh, and good news, she said she remembered breaking into your room when you slept, so you're off the hook.'

A breath that he'd been holding for a few hours finally fled him.

'But praise God, look at her now. It'll be a whole new life for her and her son . . . but hey, if you'll excuse me . . .' He checked the time again. 'I guess some of the possessed are a bit tougher to liberate than others . . . but they'll be free. Just you watch.' He clicked a finger at Matt, then danced back through the crowd, grabbing people's hands as he went, congratulating them that they were now (ironically) what Matt had been saying all along: one hundred per cent Satan-free.

The pounding music slunk into a new song. 'Celebrate' by Kool and the Gang. A part of him, a part that was drawn to retreat, told him to relax and get dancing. Maybe it was over. But the night remained dark, and the sun showed no true sign of being closer. So he pushed through the crowd towards the windows, jerking away from a hand that slapped him on the backside, tugging him into a dance. He was worried they'd feel the knife in his pocket after all. Or that they'd see it, at least. His hip certainly bulged with it.

When he reached the two women, Abby was laughing, with one hand on her hip, and the other buried into her hair.

'Ladies,' Matt said as he came near.

Abby spun around so quickly that when she stopped she looked a little dizzy.

'Excuse me,' Claire said. 'I'll let you two talk.'

'You don't have to go,' Matt said.

'Stay!' Abby laughed, and her face really did fill up with light and life. 'Matt, it's amazing. It really is.'

'It worked?' he said.

'Totally.' She took Matt's hand in hers and reached for Claire's with the other and held it. 'I feel so much better. It's like this cloud has gone. This weight.' She laughed. 'Sorry, but I can only think in clichés right now. It's just . . . so overwhelming. I can't wait to see my son.' She took his hand. 'Matt?'

'Yeah?'

'Are you pleased for me?'

He looked at her.

'Surely, you can see I'm better?'

He threw a fake smile on his face. 'It's good to see you smiling. But can I just ask . . .'

'Uh-oh . . . what now?'

'Your medication. You said you'd take it.'

She crossed one finger over the other and pushed a crucifix at him. 'Get thee behind me, Satan.' She said it with a guffaw while he stared back, baffled. 'Sorry, Matt, I didn't take them, but,' she raised a finger to calm him, '*but* . . . that's fine, because there's no need for those pills anyway. Not now.'

Matt let his gaze drop to his own shoes and tried all he could not to shake his head.

'Thing is,' she went on, 'I'm thinking Perry was right and the meds were the doorway in.'

'For the demons, you mean? He said that?'

She nodded. 'Pretty interesting theory.'

He shared a glance with Claire, and he realised then that both he and Perry's wife probably shared the exact same look. They were both smiling at Abby, sure, but these smiles were cautious and assembled, looking for cracks in Abby. They both had that slight bite of a nervous lip.

Abby grabbed his hand. She felt clammy. 'And Matt, I'm so sorry about what happened in your room. I think I just needed to be close to someone I trust. But you didn't do anything wrong, and I'll make sure they all know that.'

'Thank you, I appreciate that.'

'Awesome. Then if you don't mind, I need more champagne!' She giggled and went to turn, but something odd happened. Her body turned, and so did her head, but her fingertips stayed laced into Matt's hand. So that she felt her arm lock back as she tried to walk away. Matt frowned and Claire did too. And they all looked down at her hands, which seemed to tremble, stuck there with invisible glue.

'Abby? You okay?' Matt caught a shadow of something crossing her face. A dull click of fear in her eyes, as she stared at her own, disobedient hands.

Then she blinked slowly, like a robot resetting itself, and when her eyes opened again her hands were free. 'I'm gonna dance all night.' Her smile was wide. So wide. *Too* wide. Then she spun and skipped towards the others. Multiple hands thrust champagne her way, and she grabbed two. They cheered at that.

'So . . .' Matt turned to Claire. 'Opinion?'

Claire bit her lip.

'You can be honest.'

'She's not right.'

'Then you need to talk to your husband, and tell him this is dangerous . . .' He tilted his head. 'Why did you meet him, Claire? On the day of the murder. Why did you lie? And why is it your fault she died?'

'Because I chose my pain over hers,' she whispered, then suddenly, 'oh and if there's anybody dangerous here, why can't it be the guy with a knife in his pocket?'

She nodded at the bulge in his side; the blade had worked itself out of his pocket so that it was hanging a little, mostly unravelled and ready to drop. He pushed it back inside, and just watched her walk off, despite his calling her name. She didn't head towards the dance floor where the others were, but back out into the lobby. Maybe she was going back to her husband, in the suite of exorcism.

310

He couldn't be sure. He didn't follow her, though. Because his eyes were distracted by something that didn't sit right.

It was Abby, dancing near Ethan, who had changed out of his Pokémon pyjamas, and was back into black skinny jeans and a short-sleeved white shirt, smattered with cactuses. He must have come in a few moments ago and she'd dragged him on to the dance floor. Now she was draping her hands across his shoulders, fingertips gliding across his cheek and neck.

Nobody else seemed to notice. Perhaps because by now there were other sounds amongst the disco. The wailing screams were back, as Kissell and Perry went to round two. So now, the recently free were slowing their dance, and staring at the door towards the lobby, and the Ash Suite beyond it. Raising a glass in a bizarre prayer, that their still lost comrades would join them soon.

Staring at that door meant that none of them saw Abby slide a hand into the open collar of Ethan's shirt. Matt took a step forward, just as she pulled Ethan away from the others, towards the kitchen door where he'd just been.

And nobody saw Abby and Ethan vanish into the kitchen, because by then the muffled screams had reached such horrendous levels that people were looking suddenly guilty for their premature celebration. In fact, somebody was turning the music down, and it seemed that nobody wanted to dance to a melody of sheer pain and lament.

God, that sounded loud out there. More chaotic than ever. Sounded like things were being smashed.

Matt ignored it all, as best he could. Because right now all he could think of was that wide, mannequin grin of Abby's. And the way she'd been unable to move her hands, and had looked at him and Claire with eyes made of wood. When he rushed through the crowd into the kitchen, he thought he might see them in there just talking or kissing in the corner. He wondered how he'd explain his

311

insistence that Ethan stay away from her. But when he got inside the room it was totally empty. The only reflection in the sheer metal panels was his own distorted face, warped and deformed and worried-looking as he walked through.

Then he saw a door, which he thought had been some sort of fridge, earlier. But when he got closer, he felt a cold breeze seeping through the gaps. It was locked, and when he looked around, he saw a rack of keys, but one hook was empty.

He had no other option than to run back through the dining hall, where the music had stopped altogether and lights were now on full. The others were on their knees now, drinks discarded, and heads bowed in prayer. Though he didn't like the way some of them were rocking back and forth with it. He headed back into the lobby, wondering if Claire might be there too. She wasn't, in fact nobody was.

So he ran through the deserted sofas and armchairs and headed to the lift so he could head down and check outside. Just to make sure Ethan was okay with her. That Matt's instincts were hopefully incorrect. At one point, he had to physically cover his ears with his palms, as he crossed the lobby floor, to block out the awful sound of unseen souls screaming from the depths of agony.

CHAPTER FIFTY

Matt stepped out of the thankfully rabbit-free lift and into the chilly night, then he broke into a jog around the building. The dining hall was on the other side, and when he got there he found a metal staircase, like a fire escape, leading up to the kitchen. They must have come down—

He froze. It was a sound, unlike anything else he'd heard so far tonight. A splash of water.

The boating lake.

He spun around and jogged back the way he'd come, only this time he ignored the lift doors. He rushed straight down the path instead. When he reached the water's edge he squinted into the darkness. Something was bobbing on the moonlit lake. It was one of the boats. He couldn't see either Abby or Ethan, but then he figured it was entirely possible they might be lying down in that boat right now. Kissing or undressing or doing whatever else those crazy twenty-somethings do, these days. He felt like a nosy dad spying on his kid, and was very tempted to turn away, until he saw a strange surge of white foam bubbling in front of the boat.

What if she's jumped in? What if she's drowning?

He cupped a hand around his mouth and shouted, 'Ethan? Abby?'

In response, muffled screams came from behind.

He looked back over his shoulder and stared at the mushroom of The Reed. It glowed against the trees now, and it looked utterly surreal. A UFO, landed in the forest. He could see the disconcerting sight of silhouettes, moving about at the windows. Some in rooms with lights on, and some in rooms that didn't have lights on. That last part unsettled him. All those black shapes creeping and walking and . . . hunched. The muffled roars went on, and in some ways they were like the normal soundtrack of life here. Yet he wondered if their frequency – and urgency – seemed much more intense right now.

Was that the sound of glass shattering, up there?

He turned back to the lake, which was nothing but an ominous, deep and silent disc. A mute mirror distorting the sky. He still saw no sign of them on the water.

Better check.

He slammed both heels into the sand and pushed at the rim of one of the other boats that were left. His shoes loudly splashed into the water and he hopped up over the back end. The craft dipped and bobbed madly as he scrabbled into position and he felt the front of his socks instantly contract with the soak. He grabbed both oars and started to row, as fast as he could.

For a few moments, there was an almost pretty sense of peace about it. The fast, rhythmic splashing of the oars soothed him. And so did the low breeze that was rolling all the trees to the side. The smell of the ferns. But most of all, he liked that sense of distance he was building between him and that place. What if he just rowed out here and waited till morning?

The other boat wasn't that far out, so he got there pretty fast, but he was still panting by the end of it. He let himself slowly drift towards the other boat. He heard his wake send water sloshing under the other hull. He unhooked one of his oars and scanned the water.

Not wanting to get too close, he pushed the oar towards the other boat. Leaning forward, he gave it a little prod.

Thud.

His own boat drifted back with the impact.

And then . . . and then . . .

Pssssssssssssshhhhhhhh!

When the water erupted, Matt yelped and threw himself back. So hard that he almost tossed himself completely overboard, sending his boat into a violent rocking. And who cares if the cameras and the world heard him shriek. Because it was a perfectly acceptable thing to do in such situations.

The water between the boats exploded in a whoosh of freezing spray, and somewhere in the white fuzz of it all, he saw an arm shoot up and soon after – for a horribly brief second – he saw a face contorted in shock and terrified pain. It was Ethan, breaking up through the water. His flailing arm reached for the moon, but then it slammed down hard against the rim of Matt's boat instead. There was a nauseating crack. He knew it was bone, not wood. Ethan suddenly couldn't grip, and in seconds his face was swallowed in the water again.

Finally, through the shock of it, Matt flung himself forward to grab Ethan's hand, but the arm slithered out of his. It was lost under the surface, like an alligator tail sinking into a swamp.

As quickly as he'd come up, Ethan was gone.

Wait.

Another splash of water.

Shit. This time, it was Ethan's foot thrusting up, his body moving in a delirious dance of panic and now moving in what seemed like the wrong direction.

'*Don't swim down!*' Matt hissed at the water.

Matt did what felt right. Though what is truly 'right' at such times is too nuanced a concept to pin down. He was a good swimmer. He always had been. Growing up on the Dunwich coast had taught him that. And he'd be careful to make sure his feet didn't get tangled in any vines. He sucked a deep breath in, and before he knew it, he was up and over.

He remembered his hand leaving the rocking boat. That feeling of his skin touching wood and then not. The next sensation was an all-out assault on his nerve endings. His head and shoulders plunged under and the sheer bite of cold flooded into his face and body. It took his breath away. Literally.

God, it was like fire. Like a cold, biting fire.

He surfaced again, gulping in a ravenous breath, his entire body shuddering. He frantically looked around for bubb—

There!

He burst into a front crawl, and he flailed his hands under the water, grasping, grabbing. His fingertips slid through something strange.

Reeds . . .

Hair.

It was all he could do. His fist closed and he yanked up. Hoping like hell that Ethan's silvery scalp wouldn't come out in a clump while his body headed down into the dark. The tug brought something heavy with it, and Matt could finally scoop his arm under the armpits. Ethan's face broke through the water and Matt instantly slapped it.

'Hey,' Matt's limbs ached as he kept them both afloat. He kept swallowing water. 'Hey. Wake . . . up. Breathe . . . Ethan. *Breathe.*'

But then it didn't matter any more, because when Matt lifted him from the water, his head lolled back. And something horrendous opened up under his chin. Matt's immediate thought was that it looked like an overstuffed cushion, bulging apart and tearing open at the zip. But inside this cushion was pure blackness, which bubbled and turned the rest of his neck black. Horrified, Matt flung himself back in an uncontrollable shudder of disgust, and deep guilt for letting go. The last he saw of Ethan's dying . . . no . . . Ethan's dead body was the matted wisps of wet silver-grey hair being swallowed by the black.

Horror and sadness pummelled through Matt, and it only got worse with every blind flail and plunge under the water. The thought of Ethan drifting down, and down, got too much. And so Matt gripped the rim of his own boat, about to pull up. Until a new sight came, when he looked back.

A slow black mass was rising from the rim of Abby's boat. It slid slowly up, and for a sickly second he thought it was the black rabbit from the lift again, sharp claws fresh with Ethan.

It was so dark, and his eyes were so filled with dirty water and maybe even tears, that her silhouette took a while to look distinct. But a wipe of his eyes made it clear.

It was Abby, hair hanging wet and she was grinning in the moonlight, just like she'd been doing before. Only this time, she looked at The Reed while her shoulders rocked with silent laughter. Or was she crying? It was hard to tell. Whatever it was, it flooded him with a much deeper cold and he kept having flashing images of her suddenly leaping from her boat and springing into an impossible, nightmarish, whip through the sky towards him.

Shivering, in every way that was humanly possible, and with his muscles close to explosion, he started the desperate, squeaking crawl back into his own, now madly rocking boat. When he finally dropped into it, drenched, gasping and freezing, he felt an urge to call Abby's name. To snap her out of it. But his brain and logic were insistent. Get away. Get back to The Reed and tell them. And get them to lock the door, and call the police if they could. Or at the very least, for them all to bundle into the cars and get the hell away from here.

He took one last look at her and was surprised to see that she'd now stood up in the boat. She was neither laughing or crying, rather she was lifting the material of that ruffled white shirt of hers, higher and higher so her midriff showed.

Her voice, smooth and warm, did not sound like an old man. But like the beautiful young woman she was. She said, 'Don't leave me, Matt.'

He looked away. Not for modesty. That wasn't it. It was the shard of glass in her hand that did it, still glistening with Ethan's blood. He looked away because, framed in moonlight, she'd already started to splay the skin of her flat stomach, so she might patiently carve the first letter deep into her skin.

CHAPTER FIFTY-ONE

A sure-fire way of knowing that something is very, very wrong, is when there's blood in the lift. Matt didn't even see it at first. He flung himself inside it breathless, shaking and soaking wet, and he turned to keep an eye on the slowly closing door. He saw the very dim outline, there on the lake, her black shape still standing and bobbing out there on the water.

Without properly looking, Matt jabbed his finger against the panel, but his fingertip slipped off with a squeak. When he looked down, the reaction was immediate and primal. He went back in a clumsy stagger, his soaked back pushing into the mirrored wall.

There was a chest-high arch of blood across the buttons. It was seeping between the gaps in the metal and illuminated plastic. And when he looked at the floor he saw a thick, glistening puddle of it, and a handprint, very low down.

He felt that instant tingle you get, when you see blood. That evolutionary warning signal that says – *There be danger in these parts. Best skidaddle.* So when he lifted his hand, and saw his own sticky red fingertips, he started desperately smearing them. Damn those designers for not putting carpet in here. He had to wipe his grotty fingers on his own wet trousers.

He was so distracted by this blood that he hadn't even noticed that his initial button press had actually made contact. The lift had already started to rise. So he felt a shudder of fright when it rang its cheerful little digital bell, for the lobby floor.

Crap. He should be running away from here, not going in.

The doors started to open, and he thrust out a hand towards the panel to close them. After all, he really had no desire to see a band of shuffling maniacs snap their heads his way, and come scrambling over the lobby sofas to get him. But when the doors slid open, he saw only the lobby, with upturned chairs, and a spray of something against one of the far windows. It could have been red wine he supposed. But then red wine didn't really cling to glass, did it?

At first he thought the room was empty, until he saw her, crouching behind the counter where the coffee machine was. It was Suzy, his camerawoman. She was on her knees, holding a thin camera tripod. A weapon. She'd heard the doors open, so she was looking at him before he saw her. She was shivering, she'd been crying. Her eyes had clearly seen things that he didn't want to think about.

He looked both ways, then waved her towards the lift, mouthing the silent words, *Come on!*

She pressed her lips together, unable to move anything but her head. Then she mouthed, *I can't.*

The lift doors suddenly started to close, and some selfish little imp deep in his brain said, let them close. Go downstairs and grab a car. Figure out how to hot-wire something and drive off. But the imp was little, and its voice was slight. He put his hands out to stop the doors closing. Cold metal pressed against his wrist and fingers, which were still damp with water and now, he supposed, blood. The door bounced off him and dutifully opened again.

She was about fifteen feet away. As he drew closer, he started unravelling the kitchen roll in his pocket. He left it strewn in a long line. The sharp little knife gleamed in his hand. When she saw the blade, she went pale with shock and seemed to grip her tripod even tighter, ready to strike. She kept staring at his face, searching his eyes for some sign of humanity. Making sure he wasn't one of *them*.

So when he reached her he spoke calmly and very, very gently indeed. 'Are you hurt?'

She shook her head.

He dropped behind the coffee counter. Took a second to catch his breath. 'Where is everybody?'

'It . . . it happened quickly . . . they . . . they . . .'

'Breathe,' he whispered. 'Is there anybody else we can grab? We could get to the lift. Find a car.'

'No!' Her eyes bulged. 'Do *not* go outside.'

He looked to the windows.

'They're out there. Loads of them. They chased the crew out.'

'I didn't see anybody come out.'

'No . . . no, they went through . . . through the kitchen.'

He leant out a little from the counter, spying across the lobby. 'Just tell me what happened.'

'It was so fast. I was checking the camera feed for the after-party in the dining hall. They were praying or something until the screaming started in the main hall. We thought it was just . . .' she took a shuddery breath, '. . . that it was just the exorcism getting intense, but then a few of our camera guys ran out. They said some of the clients, not all . . . but some, just went berserk. Started attacking each other, and the crew. They smashed a mirror. One of them grabbed a big chunk

of it. And he started . . . cutting people. Jesus. He was stabbing them.'
Her body shook again, with the trauma of it. 'Some came running
into the dining hall. One of them found us in the tech room. I saw
Jonas Fuller, our sound man. He was stabbed right in front of me.'

Matt looked at her and waited for a moment. 'By who?'

'That Richie bloke. The big guy. He looked crazy.' Her cheeks
seemed to hollow at the thought of it. 'So I panicked and ran.
We all did, and the only clear way looked like the back door in
the kitchen. Some of our guys kicked it down, and they ran out
there. But I wasn't fast enough. Those crazy fuckers . . . they just
chased them, laughing and screaming and grabbing knives from
the drawers. So do *not* go out there. They're in the car park, I
think. And the woods.'

'Suzy,' Matt whispered, eventually. 'Who's left in the building?'

'I think Nupa's trapped in the main hall, the Ash Suite. Perry and
Kissell are there too, I think.'

'And Perry's wife?'

'Claire? I don't know. I think most of the possessed are outside,
but some of them might still be in the building. I heard footsteps
upstairs and singing . . . God that *singing*.' She pushed her fingers into
her eyes, and squeezed the bridge of her nose. 'There's no reception,
the Wi-Fi's still out. We found the media plate for the whole building
smashed to bits. There's a backup system somewhere, but I have no
idea where. So we're alone . . . and we're gonna die here alone.' She
crumbled into sobs.

'Hey. Look at me, you need to find a better place to hide. There's
a toilet right around that corner. Crawl over and lock yourself in.
And take this . . .' He handed the knife to her. 'Use it if you have to.'

'But . . . what about you?'

He shrugged. 'I'll take the tripod if it's going spare.'

'Hide with me.'

'If Nupa's trapped, I have to help . . .' He shook his head. 'Just get in that toilet. I'll get Nupa and come back. I'll knock like this.' He tapped a silent but recognisable pattern against the back of her hand. Then he leant out and took one last scan of the lobby. Still empty. 'Go. *Now*.'

She burst into a quick scramble towards the door. He waited to make sure she went inside the toilet. He heard the lock click into place.

Jittery with the risk of it, he pulled himself up, and gripped the tripod like a baseball bat. Then he made a swift, hunched run towards the glass door that led into the Ash Suite corridor.

CHAPTER FIFTY-TWO

Oh, no.

Matt stopped dead at the glass door and stared through it. One of the security guys was lying motionless on the corridor floor. The man who had told Matt to step away earlier. The other one was missing and Matt saw another body collapsed in a heap against a wall. When he saw this one, Matt's chest lost its air. It was Deron Johnson, sitting on the carpet, like he was just taking a moment to chill. Only he had a long smear of red running from the back of his head. It shot up the flowered wallpaper in a strangely neat line. He must have slid down the wall like this.

Was Deron a victim? Or had the security guard done this to him in self-defence?

Matt pushed the glass gently, knuckles white.

He lifted the tripod, slowly creeping towards the bodies, to check for signs of life. He saw a huge hunk of mirror wedged into Deron's shoulder, pinning that velvet scarf of his for ever in place. But the guard made a noise as Matt came past. He dropped to his knees, and whispered, 'Can you move?'

He groaned and shook his head. He was crying.

'Okay . . .' Matt looked around, baffled as to what to do, then he jumped when a voice crackled near him.

'Ash . . .' It was Deron, fluttering his eyes open. Wow.

'You're alive!'

'Still . . . truckin . . .' Deron, said, eyes still closed. He attempted a smile, but it only made him wince in extreme pain. 'Just get in the Ash Suite . . . people in there.'

'Anybody dangerous?'

'No. But they'll be back.'

'Okay. I'll be straight—'

The words caught in his throat, as he flicked his gaze to the glass that led back to the lobby. The one he'd just come through. His skin prickled, all hair standing. Could almost hear it bristle, too. He was sure he'd just seen a huge shadow pass by, out of the corner of his eye.

Deron groaned quietly, '*Hurrrrrrry.*'

Matt pushed himself up. His kneecaps thick with Deron's blood. Then, once he was standing, he gulped down breath and pushed the door to the hall.

He stepped inside and—

Something slammed into him.

He staggered sideways and crashed noisily into a chair. He twisted back and went to swing the tripod, but he heard a familiar, panicked voice.

'*Wait, wait!*' she said. '*It's me.*'

He let his arms drop, just on the swing.

Nupa gulped. 'Sorry, I thought you were one of them. Are you injured?'

'No. You?'

She shook her head. 'We've got to get out of here.'

'Ya think?'

'Have you seen anybody?'

'Suzy's in the toilets near the lobby . . . but Ethan . . .'

'What about him? . . . Wait . . . Hey, don't look at me like that . . .'

'I'm sorry, Nupa. He's dead.'

She pressed her hand against her mouth. He noticed her meticulously manicured nails were all chewed. 'How did he die?'

'Abby killed him on the lake. Look, let's focus. Who's left in here?'

'Jesus . . .'

'Nupa. Listen to me. Who's left in here?'

'Just Reverend Perry. He's right there.' She pointed at the stage.

Matt saw nothing on the stage except Tom Riley's stupid box, still spot-lit on a plinth. 'I don't see anybody.'

'Under. He's hiding under the stage.'

They shared a glance. Even in the midst of this, it was hard not to roll eyes.

Matt rushed to the front and dropped, tugging at the little blue curtain that hung from it. He yanked it back and saw Perry lying on his side. A man-sized embryo with a ginger beard. 'Come on. We need to get moving.'

'Oh, not you.'

'Fuck's sake, Perry. This isn't time for a tiff. We need to stick together.'

'They've gone wild, they've gone insane.' Perry's cheek was pressed into the carpet. 'Do you see what you've done?'

'What *I've* done?'

'You let the darkness in, not me. Your negativity. This was you.'

'Yep, all me. Now, let's get moving. Where's Claire?'

'Who?'

'Your wife, dimwit. Where is she?'

'It's people like you . . . the atheists, the heretics. You bring the Devil in.'

'Leave him,' Nupa hissed behind him. 'He's lost it.'

'That's why exorcisms are rising. That's why Tom did what he did. It was nothing to do with me, it's people like you . . .' Perry mumbled. 'It's the atheism.'

Matt was about to reach in and drag Perry out, but something made him stop. It was Nupa. She made the strangest little yelp sound. He could have sworn it was the sound of a piglet stepping on a pin.

When Matt looked back, he knew why she'd made that sound. He felt like making it himself.

The double wooden doors were rattling, and though they heard no voice and no scream, they could hear the frantic thud and drag of heavy things being pulled and ransacked out there.

Oh, shit.

The handle started to jerk up and down frantically, which wasn't just scary, it was weird. These doors didn't even have locks. He heard Nupa shriek as she flung herself towards the stage. Then the doors just smashed open, wood splinters spinning through the air, and standing in the frame, hulking and panting, was Richie. He was butt-naked, looking strangely pale like he was covered in flour, and yet he was splashed with blood. Probably not his. He had so much on his chin it looked like a thick, red goatee. Each of his hands held two hefty shards of . . . oh God . . . of *mirror*. They were dripping onto the carpet, and his eyes were cocked and crazy.

Stomach rolling, Matt looked at the corridor outside where Deron's hand was twitching in a black, wet, rapidly growing puddle.

Richie saw them looking at him and he tilted his head. Which made Nupa scream. It was an ear-splitting squeal of uncontrolled fright. The sound did something strange. It made Richie start to sway from side to side, like a giant white monkey, genitals

327

swinging. He put his ear to the air, as the scream echoed. Matt thought of the rabbit in the lobby, drawing in pain.

'Oh God, oh God, oh God,' Perry was frantically pressing himself further back under the stage. 'Matt. Drop the curtain. *Matt!*'

It was too late.

Richie lifted both shards of mirror high into the air and let out this godawful banshee wail. Then with the massive hammering of bare feet he ran towards them all at the stage, arms up and screaming.

CHAPTER FIFTY-THREE

Richie left a trail of tremors as his tree-trunk feet pounded towards the now hysterical Nupa. The floor shook with the wet, heavy smack of him. Matt leapt to the side out of his way, which to any passing witness – or indeed to the ever-watching cameras – could have looked like he was simply letting this beast get what it wanted: Nupa.

Yep. I'm a modern, equal opportunities fella, me, Matt might say in the talking-head interviews after. *I'm a big believer that women should be granted the equal opportunity to be the first person murdered by a naked psychopath.*

But there was a much more important reason for the leap. He had a plan. He'd tossed his tripod to the floor earlier and it was way out of reach now, but when he hit his knees he grabbed something more substantial instead. The front two legs of a steel-framed,

329

comfy banqueting chair. Just as he got it, Richie slammed into the stage, grabbing frantically for Nupa, bare blood-soaked backside flexing as he pushed. The entire platform shook, even Tom's wooden box teetered for a moment. Nupa was scrambling backwards on all fours, mouth moving in terror. The stage wasn't deep, so she couldn't go far.

Richie raised those arms of his and swung them down. The two pieces of mirror sliced the air and one of them landed in the very tip of Nupa's Italian leather shoe. The same one she'd worn on the night they'd met in the park. She wept when she knew she was pinned to the floor.

Matt saw fresh blood splash against those shoes, but it wasn't hers. The impact of the mirror had slashed two deep gashes into Richie's bare palm. He was oblivious to the pain, and was about to slam those shards down again when Matt staggered forward. He lifted the chair and ploughed that thing into Richie's bare side.

Whump.

The impact sent hot agony racing all the way up to Matt's shoulders.

Yet Richie just stayed there, unmoving and rooted to the ground.

'Hit him again!' Nupa shouted.

Matt went to lift the chair, just as he heard what must have been the muffled scrape of neck bone as Richie started to turn. Matt raised the chair higher, just as Richie's mad-eyed profile became visible over the mound of his He-Man shoulder. Wild, bovine eyes strained into the very edge of his socket, so he could look back at his attacker.

Matt swung again. Arms absolutely *aching.*

Whump.

Another thundering slam sent an earthquake up Matt's arms. Like a cartoon character whacking an anvil, and Richie finally staggered to the side. Suddenly one of the mirror shards dropped

330

from his hand, which Matt thought was a sign of him faltering, but the flash in Richie's eyes said something else. This was planned. *He was after the chair.* Matt yanked the chair back as fast as he could, but Richie clamped his hand around the leg. He ripped it from Matt's throbbing hands and flung it to the side, so hard that it literally skittered across the tops of the other chairs in a tumble.

Nupa scream again. Matt backed away.

Richie was streaming cups of blood, not only from his hands, but now from a growing split on his side. He was mumbling something. '*I am roaming . . . roaming . . . to and fro, through the earth, through the earth . . . patrolling, and watching . . .*' The same words Richie had used in the TV studio that night. And Matt knew now, just as he'd known then, that these were the words of Satan in the Old Testament book of Job. '*Through the soil . . . I am roaming . . . coming up from the soil, I come from the fucking soil . . .*'

Matt staggered back from this lumbering, naked monster of a man, and figured that the best bet was to grab another chair. But there was no time for such luxury, because Richie was coming too fast, with two industrial-sized hands that wanted to *crush* something. He saw Richie greedily staring at Matt's windpipe.

'Oh God,' Matt said.

Then something else happened. Something that threw an already terrifying moment into a cavern of pure, blind panic.

Matt felt unseen fingers slip over his shoulder, and wriggle into his hair from behind.

A woman's voice whispered into his ear, 'Shhhhh.'

CHAPTER FIFTY-FOUR

Matt span at the coldness of her fingers, dreading, *seriously* dreading to look into Abby's smiling face again. But as he stumbled into a half-circle he was startled to see it was Claire Perry who was pulling him back.

She yanked Matt backwards, then swung what looked like a black sword through the air. It was the tripod he'd had earlier. It cracked hard against Richie's jaw and his face crunched into a million agonised lines. Claire yelped with the agony in her arms – a pain she clearly hadn't anticipated. Richie staggered. A robot losing power and dripping red oil.

'He's dazed,' Nupa shouted. 'Kill him!'

Claire stumbled, looking at her hands while Matt didn't think much about it. He swung another chair up and over, and it smacked down across Richie's naked spine. There was a sickening, moist thud. If this was a cartoon, it'd be the ideal time for animated birds to tweet in circles over his head. Instead Richie just wet himself. What a thing to see. Then he finally dropped to his knees, eyes rolling up into white. Richie fell forward and the floorboards seemed to ripple across the entire Ash Suite as his hefty chest hammered into the floor.

Everybody stood there for a moment, utterly silent.

It was a weird moment that. Staring at what Matt simultaneously assumed, hoped and dreaded was a dead man. And maybe it was this latter feeling, the throb of fear and guilt, that convinced Matt that it'd be right and proper to tie Richie up. Even if he did just look like a wet, broken corpse at their feet. Tying him up wasn't just a good precaution, it did welcome things to Matt's brain. It helped him imagine that no, no, he had certainly not just killed a man with a chair. Not at all. He'd only knocked that sucker out, *Tom-and-Jerry*-style. Richie would be fine by the next episode.

He shivered at the existential throb of it. At the pain in his arms, sure, but mostly at the panic untying his own ideas of who he thought he was. Had he just killed a person? He yanked a power cable from the floor and whipped it back like a snake. He bound Richie's hands and ankles together – willing them to move or quiver, yet they didn't. The hands were especially slippery to hold on to, so deep and ragged were the cuts from the mirror's edge.

He turned to Claire. She'd already sunk into one of the chairs, panting.

'You saved my life,' Matt said, nodding at the tripod in a stinking puddle. 'Thank you.'

'I think we saved each other's . . .' She turned her head to the stage. 'Is she okay?'

Matt looked back to Nupa. She was now curled into a ball, pressed against the back of the stage. In any other walk of life, the answer to Claire's question would have been, 'She's clearly not okay. Look at her.' But in the upside-down economy of a murder outbreak, she was actually doing pretty damn well. She was even reaching forward to retrieve her shoe. It did look expensive, after all.

'I'm pretty sure Richie here was the last one inside.' Claire leant forward, elbows on her knees. 'The rest are out there. Wandering the grounds.'

'Then we need to lock the doors,' Matt said.

'Already done. Me and one of the security women did it.'

'That's good. Where's she now?'

Claire looked down at the hunk of meat, oozing into the floor, and just pointed at him. Her voice was a whisper. 'He broke her neck. I took her keys.' She held them up. They made a tinkling sound.

Matt pulled the cord tight one final time, then he clambered back up onto a chair, desperately wiping his bloodied hands on the carpet. Kneecaps soaked with blood, Matt turned to the stage.

'Nupa, we have *got* to find a phone. Like pronto. Do you know how to get this place back online?'

'Yeah. There's a backup hub, on the second floor. Maybe the third.'

'Well, which is it?'

'I'm not sure. My tech guys dealt with that . . .'

Matt and Claire sighed at the same time.

'We'll just have to search. And when we find it, we can get the Wi-Fi back online at least.'

'*Wi-Fi?*' Claire tutted. 'We need a phone line not Facebook.'

'Oh, shush,' Nupa started to stand. 'We'll try and get the phones on too, but listen. If we get Internet, we can contact the outside. Okay?'

Claire sucked the inside of her mouth. 'I'm sorry,' she said. 'I'm scared.'

Matt nodded. 'We all are. Nupa, lead the way . . .' Matt trailed off when the curtain moved under the stage. Claire saw it too, so she instantly grabbed a chair to swing. Matt put up a hand. 'Relax. It's your husband.'

'Simon?' Her eyes filled with tears, and she rushed to the stage.

A pink, trembling hand slid out from the curtain, and a face followed. They all just waited while Perry clambered out, all squinty-eyed. A mole, up from the depths. He stood to his feet and brushed the dust from his trousers. On the one hand, it would have been very easy to call the guy a coward, for hiding under the stage the entire time. But on the other, what Perry had done looked like pure and brilliant logic right now. Perhaps if they'd all just hidden under there, Richie would have passed them by completely, and Matt wouldn't have killed a human being—

Stop . . . stop . . . thinking about it . . .

Maybe a little pettiness would distract him from the guilty sense of panic. So he looked at Perry, and said. 'Glad you could join us.'

CHAPTER FIFTY-FIVE

'Go ahead.' Reverend Perry straightened his shirt and shook his head, while Claire hugged him. 'Stand there all smug. Go ahead and sneer.'

'Sorry. It's not a sneer. Let's just get—'

'Then what is it?'

'Stress! I'm stressed out. Aren't you?'

Perry opened his mouth to snap some caustic comment back, but he seemed to lack the energy, even for that. He looked at Richie on the floor for a few seconds. 'I'm sorry, I'm stressed too. So much for my faith, eh?' Claire rested her head on his chest.

Finally, some humanity.

Matt put a hand on his shoulder. Gave it a little grip of reassurance. 'What happened in here?'

'It was all working so well. People were being set free and it was beautiful to watch but . . . then . . . it just all changed.' He looked around the room, eyes scanning the ceilings and the doors. It was as if a wasp had been loose in there, and he wasn't entirely sure it had actually left. 'The room started to shake. I saw pictures dropping from the walls. You could feel the evil in the room. The type of cold that gets right inside of you. I can *still* feel it.' His eyes passed across Tom's wooden box, but he quickly looked away. He wheezed and touched his chest. 'We better get going.'

'Then shouldn't we just destroy it?' It was Nupa, standing on the stage. Arms folded, she stared at the plinth. 'Maybe if we smash it to bits, then all this will stop? Kinda like pulling the plug out.'

Perry shot out a hand. 'Do *not* touch that!'

'Hey,' Matt hissed a nervous whisper, eyes on the door. 'Keep your voice down.'

'Sorry, but don't even look at that thing. The possessed may well be in the forest now, but if you smash that box they'll come flocking back in. Kissell told us if it breaks, it'll be like ripping down the wall of a dam and . . . Nupa . . . *Nupa, what are you doing? Stop it.*'

'Listen.' She was unfolding her arms, her jaw dropping as she leant towards the box. '*Listen!*'

'What?' Matt said.

Perry stamped his foot. 'We've got to go, now.'

'Something's making a sound in there.' Nupa leant closer to it. 'It's quiet but . . . Matt, come and hear this . . .'

'No!' Perry shouted. 'It'll lie. It'll suck you in.'

Claire said, 'Listen to him, please. Don't touch it!'

'It's *whispering*.' She started to reach one tentative arm out as her head tilted. 'We should open this up.'

'Nupa, no!' Perry was clambering up on the stage.

Matt sprang up there after him and for a moment, Matt heard it too. The slightest hiss of whispering. It was coming from the box.

Perry was already next to her. He grabbed Nupa's arm and yanked it to the side, pulling her away with a hard and painful snap. He was so frantic with it that they both stumbled and fell in a crunching heap at the edge of the stage.

Perry looked up to the box and gasped. 'For God's sake, Matt, don't. Leave it alone. Please . . .'

Matt slapped his hands on each side of it, and he felt that familiar scratch of the dry wood, from when he had it in his house last night. Was that whispering . . . or singing? He pulled it close and pressed his ear to it, which was when the whispering seemed to stop.

There was definitely something in there. He started to raise his hands in the air.

'I'm begging you.' Perry crawled closer. 'You'll kill us all.'

'Stop it, please,' Claire Perry was on her knees now, crossing herself. The box was over Matt's head.

Perry's pleading switched to pure aggression. *'Don't you dare!'*

'Dammit, it's a box!' Matt hammered it downwards.

There was a split second of silence, and a strangely long gap, as if gravity itself was trying to cushion its fall. But then the air burst with a splintering snap and the cracking of old wood.

Nupa stepped backwards, and Claire immediately turned towards the smashed double doors, watching for the hunched shadows of the summoned. But nothing happened. The air didn't change. The lights stayed on. Heads remained fixed and in natural positions, all unspun.

'Fine, you've done it now. Now we just get away from it.' Perry was tugging Claire to her feet. 'Come on, love.'

'Wait.' Matt was frowning. 'Look at this thing.'

'Don't even look at it, just—'

'What . . . wait . . . what?' Matt frowned. 'What is *that*?'

Perry buried his fingers into his hair. 'Please . . . it's making you hallucinate.'

Matt dropped to his knees, flinging bits of splintered wood to the side.

Then Perry's face, so full of fear and foreboding changed too. He took a few steps forward and said, 'Dear God . . . you're right. There's something in there. Pull it out.'

Perry dropped to his haunches and helped pull one of the panels back. When it was fully visible, he shook his head in confusion. 'I don't understand.'

Matt lifted the little metal mechanism up to the light. A small, soldered box, with battery wires sprouting from one end, and replanting themselves into the other side. He went to prise the metal open with his fingers, but it was stuck tight.

'Oh my God,' Nupa said. 'A bomb.'

Perry shook his head. 'That's no bomb.'

Matt slammed it against the stage and the metal box cracked open instantly. Inside was a small and retro Olympus dictaphone, strapped to what looked like a digital watch and a hefty little battery pack. Matt moved his thumb, smeared brown with blood, towards the play button.

'Play it,' Perry said, voice low and monotone.

Click.

The spools of micro-cassette started turning and a low, barely audible hiss fuzzed up the speakers. Matt flicked the volume dial up. Which is when the words began. Indecipherable at first, but rhythmic and consistent. The sound of whispering.

Qui intus incolit ego daemon . . .

The others frowned, but Matt just pushed it closer to his ear. He felt the cold metal touch his lobe.

. . . Baalberith lux te perducendum

'What the hell is going on?' Nupa said.

When Matt was sure it was the same phrase over and over, he clicked the tape off, and looked back at them. 'It's Latin.'

'Meaning?'

'Roughly . . . I am the demon who lives inside you. Baal-Berith, a light to guide you.'

339

Perry's mouth dropped open, and he looked at Claire. She was staring at the carpet in shock. Actually, Matt noticed that her face was now a mask of white. Her eyes, unblinking.

'Why is there a tape in . . .' Nupa trailed off when she saw Perry put a hand against his forehead. He fell back a little.

'My God, Matt . . . you were right,' Perry said. 'I'm so sorry . . . but you've been right all along. I saw his hand . . .'

Matt turned to him. 'What?'

'Earlier tonight, when you said Pastor Kissell had something in his hand. I . . . I looked. And I was ashamed to look, because I thought it showed doubt. In fact, I was worried my doubt might have caused all this to go wrong tonight.'

Matt stared at him. 'You *saw* something in his hand. The device?'

He closed his eyes and nodded.

Nupa was on her feet. 'Then why didn't you say anything?'

'I thought it was a trick of the Devil. An illusion . . .' Perry shook his head. 'So *this* is why tonight's exorcism failed. Dear God . . . Kissell's a fraud. And all these poor people. I should have known . . . when he said love was the aim of everything, and not God. I should have known he wasn't holy . . .' He looked at the body on the floor again. 'My God, I was part of this. I'm sorry. I didn't know.'

'Where is he?' Nupa said.

'Upstairs somewhere,' Perry said.

'Well, listen. This is going to have to wait. If we see him on the way, fine. But for now, our focus is to get help here. Nupa, you said you know where the comms room is?'

She was staring at the box, not speaking.

'Nupa? Can you take us there?'

For a second Matt thought she was so traumatised by all this that her brain had finally shut down at the horror of it all, but

340

then he saw her eyes glance up to the camera, fixed to a high beam, and then back to the broken box again. He saw a sigh of relief on her lips.

'Yeah, I'm sure that box smash was captured on film,' Matt said. 'Now can we go?'

They held each other's gaze for a moment, then she looked away. She pointed to the smashed-open doors. 'Come on.'

When Perry stepped down from the stage, he went to hold Claire's hand, but Matt noticed her snap her fingers from his and step to the side.

'I'm sorry,' Perry pleaded with Claire and then he turned back to Matt. 'I swear I thought I was helping. I swear, I've just been blind.'

'Later . . .' Matt said. 'For now, we find this room. Make sure you bring those keys, Claire.'

'We're right with you, Matt,' Perry said. He was like a sudden obedient soldier, ready to fall in line. They all headed for the doors, but Matt held back, just to catch Claire's eye.

'Are you okay?' he whispered.

'He isn't blind. That's not his problem.'

'Then what is?'

'He sees what he wants to see.' She blinked, and when her lids came back up her eyes glistened with moisture. She sniffed and walked on.

Perry, oblivious to all this, was waiting at the door. He turned, seeking their approval. Voice slipping into what he might think sounded heroic. 'Okay, we're ready.'

Matt took one last look behind him, at the box shattered on the stage, and the upturned chairs. And the image he was so keen to forget. The large heap of body that lay on the carpet.

For a little bit there he'd forgotten that he might have just killed somebody.

His stomach dropped at the reminder, and maybe Claire heard

341

it sink. Because she touched his arm and said, 'You had to. Now come on.'

He felt the cold of her fingers as she pulled her hand back. Then he turned from the accusing glass eyes of Richie's corpse and followed her out.

CHAPTER FIFTY-SIX

When they finally got out into the corridor, they had to step over each body in turn. Two humans, who had now become just two silent bundles of cloth and bones. The security guard first, and Deron, who was thankfully now face down. Matt still checked them both for a pulse, just in case. Though he really didn't want to touch them. They were both very dead, so neither he nor the others let themselves look at the guard too long. Seeing a man lying flat on his stomach, with his face pointing mostly *upwards*, was simply too much for the brain to bear.

So they all just kept their eyes up, holding their breath as they stepped across one, then the other. Shoes picking up blood and sleepless nights on the way. When it was his turn, Matt felt the curve of Deron's lifeless finger stroke his shoe, and he had to swallow down something he'd rather not. When they finally reached the lobby, he was shocked to see how many of the sofas and lamps had been overturned. It looked like a tornado had torn through, and the sticky footprints, and long lines of dripping blood suggested that Richie had stomped through here in a mad frenzy, before finding them in the Ash Suite.

He headed straight for the disabled toilet and tapped out his signal with a knuckle. This had been his signature door knock ever since he was a teenager. A secret code his mum had worked out to show that it was *her* at his bedroom door, and not Matt's dad, spitting out cruelty. Matt still used that knock on most doors, even today.

Perry came close. 'What are you doing?'

'Suzy's in there.'

Nupa's mouth dropped. She rushed forward and hammered her fist at the door. 'Suz, it's me, Nupa. Open up.'

'Not so loud.' Matt listened for the locks to start sliding. When they didn't, he pulled at the handle. It wasn't locked. That was odd. He felt his spine tense as the door swung slowly open and he prepped his eyelids for a speedy shut. But the room was empty.

Matt stared at the toilet floor and thankfully found no blood. He scanned the lobby again, then froze when he saw Perry way over on the other side of the room. He was peering through the glass, hands cupped over his eyes.

Matt rushed over in a crouch. 'Stay away from the windows. With these lights on, they'll see us.'

'Oh, of course, sorry . . .' Perry instantly shrank back. 'Just looking for signs of life.'

'And was there any?'

'I see shadows moving in the woods, lots of them . . .' He turned to his wife. 'And you're *sure* you locked all the doors, Claire?'

'Don't you raise your voice at me.' She glared at him.

Perry seemed genuinely shocked at this. 'Don't be like that, love.'

'Don't you patroni—'

'Children, please.' Nupa put a hand between them. 'Save the domestics till later. Let's just get upstairs and find that room.'

Matt nodded. 'She's right.'

'Then at least give me those keys.' Perry snatched them from Claire's hand, and slipped them into his pockets. 'It'll be best if I have them.'

Claire shook her head in what looked like despair. 'How could you possibly know what is best for anybody?'

Matt looked at them both in turn, confused by this sudden frostiness, but then Nupa pushed between them and said, 'Come on . . . Just grab a weapon and move.'

They quickly scrabbled through the debris of the lobby, scooping up metal ornaments mostly. There were so many of those at The Reed. Matt found a tall, pricey-looking floor lamp. He snapped off the chrome pole from its moorings and prised off the light from the top. It felt strangely satisfying to wreck something expensive, even tonight, and he was left with a long pole, with a sharp, jagged edge. In an action movie, he'd have thrown this like a javelin and hit a demon right between the eyes from across the room. But he reckoned he'd just do some swinging and jabbing with this, if it came to that. He bobbed the pole in his hand a little, checking the weight. Everyone was doing that with their weapons. Passing them from hand to hand. It may have looked a little dumb, but it was reassuring all the same.

'Ready?' Matt turned to the little troupe, all tooled up. Nupa held, of all things, a large glass coffee pot, shaped like a fishbowl. She'd poured out the trickling contents onto the floor, and for the briefest of moments, Matt's nostrils caught a whiff of heaven. 'Wish you'd poured that into my mouth.'

She smiled. 'When we get out of here, I'll buy you a thousand lattes.'

'Noted.' They started to move. 'Okay, so we'll try the second then the third floor.'

They all nodded at each other: a kind of silent, tactical vocabulary that was starting to grow between them all. Then they trotted out through a door that led to the staircase, as silent as they could move.

They skipped the lift. Being trapped in a metal box did not sound like the healthy option right now. Not when it might, at any time, drop downwards to the ground floor and open its doors to the outside. He had a mental image of all those possessed people shuffling through the trees and stooping past hedges. Slowly turning their heads as the lift door pinged to the world that it was dinner time.

So they found the staircase instead. It was enclosed and windowless, and they crept up it in single file. Nupa pushed Matt into the front, and Claire insisted she watch from the rear. There were motivational posters on the wall. One of them showed a blank diary lying on a desk, with the ominous slogan, *You will never have this day again, so make it count.*

They reached the plain, windowless door that led to the first floor. His corridor and his room were beyond that. But they stayed in the stairwell, tiptoeing past it. When they got to an identical-looking door on the second floor, he pressed a finger to his lips to shush them all. He pulled the door handle back very, very gently indeed. A tiny crack opened, like the thinnest of lips. He pressed an eyeball at the gap and saw an empty corridor. There was no blood on the walls. No broken glass or smashed mirrors. All the lamps and pictures seemed to be in place, too. It felt like a good sign.

He pushed the door open and they crept through. As they moved along the corridor, Nupa accidentally knocked her coffee pot against a radiator. The god-awful clanging sound was so harsh that it froze them all into an instant, pantomime pause. She mouthed, *Sorry*. They waited for a moment and then, with gritted teeth, set off again.

It was only as they turned the corner that he first heard the sound of muffled sobbing. It was coming from one of the doors, way down the corridor. He could already tell which it was. They shared nervous glances, then slowly approached it, more cautious than ever. At least their footsteps were lost in the silence of such thick carpet. When they reached it, Matt saw the word CHAPEL etched into the door. There were bitter tears flowing in there. Was it a victim of the possessed, or one of the possessed themselves?

'It's him.' Perry jostled himself through. 'It's Kissell.'

'How can you tell?'

'I've heard that man cry before.' Perry reached the chapel door, but rather than knocking, he turned towards them and blocked it. 'Listen. I've got this. You should go and find that Internet room thingy. Get us connected. That's the *top* priority – am I right, Matt?'

'Right,' Matt said, awkwardly. 'So what are you going to do?'

'I'll talk to Kissell. I'll tell him the damage he's done, working these people up. I'll tell him he's in the wrong.'

'Oh, will you now?' Claire said. Her eyes were glistening, and Matt heard her sniff.

Nupa shrugged. 'Fine. Stay and give him a slap from me.' She span from the door and started walking down the corridor. She paused halfway when she realised she was alone. 'Hello? Matt? Claire? You coming?'

Matt didn't move or speak. He just stood there, thinking. Eyes gliding back and forth between Perry and Claire. Trying to understand the tension there. The coldness.

'Claire, Matt,' Perry said, 'you two need to go with Nupa. Those things could be crawling up the struts by now.'

Matt shook his head. 'Let's stick together.'

'And let Kissell get away? *I'll* keep him here. You go.'

Matt just stood there frowning. Thinking.

Nupa sighed. 'Matt. You're buffering. Now come on.'

'Wait . . .' Matt said. 'Something's not—'

The chapel door suddenly opened and everybody but Perry stepped back. They gripped their makeshift weapons – pole and coffee pot at the ready – but Perry's ears were correct. This was no raging demon. It was Pastor Kissell, wet eyes puffed, with a damp comb-over. He poked his head through the gap, glasses so crooked he could have just escaped a comedy earthquake.

'Told you,' Perry said. 'Now go on . . . shoo. Call the cavalry.'

'Pastor Kissell?' Matt said.

Kissell stared off into space.

'Can you hear me? Are you hurt?' Matt leant forward a little. 'Bernie?'

His eyes flickered behind half-fogged lenses, then he turned his jerky gaze to Matt. 'Professor . . . Matt . . . oh good. Are you . . . all right?'

'We're okay. You?'

'I'm not hurt.'

'Good. Then come with us. We're going to get help.'

'But,' his eyes rolled towards the empty corridor, 'I'm afraid . . .'

Perry shook his head, tutting loudly. Matt ignored him and reached a hand to Kissell. The door swung open, and he saw candles burning on the chapel altar.

Matt had to guide Kissell out because his footsteps were so unsteady. At times, he walked like a fawn, finding its way. His knees gave way at one point, and as Matt scooped him up, he noticed a thick and congealed gash under Kissell's hair. He gripped Matt's hand tighter.

They headed down the corridor, checking each room, and as they walked, Kissell sometimes mumbled things under his breath. Every time he did that, Matt noticed Perry's face. He didn't see irritation there. He saw something else. He saw fear.

'Why do you keep staring at him?' Matt whispered to Perry.

'Because I think we should leave him in the chapel.'

'Why?'

'Just in case . . .' Perry quickly said. 'I mean, what if *he's* possessed now, too?'

CHAPTER FIFTY-SEVEN

They guided Kissell round a curve in the corridor and immediately spotted Nupa. She span around with a huge smile and jabbed a finger at a small half-flight of stairs to her left. The one that had all the cables and wires on when he was exploring yesterday. She vanished up them. Matt tugged Kissell along, helping him lift his shaky legs up the steps. At the top, they finally found the room they were looking for.

The glass door said HUB.

'Stop the clock. We've found it,' Nupa jabbed a code into a keypad. It glowed a dull blue in the dim light, then turned green. Something clicked, and within seconds she'd vanished inside. Matt watched her through the glass, flicking switches and frantically trying out possible passwords and figuring out the backup system. Her hasty fingers kept mistyping. It was the first time he'd noticed how much she was trembling. At one point, she smacked a fist off the desk with frustration. Then she'd take a breath and try again.

While all this happened, Matt, Perry, Claire and Kissell just stood waiting on the staircase outside. Matt kept staring at the bottom of the stairs, where the corridor was. Dreading the flicker of a shadow.

'Bernie . . .' Perry said suddenly.

Kissell looked up. 'Mmmmmm?'

'I have a question and I'd appreciate a straight answer. Did you have a machine in your hand tonight or not?'

There was no hesitation. 'Yes.'

Perry's lips tightened. 'And have you always used one of those gizmos, or was that just for—'

'Always.'

The anger in Perry's face seemed to fall away. Matt saw pain there instead. Shame, even. 'But *why?* We all trusted you. You've lied to the whole world . . .'

'Perhaps . . . but what was the alternative, Simon?' Kissell leant a shoulder against the wall. 'When a mental health case doesn't respond to medicine, or counselling. Do we leave them alone in the dark? Or do we offer them something old? Something ancient. Exorcism – no matter what you think of it – has a genuine psychological power . . . but they have to believe it for it to work. The thing in my hand . . . it helped them have faith in the treatment.'

'I don't believe I'm hearing this.' Perry looked away. 'You're mad.'

'No, not mad. I've seen people puke their negativity into a bucket, and God help me, they're better. Placebo or not, they're free at the end.' He bit his lip hard. 'And I will not apologise for giving people hope. And for telling them they're not alone. If I'd maybe done the same for Sandra, then . . .' His words caught in his throat and he winced.

'Your wife?' Matt said.

Perry groaned in frustration.

351

Kissell caught Matt's eye. 'She always said he sounded very polite and kindly spoken.'

'Who was?' Matt said.

'Satan. She said he called her on the phone and told her he'd live inside her for a while. That he hoped she didn't mind, but it was for her own good. Told her to cut her hair, her clothes, her wrists. And I'd find her crying with the phone in her hand, and she'd ask me to drive her to the church and of course, being a good atheist I refu—'

'You're an *atheist*?' Perry grabbed a handrail to steady himself.

'I was . . . till tonight.' Kissell stared at the carpet.

'What's that supposed to mean?' Matt said.

'It means I refused to take her to church even though she wanted me to. She'd take the pills and I'd rock her to sleep. And when those pills didn't work, I tried new ones, and when they didn't work, we'd try more. But the calls from hell kept coming, she heard them, even when I yanked the cord out. I'd find her curled up in the corner, with that damn phone at her ear, listening to him persuade her. And she kept asking for an exorcism. Course, I said that would be dangerous and I kept on refusing. Just as I'm sure you would have done, Matt, if it was for your wife, or your child. You think there's a higher ground, don't you . . . but listen to me . . . what if the better way is to give people therapy that makes *sense* to them. That plugs in to *their* hope, and *their* fear? What if the truly rational thing is to allow the irrational its moment in the sun.'

'Bernie.' Claire's eyes were glistening. 'What happened to your wife?'

'I kept on refusing to take her to a priest . . . and I said I'd cure her with medicine. And one morning we stopped for gas and they still had one of those public telephones. It was ringing. She answered it while I was paying and then I heard the tyres soon after. The screams of the other drivers. When I looked back, she was out on the highway. Standing with her arms out.' He stared at his palm. 'She didn't last long.'

352

'I'm so sorry,' Matt said, 'but I still think you did the right thing . . .'

'I did the right thing for *me*. But dammit, I should have taken her to see Santa Claus or the Easter Bunny or Wiley Fucking Coyote or whoever the hell else she wanted. But I didn't and she's gone – but hey, Matt, at least my principles weren't compromised, so there's always that, huh?' A tear dropped from his eye.

'You said you were an atheist till tonight,' Perry said. 'What do you mean?'

'Well, that's the biggest irony of all, isn't it? See most of my clients just spat on crosses and swore in my face the usual stuff. Fine. Then after the ritual, trick or not, they were cured. Most of them did the same tonight, and they wound up dancing and celebrating and it was beautiful. But a couple of them . . . Jesus . . .' He didn't just shudder, he seemed to jerk at the thought of it. 'Firstly, it was Richie . . . my God, he did the things you see in the movies.'

Claire hugged her arms into herself. 'What things?'

'I mean his eyeballs . . . they rolled up white.'

Matt said, 'People sometimes do that in a heightened state of—'

'Dammit, Matt, I saw him lift off the ground, right in front of me. Do you hear me? I said he *lifted* off the ground and I saw the space under his feet. And he's as big as a bull but he just came drifting towards me. So I ran. I screamed and I ran . . . and then later on, just now, I saw the girl . . . Abby. She was wandering barefoot in the corridors, doing the same with her eyes, and when she saw me, she turned and floated towards me. She was saying Bennie . . . little Bennie. My grandad used to call me that. And I just wanted to keep running until I came up here to hide. And my phone kept ringing the whole time. I was too scared to answer it, because I knew who'd be on the line. Who was on the line every single time she picked up that damn—'

He jumped, they all did, when the door suddenly opened. Nupa came out, still shaking. 'All done. Took a while to figure it out but I've found their backup system for comms. The police are on their way.'

'Thank God,' Claire said.

'Thank Wi-Fi.' Nupa's half-smile faded. 'What's up with him?'

'Ignore him,' Perry said. 'He's lost his mind.'

'Let's go back to the chapel,' Matt said. 'There's space for us all and we can barricade the door.'

Perry nodded. 'Excellent idea. You folks head there now, and I'll stay and talk to Bernie for a bit. Alone. I'd like to pray for him.'

'Then pray for him in the chapel,' Matt said. 'It's a good place for it.'

Kissell nodded. 'Matt's right, Simon. We should all stick together.'

Perry's eyes started darting a little as they all started to walk back down the stairs. They moved through the corridor as quietly as they could and reached the chapel. Matt held the door open as the others filed in, then he went in too. They were all inside when Matt noticed that Perry was the only one still out in the corridor, hands on his hips. 'Please, just let me pray for my old friend in private. We'll follow you in.'

'What are you doing?' Matt frowned at him. 'Why are you so desperate to be alone with him?'

'Because he deserves forgiveness . . . for all of his tricks, I mean.'

'Simon, I've already explained about the hand thing.'

'Just get inside,' Matt said, then he froze. '*Wait . . .*'

Perry's face dropped when Matt turned back to the others.

'The box,' Matt said.

Perry said nothing.

'What box?' Kissell was settling a shaky hand onto one of the chapel chairs. 'You mean Tom's box?'

Nupa nodded. 'Yeah. Your other gizmo. The one you put a tape player in. Remember?'

Kissell blinked a few times. 'I didn't put anything in that box. I swear.'

'Get in here, Perry,' Nupa said, 'and close that damn door.'

Perry laughed, still in the corridor. He pointed through to Kissell. 'Look at him, he's had a nervous breakdown. Can't remember anything he's—'

'Wait . . . *wait*.' Matt put his hand on the door frame. 'He *couldn't* have. We picked him up from the airport. Then we went to the prison, which is where we heard about the box . . . yeah, that's right. Then we dug it up and *I* took it home straight after. The tape was already inside. He couldn't have put something in there.'

'He could have put it in there today,' Perry said.

'No . . .' Matt shook his head. 'Because my daughter said she heard that box singing.'

Perry's face dropped.

'Close the fucking door,' Nupa said.

Claire suddenly stood next to Matt, staring at Perry. 'And when we dug that box up, you said you wanted to destroy it, didn't you? You said you wanted to take it away and burn it, all by yourself. But Kissell was the one who said no. He said we should bring it here to The Reed. And I remember how scared you were, when he said that. Like you wanted this box gone . . .'

'Holy shit . . . *you* put that tape in there.' Matt felt his grip on his pole tighten. 'You must have. Before Tom even buried it. Before Kissell even came into the *country*.'

Perry started backing away, and his shoulder pressed against a small painting of a jetty of boats. The frame slid to the side, until it fell to the floor. 'No, you're wrong. Tom must have put the tape in there. That explains it.'

Matt shook his head. 'No, it doesn't. You wanted that box destroyed without anybody seeing . . . and now that we've found the tape you want Kissell gone so he'd be blamed for putting it there when—fucking hell, Perry. *Why?*'

Perry said one thing before he turned. 'You're all crazy. You're all . . . demonised.' Then he ran away, unsteady feet stomping against the carpet. His loping shoulder dragging against the wall, knocking picture after picture to the floor.

Matt turned to Claire. 'Sorry, I know he's out there but we're going to have to close this door.'

'Screw him. Close it,' she said.

He blinked, closed it, then for a moment they all stood in the chapel, trying to get their brains around it all. Nupa was shaking her head. 'I'm lost. Why would Perry put a tape in the box?'

Matt was about to speak, but Claire had already picked up a candle. She looked into the flame and spoke to it.

'I know why,' she said.

CHAPTER FIFTY-EIGHT

She didn't explain it straight away, because Matt and Nupa knew they'd already been distracted enough. They started looking for things to drag towards the door, to barricade themselves in. There was hardly anything to use.

'Where are the bloody pews?' Nupa said. 'Where are the chairs, at least?'

'There are none,' Matt said. 'They've gone trendy. It's all beanbags and cushions. Apart from . . . *that*.'

Nupa followed his gaze to an oak table, sitting near the back of the room. They all dragged it towards the door, including Kissell, who wiped his wet cheeks as he went. It wasn't the biggest of altars, and it wasn't that heavy either. But it was better than a pile of beanbags, that was for sure. They lodged it into place against the door, and with a sigh Matt took a quick glance around the chapel, just to make sure it felt secure. At least the window in here had its thick curtain closed.

There was a strange-looking water fountain buried in the wall, with water trickling over a pile of smooth white pebbles. The sound spoke of tranquility and peace. It sounded terribly out of place in this hellhole. Each corner had candles on long metal poles, burning softly. He went to blow them out, but Kissell put out a hand and said, 'Please, let them shine.' Matt shrugged and said, okay. He'd already decided against turning the main electric light off. He was worried eyes outside might see it click off. He didn't want to give any reason for any of them to come up and find this room. Not before the police got here.

He saw Nupa sinking into the circle of cushions, where Claire sat staring. 'Well?' Nupa said. 'Out with it.'

Matt joined them and waited.

Claire took a breath. 'You were right, Matt. I did see Tom that day.'

'What day?' Nupa asked.

'The day Justine was killed,' she said. 'I was painting at home and I saw Tom standing in the fields near our house. He was watching the windows and so I was scared. Simon already told me that he was probably possessed.'

'And you believed him?'

'I wasn't sure, but Simon was in London all day and Tom was out there watching me. I was scared, so I just got in my car and drove to the next town, Sneddon. He followed me. He must have had his car. He found me in the park, sitting by the lake . . .' She trailed off and touched her chest.

'What did he want?' Matt said.

'He was upset. He asked me if I knew, and of course I said, did I know what . . .' She sniffed and reached for one of the free cushions. 'He thought that Justine was having an affair with Simon. Had done for months.'

Nupa's eyebrows shot up, and looked at Matt.

'Course, I didn't believe him. Simon always told me that the possessed tell lies. And Tom really was mentally unstable, you could see that at church sometimes. So I just . . . kinda . . . snapped. I shouted at him. I said he was a mess. That he needed help, and whether it was the Devil or his mind talking, he had to stay away from me and Simon. I was . . . cruel, I think. I thought that he might respond to a stronger message. Simon was always so soft with him. So kind.' That last word made her laugh, bitterly.

'So how did Tom react?' Matt asked.

'He sat there and scratched his face till he bled. Called himself horrible names. So, I *ran* to my car. I drove home and that night Simon came straight from London to the pub. We'd started doing that once a week. It was my idea . . . to help us get closer.'

Matt shimmied forward a little. 'And did you tell Simon, about what Tom said?'

'Of course. A rumour like that could have ruined his career. I just figured this stuff about Justine and Simon was another part of the possession . . . a lie . . .' She stopped talking and stared up at the candles.

'And yet . . .' Matt said. 'Part of you thought Tom might be right, didn't it?'

Her eyelids fluttered. She sucked her lips in and slowly, with much pain, nodded. 'I guess it was just the looks Simon gave Justine sometimes, in town. That and his . . . his distance from me . . . you know? We hadn't . . .' Her voice caught and she looked at Nupa. 'We hadn't in a long time.'

Nupa covered Claire's hands with hers. The touch brought Claire's tears out.

'But Tom had no evidence and the main thing was he really *was* losing his mind, and me . . . I'm not very . . . confident in myself. So when I told Simon that same night at the pub, he was horrified. He said Tom was completely wrong and that the demon must be going after *us* now, with a pack of lies to hurt us. So he went straight over to do the exorcism. He came home and said it worked . . . until . . .'

'Till what?'

'Justine called him. She got back from Brownies that night and said Tom was acting wild and strange. She asked Simon to come round again and he did—'

Matt's mouth was open. 'He went round, *later*?'

'Yes, but he didn't stay long. I couldn't handle it. I kept pacing the floor at home, then I called him. I told him it wasn't his business and he should leave them both alone. He said he was still in the car outside their house, praying before going in. He was worried about her, and I guess I got angry, or jealous. I told him to come home straight away.'

'And did he?'

'He didn't want to. He was scared for her, but I was insistent. So he started the car and came straight home, and all this time I thought he could have saved her life, if it wasn't for my jealousy. But now I know. It wasn't my fault, or even Tom's . . . it was his. Because it was Simon who killed her.'

'What? This doesn't make any sense,' Nupa shook her head. 'Tom confessed. Simon didn't kill her.'

'Not with his own hands . . .' Matt was starting to nod. 'But think about it. Perry has an affair with a parishioner but he's petrified he'll be found out. If he is, he'll lose his wife, his job. Along comes this woman's *husband*, seeking counsel. He's blatantly suffering from depression and paranoia. So what does Perry do?'

'He sees an opportunity . . .' Claire said.

'Exactly. Perry warps Tom's already brittle mind into some sort of spiritual conspiracy.'

'He even took Tom's medication away. He said they were making him worse.'

360

Matt sighed and shook his head. 'He tells him there's a demon in him . . . of murder no less. Baal-Berith. And you just realised this, didn't you . . . ?' Matt turned to Claire. 'I saw your face, in the Ash Suite, just now.'

Kissell spoke up. 'I don't follow.'

'When I smashed the box. As soon as that happened, you wouldn't take Simon's hand, would you?'

'What are you talking about, Matt?' Nupa said.

Claire bent over to cry.

'I'm saying that look on your face, when you saw the tape recorder. I thought it was confusion but . . . but it was recognition. Wasn't it?'

She nodded into her hands. 'That recorder was mine. I've had it for years, and I liked how retro it was. So I used it as a student. I kept it in my art room, but then it went missing . . . he must have taken it. As soon as I saw it in the box, I knew. Simon must have used it, to provoke Tom. He and Justine must have been together, after all.'

Matt started pacing, taking it in. 'So Justine picks up an innocent box from a car boot sale, and Perry somehow sticks that recorder inside it. And all the while Perry is praying with Tom, telling him that demons have voices, at the same time he finds a way of making that tape play a message in the box. Like those little gizmos he made for your paintings. No wonder he wanted to destroy it on his own.'

She gripped her folded arms to her and rocked.

'Bloody hell,' Matt said. 'And who's to say that was even Tom at your doorbell?'

Claire looked up. 'What?'

'You showed me it. It was just a figure in chef's trousers. Who's to say that wasn't your husband *pretending* to be him? It's just technique after technique, trick after trick to slowly convince a man he wasn't in control . . . but the *demon* was. Maybe there was no exorcism that night at all. Maybe he goaded him to finally do it. Like . . . like one of those damn puppets in his church office.' A sudden, ice-cold image spiked into Matt's mind – shockingly sharp and detailed. Of Perry whispering through Tom's window that night with the voice of a demon . . . the same voice that came from the box . . .

She's a slut, she hates you, she's going to humiliate you . . . and you need to stop her . . .

Nupa looked over to Kissell. 'And you are involved in this?'

'No, I swear.'

'He couldn't have been. The tape was put there before he even—'

Matt stopped dead, because something crashed outside. Claire didn't flinch or move at all. She was too lost in the nightmare swirls of memory. But the rest of them were staring at the curtain.

'Oh, no. They're at the window.' Kissell gasped.

'No, they're not.' Matt pushed himself up. 'We're too high up.'

'But they can rise up. I saw them!'

'They're not bloody flying.' Matt rushed over and peeked through the crack in the curtain. It was too dark to see outside, not with the glare of the chapel lights, so he nodded for Nupa to switch them off after all. The room plunged into nothing more than candlelight and he looked out again. Just as he did, he heard a loud shouting coming from somewhere outside.

'Keep an eye on that door.' Matt popped the latch and started to raise the window, a tiny amount. It wouldn't go far. But a small gap was quite enough to hear and enough to see, because now his eyes had adjusted to the light.

He could see some of the windows of the lobby, a few floors below. Only now, the glass was smashed and gaping. The curtains were flapping wild in the wind, and scattered on the gravel path below he saw chair after chair, where someone had thrown them through, out into the dark.

Then he saw a figure, jogging around the path, something shiny twinkled in his hands. A set of keys. It was Perry, and he was running back around the building, towards the lake, which Matt knew was where the lift door was. The main entrance to the entire place.

Just as Perry went to turn the corner, he cupped his hands around his mouth, and shouted at the black woods again. Only now, with the chapel window open, Matt could understand it.

'Come back! Come back in!' Perry shouted. 'I've unlocked the doors. And look. They're up there. In the chapel. They're mocking you!'

For a split second, Matt saw Perry slide his head back, and he looked right at him. For the strangest moment, a breathless, shivering moment, the lobby lights picked out Perry's eyes. Even from this distance, Matt saw a creepy trick of the light, as if his eyeballs were luminescent and burning with yellow fire. Then he was gone, running hunched over and around the corner, opening whatever doors were left, and all the while crying out for the possessed to come back home, to find them.

CHAPTER FIFTY-NINE

Matt took a few, unsteady steps back from the window. 'We need to go . . . now.'

Nupa stared at him. 'What's going on?'

'It's Perry. He's calling them all up here.'

A ghastly wave of fear washed across her. He saw her eyes grow fixed and forward. The halting of her chest.

He went on. 'These doors are not going to hold. Not if there's a few of them.'

Claire squeezed the pillow she was holding and flung it across the room with a grunt of anger. 'Damn him.'

'The roof?' Matt said. 'It's flat, isn't it? Can we get up there?'

Nupa stopped for a moment, bit her lip, and nodded. Locking herself back into action. 'Yeah, it's flat. We put some cameras up there. Easy to defend, I guess. There's a door at the top of the very highest stairwell. I have the keycode.'

'Then let's go.' He started dragging the altar away from the door. God, it was flimsy.

When the door was clear he went to grab the handle.

'Wait.' Kissell stared at the door. They all did. 'What if they're all up here already?'

Nupa waved her coffee pot in the air. 'Then we whack the fuckers' heads in with a Java.'

He pulled the handle down, gripped the pole.

His entire head was a heartbeat.

When he opened the door, the corridor was empty. It did look different, though. At first, he couldn't figure out why exactly, until they crept along the carpet. It was the pictures on the walls. The ones Perry had accidentally knocked down earlier. They'd all been replaced, upside down. Even the pictures that hadn't fallen before were also flipped.

Odd that such a thing would chill him so much, but it did, as they hurried past them. All those empty fishing boats hanging from the sky. Those tall trees, sprouting downwards from green clouds. It made him think of Menham, and a primary school where he'd once stood. Where a music teacher lay dead, without a throat, and all the children's pictures of animals walking had also been turned completely on their heads.

When he finally reached the door to the stairwell, Matt pressed an ear against the cold wood. He heard nothing, and pushed it gently with his shoulder, poised to thrust his pole directly into whatever might come running, but nothing did. He stepped inside and waved them all through, letting them go up to the next floor. He stayed put, so he could keep an eye on the staircase heading down, bracing himself for shadows, or a flurry of many footsteps, heading up. Was that the wind moaning down there? Or was that the entire, tumbling horde of them, following Simon Perry? Storybook images of the Pied Piper flashed in his mind, stirring up his old, childhood terror of that tale.

He stared into the inky dark staircase below, watching for glowing eyes to start appearing, then with a shiver he tore himself away and followed them up the staircase to the top floor. The Reed's almost pyramid-like design meant that the highest point of the building was little more than a concrete box. There were no more corridors up here, no windows. The only thing other than the wall was a red metal door that said the word ROOF on it. The one he'd found locked yesterday.

He reached for the entry pad and a low moan, as heartfelt as any the possessed could make, rolled out of him. He didn't bother turning to Nupa for the code because the box wasn't glowing and was crooked close up. He tapped it and the whole panel dropped off in a spring of wires.

Nupa's jaw fell with a click, and Matt saw something in her eye he didn't like. The hot, hard throb of panic.

'No, no, no . . .' she said.

'Nupa. Calm down.' He pushed on the door as hard as he could, then he nodded them all over and they tried together. So much for group effort. Turned out, they were Team Pathetic. It simply wouldn't budge. He even risked the noise by kicking it, hard. It stayed solid.

'He did this . . . I know it.' Claire glared at the broken keypad. 'Selfish bastard.'

Nupa, her stunning hair now slicked with sweat and blood spray, started shoving at the door, pressing at it with her splayed hands, heaving her hip into it, until her arms shook.

Matt put a hand on her shoulder. 'It's useless.'

She turned back towards him, opened her mouth to speak . . . and screamed instead.

He spun round and looked down the staircase at the small visible segment of the next floor down.

366

Two bare feet were standing on the carpet below.

Nupa immediately fell backwards against the roof door. The rest of them had the good sense to stay still. He thought the feet had hair at first, but it was actually dry blood, and though they couldn't see above the knee, he knew it was Abby. He wondered if that blood was from Ethan or from the word she'd been carving into her stomach. Or who knows, maybe she'd killed a whole bunch of people tonight – and they were next.

They all just stood there, one collective held breath.

Seconds passed. A minute even.

He felt a sudden movement next to him, then Kissell pressed his lips against Matt's ear, and pushed in a panicked whisper. And no amount of Matt's finger against his lips to shush him would work. *'This is how they stood, earlier on . . .'* Kissell hissed. *'Before their eyeballs turned white. Before they started to levitate.'*

Matt went to shush him, but then one of the feet suddenly moved.

Claire yelped. Nupa yelped. Kissell started to frantically cross himself.

It wasn't a zombie slide, or a Frankenstein Monster stomp. Just a careful turn towards the door they'd just come through down there. The one that led to the chapel. He saw the side of her ankles, just as he heard the metal hinges creak open. Then the bare feet dragged away and were gone.

The door closed with a dull click, and she vanished, somehow oblivious to them.

Everybody's breath finally spilt out for freedom. Only Nupa's brought something with it. She pressed her head against the wall and vomited.

CHAPTER SIXTY

'I think that was Abby,' Matt said.

Claire blinked. 'The one who passed all your tests?'

'Not every—'

Abby's muffled screams suddenly boomed from somewhere in the corridor downstairs. Then they heard glass shattering. It sounded like a windowpane.

'She must be in the chapel,' Kissell said. 'All those crosses.'

Nupa finally looked up from the stinking floor and wiped her mouth on her sleeve. 'I can't do this any more. I'm going down before she comes back.'

'But Perry's down there,' Matt said.

'And all the others too.' Claire nodded. 'We should stick together.'

'I don't care, I'm making a break for my car.' Nupa started down. 'So if you really want to stick together, then you'll have to follow me.'

Matt looked back at the roof door and the useless keypad hanging open. He sighed and followed her down.

They crept down step by step, eyes always on the door where Abby was still wailing. When he reached the bottom step, the first thing he did was repurpose his beloved lamp pole. He slid it through the handle of the stairwell door and wedged it against the frame. Not unsnappable by any stretch, but something to slow her down.

Just as he turned, Abby roared in agony, calling out a name, which confused him at first. What on earth was Tuan? His brain quickly remembered. The kid he'd met in the TV studio make-up room. Her little boy. To hear her scream her own son's name with such panic and pity was heart-wrenching. But for that terrible shout to be threaded with hatred and venom too was truly frightening. The type of sound you just had to retreat from.

Nupa wasn't thinking straight. When she reached the next floor down, she pushed through the door that led to his accommodation corridor. He rushed to her, to tell her to slow down, but something stopped her in her tracks anyway. When he reached her shoulder, he saw it too.

The lights were off on his corridor, but there was enough spilling from the stairwell to pick out shapes at the far end. Hunched in the shadows were two figures. One was collapsed in a heap by a wall and the other was nearby, crouching on his haunches, gnawing at his own wrist with a sickening rapidity.

He recognised them both: the collapsed one was a recently added client. He didn't know his name, but he'd seen him dancing the Macarena earlier in the after-party downstairs. And the other, the one eating his own hand, was Pavel Basa, who had gone missing earlier. His pyjamas looked streaked with mud and his bare feet were gashed and scraped by twigs. He'd been out in the woods, no doubt about it. And now he was back.

Was Pavel crouching like that because he'd killed people tonight, or was he as innocent as anybody else and just traumatised by the horror of it all? Matt had no idea, but it didn't matter much anyway. Nupa pushed her hand against the door and started to shove it shut. 'No frickin' way are we running into that fruit loop.'

Kissell shot his hand at the door and kept it from closing.

Nupe glared at him. 'What are you doing?'

'They need help . . . I should pray.' He started rummaging in his trouser pocket. There was a secret flap, which was barely visible. He pulled out his buzzer and blatantly started fixing it into his palm.

Nupa threw her hands up. 'Leave them!'

'No, this might work.' His face was a crumple of pain as he pushed through.

'Wait,' Matt said. 'The police are almost—'

'I will not leave them in the dark . . . look at them.'

Matt stared down the corridor, at Pavel crouching, just as Kissell started walking into the darkness, raising his hands in prayer.

'Come *back*.' Matt reached out to grab him, but Kissell slipped through his fingers.

'Love will set you free, my friend. Let me pray.'

Pavel slowly looked up and Matt thought he was about to smile at Kissell, but the lips peeled back from his teeth much further than would be normal, and a terrible sound came sizzling out of the hole. '. . . *she was alone, liar man . . . but she's not alone now . . .*' The voice dissolved into filthy laughter.

Nupa shoved the door closed. It clicked loudly as it shut. 'Screw him, let's go.'

'We can't just leave him.' Matt tried to drag the door back open. Claire helped him shove Nupa to the side, and when he did, he pulled the door back. Matt could not control the shudder when he saw. Kissell was already dead on the floor, glasses off, neck wrong, his doll eyes dripping his last ever tear. Pavel was crouched over him tapping Kissell's nose. It looked like a chimpanzee with a rubber toy. When Matt saw the growing bulge pushing up the crotch of Pavel's pyjama bottoms, he couldn't do anything else but turn away.

'He's dead.'

Claire and Nupa span and just barrelled down the staircase to the ground floor, where the double doors to the lobby waited in the gloom. Matt slammed the door and ran down too, catching up with Nupa and grabbing her arm. 'Dammit, Nupa. Slow down. *Think*.'

'Get off me, get *off*!' She dug her nails into his hand and dragged herself from him. She fell into a tumbling run, straight through the lobby doors. They both swung open, and though the place thankfully looked empty, Nupa still froze in the doorway.

'Oh God,' she said. 'Cockroaches.'

He saw the small black shapes crawling over the sofas, dripping from the curtains, and some even flying through the air in strange arcs and tumbles. They were leaves from the trees outside. Black, brown and dry, they had blown in through the now broken windows.

'Nupa. *Wait!*'

She was running towards the lift, her hand thrust deep into her jeans pocket so she could fish out her car keys. A simple plan, really. Head down in the lift, get to the parking lot outside. Drive off into the sunset and maybe get therapy. Then win an award for the world's most shocking TV show.

She reached for the lift button.

He wasn't really sure what it was that made him so certain Nupa should stop. Intuition, superstition, it was hard to tell. But he and Claire shouted her name just as she jabbed the lift button repeatedly. Then the innocuous chime pinged its greeting, and Nupa, with the slip of a hopeful smile on her face, turned back to them. Panic stepped aside for a brief moment and she was the same, strong woman again. Sanity came through. She called out, 'Come on, guys. The crew car is as fast as fu—'

The lift doors, thick and mirrored, split into a long black line from top to bottom. And there he was, instantly. So close to the opening slit that his face must have been pressed against it the whole time. Reverend Perry didn't even wait for the doors to fully open. He just seemed to spill out, shoulders heaving through the doors. His clerical collar hung open at his neck. Once he stepped out, he locked both feet into place, like he needed the ballast. He lifted his arm that held something long and sharp.

Nupa was still looking back at Matt and Claire.

Matt's mouth went to shout, *Noooo*. One of those slow-mo roars you hear in bad movies, but as soon as it happened, Matt's lungs were pumped with instant cement, and so it was impossible to fuel any word, ever again.

CHAPTER SIXTY-ONE

Nupa's face burst into a look of surprise that was almost comical. The type of look you'd pull to a friend, when a stranger farted in a lift. He saw her eyebrows shoot up and her mouth formed an 'oooo'. It was the perfect cue for the comedy slide whistle. But then Claire let her own shriek come out, as she watched. It flushed itself out from between her bared teeth, long and harsh. When she stopped screaming, the entire world plunged into a much quieter, yet infinitely more gut-wrenching sound.

It was like a cruel god might be on the decks up there in heaven, having fun with the sound mix on earth. Dropping everything else away and sliding up his favourite faders, one at a time. The loudest of which sounded like the coffee machine in the corner, starting up again, spurting out decaf into the empty space where Nupa had taken the glass pot, earlier. Even now, Matt saw that pot falling from Nupa's fingers. Yet no matter how much Matt's self-protective brain insisted he was hearing coffee spurting, he knew it wasn't coffee spurting. That sound was Perry, repeatedly and methodically jabbing the blade into her back.

Claire dropped to the floor with screams of horror and incomprehension at what her husband was doing, right in front of her. Matt saw her fingers scramble up her own cheeks, eyes shut so tight that there were now shrivelled lines where her eyes used to be. Her face had aged by decades in a single second.

Matt was aware that he was running at Perry, before he even realised it was possible to move. He bounded across the lobby floor, yelling at Perry to *sssstopppppp*. Matt reached out his hands as he ran. The type of move folks do on the motorway, when a truck is barrelling down on them. Matt's voice was the engine roar. 'Let. Her. Go!'

To Matt's surprise, Perry complied with the request. He put his hand against her shoulder and pushed her hard. Nupa slid off the blade, staggering forwards, arms flailing and eyes rolling up. Matt's kneecaps cracked with fire as he dropped to the floor to catch her. She collapsed completely onto him.

They both landed in a white-hot, gasping heap, and as his hands touched her back nausea made the room spin. He felt the hideous, rhythmic press of warm fluid gushing through his fingers.

Matt let out a loud, involuntary wail. Who cared if it brought all the other monsters running? She ended up draped across his lap and so he quickly grabbed a cushion. Anything to press against her back, which now looked like the hideous surface of an alien planet, with craters erupting. Pressure. That's what blood needed, wasn't it? Lots and lots of pressure.

He grabbed a nearby cushion, just as he heard her guzzle whatever air was left of her. He could smell that perfume of hers even now, but it was being rapidly overwhelmed by the sickening metallic odour of her blood. He noticed that Nupa's heartbeat, that had only just been pounding against his knee, wasn't pounding any more.

His hands were trembling, as he looked up.

Perry was standing there, staring at his hand in pure horror. Whether it was guilt or simple shock didn't matter much, because that *almost* human look in his face didn't last anywhere near as long as it should have. After that initial, gaping despair, he just blinked himself into reality, or perhaps, *unreality*. Perry held the knife with the tail of his shirt, and started to wipe the blade and handle against the back of a wingback armchair. Rubbing any part he may have accidentally touched with his fingers.

Claire had curled up into a silent, shivering ball.

The blade clean, Perry took a drunken sidestep, then he reached a flailing hand out. His trembling, wet fingers found the back of a moulded plastic chair. He dragged it into place and dropped into it, panting. He started mumbling . . . 'Why did you do it . . . why?' His voice kept catching with emotion. Then he looked up. 'Why did you do it, Matt?'

'*What?*'

'You should've left that box alone.' He started rocking back and forth on the chair. 'Yep. Yep, that's it. You should've let me take that box in my car, and I could have burnt it in the woods. That would have been the end of it . . . but you all brought it here, and you broke it open and you saw . . .' Perry cast his eyes to Nupa on the floor. He gripped his stomach in a sudden cramp. 'You left me no choice . . . that poor woman.'

Matt spoke, eyes hooded. 'So what . . . are you going to kill us all, are you? You're going to let us all die here tonight, just so we don't tell the world what you did to that ridiculous box? That's why you wanted Kissell alone before, isn't it? So you could kill him, before he could say the tape wasn't his?'

'You shouldn't have broken it open . . .'

Matt stared at him. 'How could you do this?'

'Hey. If you have to blame anybody, then blame Justine . . .' He looked over to the Claire ball on the floor. 'She started it, love. The affair, I mean. But I broke it off after a while. I swear I did. But she was going to tell. She was going to tell the church . . . tell you . . . tell my *parents* . . .' He visibly shuddered at that last part, and he shook his head. 'She wouldn't let me end it. She wanted to keep on sinning. And Tom was already starting to hate her so much . . . so he helped the sinning stop, that's all.'

'And killing Justine wasn't a sin?' Matt said.

'I didn't do that, though.'

'You drove him to it . . .'

'Did I?' When he said that, there was a chilling sense of bafflement to his voice. As if he really didn't know the answer to the question he'd just been asked. 'Was it really me who made that tape and put it in the box? Or was it something else making me do it? Was it really me at the doorbell?'

'That *was* you?' Claire's unsteady voice came out as a thin whimper.

He nodded. 'Sometimes Tom had doubts he was possessed. But when I showed him that video, he knew the truth. And so did you.'

'The truth?'

'Mm-hmm. That something much more horrible was controlling me . . . controlling him and her and all of it . . .' He opened his hand. His finger and thumb looked like they'd been completely dipped in motor oil. 'Like it was controlling me just now. Makes you think, doesn't it?'

'Perry, you're mad,' Matt said, starting to ease Nupa off his legs. 'You just didn't want your affair found out and so you goaded her husband to kill her. And you went along with all this TV crap, because it just played into your claims. That demons are real and drive people to murder. When the only real demon here is . . . is you.'

'What a silly thing to say. I'm innocent . . .' He pressed a finger against his temple, hard enough to turn the tip white. 'And I'll be better soon. I'll pray for the demon to leave me and exorcise it. You'll see. Just not yet. There's one more task to do, then I'll be free of him.'

'What task?'

'No one can know about the box, or the doorbell.'

'Free of who?' Claire snapped it at him, pushing herself up. 'Dammit, free of who?'

He frowned. 'Baal-Berith, of course. This is his party, isn't it? And I'm sorry, but he's made it very clear just now that I'm the one who has to walk out of here. I'll tell the world what happened. How we were overrun with the possessed tonight. That's not a lie, is it? . . . I mean I didn't kill anyone till just now and . . . hey, I just thought. They'll see the possessed on the cameras. They'll see Richie, for sure. It'll just go to prove that these people are capable of murder. That Tom was controlled by a . . .' He trailed off, realisation dawning.

Matt, eager to rub it in, said what Perry was suddenly realising. He lifted a finger and pointed up into the corner of the room. 'And they'll see you too. They'll see what just happened in every detail. They'll see you smashing the windows. Calling them in. Give them a wave, you prick.'

Matt stopped talking when Perry rushed forward in a hot panic. He bounded to the corner of the room, slipping over debris and clambering up onto a sofa. He started leaping up for the fixed cameras, yanking the cord down from the beam. The camera fell and smashed into a spray of plastic and metal on the floor.

Perry scooped it up in a bundle of pieces, and came towards Matt. He threw it on the floor in front of him. *Here's your camera. Ha!* The pathetic triumph was short-lived, because Matt just glanced across at the opposite end of the lobby. Perry flicked his eyes there too, and he saw the other camera high up on the beam. His face crunched.

'Say cheese,' Matt said.

Perry darted in the direction of the other camera, but stumbled to an abrupt stop. Claire had fully unfurled and had now stood up. She was standing directly under the second camera, leaning against the wall, one foot against the wallpaper. She was curling her finger towards him.

Come here, she mouthed. *Come here.*

Perry stared up at the camera above her, then he started a slow and deliberate stalk towards her. His face split into what was supposed to be a friendly smile. The Devil's type of friendly. 'Petal, please. Let your husband through.'

She curled her finger again. *Come here.*

Matt got to his feet, broken camera still in hand. 'Claire. What are you doing?' He started walking towards Perry.

'I'm your husband.' Perry took slow steps. She was still at the other side of the room. 'Remember you took vows. You need to submit. Now move.'

She laughed at that. 'Come here. Let me give you something.'

'Claire,' Matt called over. 'Be careful.'

Perry lifted the knife. 'You should let me through . . .'

When she still didn't move, his creepy smile finally fell away. His eyes glazed over. 'Baal Berith . . . he'll kill you, you know, Claire? He's the god of murder, after all. And so you can't expect him to listen to me. He'll just do it.' He took a hideous marionette step forward. Then the knife went up. 'Move, ya fuckin' frigid sow. Move!'

Matt bolted forward.

Perry heard him coming, and so his feet also exploded into movement. He barrelled at her like a hurricane, but Matt was faster. He still had the broken camera in both of his hands, so he lifted it high into the air. He smacked it down against the back of Perry's head, and leapt onto his back, dropping him to the floor in a tackle.

For a moment, the only sound was the grunts and gasps of two men rolling across the carpet. Matt felt an elbow cracking into his jaw, and he fell away. But when Perry went to run again, laughing, Matt just grabbed his ankle. He fell forwards, arms windmilling as he stumbled headlong towards a large glass coffee table.

His arm went through first. A wide palm shattering the glass. He screamed, and fell through it, his other hand gripping the knife. The ragged edges of glass dragged up the skin of his arms, leaving widening, gaping trails. Then he spun around midway down, and his back hit the glass-covered carpet beneath it.

Matt scrambled over and grabbed Perry's wrist. He slammed the back of his hand against the floor. His fingers unfurled and the knife skittered across the carpet.

Perry's shining eyes watched it bounce away from him like a long-adored lover, leaving for the very last time. His shoulder wound gaped, and Matt looked away when he saw the clear white of bone.

Claire dropped at his left. Matt saw her knee crack into glass, but she didn't care. She started to stroke her hands across her husband's sweat-soaked hair and down the sides of his freckled cheeks.

'I said I had something for you,' she said.

'Is it forgiveness, love?' Perry's voice seemed to bubble.

'It's this . . .' She suddenly shoved her fingers into his mouth and yanked his jaw down.

She had something in her hand, and she stuffed it quickly between his lips. She made no sound when he bit down hard on her fingers. She just pulled her hand away and stood up, holding her bleeding knuckles.

She looked down at Perry, whose lips were painted with her blood. He was choking on whatever she'd shoved in there.

'May God, never, ever, *ever* forgive you,' she said. Then she burst into tears and ran towards the lift.

Perry arched his back and turned his head, watched her step inside and press the button. The doors closed before Matt could even stand.

Head on the side, Perry vomited out a smooth, stone pebble. Matt recognised it from the chapel upstairs. From the holy water fountain. Once it was out, Perry's eyeballs slid in the sockets and found him, and he grinned towards the lift as the lights above it counted down. 'I'll chase her, Matt. Just watch. And I'll chase you, too.'

'If you think this demon bit's going to help you in court, you really have lost your—'

He laughed. 'You do know this isn't Perry talking, don't you? What's my name?'

'Simon Perry.'

'Try again. My name is . . .'

'Your name is selfish murderer.'

'Mmmm. That's closer. But you know my name. You know it deep in the crack of your calcified bones. I'm Baal-Berith. And I've been hard done by, Matt. I've been vilified by the Christians and the dopey demonologists, but really you'll find that I'm a perfectly reasonable chap. And I've been standing with you for a long, long time. Ask your dad.'

'You're pathetic.' Matt looked at him. 'And if you want to survive this, you really need to save your breath.'

'Oh, I'll survive. Daddies need to be respected . . . don't you think?'

'I'm going.'

'And mamas too. Yup. Your mama especially. She neeeeeeeds to be remembered? Don't you think?'

Matt stared at him. 'What did you say?'

'I said . . . mama neeeeeeeed . . . your respect.'

Matt stomped towards him. 'Stop talking or I'll make you stop.'

'Ooooo. Gonna punch me over and over on the carpet? Huh? Huh? You like that, don't you?'

Matt swallowed. 'Perry, Baal, whoever you are. Would you answer a question for me?'

'Fire away, friend.'

'Claire said you went *back* to the house that night.'

His eyes shone, and he smiled with excitement. Pride even. 'That's right.'

'And she said you prayed on the drive for a long time, before going in. Then she called and demanded you come home.'

He was nodding. 'That's right . . . that's right. What's your question, though?'

'Did you go inside the house?'

His grin started to grow.

'Did you go in there and kill her, with your own hands? Did you make Tom believe it was him?'

His chest started to bounce in rapid laughter. 'Well, aren't you a clever boy? And I'll do the same with you . . . *watch*.'

The room suddenly exploded with the shrill sound of a siren. Matt immediately flung his hands to his ears and winced.

For a cruel second, he thought it might be the police, but then the constant, ear-splitting drone became clear, just as soon as his nostrils started to fill with the acrid smell of smoke.

'Don't fear the fire, Matt,' Perry said. 'Fire's good. Fire purifies. It needs to be respected and loved . . . like me.'

Matt spun back towards the stairwell door they'd all come through. The one that led to the upper floors. It was laying open, so he could see the steps. But he didn't see fire. Not at first. He saw something else.

Those bare feet again were slowly and shakily moving down each step.

'Oh crap.' He sucked a breath in, and he heard Perry starting to laugh hysterically.

Matt grabbed Perry's knife and ran a little closer. He saw Abby, standing on the staircase, dressed in nothing but that thick and long jumper of hers that hung down as far as her thighs. Only the mid-section had a darker patch of blood, from where she'd cut her stomach before. She wore nothing else. He saw a few crusted red lines, snaking down her skinny legs, but not much. Maybe she hadn't cut deep.

In the floor above he saw the faint wisps of smoke. She had two hands wrapped tightly around the chapel candle, pulling it so close towards her chest that a small circle in her clothes was already starting to ignite.

CHAPTER SIXTY-TWO

'Abby,' Matt shouted at her, which made her blink. 'Blow it out.'

'I'm . . .' She swayed on the step, halfway up.

'Blow it out. Help's coming.'

'What have I done? . . . Matt? I'm scared.'

He took a few steps forward, not wanting to scare her off, but keen to get close enough to at least blow the flame out.

'I should burn.'

'No . . .'

She closed her eyes and pressed the candle towards her heart. He heard a very small *whoop* as the fire really caught this time. Had she doused herself in something? The flames instantly flared up her shoulder.

He scrambled up the steps and slapped the candle away. She barely noticed him do it. He caught a split-second glimpse of the flames trying to lick her cheek, yet she stood there horribly calm. He manically looked around, and saw a fire extinguisher on the wall, a few steps up. He yanked it from its holder and turned to blast her, but she was already walking calmly down to the lobby; her black hair was catching, now. He could smell it burning. He could hear it sizzling.

'Stop,' Matt shouted. 'Please.'

He cleared three steps and fell into a stumbling run, rushing in front of her. He opened the valve and then Abby was lost in a thick white mist. It made her stagger to the side, but at least when she dropped, the fire was out. She fell against a chair clutching her shoulder in a dawning agony.

Something boomed upstairs.

It was so loud that it made him duck. When he looked back at the stairwell, the staircase walls were now flashing with an orange glow. He could see smoke billowing down from the highest floors. She'd torched the chapel, he just knew it. She'd taken those candles and burnt it down.

His ears throbbed with the alarm. Heck, he could feel the rattling pulse of it in his bones, in his skeleton, but he still turned to her and tried to help her up.

She kept blinking. 'What did I do?'

'We have to get out. Best avoid the lift . . . the kitchen has a door . . .'

'I don't remember anything.' She winced in pain.

'Just don't let go . . .' He slipped his hand into hers, always conscious that she might flip into something savage at any moment. But he grabbed her all the same and took one last look at Nupa. She was lying in a blood-black lake, which was slowly being covered by a mist of smoke.

He groaned and turned to Perry, who was still collapsed on his back. His usual pink skin was now as white as milk, and he was twitching from the waterfall of blood from his shoulder. But he was doing something else too. He was looking straight at Matt and giggling.

Matt was conscious that he should probably drag this guy out of here and yank him down the fire escape. Make him face the police and a court and a life behind bars. But as he took a step towards him, Perry smiled and said, 'Hey, neighbour, why don't you lie on top of me?'

A belching gasp of thick smoke suddenly bloomed into the lobby from the staircase, and he heard the ominous creek of joists upstairs. Something collapsed in the stairwell. Shit. He broke into a run, darting through the lobby and dragging a dazed Abby with him. As he went he was doing everything he could to blank out the sight of Perry's face. Of those bulbous green eyes staring with blazing fury at him and that ginger jaw and those thick pink lips and worst of all the long, lolling, licking tongue from a mouth that had once so gently kissed the lips of Justine . . . and yet was now mouthing the silent, but furious words of Baal-Berith. '*Mama neeeeeed . . . mama neeeeeed . . . a good bit of tongue in her mouth.*' All mixed with a terrible, bestial laughter.

When they pushed through the glass doors, and then through the corridor to the dining hall, where they'd all been dancing before, the disco lights were pulsing again. Pretty rainbow colours, flashing up the floor. But at least there was no music playing. That was good. Hearing 'Crazy Frog' right now would flip Matt's sanity completely over the edge. As he tugged her through the swirling colours she slowed down, whimpering for a moment. He turned to her, and it was the only time he considered pushing her away and leaving her for the fire.

It was the strobe light. It was making her head move in strange, mechanical movements. And when she slowly opened her mouth, he saw her form an 'm' and he was convinced that if she said the same thing that Perry was saying, Matt would leave her completely.

But she said, 'M . . . m . . . my shoulder . . . oh God, it hurts . . .'

Something else boomed and they both instinctively went to duck. Matt looked up at the ceiling and saw steam misting down from the plaster.

'Quickly,' he said.

They pushed on, smashing into the kitchen and then straight to the back door, which lay wide open now, wedged with a heavy pot on the floor. Perry must have done that earlier, when he'd called the possessed back inside to kill them. He rushed out onto the fire escape and drew in a breath of night air. It lacked any of the biting cold he'd felt earlier; it felt the opposite in fact, because now the sky was filling with fire. His right cheek burnt as their feet rattled down the rickety metal steps, handrail shaking like it might snap off completely.

As they hurried downwards, he looked out across the woods. Tree trunks were flickering and swaying in The Reed's glow. He thought of old Disney cartoons, where the forests came alive. It was only when he hit the last few stairs before the ground that he dared look fully to his right, and into the scorching blaze.

The top two floors of The Reed were a swirling cauldron of flames and Matt saw thick black smoke rising and funnelling high up into the night, blocking out the stars. Another sound of glass shattering made them both duck, as another one of the windows up there shattered. He saw glass, glittering like confetti, from a top floor room, scattering into the air, and vanishing into the smoke. A moment later, it crackled as it fell onto one of the upper level roofs.

Abby moaned in pain and lost her footing. So he linked her arm and helped her make the last step.

Their feet hit the gravel, but Matt kept them running, getting them clear of The Reed, which might teeter on its stalk and collapse at any second. He headed for the boating lake, and even though his lungs screamed for rest, he didn't stop until their crunching shoes crashed into the bitterly cold water.

Abby flung herself into the black, quaking mass, wincing at the coldness of it. But it seemed to soothe her shoulder. God, he thought, how bad was she burnt? Then he saw her turn away from him to stare across the lake . . . out where Ethan must be . . . right now.

Something else caught his eye. Things were moving in the forest. Figures. Just one or two at first. He sucked in a breath and grabbed one of the oars from the boats. Just as multiple black shadows came seeping out from the trunks.

I can't do this. It's too much. I can't handle this, he thought, but then he felt that same burst of relief that he always felt, whenever he swam up from the bottom of a swimming pool, and broke back into air. Because all those shadows were crew members and just a few of Kissell's clients. They all had their palms across their foreheads in shock and awe and tears of trauma too. Staring at The Reed as it lit up the sky.

CHAPTER SIXTY-THREE

'Jesus. I thought you were dead . . .' It was Suzy, running over and hugging him. She squeezed hard, and he squeezed hard back.

He glanced at the five or six others over her shoulder. 'Is this everybody?'

'No. Most got away, thank God. They got in their cars and drove off. But they say he rushed out into the car park, smashing everything up. So everybody else just ran into the woods.'

'Who?'

'That Richie guy. He went absolutely berserk and lost it. I think he might have killed some more people in The Reed. He tried to get into the toilet where I was hiding, but after a while he just stopped trying. I think he must have heard you guys in the Ash Suite. I heard him running over there, and then the commotion. So I just got out and ran.' She looked at the floor, started to cry. 'I'm sorry I left you in there, Matt. I'm so—'

'You did the right thing. And the rest? The . . . possessed?'

'The clients? They came with us. Most of them freaked out at first, but once we calmed them down they've been as shit scared as us.'

Matt leant to the left and saw even more figures, back in the depths of the forest. Their shapes, now visible in the flickering light. He felt a sudden and profound wave washing across his entire body. Something unexpected . . . it was guilt. How quickly he'd assumed these people could turn into a horde of psychotic zombies. He shook his head in shame. 'You're saying there was just one of them who turned violent?'

'Richie, yeah, but Pavel was acting weird too. We found him out here in the woods, hiding. When he saw us, he just started singing and ran back into The Reed. We couldn't stop him . . . hey, what's wrong?'

'We thought . . . we thought there was a whole bunch of them out here who must have gone crazy. It's why we never came out. It's why we stayed in there. I saw Pavel. He killed Kissell.'

'Jesus . . .' Suzy said.

'And Abby over there . . . we have to keep an eye on her.'

'What a mess. Oh, and we saw Reverend Perry. He started smashing the windows, telling us all to come back inside. We stayed put. He's loopy . . .' She trailed off, and frowned. 'Did you see Nupa in there?' Her voice cracked on the name. Maybe she could tell.

'She didn't make it. And Ethan too.'

'*Ethan?*' This whisper of his name made Suzy's mouth fall open, and she seemed to lose her footing. He caught her and held her up.

Matt turned back to The Reed, an inferno now. The first time he'd seen it, it looked like a mushroom, but now, filled with fire, and plumes of thick smoke, it looked terrifyingly nuclear. Like something straight out of the cold war.

He looked across at the others. The survivors.

Sensing it was over, they'd come out from the woods, and were looking up at the final conclusion of what had turned out to be an eventful slice of TV. He wondered if the mournful screech of bending metal might be all those cameras, perishing in the flames. He knew the footage was being streamed to off-site hubs as well as here. So the fire wouldn't ruin it. And that footage would be helpful, if they wanted to make sense of this night. But if this was the funeral for all those cameras and lenses, and this entire attempt to make TV history, he was happy to dance at its cremation.

The flames had reached down to the lobby now, and he could see the curtains licking the air, desperate for escape. And as the smoke belched up and out of the broken windows, he thought he saw a figure rise up, just for a moment. He thought he saw Perry walking calmly through the flames.

No wait . . . he wasn't walking any more. Matt squinted and took a step forward. Perry was dancing in happy, twirling circles. And the crackle of the fire sounded like his laughter, filling the hot air. Matt pressed his finger and thumb into his eyes, and when he looked again, he saw flames and only flames.

So they all just stood there, watching and waiting, tilting one ear to the sky in the hope that they might soon hear the sirens from the promised help. Some of them even sat on the ground, like this was bonfire night. Though obviously without the cheers or the clapping hands. Sobs and whimpers were the only real human sounds here.

'I think you can put that down now,' Suzy said.

He hadn't even realised he was still holding the oar in one hand.

He went to let go, but he was too afraid to put it down. Too confused at what could happen. Like this entire clan were just waiting for him to drop it, and then as soon as he did, their eyes would roll over white and they'd tear him apart. And if he turned to see Abby, he wondered if he might see her hovering over the waters, toes cutting a line in the surface as she drifted towards the shore.

Such thoughts made him groan in self-disgust, but he still didn't throw it away. 'I better keep it. In case she does anything.'

He turned back to see where Abby really was. She was still in the water, but she was no longer crying. She'd turned back round, and had joined with the rest of them, and together they watched The Reed groan, scream and die, and the flames were simultaneously frightening and beautiful, and very, very bright.

CHAPTER SIXTY-FOUR

Professor Matt Hunter, in a white shirt, jacket and dark blue tie, sat in a single black chair, floating in space. Around him was nothing, a pure black void. He heard a voice murmur somewhere in the darkness, and then a mechanical click echoed through the TV studio.

Boom.

A pure circle of bright light lit him up with a buzz, and he had to squint at first and hold up his hand to block out the glare. Like a farmer blinking into the beam from a flying saucer.

This was exactly how they wanted it. No audience, no backdrop. Just each of the guests, one by one, alone in a chair. Simple and discreet, they called it. Stripped down and raw. Spooky and mysterious was the core intention, he knew that.

No matter. He wanted to speak. He had to speak.

He shifted in the chair, blinking his eyes as the spotlight beam grew more diffused, more gentle. He saw a barely visible shape moving through the abyss. The black shadow of a producer, whispering. Then the shape lifted its arm up and a new light, a red light, blinked into life under the camera.

The hand dropped down, and there was a long, elongated moment of quiet.

Matt just sat there, waiting, aware that his body and face were being captured in every minute detail. By now, that really didn't bother him. He was happy to just sit now. Just him, the chair, the lens and the alien mothership light.

A voice broke through the black and empty universe.

'Professor Hunter,' she said. Freya Ellis again, hidden in shadows. 'Thank you for joining us.'

He nodded.

'Tell us. In your opinion . . . what do you believe happened at The Reed last Saturday night?'

Matt stared into the light.

'Professor? Would you like us to rephrase the—?'

'I believe what happened was what I dreaded would happen. What I warned would happen. Only, it was much worse than I expected.'

'You've said the security level was not as you'd hoped.'

He raised an eyebrow at the understatement. 'It was *way* off, and I still feel partly responsible for that.'

'Even though you repeatedly asked for more security? We have your footage of that.'

He shook his head. 'They said it'd be at least twelve. I should have double-checked the actual numbers when I turned up, but I didn't.'

'Do you know how many there actually were there?'

'Three. There were three security guards. I was naive . . .' He shook his head and glanced off into the darkness. 'No, actually. I was foolish.'

'And two of those security personnel died.'

Matt looked back at the camera and nodded. He shifted in his seat again. 'It wasn't just the security that was the problem. The medication issue was a massive factor.'

'Can you explain that? For the viewers?'

'Oh, okay. We've since learnt that for the week leading up to the event, most of Pastor Kissell's clients had voluntarily refrained from taking their medication.'

'And that turned them violent?'

'Not all of them. For most it just left them more vulnerable. More confused. Throwing them into a traumatic situation like that must have been an absolute nightmare for them. It certainly was for the rest of us. But yes, for a handful of Kissell's clients, the lack of meds led to violence.'

'You're referring to Richie Gregor and Pavel Basa. They were the main source of the killing that night.'

'That's right, but there's Abby too. But I have to say, the amount of strain she was under, and the lack of med—'

'You haven't heard?'

Matt blinked into the lens. 'Heard what?'

'The footage from the external camera?'

'I'm sorry, I don't understand.'

'Then watch . . .'

The inky black space around him changed, when a bright, glowing rectangle suddenly flicked on. He hadn't been able to see that screen before. Now it just looked like a floating window into another world.

His eyes adjusted, and he saw footage from two of the fixed cameras, with a rolling time code beneath it. The angle kept switching between one and the other. The first was near the lift. Looking out onto the path that led to the boating lake. And then click . . . the other must have been attached to one of the lamp posts,

394

high up, because it looked directly down on the shore, where several boats lay in the lapping water, waiting to be boarded.

He thought he could see the dull pulse of light on the shore. That'd be the disco lights from the dining hall.

'Keep watching,' she said.

The image flicked every five seconds.

path, *click*, shore, *click*, path, *click*

It looked like a pair of creepy, unwelcome postcards, sent from inside his subconscious. But then two figures were strolling from the building. Ethan and Abby, fresh from the dance floor, heading for the lake.

Matt put up a palm. 'I don't want to see this.'

'You ought to. Keep watching.'

'Turn it off. Turn it off or I'll leave right . . .' He trailed off.

'Keep *watching*,' she said.

He saw it just as the camera changed from shore back to path. The split-second glimpse of another shadow. Not coming from the lift, but from behind one of the concrete struts.

Click.

Ethan and Abby were now at the shore, looking out across the water. Pointing and staring up at the sky. Ethan leant over one of the boats. It looked like he was saying they should climb in. He started shoving the boat into the water, laughing.

Click.

Bare feet running along the path.

Matt felt his chair press into his back.

Click.

Abby was in the boat now, and Ethan was climbing in. Then suddenly he saw Richie Gregor, naked and wild, lunging into shot with both arms raised. Richie who had, thank God, died of blood loss, and not from the whack of his chair. In the video, he had black crab claws sprouting from each hand – the shards of mirror he would soon kill the others with. The fists hit Ethan, who spasmed and tumbled forward into the boat. Matt saw the rippled shoulders and bare backside of Richie leaning over Ethan. Hefty arms hacked and dragged in frantic, arching circles. Matt had been deliriously relieved when it was confirmed he hadn't killed Richie, after all. But watching this right now made him think he'd have gladly run this guy down with a truck.

There was no sound to this footage. And the silence of it was both helpful and hideous.

Click.

A five-second reprieve showed nothing but the path by the lift, except for some sort of animal springing across it from one shrub to another. He knew what animal it was. Then it clicked back, and Richie was gone. Whether he'd pushed the boat into the water, or she had, it was impossible to tell. But Matt just saw the edge of it bobbing out into the water, with Abby sitting up in the boat, and Ethan lost in the murk of shadows and blood. His hand kept frantically reaching out over the side, trying to climb out.

The screen clicked off, and Matt blinked himself out of its reality.

Oh, he thought. *I'm here . . . and not standing there. I'm here . . . and she's innocent.*

'So as you can see, you were wrong. She didn't kill him. In fact, she didn't kill anybody. She was in a post-traumatic trance for most of the night.'

He waited for a while, letting it sink in. There was no rush to comment, or answer. They could edit out dead air. As the seconds ticked by, he happily felt the corner of his mouth go up. 'Well, I am delighted to be wrong.'

'With that in mind, can you explain these pictures?'

Two video clips flicked up on the screen simultaneously. One had Richie Gregor sitting on the lobby sofa, and the other had Pavel

Basa standing in the corridor of his room. In both shots, Abby Linh was whispering into their ears.

'We have no footage of Abby doing this to anybody else,' the interviewer said. 'So why do you think she's speaking in secret to the two clients who would kill that night?'

He stared at the clips. They'd put them in a loop. With a shrug he said, 'This means nothing. Move on.'

'Twitter is lighting up with these shots today. They're saying she goaded the two men into violence. That perhaps the demon was in her, after all. Thoughts?'

Matt shook his head. 'How could they possibly know that? Plus, I'm not convinced that Twitter is the place for truly nuanced argument. Are you?'

'Very well, Professor. Who would you say holds the most blame for what happened that night?'

His smile slipped away, then he sat up straighter. 'All of us, in our own way. But if you're asking for the lynchpin, it's obvious.'

'Can you say his name? Say his name, Professor.'

'Simon Perry.'

He heard a slight rustling of papers, and after a shared whisper she said, 'But what about Pastor Bernie Kissell? Don't you see him as the main cause of all this?'

'He certainly didn't help, but his motivations . . . they were different to Perry's. Kissell was playing with fire, but . . . I do think his intentions were genuine. I think he wanted to help.'

'Does motivation matter, after what happened?'

'I think motivation always matters. But Perry? He convinced a mentally ill man into thinking he was possessed. Then he pushed that man, through tricks and lies, into psychosis, so he could blame him for murder. And all to cover up an affair? That motivation is as cold and as calculated as it gets, don't you think?'

'Would you use the word "evil", to describe such deception?'

'I think that's an extremely unhelpful word.'

'I see . . . and Perry's claim to have been possessed at the time?'

Matt started chuckling. 'Don't. Please. You're hurting my side.'

'Are you relieved that Reverend Perry survived the fire? That he was rescued in the end?'

Matt waited. Then he waited some more.

'You'd rather he died?'

'I'm relieved that he has to stand trial, put it that way. I'm relieved that if a jury has any sense, they'll put him away for a very long time. Because—'

'Are you aware of what he did in his cell, last night?'

Matt opened his hands. 'Nope. But I'm sure you're going to tell me.'

Click.

The white hovering rectangle returned for a moment. Then a photograph appeared. He was about to tell them they'd screwed up. That they were showing him a shot he'd already seen days ago. The photograph of Tom Riley's carved midriff that started all of this off. But this belly was different, more hairy, and a little more curved. This was Simon Perry's body. And his body said, 'Baal-Berith'.

'Is this evidence that the demon in Tom Riley has moved to Simon Perry?'

Matt winced at it, then laughed. 'All this proves is that Perry is either bat-shit crazy, or he'll go to extreme lengths to shift people's focus. And do you want to know something? My bet's on the latter. In fact, I think this entire disaster happened precisely because Perry wanted to shift the focus from his affair. That was in his mind, right up until the end.' Matt frowned for a moment and looked back at the picture. 'How did he carve that, by the way? If he's in a police cell? What did he use?'

'He says he didn't carve it at all. He says a tall animal figure with a claw wrote on him as he slept.'

The screen clicked off, and the void returned.

Matt thought for a moment, then shook his head. 'Probably prised a bit of metal off his bed. Anyway, I know you TV people like a baddie, and while we're all responsible for what happened, in our own way, Perry started this. And remember he was the one who insisted they stop taking their meds.'

'Why do you think he did that? Do you think he wanted the event to go wrong?'

'Yes, I do. He wanted those people acting in ways the world could call demonic. That fitted into his plan. Maybe he was worried people were going to dig into what happened to Justine.'

'And you believe he was the one who killed her in the end? With his own hands?'

'That's what he told me, but then I guess we might never know what really happened. But at least the world's been reminded . . . that exorcism is a very dangerous game to play, precisely because it's unreal.'

'So after all you've seen, you're still an atheist?'

'Are you kidding?'

'But what about Abby Linh? She passed your holy water test with flying—'

'I've explained that already. The temperatures must have been different . . . and that's my bad.' He opened his palms. 'But of course I'm still an atheist. How could I not be?'

Another whisper came from the dark, and then the screen was back.

'What now?' Matt said.

'Keep watching.'

Still photographs started flicking up. Cycling from one to the other. All of them showed Matt at various stages of the filming. There was one of him standing at the airport, waiting for Kissell. Another at the prison gates, just after Tom's exorcism.

Matt laughed. 'What are these? My best bits?'

'These screenshots were taken directly from the footage in the show.'

'So?'

'Keep watching.'

Another shot appeared, of him speaking to the group at the test he ran at the university. And then a few of him at The Reed. Chatting to clients, sipping a coffee on the sofa. As he watched them cycle through, his bemused smirk started to falter a little.

'Can't you see them?'

'See what?' He knew full well what she meant.

'The shadows, in the shot.'

He leant forward in his chair, looking at a picture of himself standing in Tom Riley's front garden at night. He was digging a shovel into the ground and looking for that wooden box. He counted seven people in that image. Two women, five men. And only one of them had the strange black smudge, standing next to him.

Matt shrugged. 'Trick of the light?'

The picture flicked again. Matt was addressing his test subjects at the university experiment. A very faint shadow stood behind him..

'Your camera crew need to clean their lenses—'

Matt in the back of a car, talking to Nupa. Laughing about something, but with a faded black ghost, hovering between them.

'This shape doesn't appear in the moving footage, so we never noticed it until a day ago. But when we took screenshots of the film for promo, we kept seeing . . . this shape.'

'I think you're letting your imaginations run away with you.'

'It's always with you, Professor. Nobody else. What do you make of that?'

'Like I said, the marks are too faint to be meaningful—' He stopped talking when he saw the next picture. It was him, standing outside his daughter's school. The night of the play when they turned up and dragged him into this whole thing. He saw a tall figure standing next to him, still faint, and clearly not actually there, but it was more pronounced than any of the others. He saw a spindly

400

man, or was it an animal on its hind legs, standing like a friend at his side. And what looked like a black transparent hand was curled across Matt's eyes, blocking his sight.

He turned to the camera lens and started to clap his hands together in hard applause. 'Well, there you have it, folks. Proof that all that matters to you people is getting more viewers. This is a very cheap, and very ropey bit of photoshop and it's—'

'We didn't touch—'

'Shameful, that you'd stoop this low.' He grabbed the lapel of his jacket.

'Professor? Please . . .'

Matt started tugging at the microphone, as more and more shots flicked by in rapid succession. All with the figure by his side. 'How do I get this damn thing off?'

'Just a few more minutes? We'd like—'

'No more minutes. I have *tried* to offer a rational explanation, but . . .' He turned to the camera again and spoke directly into it. 'But the simple fact is, rationalism doesn't sell, does it? The truth doesn't' – he threw up finger quotes – '*work*. But demons, oooo, and ghosts, ahhhh, and miracles and God . . . hallelujah, the paranormal. *That's* news. *That's* got media currency.'

'We didn't touch those photographs.'

He shook his head. 'Shame on you. You are fuelling the very thing that caused those people to die. Shame on you.' He dragged the microphone from his lapel, too angry now to care if he tore the cable. It flung off and took one of his buttons with it.

He heard a voice, a male voice, call out from the darkness. 'Professor. Don't be like that.' Matt didn't reply, because he could hear the smirk in that voice. The pleasure of capturing a decent scene.

He pushed his chair back and walked off into the void. He paused. 'Can someone please switch a light on?'

401

He tapped his foot impatiently, heard some movement, and then someone finally pulled what must have been a hefty-sized switch. The world came into view. Wincing with the new light, he looked around, and saw wires and cables strewn on the floor. And people, way more than he'd expected, were scattered holding clipboards and wearing head mics. Looking at him awkwardly. But at least he could see what was actually there.

He tutted loudly and headed for the door, wondering if anybody might come up behind him and put a hand on his shoulder. Maybe to apologise for their crass bit of sensationalism. Maybe to check he was okay, at least. But nobody came. They had what they wanted. Though as he looked at them, standing there, he got the uncomfortable feeling that there was more than awkwardness in their eyes. Was that fear, too?

He noticed one of the crew, jogging behind him. Matt thought he was filming him, but the rhythmic tap of the guy's thumb at his screen suggested he wasn't. He was taking a series of still photographs as he left.

Matt stopped in his tracks, threw two thumbs up, and gave him a massive, winking grin. 'Hey, why don't you paint a big old demon sitting on my shoulders? Like I'm taking him to the zoo for the day. That'd grab attention.'

Then he walked out the door and into the daylight.

CHAPTER SIXTY-FIVE

Wren was sitting in the car outside, reading a magazine and chewing on a cereal bar. When she saw him turn the corner on the pavement, her face lit up and she tossed the magazine into the back seat. She reached over to open his door. He heard the engine kick in as he climbed inside.

'Hey, you're that fella off the telly.' Her laughter sank like a stone when she saw his face. 'Oh dear . . . didn't it go well?'

'I walked out.'

Her mouth started to drop. 'Don't kid.'

'I threw my little mic on the floor and everything. Full-on diva . . .' He started to massage his neck with a sigh.

'Are you serious?'

'Yep. So it's probably a good job they didn't let you in, after all.'

Through gritted teeth she said, 'What on earth made you do that?'

He turned to her. 'I don't know what . . . possessed me. Geddit? *Geddit?*'

She punched him in the shoulder. 'Seriously. Why'd you walk out?'

'Because I told the boring, tedious truth and I guess they don't like that sort of thing.'

'Come here.'

He scrunched up his nose. 'Wren, I'm ready for home.'

'Come here.' She yanked his shoulder and he let himself lean over towards her. She pressed her lips to his temple. He felt the warmth of her breath for a blissful few seconds, and then when he turned to face her, she set her forehead against his. He could smell her perfume. His fringe was lost in hers. 'You're a good man, Matt.' And then, the words she'd said to him, every single day since The Reed. 'This wasn't your fault, okay?' He felt himself shudder against her, and so her hand found his. Since the beginning of time, these hands were meant to be clasped together, just like this.

They listened to each other breathing until she leant back and knocked the car into gear. 'Now,' she said, sniffing, 'let me tell you what one of my clients said to me today. Matt, you are gonna wet your knickers . . .'

They drove straight home and they spent the rest of the afternoon working their way through the giant box of chocolates that DS Fenn had sent over. It was great to hear Pamela was doing so well. Matt also helped Amelia build the International Space Station out of plastic milk bottles and chopsticks. She took selfies of them both holding it, insisting that Lucy and Wren join in since it was too long for one person to carry. They stood in a row, holding it up, and it collapsed just after the picture timer went off on her phone. There was a lot of mess on the kitchen floor, and Amelia cried, yet he was the first to scoop it up and start again. He was happy to rebuild a strengthened 2.0 version with her, even as the task spilt into his evening. They laughed a lot, as it came together. And as crappy and juvenile and unslick as it looked, it was a true attempt at depicting reality and so he loved it very much.

He was amused with Lucy's reaction when he told her about that wooden box having some sort of recorder and a timer in it. She burst out laughing and called herself a 'dickhead' for being scared by its singing. But then she went quiet for the rest of the night, and he wasn't sure why. Maybe she was embarrassed, or perhaps understandably freaked out that a little murder device had been in her house . . . in her hands.

Later that night, he called Abby Linh at the hospital again. He'd been trying for days and could never get through. He left her a message, saying he'd just seen the footage, and that he was delighted that she hadn't done what he'd said she had. It was an awkward thing to say to a person. After a few fumbled attempts to phrase it right, he just flat out apologised for getting it wrong.

He wondered if she might call. He hoped she would, but then he really, really hoped she wouldn't. He'd had enough of demons for the week, for a year, for a life. As long as she was getting the help she needed, finally. That's what mattered. He reminded her of the free university counselling. That he was there if she needed him. Then he hung up and stared at the phone for a while. Hovering his thumb over the text message that had come from his mute counsellor, Jeff. Speaking in his usual kind and thoughtful manner.

You missed your appointment.

It was only when they were going up to bed that he leant into Amelia's room. She was fast asleep by now. She had a habit of making the slightest-sounding snores you ever heard. It was a family joke. Whenever Amelia snored, tiny dolls were dragging their house furniture.

He could hear Wren brushing her teeth as he reached for Amelia's phone. It was lying by her bedside, plugged in and charging, as usual. It was already a hundred per cent, so he tugged the wire out to conserve energy and protect the planet. *Got to save those polar bears* – another family motto.

They had an 'open phone' kids' policy in the Hunter household. So his thumbprint was on her system. He pushed it into place and the phone flung wide its gates. He saw her screensaver and almost baulked with laughter. Where did she find this stuff? A bizarre photograph of an oven-ready chicken with a fish sticking out its mouth. And in the fish's mouth, a cigarette was hanging.

He snorted a quiet laugh, then he deliberately kept the smile plastered as he tapped on her photos. His thumb hit the latest.

There they all were, Wren and Lucy holding one half of the ISS and Amelia and Matt holding the other. It was sagging so much in the middle that they should have realised that within a second of the camera timer going off, the middle section would break apart and come crashing down to earth.

He swiped his thumb towards himself. Then he pinch-zoomed. Wow, he thought, if Wren walked in now, she'd think this TV thing had turned him into a regular Vanity Fair, obsessed with his own image. But actually, he was looking *around* his own image instead.

Every pixel was as it should be. Every colour, every shade, to be expected. And yes, there was a shadow on the wall behind him. But that's what lamps do, they cast shadows.

The only thing you could call remotely spooky was when he was brushing his teeth and staring into the bathroom mirror; when a sudden low breeze started to moan through the frosted windowpane. It made him turn around. He could just hear the outside world, pushing the sound of its melancholy through a tiny gap somewhere. If he was one of those idiotic, dumbo types from that studio today, he might think his old friend Baal-Berith was out there, climbing up the vines and coming home.

But he wasn't one of those idiotic dumbo types. So instead he ignored the breeze, even when it turned into cruel whispers. Such sounds were made by the leaves outside, and it could only ever be so. He brushed his teeth, quicker than usual. And didn't look at his reflection too much, because he really was tired and preferred to rest his head.

He headed back to bed to find Wren waiting for him, sitting up, with the pillows plumped around her. She gave him an exaggerated wink, and he laughed. He closed the door and for a while they made giggly, quiet, healing love. After they lay on their backs, they decided that tomorrow they'd play squash together. They hadn't done that in such a long time. The university had insisted he take at least a week off, and so Wren had taken some days off to be with him.

These days, they didn't normally cuddle at night. There was an efficiency to their sleep patterns that was perfectly acceptable, and hardly a sign of dying love. There'd always be the little chat. Maybe more. Then the kiss and the smile, followed by the usual retreat to each other's pillow. But tonight, after the goodnight kiss part, she slid her arm under the back of his neck and her hips shifted along the mattress. Her head joined his pillow.

They didn't say anything. They didn't need to. They just lay in the dark, breathing and loving and living. In the quiet, he noticed that the same breeze from the bathroom was at his window now. He could hear it whistling and crying his name. But he'd be damned if he'd let simple physics keep him awake. He phased it out with the sound of her breathing, and he let himself drift, knowing full well what dreams were coming. He thought he heard the voice at the window, full of mischief, quoting Dr Seuss of all things.

Oh, the places you'll go.

He let a breath out, drummed up courage, and finally closed his eyes. He gripped her a little tighter as she slept. He thought of an old dream experiment he'd read about. Where external stimuli, like sound or temperature, could influence the dream itself. An interesting idea, worth exploring, and he wondered that perhaps it'd be interesting to put it to the test right now. That if he fell asleep like this, very close to her, he might still feel the sensation of her arms holding him. Maybe if he did that, he might not feel so alone tonight, when his faithful monsters came.

ACKNOWLEDGEMENTS

Did you know that I'm 'The UK's Leading Exorcist'? Well, I didn't know I was either until I read it in a newspaper headline a few years back. A UK tabloid did a full-page interview with me after I was asked to speak at a film premiere in Leicester Square. It was a demonic possession horror movie about Satan running riot in the Vatican. I guess I seemed like a good fit for the pre-popcorn spiel. The paper sent me an initial mock-up of the article, complete with a moody, pasty-faced shot of me folding my arms and staring hard into the camera. I looked like I'd just gone ten rounds with Beelzebub, but in reality, the pic was taken on the morning after a particularly raucous karaoke night in my hometown, Chester-le-Street. But yes, there in bold black and white, next to my glassy-eyed glare, was the name Rev. Peter Laws and along with it . . . 'The UK's Leading Exorcist!'

Course, I spat out my tea in shock and called them immediately – the power of embarrassment compelled me. 'I'm not even an Exorcist', says I, 'never mind a leading one!' They apologised and dropped that claim before it went to press, and just like that, I was back to your bog-standard pastor fella. So just to be clear . . . if your kid's head starts spinning, I'm not the guy to call. The thing is though, you might think I overreacted to all of this . . . after all, nobody's going to actually ask for an exorcism anyway. Not these days . . . well, you might be surprised.

You see, requests for exorcism are actually on the rise today. Remember that bit in *Possessed* in the TV studio? Where Bernie Kissell starts spouting statistics about a worldwide boom in exorcisms? I didn't make that stuff up – it's real. Some churches are struggling to keep up with demand. The idea that an ancient religious ritual is not only surviving but *thriving* in the modern, rational world fascinates me. I just knew I had to write a novel about it. So, ta-dah . . . here it is. My Matt Hunter book on current affairs.

Now, what's behind this exorcism spike? Simple. A society that 'doth turneth from the Lord' has effectively invited the demons in. At least, that's what some Christians will tell you. Others, like Matt Hunter, take the more rational approach. That these are demons of the mind, not the soul. Being a Christian myself I'm theoretically open to the possibility of demonic activity, but I have to say that on this topic I tend to sit with Matt on this. When I'm contacted by folks who suspect possession (it happens sometimes), the doctors are always my first recommendation. To ignore or misdiagnose mental health issues can be deadly, and it's a key theme of this book. Please don't dismiss these risks as fiction. There are real-life cases of exorcism that have ended in shocking, heart-breaking tragedy, even at the hands of the well-meaning. I read such cases while researching this novel. They made me feel cold in my bed at night. They still do, when I think about them. Yet, despite this rational caution, the complexity of possession still fascinates me, especially the idea that for some people today, the idea of an ancient demonic invader can be psychologically preferable to a medical label. Such is the continuing stigma around mental health.

As I wrote *Possessed*, however, I sensed a wider theme developing: the scandal of demonising others. Of taking somebody who may be innocent, and turning them into a monster. In the book, Matt claims Christianity did this exact cosmic switcheroo to an ancient, possibly benevolent deity like Baal. While simultaneously, under everybody's noses, the exact same thing is happening to an insecure pub chef who just wants his wife back. That notion of turning a fellow human being into a one-dimensional beast troubles me. Perhaps because I see it happening around me all the time.

The Puritan witch trials of the Middle Ages was one of the themes of my second novel, *Unleashed*, and I see that Salem spirit alive and well in our modern times – maybe more than I've ever seen in my life. You see it in politics, in conversations at dinner parties, at the school gates, in social media especially so. We shame, vilify and 'cancel' others in full view of the gathered mob (who often observe it all by looking through screens and lenses – devices that litter this book). I'm not sure why we demonise the people we don't like, but we do. Maybe we just yearn for a simple dualistic world of goodies and baddies. Or maybe we're so insecure that we can only raise ourselves up by pushing others down. Whatever it is, we've become one-click experts at slotting others into the demon file. Now relax . . . I'm not trying to get all preachy here. This book is essentially just a pulpy bunch of chills and kills, peppered with a few laughs, a bit of theology and a few cheeky nods to *The Love Boat* along the way. Forgive me . . . I watched a bunch of those on reruns during the writing of this book.

But here I sit at the end of *Possessed*, trying to figure out what the heck just happened to me. It's odd saying this . . . and maybe other authors will give me a slow nod of understanding as I do, but writing a novel is a bit like being possessed. Only not by just one entity, there's a whole bunch of them. At some points with this book I just sat at my desk and heard the keys tapping, while I read what happened next. During one of the later death scenes I even remember thinking, dang, this is *disgusting*, I feel sick, I should probably stop. Yet those fingers refused, and tapped on. Course, I'm not actually possessed – it's just called imagination, and I promise you, my head DID. NOT. SPIN. But yeah, this story seemed to unfold itself to me and if there really is a ghost of a message in this book, I wonder if it might be simply this: a nod and a nudge to remind me of something so easily forgotten in this Salem age. That if I ever start treating another human being like a one-dimensional monster – no matter who they are – I may have lost what it means to be human myself.

So let me leap up from my desk in a crash of spilt tea as we enter the applause section because the following multi-dimensional gems deserve every clap. To my lovely literary agent, Joanna Swainson, and my foreign rights agent, Therese Cohen – you prepare the way for these books, and I'm grateful. To Susie Dunlop, Lesley Crooks, Kelly Smith, Daniel Scott, Christina Griffiths, Kirsten Munday, and Simon and Fliss Bage – this is the team at my publishers, Allison & Busby. You guys will probably never know how much it meant to me when you said yes to my first novel *Purged*, and now look – you've given Matt Hunter a *fourth* ride on the carousel? Wow.

I want to thank my family too: my mum Jean, my sister Julie and my brother Norman (to whom this book is dedicated). It's been a heck of a stormy year, hasn't it, but your lights keep on shining. What an inspiration you all are. I want to thank my dad too.

Thanks also to my wonderful, beautiful wife Joy, who just poured me a red wine (about three minutes ago). My talented and brilliant daughter Emma, who helped me get a moth out of my office just now, then hugged me goodnight (about ten minutes ago). And to my whacky and kind-hearted son, Adam who I was tickling on the bed (about thirty minutes ago, while he wore an Ikea lampshade on his head). Crikey, I love you lot.

Then finally, to you the reader, who I could easily just see in one dimension I suppose. After all I'm the author, and you're the kindly punter who bought this book (for which I'm grateful). But of course, it's way more intricate than that, isn't it? Who knows what you'll be doing when you put this book down, or what life lies at the other end of these words. I've no idea, but what I do know is this: I'm not just an author, and you're not just a reader – we're both wonderfully complex characters with noble traits and significant screw-ups. There are no bit players in this world, after all. I think of that sometimes: of where these books end up, and who reads them. Yeah, I'm talking about you sitting or lying there right now, somehow hearing my words playing through your brain system, in *your* choice of voice. Letting *my* spirit possess *your* mind, if only for a few hours. Thanks for letting me into your head again, but now, we must get the spirit of *Possessed* from out of your body. So that you can carry on with your life. So are you ready? Good . . .

Close your eyes, and hear this prayer . . .

'Spirit of the fourth Matt Hunter book, listen to me. You cannot live in this reader any longer. I CAST THEE OUT! You are condemned to wander the earth until you find some other reader to climb inside. But for now set this prisoner free. Amen.'

There you go. All clean again. Now go and eat chocolate and watch some telly.

Peter Laws, at home, drinking red wine and eating Ben and Jerry's cookie dough ice cream (which is, I reckon, the most convincing proof of a deity that I know of)

PETER LAWS is an ordained Baptist minister with a taste for horror. He writes a monthly column in the *Fortean Times* and also hosts a popular podcast and YouTube show which reviews thriller and horror films from a theological perspective. He is also the author of *The Frighteners* which explores our fascination with the macabre. He lives with his family in Bedfordshire.

peterlaws.co.uk   @revpeterlaws